Fan Favorite

FAN FAVORITE

ADRIENNE GUNN

GCP
GRAND CENTRAL
New York Boston

This book is a work of fiction. Names, characters, places, and incidents are the product of the author's imagination or are used fictitiously. Any resemblance to actual events, locales, or persons, living or dead, is coincidental.

Grand Central Publishing
Hachette Book Group
1290 Avenue of the Americas, New York, NY 10104
grandcentralpublishing.com
@grandcentralpub

First Edition: June 2025

Grand Central Publishing is a division of Hachette Book Group, Inc. The Grand Central Publishing name and logo is a registered trademark of Hachette Book Group, Inc.

The publisher is not responsible for websites (or their content) that are not owned by the publisher.

The Hachette Speakers Bureau provides a wide range of authors for speaking events. To find out more, go to hachettespeakersbureau.com or email HachetteSpeakers@hbgusa.com.

Grand Central Publishing books may be purchased in bulk for business, educational, or promotional use. For information, please contact your local bookseller or the Hachette Book Group Special Markets Department at special.markets@hbgusa.com.

Print book interior design by Marie Mundaca

Library of Congress Cataloging-in-Publication Data
Names: Gunn, Adrienne author
Title: Fan favorite / by Adrienne Gunn.
Description: First edition. | New York : GCP, 2025.
Identifiers: LCCN 2024059605 | ISBN 9781538768259 trade paperback | ISBN 9781538768266 ebook
Subjects: LCGFT: Romance fiction | Novels | Fiction
Classification: LCC PS3607.U54763 F36 2025 | DDC 813/.6—dc23/eng/20250211
LC record available at https://lccn.loc.gov/2024059605

ISBNs: 978-1-5387-6825-9 (trade paperback), 978-1-5387-6826-6 (ebook)

Printed in the United States of America

LSC-C

Printing 1, 2025

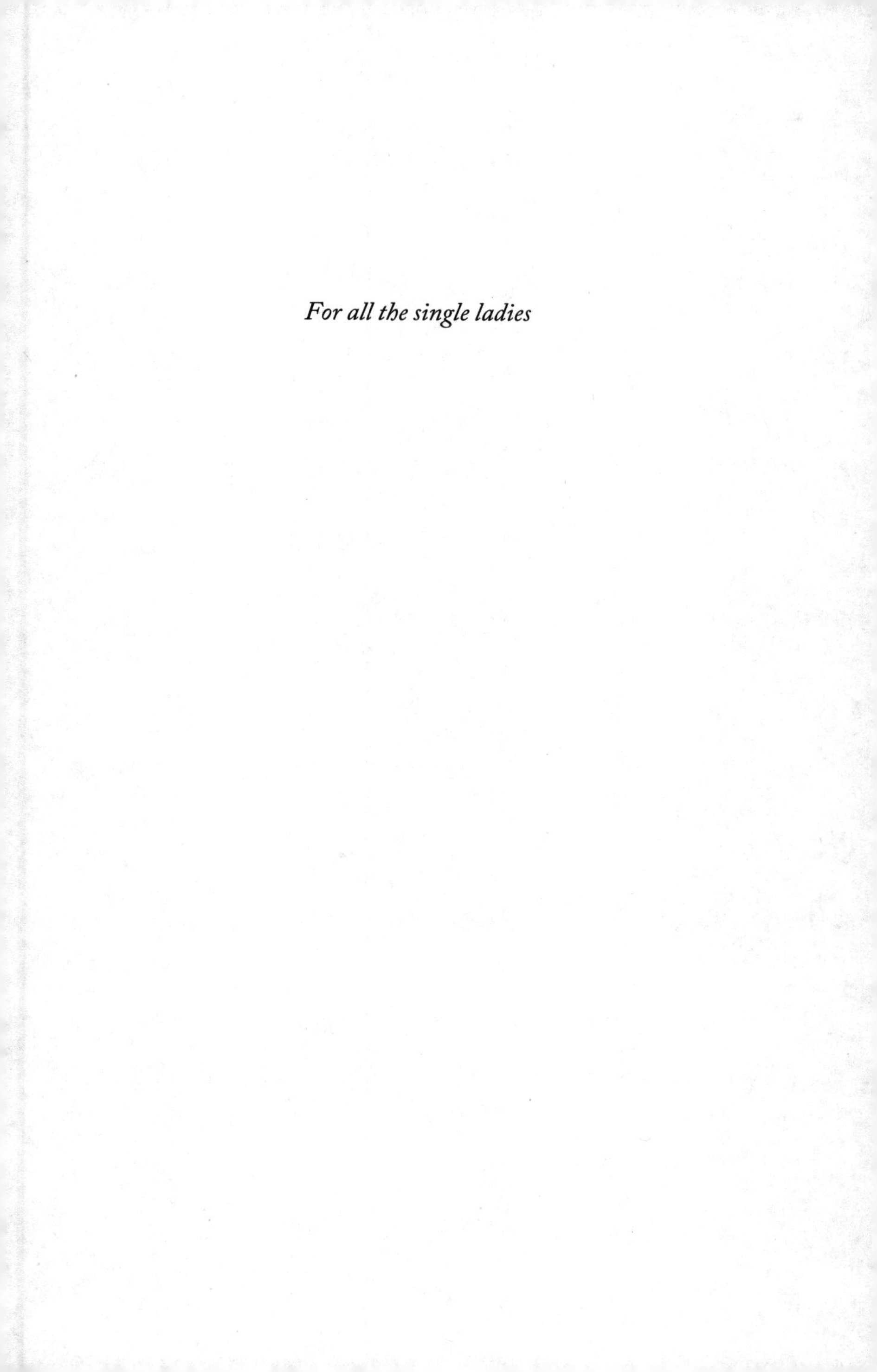

For all the single ladies

Fan Favorite

"All I'm saying is, somewhere out there is the man you are supposed to marry. And if you don't get him first, somebody else will, and you'll have to spend the rest of your life knowing that somebody else is married to your husband."

—Marie, *When Harry Met Sally*

1

Edie Pepper was starting over. Again.

"I *never* do this," she mumbled through a mess of sloppy kisses. "Seriously, this is like *so weird* for me."

"Yeah, sure, of course," Dave said, tracing his tongue down her jaw. "Me too."

"Did you have fun tonight?" Edie pulled away from Dave's licking to evaluate him one more time. He was handsome in the way that white guys in polo shirts with crossbody laptop bags emblazoned with their consulting firm logos were handsome—that is to say, unremarkably, without even an artisanal beard to indicate an interest in urban beekeeping or Proust. Dave was clearly a Dave—someone who loved the Cubs, who drank IPAs as a cornerstone of his personality, who had his fraternity letters tattooed on his ankle (Spring Break '02!), and who threatened to move to Canada after every episode of *Pod Save America*, which he listened to on his AirPods during thrice-weekly jogs along the lake.

Edie had been trying to marry a Dave for many years.

"So much fun," he agreed.

"The great thing about breakups is they give you the opportunity to explore." Edie smiled as sexily as she could with one eye blinking rapidly to keep in her contact lens. Happy hour had been brief—three glasses of rosé and Dave's hand inching up her thigh while he educated her on the history of Chicago's improv scene. But Edie hadn't thought about Brian once! And now here she was in Dave's apartment, still not thinking about him. "Like, now that I'm single again, I get to explore you."

"Explore this, Evie," Dave growled, placing her hand on his crotch.

"It's Edie, but that's cool—Starbucks never gets it right, either." Edie moved her hand back to his hip. "My mom was forty-four when she had me, hence the old-timey name. I always wanted to be a Kelly." Dave was busy palming her left boob, pushing and turning it like the lid of a jar that just wouldn't catch. "Anyway, you learn so much from breakups. Like, for one thing, you can't control other people," Edie mused while Dave attempted to wedge her tit up and out of her shirt. She twisted her head horizontally to catch his eye. "You can only control yourself. Know what I mean?"

Suddenly Dave released her, and Edie toppled into a mountain bike that was propped against an exposed brick wall. He took a big step back.

"You know I'm a feminist, right?" he asked, hands in the air.

"Oh! Yeah! Of course," Edie assured him, rubbing the side of her ass where the bike's handlebar had skewered her butt cheek. "Me too. Obviously."

"Cool, cool, cool. I mean, I thought you knew, 'cause I let you pay for the drinks. And the Uber."

Edie waved her hand. "The bar was so close to your house, it was, like, nothing. Thanks again for setting it up. So many guys don't want to make an effort."

"No problem." Dave grabbed the waistband of Edie's jeans and pulled her to him again. "Time to sit on my face."

"Oh…wow…maybe…" Edie placed her hands on Dave's chest, atop the navy gingham button-down that guys in Chicago reliably wore on first dates. She didn't want to sit on a face. She wanted to get married. His mouth found her neck again and started sucking. Edie squirmed. There was just so much saliva—it was like being licked by a Saint Bernard.

Nevertheless, she persisted.

"Being a single woman in the internet age is so empowering," she continued. "Like, yesterday, I didn't know you, but today, here we are, making this connection." His tongue slugged hot and wet in her ear and a wave roared against her eardrum. She rose onto her tiptoes to escape. Edie had been dating in her thirties for the past five years—tolerance for a potential husband's flaws was just, well, *part of it*. "And I haven't thought about Brian all night."

Dave burped hot in her ear. "Who's Brian?"

"Fate doesn't bring people together by accident," Edie continued firmly. "That's like, the opposite of fate. Accident. Do you think this is fate?"

"What?" Dave asked, pulling her by the wrist toward his bedroom.

"Us."

"'Us' what?" Dave dropped her hand, and they stood in the middle of the living room, staring at each other.

"You and me, 'us'?" she said, confused.

"Oh shit," Dave said, running a hand through his short brown hair. "Don't get the wrong idea—I had a great time at happy hour, but like, this is no big thing. I'm not looking for anything serious."

Edie's face went incredulous. "But that's not what your profile said *at all*." She scanned the living room for her purse, finding it tossed on Dave's game day recliner, the ChapStick and credit cards and ragged Rothy's she used for commuting spilled across the faded velour. She fished around for her phone and tapped the screen until Dave's Hinge profile came up. "Look, it says right here: 'Looking for my partner in crime. Help me get off this app for good! Work hard, play hard.'"

"Okay, sure, but then look at the messages." Dave took the phone from her and toggled to their exchange. "See, here you said, 'Hey, Dave, how are you?' And I said, 'wsup.' And you said, 'Very important question: What's the best Tom Hanks film?' And I said, 'saving private ryan.' And then you said, 'You can tell a lot about a person by their favorite Tom Hanks movie. I can tell you have a strong masculine spirit,' and then I didn't respond for three days. Then you said, 'Hey, Dave! How's it going? Wanna grab a drink sometime?' and I said, 'sure, but I have to warn you, I'm easy on the eyes and hard on the pussy,' and you said, 'ha ha ha, how's Tuesday?'" Dave handed the phone back to her with a shrug.

"What?" Edie exclaimed. "I thought you were kidding! You weren't kidding?"

Dave sighed and looked her up and down. "Aren't you, like, thirty-eight?"

"I'm thirty-five!" she said, throwing her shoulders back to present herself at her best angle.

"Yeah." Dave grimaced. "There's no way to say this without looking like a dick. I'm looking for someone more like twenty-eight."

Edie shoved Dave's profile in his face. "You're thirty-nine!"

Dave shrugged again. "Look, twenty-eight's the sweet spot—not young enough to be ridiculous, not old enough to be neurotic." When Edie looked like she might cry, Dave's voice took on a soothing tone, and he started to rub her arm encouragingly. "I'm sorry, you're great, but I'm about to turn forty, ya know? I gotta think about getting married. I don't want to be one of those dads who's too old to coach Little League 'cause his shoulder or knee is blown out or whatever. I can't waste time on relationships that aren't going anywhere."

"But I want to get married!" Edie exclaimed. "I want all of this!" But as she gestured at Dave's "all of this," for a second Edie wasn't so sure. Did she really want Dave Last-Name-Unknown's framed Wrigley Field "art" on her living room wall? Was she even capable of smiling-smiling-smiling through dinner while Dave lectured her about the comedic superiority of *The Good Place*? Could she spend the rest of her life listening to *Under the Table and Dreaming*, or tolerate being finger-banged like it was a search for lost change? Or had Edie Pepper finally—*finally*—become too old, too tired, too brokenhearted to give a shit?

"Hey, look, you're dope. You're gonna meet someone great." Dave smiled the smile of a really chill dude. "Sorry about the miscommunication. For real. And I'll still go down on you. Or you could blow me. Honestly, it's cool. I'm down for whatever."

"You, *Daayyvvve*—" Edie said, drawing out each smarmy syllable of his dumb, stupid name while gathering her shit from around the apartment: coat on the couch, purse on the recliner, kitten heel under the table. She clambered beneath it on her hands and knees and reached for the shoe. "—do not *deserve* my *orgasm*." She jabbed the shoe at him emphatically before accidentally banging her head on the table. "Fuck me!"

"Literally just offered to." He winked.

"Aargh!" Edie screamed as the heel of her pink Jessica Simpson pump—the one that had been worn so many times a nail stuck out of the stiletto—struck Dave Last-Name-Unknown right in the middle of his forehead.

Bullseye.

2

Edie got into an Uber bound for the too-big, too-expensive apartment in Roscoe Village she was supposed to be sharing with her ex-boyfriend, Brian, and his two-year-old son, Cayden (every other weekend, alternating holidays, and for six weeks in summer), desperately brooding over this latest dating debacle. Fucking Dave Last-Name-Unknown! Why were men like this? Sure, yes, Edie scrolled past articles about patriarchy and misogyny and emotional labor and the mental load on social media every single day, but sociological research didn't interest her like the smiling photos of couples and babies and couples and dogs and couples at birthday parties and on New Year's Eve. She refused to believe that a loving, fulfilling relationship between a man and a woman was impossible. What about George and Amal? Tom and Rita? Barack and Michelle? Harry and Meghan! But keeping hope alive amid all this die-alone energy was getting harder and harder. Edie was at the end of the line, and there were only two options: psychotic optimism or total spinsterhood.

"Hey, girl, hey," Daryl R. said from the front seat of the Kia as they pulled away from the curb and headed north. He popped his chin at her. "Where you goin' lookin' so fine?"

"Sir," Edie said with her talk-to-the-manager-hand in the air. "No, thank you. I've had enough for one night."

Edie put in her earbuds and sighed as she collapsed against the back seat. Perhaps being a spinster wouldn't be so terrible. Wasn't it true that no one added stupid shows like *MythBusters* to her Netflix watchlist, forever tainting her algorithm? And couldn't she come home after work and throw her bra on the living room floor and watch all her reality shows with one or two or three glasses of wine without anyone criticizing her choices? And couldn't Edie order plain cheese pizza and not defend it to anyone or have to compromise and order half mushrooms or onions or olives that never stayed on their half and always contaminated her side? And didn't she sleep until seven thirty on weekdays while all her coworkers got up at like five a.m. to deal with their children and commutes from the suburbs? And couldn't she do absolutely whatever she wanted in her very own bathroom, including, but not limited to, staring at her pores in a magnifying mirror or periodically shaving her asshole? And with nothing tying her down like a husband or children, couldn't she drop everything at a moment's notice and go on an adventure? Sure, she'd never done that, but the point was, she *could* do that. Maybe she'd spend Christmas riding elephants in Thailand. The world was her oyster.

Edie poked at her phone until the soothing voice of Oprah filled her ears. "I'm Oprah Winfrey. Welcome to *Super Soul Conversations*, the podcast. I believe that one of the most valuable gifts you can give yourself is *time*. Taking time to be more fully present. Your journey to become more inspired and connected to the deeper world around us starts right now."

But who wants to go to Thailand *alone*?

Edie opened Bumble and started swiping. What was *wrong* with her? Bad dates, bad boyfriends, bad choice after bad choice—until here she was, buzzed in the back of an Uber at 9:13 p.m. on a Tuesday, reckoning with the fact that if something didn't change soon, she was absolutely going to die alone, most likely crushed to death by her bookshelf while reaching for a tattered copy of *Little Women*. She'd be found weeks later, nibbled to the bone by cats. Because surely by then she'd have multiple cats. Left, left, right, left, right, right, left she swiped. Guys who "just wanted to fuck." Guys in "consensual non-monogamous" relationships. Guys looking for someone "spontaneous" to travel and run with, #fitlife #vegan. Guys in cars. Guys lounging against cars. Guys holding fish. Guys holding a woman's hand, the rest of her body amputated out of the photo. Guys pulling down the waistband of their jeans to present the top of their pubes. It was exhausting. But she was thirty-five years old, and as Dave had just reminded her, there was literally no time to waste. Suddenly Edie wondered if a thirty-five-year-old woman who'd had the kind of one-night stands she'd had—where a man spooged in her hair with complete disregard for her wash cycle, or who'd penetrated her anally with his thumb after buying her a single Coors Light at a street festival—could even wear a white dress down the aisle. Everything was starting to feel *too late too late too late*, and the more Edie felt her dreams slipping away, the more frantic she became.

She needed more wine.

"Learn from every mistake," Oprah said as Edie trudged up the steps to her apartment, "because every experience, particularly your mistakes, are there to teach you and force you into being more of who you are."

Edie paused and stared at her front door. This apartment had been a real fucking mistake. "If you're still breathing, you have a second chance," encouraged Oprah. Edie sighed and unlocked the door, opening it directly into a tower of unpacked moving boxes. She slid inside through a crack. The apartment was like a storage facility, crammed with boxes and bags and unplaced furniture, all of which Edie had fastidiously ignored since the movers dropped them off a month ago. Edie threw her purse on the floor and stripped off her date-night clothes, leaving them in a puddle. She plucked a T-shirt with BRUNCH SO HARD printed across the chest from the couch, put it on, and made her way to the kitchen.

"Hey, Nacho," she said to her cat Nacho Bell Grande, who was meowing and circling. She dumped food into his bowl and all over the floor.

Edie returned to the living room with her favorite CLASS OF '03 mug filled to the brim with boxed rosé. She made her way to the brand-new couch that she and Brian had ordered at IKEA on a blissful day in spring when they were drunk on the thirtysomething's aphrodisiac—Swedish meatballs and plans for the future. He'd held her hand and discussed plates and bowls like they mattered. He'd pinched her butt with a pair of salad tongs. And when they'd reached the display of sleek Swedish bathrooms, he'd unbuckled his belt and pretended to use the fake toilet, which was dumb—*so dumb!*—but had made her laugh anyway because Brian had this way of making dad jokes seem sweet and original. And when she pulled him away, laughing, he took her in his arms, right there in the middle of the aisle, with all the people rushing to make their own fresh starts swirling around them, and he'd buried his face in her hair and whispered he loved her.

But who wanted to think about that now? Edie threw herself onto the couch and turned on *E!*. Was it too much to want to love and be loved in return? To have someone to go to dinner with? Someone who'd have to text her back because *vows*? She gulped some wine and ruminated over what miracle of science had produced Kim, Khloé, and Kylie's respective asses as they appeared on-screen. Sure, of course Edie wanted an impossibly tiny waist. Of course she wanted to look like she'd shoved balloons down her bra and up her shorts, even if it did seem to make simple locomotion a challenge. But how could she be expected to diet or exercise or get plastic surgery when she had a broken heart?

Edie opened her phone and stared at the last message Brian had sent her: I think Rachel and I are getting back together :/

Edie's entire life decided by some rudimentary sad face emoji. Like clockwork, the rush of memories flooded Edie's brain, hot and shameful. There she was at her office, six weeks ago, the fabric of her desk chair itchy under her thighs because it was a Thursday and she'd dressed up for the team meeting. The overwhelming floral scent of Barb's perfume when Edie burst into the bathroom. The sweat that had engulfed her entire body as she stared at her phone, at that little colon and slash, wondering what the fuck was happening. *We are moving in together. We've just signed the lease.* The ensuing phone call, which he'd waited until the very last ring to pick up, Edie whisper-yelling in the tiny stall. He was sorry, but this was what was best for Cayden. It just *happened*. Brian had loved his time with Edie. Edie was great. But, you know, Brian *had a family*.

Now Edie felt the tears coming in hot, so she turned her attention back to the TV, and that's when, out of nowhere, the answer to all her questions—to where her life was truly headed—appeared.

Because right there on Edie's TV was her One True Love.

But then the connection dropped, the television went black, and Edie was left rubbing her eyes, wondering if she'd passed out and entered some peculiar dream. But then the screen flickered and he appeared again, inexplicably wearing a FREE TIBET T-shirt. He was standing next to, of all people, *Ryan Seacrest*. Edie sat up quickly, and the coffee mug of rosé she'd been balancing on her stomach plunged to the floor.

"Hey, guys, I'm Ryan Seacrest and this is *E! News Now*. The hunt for love is on as twenty of America's most eligible bachelorettes descend upon Los Angeles to meet Bennett Charles—"

Edie felt dizzy as she crawled toward the TV. Starring in a glossy montage of extreme sports and white-savior philanthropy was her high school boyfriend. It seemed strange that Ryan kept calling him Bennett Charles when his name was Charlie Bennett. And he was nothing like she remembered—her Charlie was shy and nervous and chewed his nails and read fantasy novels and wore weird clothes and was sort of chunky and splotchy all over. But this—this was an unbelievably grown-up, *Us Weekly* cover version of Charlie. There he was on Edie's TV, skiing off the top of a mountain, hanging from a rock face by one hand, kayaking down a waterfall, photographing children in Nepal with prayer flags flapping against temple walls, playing an acoustic guitar for tribespeople in Africa, and, with his eyes closed and a beatific expression on his gorgeous face, *taking an outdoor shower?*

Edie, rising to her knees, was suddenly self-conscious. She adjusted the elastic of her giant underpants, which despite their ample coverage had ridden into her butt crack.

"—activist, adventurer, entrepreneur, amateur photographer, musician, wow, this guy does it all!" Ryan continued. "Bennett, after scandal rocked *The Key*'s incoming suitor, Wyatt Cash, it looked like this season might be canceled. But then your popular Instagram @Sherpa4U came out of nowhere and landed you the job! Are you ready to find love on this epic ten-week journey?"

Wait, *WHAT?*

Edie's eyes went huge, and she put her hand over her mouth.

Charlie Bennett aw-shucks smiled, just a humble everyman with an active CrossFit membership. "Listen, Ryan, I've rappelled into active volcanoes, summited the world's tallest peaks, even ridden a yak across the Nepalese tundra to deliver life-saving medicine to victims of the Tibetan diaspora. And still, nothing's prepared me for this! Being on *The Key* is by far the scariest thing I've ever done, but I know"—he looked directly into the camera, and Edie felt her stomach flip—"I'm going to find my soulmate on this adventure. And that I'll give her the Key to My Heart. Forever."

Their eyes met. He smiled, revealing that one crooked tooth she'd always adored, and suddenly Edie understood that their connection transcended space and time and knew, with absolute certainty, that Charlie Bennett was, and had always been, her One True Love.

"Holy shit." She sat down hard in the puddle of rosé. "Fuck."

3

Edie paced the living room with zero chill, wildly scrolling every article the internet would give her about the new season of *The Key*.

WILL *THE KEY*'S BENNETT CHARLES FIND THE ONE?

The People.com headline screamed over a photo of a sexily smirking Charlie Bennett offering the camera a golden key from the palm of his hand. Edie texted her best friend Lauren ALERT ALERT with a link to the article, suddenly stone-cold sober and losing her mind over how in the hell Charlie Bennett—*Charlie Bennett!*—could be the star of the biggest reality show in America.

It was just so *bizarre*. Of course, Edie knew all about *The Key* and the Wyatt Cash scandal. She'd been watching *The Key* for what, a decade? *The Key* was America's most beloved dating show, the only one that really, truly believed in love. One lucky suitor romancing a group of incredibly gorgeous potential love interests in a palatial California mansion. Romantic dates, first kisses straight out of a fairy tale, tear-filled eliminations, incredible around-the-world travel locations, all leading up to one epic proposal. And the suitors were always—*always!*—chosen from the previous season's cast. Charlie Bennett had never been on *The Key*, of that she was certain. Wait—Seacrest had said something about Instagram.

Edie opened the app, her heart beating fast. First of all, Bennett Charles's account was *verified*, which was only for *celebrities*, which made no sense, because if Charlie Bennett was a *celebrity*, why was Edie just hearing about it now? 400,000+ followers! Edie suddenly felt lightheaded and grasped for the couch, which of course she missed, landing, once again, in the rosé.

"Shit!" she yelped.

Nacho Bell Grande yowled and fled for the kitchen.

Edie scrolled and scrolled through @Sherpa4U's fantasy-inducing grid, trying to piece together a narrative that would explain how over the past seventeen years, her sweet, nerdy Charlie Bennett had transformed into this snowboarding, paragliding, *Key*-suitor hunk with the bio "Live the adventure, share the love." But his Instagram was only five years old and bore no trace of the Charlie Bennett she once knew. Like Athena bursting fully formed from Zeus's skull, one day Bennett Charles just appeared, topless and grinning, on Instagram. And, *damn*, he was topless *a lot*. In between feats of extreme sport, vistas worthy of travel magazines, food porn, and shots posing with Vitaminwater near rock formations (#ad #sponsored) was a half-nude Bennett Charles, a lotus tattoo on his forearm on full display and drool-worthy abs glistening in the sunlight.

Edie swallowed hard. Typically, she found a display of body-ody-ody sort of silly and self-indulgent, but suddenly all she wanted to do for the rest of her life was glissando her fingertips down Charlie Bennett's torso. After a particularly jarring photo of Charlie standing on a mountain top in hiking boots and a lime-green Borat-style mankini—*chest and abs and hips and goddamn those divots on the sides of his ass*—Edie, dumbfounded by Charlie's inconceivable glow-up, foolishly opened her own grid, as if there she would find answers.

Suddenly the selfie she'd taken yesterday with the caption "'If you're going through hell, keep going.'—Winston Churchill" seemed not only maudlin and desperate, but also unbelievably pedestrian. There were also a lot of pics of Nacho that she'd thought were totally cute, but now looked more cat-lady tragic. Last week she'd posted a photo of her Moleskine planner and a cup of coffee that she'd Clarendon-filtered for the gods. She'd thought it looked like something out of Reese Witherspoon's feed. But now Edie was horrified to realize that she was not, in fact, Reese Witherspoon; she was just a regular person with nothing better to share than this picture of a coffee and her planner artfully lit on the kitchen table. It had seventeen likes. And then, of course, there were the pictures of Brian and Cayden that she'd wanted to delete and should've deleted, but that were too painful to delete—like erasing them entirely would mean erasing those five months of her life, like they had never happened at all. Those pictures were proof that she wasn't crazy for believing him when he'd said he loved her.

Edie pulled her shirt over her face in shame.

A brief investigation into *The Key*'s cast further underscored Edie's general failings. Not enough gorgeous friends. Not enough bleached-blond hair. Not enough glam portraits of herself smiling, laughing, pouting. Not enough smirking selfies, travelogues, or exercise photos that showed off her hot bod in matching sports bras and leggings. Edie clambered over the moving boxes and ran to the foyer for a good, hard look at herself in her full-length mirror.

Her dark blond hair shot every which way, and suddenly, her T-shirt's BRUNCH SO HARD slogan seemed like a really stupid thing to wear on one's chest. Upon inspection, her underwear was unbelievably large and of the blood moon variety, even though she'd finished her period last week. She'd worn it because, typically, the mental image of a man tearing it off was a good deterrent against casual sex. Now this seemed less like a sensible plan (which clearly she was prepared to abandon) and more like another reason, among a myriad of reasons, why Edie Pepper was still single.

Edie turned sideways and lifted her shirt to inspect her belly, sucking it in and sticking it out. Not great. And why were her tits suddenly falling into her armpits?! She looked over her shoulder to examine her wine-covered ass, picking up her cheeks one by one and then dropping them. She stood on her tiptoes to see if that perked them up. It did not. Gah! Back rolls! Over the past few years, Edie had noticed herself developing an adult woman breeding body, but she didn't think of herself as fat, more like...*Midwestern healthy*. Hearty enough to survive a long, cold winter. But it occurred to her now that all her friends skipped the breadbasket and the women at her office ate lonely forkfuls of field greens at their desks, maybe with a touch of tuna, and went to places called "barre" and "SoulCycle" after work. Most of them were already married.

Edie leaned closer to the mirror. Her nose wasn't too big, so there was that. Her eyes were gray and that was...fine? At any rate, it was her smile that she'd always thought captured her inner whimsy. Edie tossed her hair back and smiled her most beautiful smile, and a shock of previously undetected wrinkles exploded across her face. She stumbled back, dazed and wondering, *Should I be using a cream for that?* She grabbed a pair of tweezers from her purse and started yanking at her eyebrows wildly. For the love of God, what was growing out of her chin? Edie angled her head around for a better look and eventually plucked a black whisker, at least half an inch long, from her jaw. She laid down on the floor and sent Lauren another text: WHERE ARE YOU, THIS IS A CRISIS, I NEED YOU.

It took Edie a moment to decide what to do next, but finally she got up and scoured the entire apartment for a box labeled "Old Shit." She found it in the bathroom and dug around until she found her senior yearbook under a binder of *Sweet Valley High* fan fiction she'd written when she was twelve. She was definitely going to need more wine, so she paused in the kitchen to dump a glug of rosé into her mug before settling back on the couch with the yearbook. Edie closed her eyes for a moment, trying to picture Charlie Bennett, but all she could see now was Bennett Charles. The wine and cognitive dissonance were too much—she felt like she was going crazy, like she couldn't trust her own memories or what was real. Edie took a deep breath and opened the yearbook to the Bs, and there he was, CHARLES BENNETT, sandwiched between Carly Bateman and Daniel Benson.

Looking at his senior portrait, Edie felt a rush of the purest, warmest love. He had a bowl cut of brown curls, and his face was plump and shaped like a potato. He wore wire-rimmed glasses that were too small for his features, and his expression was blank, except for the tiniest purse to his lips that exposed an earnest but unsuccessful imitation of cool. He was wearing a suit, which Edie had forgotten and found extra endearing because he looked so young and silly. Under his name was his senior quote:

> "Home is behind you, the world is ahead."
>
> —*J. R. R. Tolkien*

Edie clutched her heart. Suddenly it seemed impossible that life could've continued all these years without him. They met when they were five. The Bennetts lived just a couple of blocks away from the Peppers, in a classic midcentury with, according to her mother, Alice Pepper, "inexcusable landscaping." As the president of the Wilmette Garden Club, Alice attempted to thwart the budding friendship on horticultural principle alone. "What sort of people don't edge their lawns, Edith?" she'd said, brows raised. "The very least they can do is hire someone."

But there was something about Charlie that Edie always liked. He was guileless and sweet, and despite Alice's oft-repeated disapproval over a close friendship *with a boy*, Edie and Charlie quickly became fixtures in each other's backyards, kitchens, and basements. Charlie never complained when Edie and Lauren gave him makeovers and poked him hard in the eye with a mascara wand. He could always be relied upon to make Monopoly trades that improved Edie's or Lauren's position and diminished his own. He loved *Troop Beverly Hills* and *Don't Tell Mom the Babysitter's Dead* almost as much as they did. And even as time went on and they got older and their interests diverged—Charlie: fantasy novels and Dungeons & Dragons; Edie: boy bands and, well, *boys*—their friendship had always remained. They were bound by shared history and an unwavering commitment to life as indoor kids. They weren't sports people; they were marching band people. They weren't pool-party-this-weekend-at-Maddy-Morrison's-manse people; they were drama club people. They walked through high school like this—*just as friends!*—until one particularly miserable summer day, right before senior year, when everything changed.

Edie and Alice had been running late. Typically, Alice ran the household with military precision, dragging a wild-haired Edie along behind her. But today, the day of Bill Pepper's funeral, it was Alice who seemed to have no concept of time.

She stood at the bay window in the living room, in her neat black dress and heels, staring into the abyss. *We have to go*, Edie called. She crossed the Oriental rug and placed a hand on her mother's back and Alice startled, as if she'd forgotten who, or where, she was entirely.

"Every home needs a man," Alice whispered.

Edie looked out the window and there was Charlie Bennett, mowing the grass that had gotten much too long in the blur of her father's heart attack and death.

"I'm alone now," Alice said.

"That's not true," Edie said. "You have me."

But Edie would leave for college in less than a year. And her father—a man who wore bow ties, who read the paper every night, who slipped her a good luck Werther's Original before her drama club plays, who'd been an old man her entire life, but who'd always loved her—was gone. And somehow her mother already seemed smaller.

Alice took Edie's hand and looked her in the eye. "Find someone to love you," she said. "I won't be around forever, and I don't want you to be alone."

Another memory came to Edie now of Charlie, in the fall of their senior year, right before they were officially boyfriend and girlfriend. They were on a school bus after an away game, sitting together on a pleather seat sized for elementary kids. He'd taken off his marching band jacket and his T-shirt was sweaty from where the bass drum had hung from his soft chest; his neck was splotchy red. He smelled liked fall. When they'd performed the Backstreet Boys' "I Want It That Way" at halftime, she'd matched her steps to the thud of his drum and thought it was unbelievably romantic. It was dark on the bus, and when he'd taken her hand and held it on the seat between them, she could hear Cassandra Bernstein and Jonathan Nash making out in the seat behind them. Charlie had looked at her then, shyly, and smiled. He'd had that one crooked tooth.

Edie's eyes were bleary from wine and despair when Lauren finally walked in, jingling her pet-sitting keys.

"I almost crashed my car into the side of a Walgreens, so thanks for that," she said. "Charlie fucking Bennett, I literally cannot." Lauren kicked off her shoes and pitched her purse on top of a box. "Seriously, when are you going to unpack this place, it's been, what, a month?"

"Charlie Bennett's going to marry a fitness model and have five perfect children and live in a mansion and be rich and tan all year round and I have thirty-eight dollars in my checking account and no one loves me or will ever love me and I'm going to fill my pockets with rocks and throw myself in Lake Michigan. Take care of Nacho."

"Oh, please." Lauren plopped down on the couch and took Edie's mug of rosé and drank. "Charlie Bennett. Charlie Bennett! I mean, when I think about Charlie Bennett, I think about that time he dressed up as Severus Snape at the premiere of *Harry Potter and the Chamber of Secrets* at the mall. Like, this fool was walking around with a wand and shit. This is so weird. I mean, didn't he have, like, a severe skin condition or something?"

"*Yes.*" Edie was completely relieved to be seen again. "He *totally* did. He was always breaking out in hives. And you know what? It never bothered me. Because I loved him."

"Girl."

"It's true," Edie pouted.

"Let me see that." Lauren took the yearbook and began flipping the pages. "Oh my god!" She doubled over with laughter. "Look at you! 'Most Likely to Win the Lottery but Lose the Ticket.' I completely forgot about that! Too good."

Edie looked over Lauren's shoulder at the photo.

"That was during my Christina Aguilera phase. Look at that cropped cardigan. Fuck, have I always been awful?"

"Don't be an idiot. Everyone is awful in high school."

Lauren, of course, had never been awful in high school. Lauren had always been effortlessly cool. A couple of months ago, she'd chopped her hair into a short mullet and dyed it lilac. Tonight she was wearing high-waisted denim shorts over black pantyhose, combat boots, and a preppy striped button-down with her favorite leather jacket on top. Edie would look like she was cosplaying *The Craft* if she tried to wear that get-up. But Lauren just looked like someone you might talk to about bourbon. Or the best BBC deep cuts on Netflix. Or her favorite tattoo artist specializing in intricate floral work. Fucking Lauren.

"Apparently, some people change," Edie said. "Where were you tonight? You're cute."

"I joined a feminist pinball league in Logan Square," Lauren said with a wave of her hand. "I was on my way home when I saw your text. Obviously, I couldn't let you live through this trauma alone. Anyway, I did some googling at the stoplights—did you see he was on *Good Morning America*?"

"What? No. Show me."

Lauren got out her phone and they watched Bennett Charles strut onto the *GMA* set in a gorgeously tailored black suit. He hugged Robin Roberts and flashed a million-dollar smile and a magnanimous wave at the squealing ladies in the studio audience. His bowl cut had been replaced with a trendy pompadour, short on the sides with a deep part, deliberately messy curls cascading over his right eye. The total effect was very sexy-surfer-investment-banker, and *damn* it was good.

"He's seriously so hot now, it's mind-bending," Lauren said. "Literally cannot believe I just said that. I don't even like men. But objectively it's true. Do you think he had plastic surgery?"

"Lauren." Edie chewed her lip. "Don't make fun of me, but I think maybe Charlie Bennett is *The One*."

Lauren squawked with laughter. "Girl, no, he is not. Honestly, he seems pretty douchey."

"Don't say that! Why would you say that?"

"Edie, c'mon! The whole thing is pretty douchey. What kind of person turns their name backward and chugs Muscle Milk 'til they're culturally relevant? It's weird."

On Lauren's phone, Charlie and Robin took their seats. Golden locks and keys fluttered digitally on a screen behind them. Charlie and Robin chatted, but Edie couldn't really concentrate on anything they were saying. All she could think about was all the terrible boyfriends she'd had, all the guys who'd cheated on her, or ghosted her, or dumped her via text, and all the guys to come who'd be exactly the same. What if Charlie Bennett was the only real, true relationship she'd ever have?

"This whole time, all these years, I've been searching for something I already had," she whispered, her fingertip caressing Charlie's yearbook cheek.

"Well, you don't have it anymore!" Lauren burped and wiped her mouth with the back of her hand.

"That's mean!"

"Uh, he's the star of *The Key*—it's all about getting people engaged! Robin just said, 'Are you hoping to end this season with a proposal?' and he said, 'Absolutely.' So, since you're not on this show, you should probably let that shit go." Lauren slung her arm around Edie's shoulders and gave her an encouraging squeeze. "But I promise to watch this trash with you every single week. That is, if you ever unpack this apartment. Seriously, what the fuck, Edie? It's going to be hard to move on if you don't ever put your shit away."

Edie considered this, but really, she didn't want to let it go. Somehow seeing Charlie Bennett on her TV clarified that she'd never really fought for anything of any importance. That she'd just been floating through life, taking it as it came, and that's why she was here now, in this messy apartment instead of a beautiful house. Alone instead of with her husband. Old and dried up and probably barren rather than at Chuck E. Cheese with her adorable children. What was it Lauren had said? *Since you're not on this show, you should probably let that shit go.* Lauren was right! Not about letting it go—why the hell would Edie do that when right in front of her was the guiding hand of fate, shoving her toward the life she was meant to live all along?

Lauren was right that she wasn't on the show. But she *could* be.

"Lauren!" Edie squealed, clutching Lauren's arm. "I'll go on the show!"

"Absolutely not." Lauren gave Edie a look. "Call 911, you've lost your mind."

"Be serious! What if my entire life's happiness depends on me getting on *The Key*?"

"Edie, first of all, it does not. Second of all, they've already started filming. I looked at the website and all his contestants were already there—a bunch of Beckys with Karen moons. And then I looked at *The Key*'s Instagram and there was a pic of him in a hot air balloon with some girl. Like, it's already started. It's happening."

"I know, I saw." Edie felt incredibly dejected.

"Besides, what about that guy you were talking to? That PhD dude? Didn't he have potential?"

"Chemistry Jim dry-humped me to the Talking Heads for like an hour two weeks ago and I never heard from him again."

"Okay, that's bleak," Lauren said. "Wait—didn't you have a date tonight?"

"He said I was too old to get married. I threw my shoe at him."

Lauren raised her eyebrows, impressed. "Good. Fuck him. But also, the entire point of being old is knowing deep in your bones just how great you are and that you don't need to be married!"

Edie grabbed Lauren and held her face in her hands.

"Bible: Do you think I could get on that show?"

Lauren, held captive, mumbled out of puckered lips, "Bible: You're being crazy. Is this about Brian?"

"Of course this is not about Brian!" Edie said. "And it's very rude to insinuate everything in my life is about Brian. I am way over that, and you know what, if me and Charlie falling in love all over again on national television makes Brian feel some kind of way, well, I can't control that." Edie pressed Lauren's cheeks harder. "This is about my One True Love! Don't you want me to be happy?"

Lauren, reluctantly, nodded her head.

"Promise you'll help me," Edie said.

Lauren tried to shake her head no, but Edie persevered and made Lauren's head nod yes until Lauren finally relented and Edie released her.

"I don't understand what you think we're going to do." Lauren said. "Drop him a DM, like, 'Oh, I saw you on TV, can I hit that again?'"

"We should do whatever a fabulous, modern woman would do." Edie paused. "What would a fabulous, modern woman do?"

"I have no idea—I'm not fabulous!"

"Lies! And you're a journalist! You're always making things happen."

"How drunk are you? I can't tell if you're Fun Edie or Throw-Up-in-the-Bathtub Edie."

"Oh my god, I've had three glasses of wine, maybe four. I'm perfectly in control of my faculties. Stay focused! What are we gonna do to get me on that show?"

Lauren sighed. "Well, I guess we could like, find a producer? Tweet at them? Are you sure you want to do this? This seems like a bad idea."

"That's perfect!" Edie squealed. And before Bennett Charles could finish his interview, Edie and Lauren had tracked down a *Key* producer on Twitter, taken a photo of a picture of Edie and Charlie in their dorky marching band uniforms from the yearbook, and tweeted it at @jessa.johnson with the caption, "Hey, Jessa, why you stealing my boyfriend??? I want him back, DM me!!!"

Edie fell back on the couch and sighed. Her journey to true love was about to begin. Again.

4

The first thing Edie remembered when she woke up the next morning was tweeting at that *Key* producer. She shot up in bed, startling Nacho Bell Grande, who jumped three feet into the air and took off yowling down the hall. What kind of person sends mortifying high school photos across the internet to some glamorous Hollywood producer? What the hell was wrong with her? Why would Lauren let her *do* that?

Edie's yearbook was splayed open on the bed, a Sharpied heart freshly drawn around Charlie Bennett's senior pic. She was so stupid! Obviously there was no way Edie Pepper could reclaim the new and improved Charlie Bennett. The wretched unfairness of not being born a supermodel or exceptional in any way really pissed her off, so she kicked the yearbook off the bed and it slammed to the floor. Why-oh-why was it that every single time Edie thought she'd suffered enough, endured the ultimate embarrassment, *there was more*.

Edie looked at her phone warily, racking her brain-catalog of *Super Soul* episodes to guide her through this moment. There was something about everything in your life being a teacher. Sigh. Edie picked up the phone and began to cycle through her notifications.

Holy shit!

She had a DM.

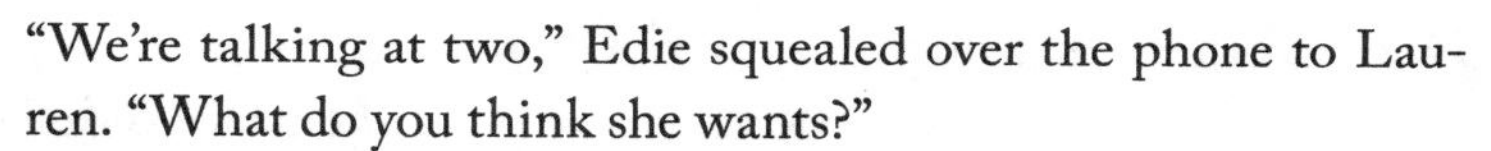

"We're talking at two," Edie squealed over the phone to Lauren. "What do you think she wants?"

"I mean...probably she wants to talk about you joining the show?"

Edie almost passed out on the kitchen floor.

"But, Edie, seriously, don't you think this is going too far? You've watched enough reality TV to know they probably just want to put you on for shock value, like 'wocka-wocka, here's your ex-girlfriend!'"

"You're so cynical!" Edie was already envisioning her spring nuptials to Charlie Bennett. She would carry a bouquet of calla lilies and wear her hair down because wasn't it true that her neck was too short and calla lilies were the most elegant wedding flower?

"They'll make you look stupid. You know the kinds of girls who go on these shows, Edie."

"Lauren! Why would they do that? *The Key* is all about love!"

"Alice will never approve."

Well, that was definitely true. But Alice could be managed. "If I end up married, Alice won't care how I got there. You think Alice is clinging to life to play bridge? She's waiting for me to get married."

"But what about your job? You have an actual life, Edie. You're just gonna drop everything to date Charlie Bennett? On TV?"

"Drop everything? What's there to drop?" Edie's life suddenly slid into focus and she felt incredibly clear. "You've got a career, Lolo. I've got *a job.* And I couldn't care less about being a copywriter for an insurance company—all these years I've just been going to work, waiting for my actual life to start. Even this apartment, all the boxes. It's like, here I am, ready to *go*. Don't you think it's a sign? All I want is for my big love—for my *life*—to begin. And if Charlie Bennett can transform himself into a Hemsworth brother on prime-time TV, why can't I?"

The more Edie thought about it, the more she realized this was exactly right. She'd always understood Charlie, understood that they both had that thrumming thing inside, that constant *not enough not enough*, but he had battled it and *won*. Edie felt a surge of confidence—maybe she would never be a model, or a fitness instructor, or a manic pixie dream girl, but adorable blast from the past ex-girlfriend, the one you were supposed to be with all along? That she could do.

She might even be great at it.

"Edie, you're super talented in all sorts of ways. What about investing in yourself instead?"

"Love doesn't just disappear. Charlie and I were in love before; why can't we be in love again? And get engaged!"

"Marriage is oppression," Lauren said with authority.

"You're ridiculous. Who even says that?"

"Literally every feminist thinker ever."

"Well, Nora Ephron didn't say that, and I worship at the altar of Nora Ephron."

"It might be helpful to stop internalizing fiction like it's a template for real life."

"Instead of *When Harry Met Sally*, it'll be *When Charlie Met Edie*. Again!"

"I read this article that theorized that our mothers told us we could do anything," Lauren continued, as if she hadn't heard

Edie. "That we could have it all—careers, husbands, children. And then they told their sons to go out and find a nice girl to take care of them. It made me so grateful to be a lesbian. And unlocked why all the hetero marrieds we know can't figure out who should unload the dishwasher."

"I don't mind unloading the dishwasher," Edie said, biting her lip and staring at yesterday's dishes.

"Don't get mad, but I'm gonna ask you again: Is this about Brian?"

Edie huffed. Just because the breakup with Brian had broken Edie into a million little pieces didn't mean *every* decision Edie made now or in the future was about Brian! And those million little pieces weren't even really about *Brian* as much as they were about the existential crisis the breakup with Brian had caused. Sure, Edie had been hurt many times before, but this was a thirty-five-year-old woman's hurt. A hurt that encompassed every disappointment, every broken dream, and every bad decision she'd ever made and knotted them up into one big blanket of despair that Edie had wrapped around herself like a shroud. For two weeks after he'd broken things off, Edie had told her boss she had mono and laid in bed watching *The Great British Bakeoff* (when she needed to be soothed) or early seasons of *Grey's Anatomy* (when she needed to sob). Periodically the iPad would go black and demand to know "Are you still watching?" and Edie would watch the tears snake down her face in its murky reflection.

She looked like an old, sad person.

She *was* an old, sad person.

Eventually Edie had been forced from her bed when the movers started pounding at the door. She'd stupidly given up her apartment and signed the lease and paid the deposit on the new place herself because Brian was mid-divorce and blah blah blah it would be easier that way. And so, when he'd left her, she'd still had to move. Move out of the little one-bedroom in Lakeview where she'd become an adult. Edie suddenly felt nostalgic for every part of her old apartment, even though every spring it had ants, and the bathroom was tiled pea green, and it was on the third floor and hauling groceries up there was a real pain in the ass. The day the movers arrived, Edie had done such a poor job of packing that they'd just started shoving her things into boxes while grumbling and exchanging angry looks. Edie had stood in the kitchen, sort of wrapping dishes but mostly just standing there with a tape gun stuck uselessly in her hand, until Lauren had shown up and taken over.

It wasn't that Edie didn't know she was a mess. She did. She was just somehow helpless in the face of it.

The thing was, for the past thirteen years Edie Pepper had lived in a major city filled with men. And for the past thirteen years, she'd been dated and dumped and dated and dumped, yet somehow, after every bad date or unreturned text or bad sexual encounter where some man tried to gag her with his dick, Edie had always been able to replenish her wellspring of hope. Because facing the possibility that this might be it, that none of life's big joys were meant for her—no husband, no house, no babies, no family vacations, no Disneyland!—was even more painful than nursing her hope for a great big love back to health over and over again.

And then she'd met Brian.

Their first date was at Guthrie's, a bar in Wrigleyville that had endless stacks of board games. Edie thought it was perfect and adorable as they drank draft beers and played the game of Life. At the end, instead of counting their individual monies and assets, he'd taken his little blue peg man and his little blue peg child out of his little blue car and put them in her little pink car with her little pink peg woman and said, "Life's better together, dontcha think?" And then he'd leaned over the board and kissed her. Can you even imagine? He was smart and thoughtful and laughed at her jokes, and even though he preferred to have sex the exact same way every single time, she always came.

This is it, she'd thought. *This is finally it.*

On the day she moved to the too-big, too-expensive apartment in Roscoe Village, she'd told the movers somewhat hysterically not to put anything in the second bedroom that had been meant for Brian's two-year-old son, Cayden. After the movers left, she'd stood in there, running her fingers over the vintage built-in bookshelves she'd planned to fill with books about bears and frogs and pigeons finding their way in the world. Losing Cayden, a little person she had absolutely no claim to, broke her heart. For the love she felt for him, for the warm feeling of family she felt when the three of them were together, and for the ever present and suddenly screaming fear that because of all of her flaws, she would miss out on the fundamental human experience that was motherhood.

But that had been weeks ago, and Edie was basically all better now.

"It was literally the craziest thing I'd seen on television since that dragon burned up the Iron Throne—like, it understood the quest for the throne itself was what killed Daenerys, which was like, wait, does this dragon *actually* understand Westerosi politics right now?" Edie said in a rush. She paused and took a breath. More calmly she continued: "What I'm trying to say is, I was a teensy bit drunk and a whole lot shocked to see Charlie Bennett on my TV, and I'm sorry I wasted your time. I was out of my mind tweeting at you last night."

"Are you kidding me? We're *thrilled* you tweeted at us," *Key* producer Jessa Johnson enthused. Her voice was bouncy,

Californian. "Peter—that's our showrunner—thinks you're the rock Bennett needs to get through this process, and he can't wait to meet you!"

"Wait, what? *Really?*"

"Oh, yeah, of course. We're hoping you'll come to LA tomorrow for a chat."

Edie could not believe what she was hearing—fly to Los Angeles in what, less than twenty-four hours? "Are you serious?" Edie asked. "I have to work tomorrow."

"I don't know how familiar you are with the show," Jessa continued, "but after Wyatt Cash, we're more focused than ever on telling stories about true love. And you and Bennett have all this *history*—I just loved that photo of the two of you. Can you send more? We really think you would inject the show with authenticity, you know? Totally different from the other girls."

Oh, yes, Edie did know. Obviously, the other girls hadn't known Charlie Bennett since kindergarten like Edie had. She could already envision the kind of conversations they were having, sitting on some romantic moonlit patio.

The other girls: So, what's your favorite color? What's your favorite food?

Edie: Remember that time we learned all the moves to *Dirty Dancing* in my basement? Except I was Johnny and you were Baby because you were still smaller than me, and that's the only way we could execute the lift?

"I don't see this as just a one- or two-episode arc," Jessa continued. "I see you and Bennett engaged. What's more romantic than falling in love with your high school sweetheart all over again? I'm excited just thinking about it."

As much as Edie tried to keep Lauren's warnings top of mind, Jessa's enthusiasm easily ignited Edie's manic optimism all over again. What *was* more romantic than falling in love with your high school sweetheart all over again?

"It's a once-in-a-lifetime opportunity," Jessa added.

Edie pictured her life as it was now and would be in the foreseeable future. Snooze her alarm five times instead of getting up and working out (even though her intention was always to work out). Finally roll out of bed. Commute downtown. Arrive at cubicle. Scour the internet. Write and copyedit boring things until lunch (the highlight of her day, because Edie always paid extra for guacamole). Return to office. Scroll on her phone. Sit in boring meetings about boring things. Try to find someone to go to happy hour with, but everyone's married. Go on an internet date that would inevitably be awful, even though she'd put makeup on. Return home. Pizza. Wine. Bravo. Despair. Go to bed with a cat instead of a man. Rinse and repeat.

The way Edie saw it, there were only two options: go to Los Angeles and reclaim the love of her life, or stay here and, what, *unpack her spoons*?

What Edie understood love to be was this: Love was the future. It was the way out. Love was what would change everything. Being in love and getting married and buying a home and starting a family, this was how Edie—since she was a little kid watching *Family Ties* and *Roseanne* and *The Cosby Show*—saw her life playing out. And so, sure, the *Key* of it all seemed insane *(it was insane)*, but wasn't Edie at the end of the line? She was thirty-five years old, and she'd made enough life choices that they'd all started to stack up and stack up and now she was left trying to shove her foot in a closing door before she was locked out for good.

"We believe in your love story," Jessa said.

And just like that, Edie was calling in sick and packing her bags for Los Angeles, because she believed in it, too.

To: Peter Kennedy
From: Jessa Johnson
Subject: Show me the money

Peter,

First of all, I just want to say, words mean nothing. MONEY TALKS. And since I'm basically single-handedly delivering you the most dramatic season ever, I'm expecting a sizable bonus or raise or EP title. I just want to put that out there so we don't spend the rest of production strangling each other. Please, just make it happen.

Stop rolling your eyes. Because I found Bennett Charles's high school girlfriend and she is *desperate* to join the show and win back her man. Oh, and she is A MESS. Her entire personality is "obsessed with Bennett Charles." I got her on your calendar at 11 a.m. tomorrow. Apparently, they were deeply in love—wait till you see the pictures. Let's just say, if you crossed Screech Powers with that guy from *Frozen*, you know, the snowman who was also the original messy missionary brother in *The Book of Mormon*? And sprinkle in some asthma and psoriasis? That's high school Bennett Charles.

You're welcome,
Jessa

5

This Edie Pepper situation was giving Peter Kennedy formidable heartburn. He sat at his computer, loudly chewing a handful of Tums and anxiously awaiting an eight a.m. status call with the network. Since the Wyatt Cash incident, the network had kept Peter on a tight leash. In addition to the status calls with RX chair and chief content officer Carole Steele—now there was a woman who really gave Peter indigestion—he was also expected to check in via hot sheets and dailies, the contestants were required to meet with the resident psychologist weekly, and any deviation from the standard horse-drawn carriage, fairytale narrative was to be explicitly cleared by the top. Peter was still debating whether to tell Carole about his impending meeting with Edie Pepper—pros: honesty; cons: verbal assaults on his intelligence—but since he'd already decided to put Edie Pepper on the first plane back to wherever the hell she was coming from, he determined the juice would, in fact, not be worth the squeeze.

Peter rubbed his temples against a looming headache. Jessa was great at following her instincts in the field, and the contestants loved her, but this Edie Pepper situation reflected just how little she understood about the future of the show post–Wyatt Cash. Fleeing advertisers, budget cuts (at $2 million per viewable hour, *The Key* was not a cheap show to make), and a desperate need for sponsored partnerships with resorts, airlines, and even stupid things like Crest Whitestrips were vital just to keep them going. They had to deliver the under-budget, redemptive season that Carole Steele and the network expected if they were going to survive, and their focus needed to be on resurrecting America's faith in true love and *The Key*'s process. They were making a fairy tale about *soulmates*, not some tedious C-plot featuring a tragic high school girlfriend. Regular people ruined the fantasy—that was a fact. And from what he'd seen on Instagram, Edie Pepper was so average she could've been some girl he'd walked right past at a bar. Every time she appeared on-screen, people would think about going to bed early, not drooling over gorgeous people in a hot tub or buying product placements on their phones during commercial breaks. No, what they needed to do was *stick to the format*: fireworks and helicopters, bungee jumping and slow dancing, hot air balloons and hot bodies.

Peter's Apple Watch buzzed, and he looked away from his email to the hourly stand notification on his wrist. He retrieved his jump rope from a desk drawer and started in on a one-minute burst of cardio. He'd heard there'd been a lot of suspicion from the network about what he did or did not know about Wyatt Cash. Look, he hadn't known *anything* about Wyatt Cash. Peter began to jump faster. He hadn't known *anything* until he saw the *Us Weekly* cover with the rest of America. Well, that wasn't exactly true—they'd called him for comment a couple of days prior and he'd done his best to squash the story, calling in favors from reporters and editors who could pull strings. But in the end, it was just too big. No tabloid could be expected to shelve photos of the cattle-ranching *Key* suitor at a gay bar in Miami, making out with a man in a thong at a foam party.

Yes—*fine*—it was Peter's fault he'd let Wyatt out of his sight. But Wyatt wasn't a *hostage*, and Peter had believed him when he said he was going home for the weekend to see his sick mamaw in Abilene before they started filming for ten weeks. It'd seemed reasonable!

Had there been signs? That's what everyone wanted to know. How the hell was Peter supposed to know? Last time he checked, gender didn't exist anymore, and everyone was pan or sapio or poly or some other term he hadn't heard of yet because he was thirty-fucking-nine and worked three hundred hours a week. And he was divorced, so he didn't even have a wife to keep him in the loop on things. So how the hell was Peter Kennedy supposed to know that Wyatt Cash was gay? Or bi? Or demi? Or whatever! Sure, Wyatt spent a lot of time on his hair, but so did all the guys these days. And they were *all* on Rogaine. (Peter wasn't because he didn't need it.) (Secretly, he took pride in that.)

Honestly, Peter had always been a little suspicious of Wyatt's cowboy hats, wide stride, and hokey aphorisms, but he'd chalked it up to a Southern thing that Peter just didn't understand because he was from Connecticut. He didn't think it would benefit him to mention that now. Peter dropped the jump rope and went back to his computer.

Of course, the story exploded. Every news outlet covered it, former contestants showed up on entertainment programs and podcasts to weigh in, and for two days *Brokeback Mountain* was the most streamed movie on the internet. Even Jake Gyllenhaal tweeted about the tender way Wyatt had cupped that guy's ass. The ensuing think pieces were eviscerating:

DECOLONIZING DESIRE: HOW WYATT CASH DRAGGED *THE KEY* INTO THE 21ST CENTURY

***THE KEY*'S BIG LGBTQIA+ PROBLEM**

***THE KEY* AND THE FEMINIST WORK THAT REMAINS UNDONE**

BREAKING UP WITH *THE KEY*

GEN Z DOESN'T NEED ENGAGEMENT RINGS: *THE KEY* AS A RELIC OF MODERN ROMANCE

OPINION: *THE KEY* HASN'T BEEN ABOUT LOVE FOR A LONG TIME

It was that last one (and all the others like it) that really hurt. They argued the show had become an empty fame factory, churning out social media stars for a morally bankrupt audience. That there hadn't been a *Key* wedding in four seasons (true). That the show's lack of diversity and heteronormative, patriarchal agenda were outdated at best, corrupt at worst. The bloggers and podcasters rang the death knell for *The Key*, the advertisers panicked, and the network, struggling to forge its own identity in a new woke world, had threatened to pull the plug entirely.

But after much pleading and assuring, the network finally acquiesced to recasting the lead and moving the twenty-second season forward on a slight delay. So, while Wyatt Cash began a LGBTQIA+ press tour and inked deals for underwear endorsements and nightclub appearances, Peter scoured the Earth for his replacement. The requirements: Must be able to start filming immediately. Must have zero connection to *The Key*, reality TV, or anything or anyone in the show's universe—this time they'd start fresh. Must be willing to get engaged *no matter what.* Must be good-looking and charming enough to make the women of America fall in love with the show all over again and save all their jobs.

Peter knew that times had changed since *The Key*'s humble beginnings in the mid-aughts. Over the past few years, social media had become a major part of the *Key* experience. It was one of the few shows left on network television whose audience watched live and zealously discussed episodes in real time. The audience loved following the contestants on social and the contestants loved being followed. The people who went on the show wanted to be famous, and the show's exposure gave them notoriety they could monetize. Peter couldn't control that.

But in a particularly confounding ouroboros, the bigger the cast's social accounts became, the less earnest they appeared, undercutting the very spirit of the show, which was *earnestly* about a male or female suitor finding their *soulmate* through dates focused on discovery, compatibility, and one-of-a-kind adventures. Contestants had to at least give the *appearance* of being in it for love. Because Sydney from San Diego, who'd been on the show for two fucking weeks getting paid to schlock laxative tea to fourteen-year-olds on Instagram did not read as "here for the right reasons."

Audiences were fickle. They might give you a million followers. They might like some winks and jokes. But the second they thought you were being insincere—that you were playing them—they'd turn on you. That's what was exciting about it—finding the authenticity under the farce. (The first layer being the cameras, of course.) So, in what was a particularly genius move in Peter's estimation, he'd decided to go straight to the source and search for men already established as mid-level influencers. Men who, sure, the show could help, but who also didn't really need the show. Men who could carry an *I've got everything, I just need someone to share it with* storyline, both on the show and off.

Enter Bennett Charles.

He was well known to a niche audience—adventurers, extreme sports lovers, travel bloggers. He was a little old (thirty-five) but came with a great backstory totally new to the franchise: guy spends his twenties traveling the world, eventually turns adventure into a "career" in endorsements, inspirational speaking engagements, and some minor philanthropy, until finally rootlessness begins to plague him. A steady itch of loneliness somehow making everything less *fun*. When Peter showed up, Bennett was already looking for an answer—all Peter had to do was hand it to him. Wife up.

On their very first call, it became clear that Bennett Charles had never had an original thought in his life. But after the Wyatt Cash debacle, that's *exactly* what Peter (and the network) wanted. Sure, perhaps using words like *dude*, and *bro*, and *sick* wasn't in Peter's natural wheelhouse, but this wasn't the first meathead Sigma Alpha Whatever-the-Fuck Peter had produced, and the visuals would be stunning—mountain vistas, shirtless rock climbing, fresh water and fresh air, and Sweaters for Sherpas fundraising initiatives. Peter could already hear the opening narration: *Will Bennett Charles finally find the woman of his dreams? Is he ready to give up a life of globetrotting adventure to settle down and start a family?* What the viewers wanted was *fantasy*, and what was more fantastic than a guy who'd summited Kilimanjaro?

(Everest, of course, was at the top of Bennett's bucket list.)

Honestly, guys who BASE jumped liked attention, so it wasn't difficult to convince Bennett to spend ten weeks dating twenty gorgeous women on national TV. He wasn't entirely stupid—Bennett saw the dollar signs that came with this sort of exposure—but he also seemed sincere, hopeful that he might find the woman of his dreams on the show.

What did it matter if Peter thought Bennett was an epic douche? Epic douche was perfect for reality TV.

Still, Peter had to get Carole on board. So he took Bennett to New York for an emergency meeting. He told Bennett to just "be himself," and Bennett delivered, arriving at the RX lobby in realistically scuffed boots, jeans, and a simple white button-down that he'd left unbuttoned practically to his navel, peacocking his waxed and tanned chest in a ridiculous *Crocodile Dundee* sort of way. Conversely, Peter had dialed up the prep: Hugo Boss houndstooth blazer, light blue Gucci button-down, Ted Baker khaki slacks, brown Prada loafers, and his Tom Ford glasses. The further they'd traveled into the buttoned-up corporate offices, the more cartoonish Bennett seemed, and the more confident Peter felt. Here he was, delivering a crystal-clear idea.

After only a fifty-three-minute wait, they were ushered into Carole's office. She rose from behind her desk, tall, thin, her beaky face framed by a sleek blond bob, and at the sight of her, Peter instantly broke out in a sweat. Carole was impossible to manipulate. (Also, she kept the thermostat at a balmy seventy-six degrees to accommodate a rotating selection of tight designer dresses.) She crossed the plush rug in her four-inch heels and took Bennett's hand. Peter watched her clock the lotus tattoo on Bennett's forearm, and the bracelets in string and bead on his left wrist. Bennett bestowed upon her a roll of Tibetan prayer flags and thanked her for "trusting him with this journey." After Carole had seen enough and ushered Bennett out of her office, she'd brushed the prayer flags into the trash and dug her red talons into Peter's forearm.

"If this season doesn't give me a clean love story and motherfucking goosebumps every Tuesday night at eight p.m.," she'd said, "I'm going to stab you to death with my Louboutin."

Jesus, his esophagus was on fire.

The phone rang. "Hi, Peter, I have Carole for you, please hold," Carole's assistant said.

"Peter!" Carole trilled. "How's the wife?"

"Carole! Always a pleasure. I haven't spoken to her recently. Since we're divorced." Peter attempted a lighthearted chuckle but choked on it and started coughing.

"Oh, Peter, please, I know that. I saw Julie last week at the September issue party. She looked fabulous. So where are we?"

Peter grimaced. "Well, as I wrote in the report I sent to Stacey yesterday, overall, we're very pleased with how the girls are responding to Bennett. We've adapted the schedule to ensure extra one-on-one time to continue building strong enthusiasm."

"I suppose we're incurring extra costs as the timeline continues to shift."

"I'll have Cameron send over the detailed projections. We've attempted to offset cost with a longer production scheduled in LA and truncating the travel schedule."

"I'm told Wyatt's been all over the podcast circuit."

"Yes, but he's mostly stuck to the script—life is about discovery, learning from mistakes, et cetera. Everything's on track for Wyatt's story to be dead by Bennett's premiere in November."

"Good. I've put Tegan on PR. I want to see Bennett everywhere. The sooner the women of America forget about Wyatt Cash the better. And if the plan is to be in LA longer, she should be able to book Bennett on *Ellen* at the very least. Ask for a segment with babies. Push the 'Bennett wants to be a dad' stuff."

"We can do that."

"Any frontrunners?"

"It's a little early to tell, but there's a girl named Bailey who's very California fresh, All-American—you'll like her. We've got a possible villain in a former ballet dancer, and, overall, we're making sure the drama is all in the name of love, as they say."

"We're two weeks in and that's all you've got?"

"Well, as you know, we lost a handful of girls because of the filming delay and Wyatt's casting change, but we feel positive about the commitment from those who stayed on."

"But where's the story, Peter? Why am I watching?"

Peter didn't know what to say. He'd been playing it safe *on purpose*. No stunts, no manufactured drama, just a lot of candlelight and close shots of Bennett kissing the girls slowly. Isn't that what they'd discussed? *Sticking to the format*. "We've been focused on going back to our roots and concentrating on romance. Those storylines take a minute to tease out. It takes time to figure out who Bennett has real connections with," Peter said. When Carole didn't say anything, he added, "We're planning a pool party. Get everyone out in their bikinis."

"This sounds exceedingly boring," Carole said. "I don't care who Bennett has 'real connections' with. I said 'love story,' Peter, not 'boring shit I don't want to watch.' The emphasis is on *story*. Every time I think you understand me, I realize you're off in your own little world, skipping around the offices that I pay for, doing God knows what, when what I need you to do is *produce*. That's what *production* is, Peter. I need you to *produce* a fucking storyline."

Jesus fucking Christ. Peter had been a producer for eleven years and *The Key*'s showrunner for the past four; he knew how to create a storyline. He'd been a screenwriter, for chrissakes! Peter felt a familiar wave of regret wash over him, an uncomfortable uncertainty about every decision he'd made since he was twenty-two and broke and writing spec scripts for *The Sopranos*. He'd hustled around town during every pilot season, trying to get hired onto a show, hopefully a show that got picked up to series so he could finally have health insurance and a reprieve from his parents' glare.

But time and again he failed until eventually his options turned out to be (1) become a waiter with all the other washed-up Hollywood rejects, (2) go back to law school and become a lawyer like his father, or (3) make the most out of the PA job he'd landed through a college buddy on *The Anna Nicole Show* and, seriously, anything, literally *anything*, was better than working on that piece of shit, so when he got the chance to jump to *The Amazing Race* as a story editor and then *Survivor* and then *The Key*, it seemed like his career had finally taken off and he never looked back. Until moments like this when his own life seemed unfamiliar and disappointing, and he wondered how he'd become the mastermind behind a fairy tale he didn't even believe in.

And now, it looked like Carole Steele was going to fire him. Between the Wyatt Cash scandal and possibly being axed from Bennett's redemption season, he'd be lucky to get a job producing the local news in Omaha, because no one in LA would touch him.

He had to do it. He didn't want to do it—he knew it was a very bad terrible idea—but he couldn't end up in fucking *Omaha*.

"Well, I do have a storyline to run by you," he said. "We've found Bennett's high school girlfriend, and apparently she wants him back. I have to warn you—she's not a beauty queen. She's more like a woman you'd see at a bowling alley in Minnesota. But she's very enthusiastic."

Silence.

Peter propped his head in his hand and squeezed his eyes shut. He pulled at his hair for a point of distraction.

"Are you really this stupid, Peter?" Carole said finally. "Why didn't you lead with this? This is *perfect*. This is exactly what the show needs—a real person falling in love. This is what I want, Bennett engaged to his high school sweetheart. It's the saccharine, homegrown fantasy of every woman's dreams. Make it happen."

And with that, Carole Steele hung up.

Fuck. Peter dropped the phone and collapsed face first onto his desk. How in the ever-loving fuck had he just pinned his entire future in television on some premature cat lady he'd never even met? How could he be so fucking stupid? Peter banged his forehead against the particle board. He'd just sold the impossible to Carole Steele. It was an *impossible* love story. There was no way a guy like Bennett Charles was going to get engaged to a girl like Edie Pepper. Especially with all these supermodels around. Is this what would finally defeat him? Some copyeditor from *Chicago?*

Peter refused. Just flat-out refused. He sat up and poured another handful of Tums into his palm. Peter chewed and considered. Maybe she could be...spruced up?

Fuck.

BENNETT CHARLES PLAYS "TAKING CANDY FROM A BABY"

Added by TheEllenShow
1.9 million views / cc

[ELLEN]
Alright, after the biggest tabloid scandal of the summer, *The Key* is making its comeback with our next guest. Please welcome activist, entrepreneur, adventurer, and all-around hunk, Bennett Charles!

[MUSIC: "ALL AROUND THE WORLD" BY LISA STANFIELD]

Been around the world and I-I-I-I can't find my baby
I don't know when and I don't know why, Why he's gone away

[AUDIENCE]
(applauding, cheering)

[ELLEN]
Hi, Bennett Charles.

[BENNETT CHARLES]
I'm on *Ellen*! What a trip! Can you believe this?

[AUDIENCE]
(applauding, cheering)

[ELLEN]
Now, tell me, how are you still single? You don't look like you'd have too much trouble getting dates.

[BENNETT CHARLES]
Aw, that's so nice! But it's harder than you might expect—

[ELLEN]
—because of the muscles?

[AUDIENCE]
(laughing)

[ELLEN]
Now, Bennett, I know we just met, but can I ask you something personal?

[BENNETT CHARLES]
Of course! Nothing's off limits. I'm an open book.

[ELLEN]
It might be hard to talk about, but visibility and representation are important... are you a heterosexual?

[BENNETT]
(clapping, laughing)
Ellen! Love comes in all shapes and sizes, and you know I support all the beauty in the world!

[AUDIENCE]
(applauding)

[BENNETT]
And I am totally ready to fall in love and find my Mrs.

[ELLEN]
When did you find out you were going to be *The Key*'s next suitor?

[BENNETT CHARLES]
It was totally unexpected! But you know what I always say, "live the adventure, share the love."

[AUDIENCE]
(cheering)

[BENNETT CHARLES]
It was all super-fast and I can't wait to take America on my journey. I'm so stoked to meet my future wife.

[ELLEN]
What are you looking for in a wife?

[BENNETT CHARLES]
I'm really just looking for someone who's beautiful inside and out. Kind. Has an adventurous spirit. Wants to give back and make this world a better place.

[ELLEN]
I'm already taken.

[AUDIENCE]
(laughing)

[BENNETT CHARLES]
(clapping, laughing)
You're the best.

[ELLEN]
Now, are you sure you're ready to settle down? You seem like a guy who's always on the move.

[BENNETT CHARLES]
Definitely. I've been all around the world and had so many amazing adventures. And what I've come to learn—and this is true in every culture in every city in every nation—is the only thing that really matters is the relationships you create and the people you love.

[AUDIENCE]
(collective aww)

[ELLEN]
And I heard that you want to be a dad?

[BENNETT CHARLES]
Absolutely.

[ELLEN]
So you thought the best way to do that was on TV?

[AUDIENCE]
(laughing)

[BENNETT CHARLES]
(laughing)
You're too much!

[ELLEN]
Do you think we should find out if Bennett's ready to be a dad?

[AUDIENCE]
(applauding, cheering)

[ELLEN]
Let's play "Taking Candy from a Baby!"

[AUDIENCE]
(applauding, cheering)

[ELLEN]
Ok, Bennett, we've got three games to test your parenting skills. Bring out the babies!

[AUDIENCE]
(applauding, cheering)

[ELLEN]
Alright, you've got thirty seconds to diaper all three of these baby dolls. Do you think you can do it?

[BENNETT CHARLES]
Do you think I can do it?

[AUDIENCE]
(applauding, cheering)

[ELLEN]
Ready, set, go!

[AUDIENCE]
(applauding, cheering)

[BENNETT CHARLES]
Oh my god, how does this work? He's peeing! He's peeing on me!

[ELLEN]
That's why you have to put the diaper on him!

[BENNETT CHARLES]
I'm just going to turn him over!

[ELLEN]
Go to the next one! Hurry!

[BENNETT CHARLES]
You've got to be kidding me! She's got the runs!

[ELLEN]
(laughing)
What did they feed this baby?

[BENNETT CHARLES]
It's okay little baby.

[ELLEN]
Hurry! Go to the next one!

[BENNETT CHARLES]
Oh god, it's doing one and two! How did you make them do this?

[ELLEN]
(laughing)

[BENNETT CHARLES]
How do I make it stop? Help!

[ELLEN]
I can't help you! I only have dogs!

[AUDIENCE]
(laughing)

[ELLEN]
On to the next game! Can you parallel park this minivan while your baby is crying without hitting any of these soccer players, and deliver the team snacks in thirty seconds or less?

[BENNETT CHARLES]
(laughing)
Honestly, I don't think I can.

[AUDIENCE]
(laughing)

[BENNETT CHARLES]
I don't really drive much? I like to use my feet or take public transportation. Better for the environment.

[ELLEN]
Now you know your first question for all your dates: "Can you drive? I need someone who drives."

[AUDIENCE]
(laughing)

[ELLEN]
On to the next game! Ok, Bennett, we've got Joey the Toddler here and he's got some candy. We're gonna need you to retrieve at least one piece of candy from him—can you do it?

[BENNETT CHARLES]
Joey's my boy! I got this!

[AUDIENCE]
(applauding, cheering)

[BENNETT CHARLES]
Hey, kiddo, what's up? I'm Uncle Benny. Can I share your candy?

[TODDLER]
(sobbing)

[ELLEN]
Too creepy! Too creepy! You're scaring him! Try something else!

[BENNETT CHARLES]
It's cool, it's cool, man. Let's be chill.

[TODDLER]
(whimper)

[BENNETT CHARLES]
Lookee here, I've got something cool. It's the Key to My Heart! Let's trade!

[ELLEN]
Is the baby gonna do it? Is he gonna do it? . . . He did it!

[AUDIENCE]
(applauding, cheering)

[BENNETT CHARLES]
I'm gonna need that back later, man, but it's cool, you can chew on it for now.

[ELLEN]
What a comeback for Bennett Charles! Watch out, ladies, he's a sweet talker!

[AUDIENCE]
(applauding, cheering)

[ELLEN]
Bennett, I wish you the best of luck. We're all rooting for you to find your True Love.

[BENNETT CHARLES]
Aw, thanks, Ellen.

[ELLEN]
The Key airs Tuesdays at 8pm on RX this November. We'll be back right after this.

6

It went without saying that the women who made it through enough rounds of casting to be ushered into Peter's conference room for the final stamp of approval were the kind of women who could easily be imagined on the cover of *People* showcasing a three-carat rock next to a LOVE AT FIRST SIGHT! headline. So when Edie Pepper walked in with her runny nose, messy ponytail, yoga pants, and bright red University of Wisconsin sweatshirt with a strutting badger across the chest, Peter couldn't help but think she looked less like a luminous fiancée and more like—as Wyatt would say—she'd been rode hard and put away wet.

"Welcome to Los Angeles," Peter said, extending a hand.

Edie sneezed loudly three times. "Oh my god, so sorry. I must be allergic to Hollywood." She laughed and wiped her nose with the back of her hand before shaking his. "It's been like this ever since I got off the plane."

"Yes. Well. It's a desert. It can be dusty."

Peter wiped his hand on his pants and wondered just how badly Bennett was going to react when he saw Edie on set for the first time. A couple of years ago, Peter had seen his own high school girlfriend, Claire Martin, at a Whole Foods in Greenwich, and he'd immediately thrown down his avocados and fled. Wasn't this the response most people had when confronted with a former flame and, by extension, a former version of themselves? Over Edie's shoulder, Jessa was waggling her eyebrows like *See! See!* Yeah, Peter saw. He saw disaster. Peter wasn't especially worried about getting Bennett back on track once the Edie Pepper bomb dropped—working leads was Peter's specialty—but getting Bennett to forget about all the other girls—girls who were much more suited to him, frankly—and make him fall in love with this middle-aged, Midwestern Cinderella? Now *that* was going to be a problem.

"I thought I'd have time to change before I got here." Edie sneezed again. "I brought a dress, but there was so much traffic—"

"I already told her it's no problem," Jessa interrupted, shooing Edie farther into the conference room. "This is LA! The biggest directors in town run around in flip-flops."

"Of course you'd say that," Edie said. "I've literally never seen anyone look as good as you do right this second."

Christ, Peter didn't even need to hear what came next. Over the past few years, he'd sat through a ridiculous number of conversations about Jessa's beauty routine. "Looking good is about access, Peter," Jessa had said to him once when he complained about yet another fifteen-minute conversation about eyelash serum. "Which is not something *you*"—she pointed her bourbon at him over the editing desk—"a white, cis man has to worry about." Peter didn't think this was entirely true but knew better than to say so to Jessa. He'd traded on his relatively good looks his entire life. He knew how to wear his hair, put together an outfit. (Today's look was casual but crisp—cashmere sweater, jeans, five-hundred-dollar loafers, and the Apple Watch on the upgraded Hermès band.) Undoubtedly, it was more difficult for women, but this was LA—everyone had a stylist on speed dial.

"It's a capsule wardrobe. You could totally do it," Jessa said.

Jessa was sort of generically beautiful—long blond hair, full lips, simple nose—but with little geometric tattoos on her fingers, a nose ring, and, most of the time, a mischievous look in her eyes, all of which lent her an effortless California cool. "Every day I wear a good pair of jeans, a bodysuit, mules, and a jean or leather jacket," Jessa continued. "Then I pop on a bold lip, a high pony, and big earrings. Done and done!"

Peter gritted his teeth and went to set up the camera.

"A bodysuit? I could never." Edie laughed, taking a seat at the table. "Seriously, I'm having so many feelings right now." She started singing, "You're the meaning in my life, you're the inspiration..."

"Is that Chicago?" Peter asked from behind the camera.

"Respect Peter Cetera, please." Edie laughed. "Oh! I almost forgot—I brought you something." She dug around in her backpack and retrieved a small plastic snow globe of the Chicago skyline. She held it out to him and smiled. She had a big smile, a toothy smile. A genuine smile. Honestly, it was a nice feature, but still, Peter found it off-putting. He was used to fame whores and sycophants—he knew how to handle fame whores and sycophants. But Edie's smile reminded him of things he never thought much about at all, like pancakes and Sunday afternoons.

"It's dumb. It's just from the airport," she added when he didn't say anything.

Peter realized he was being weird. He came out from behind the camera and took the globe. "You're hitting the Chicago theme hard," he said with a muster of charm. "Has anyone ever loved the Windy City more?"

"Barack Obama?" she said with that smile. "Oprah? Ira Glass? Kanye? All of the Cusacks? John Hughes? Chance the Rapper?"

"Don't let him give you shit, Edie. I know for a fact Peter loves Chicago," Jessa said, twirling the end of her ponytail. "Both the city *and* the band. He's basically America's dad when it comes to music. If they're playing it at the grocery store, he loves it." She leaned over and stage-whispered, "I swear to god, he has Journey on vinyl."

"Oh, I love Journey," Edie said, smiling at him again. "Respect Steve Perry."

"I haven't seen snow in years," Peter ruminated, shaking the globe.

The three of them watched the snow float down over the Chicago skyline. Contestants were never this earnest. Contestants never brought gifts. Peter looked at Edie again. She seemed to be looking at him with some sort of elastic openness that made him deeply uncomfortable.

"Thank you," he said finally, returning a tight smile and trying to remember what he usually said to contestants when they appeared in his conference room and he wasn't afraid of them. "Well. We're so glad you're here."

"Thank god," Edie said, sagging in her chair with relief. "I spent the entire flight worrying you were going to hate me and that this was a terrible idea."

"Why would you think that?" Peter asked, his gaze meeting twenty headshots of this season's contestants affixed to the wall behind her. Jumbo index cards were taped underneath each photo with information like:

LILY, 26, Aromatherapist, Portland
Always saying things like, "Everyone's a teacher, what do you teach?"

Five of the headshots already had Xs drawn across the faces in Sharpie. Potential storylines, date details, and elimination strategies were sketched across the neighboring whiteboard. Peter suddenly felt embarrassed. This was exactly why contestants were not supposed to be in here after production began. And then he felt oddly ashamed. And then annoyed because this was his fucking show—he was supposed to be making the decisions.

"I mean, I've seen *The Key*. I know I'm not exactly like the other girls," Edie continued. "I don't own a single crop top. I've never injected any paralyzing agents into my face. And I legit enjoy a night at Olive Garden."

"At least it's not a Red Lobster," said Jessa.

"They have good biscuits," Edie and Peter said at the same time. Their eyes met again, and this time when she gave him that toothy grin, for a second Peter forgot how terrible this all was and smiled back. What could he say? He grew up in a suburb. They *were* good biscuits.

Jessa bounced her eyes between them, curious, before soldiering on. "I can lend you a crop top," she said with a wink. "No worries."

Edie and Jessa glowed at each other, and Peter's heartburn surged. He dug in his pocket for some Tums, already hating himself for all the terrible things he knew he was about to do to ensure Edie Pepper and Bennett Charles ended up on the cover of *People*. He chewed the Tums and reminded himself that absolutely none of this was his idea.

"Well, then," he said, clapping his hands together, "why don't we get started?"

"So, Edie," Peter said, turning on the camera and joining them at the table. "We're just going to ask you some questions, get to know you better. Nothing too serious, we just want you to get used to the camera." Peter opened his laptop so he could take notes on Edie's pain points. As long as they stuck to the script—scare the shit out of her and then offer her a solution—everything would be fine. "Why don't you go ahead and introduce yourself: name, age, hometown."

"Oh, okay, sure," Edie said. She made an attempt to fix the messy bun on top of her head and straighten her sweatshirt before looking into the camera. "I'm Edie and I'm from Chicago. And, just so you know, Chicago pizza is not deep dish. Real Chicago pizza's a thin crust, square cut. Tavern pizza. Thank you for coming to my TED Talk."

Jessa laughed. "L-O-L, girl, you are a delight." Jessa elbowed Peter in the ribs. "Isn't she a delight?"

"A delight," he said mildly. Even he knew that no one said "thanks for coming to my TED Talk" anymore. "And how old are you?" he reminded her.

"Oh! I'm thirty-five." She looked away from the camera and back at them. "Is that, like, sixty-seven or something in *Key* years?"

"A bit older than our usual demographic, but it's not a problem," Peter said. "Remember, don't look at me. Look at the camera."

"Oh, sorry." Edie shifted in her chair.

"And what do you do? Your job?" he asked.

"I'm a content writer and copyeditor for an insurance company. So, I'm the one writing those emails and blog posts you're probably not reading. You know, about new guidance on colonoscopies, that sort of thing. Really scintillating stuff."

"Uh huh," he said, typing "depressing job" into his Word doc. "Hobbies?"

"God, Peter, these are the worst questions," Jessa finally interrupted. Peter and Jessa had a great success rate with their good cop/bad cop routine. "Let's talk about fun stuff. Tell me about your worst date, and I'll tell you mine. Maybe we'll let Peter judge whose is worst, even though he's basically a monk. Oh my god, Peter, you should have your own reality show, *The Monk of Malibu*. They could film you sitting on your balcony, staring at the ocean. Like an art house picture of privileged melancholy."

"I don't stare at the ocean," Peter said, watching Edie closely. He was definitely interested in hearing who this girl had been dating.

"The worst date I've ever been on?" Edie paused to think. "I mean, there've been a lot. Once I went out with this guy who said he was allergic to cheese and then he ordered fettucine alfredo and got all sweaty?"

"No!" Jessa exclaimed.

"I just threw my shoe at a guy who said I was too old to get married..." Edie clapped a hand over her mouth and turned to them again. "You don't think I'm too old to get married, do you?"

"Of course not," Jessa said immediately. Peter said nothing.

Edie looked at him questioningly. "You know Charlie and I are the same age, right?"

"And we *love* that," Jessa assured her, slapping Peter on the arm. She picked up her phone and shoved the photo of Edie and Bennett in their band uniforms at Peter. "Aren't they the cutest?"

"The cutest," Peter agreed in an indifferent tone. Sometimes he worried about how easily being a dick came to him. "Your worst date?" he said again, pointing back at the camera.

"Right," Edie said, gathering herself. "There is one that sort of sticks out. I've gone over and over it in my mind, you know? Like, what went wrong? If I should've done something... different?"

"Ooh, do tell," Jessa said.

"It's really mortifying."

"We've heard it all," Peter said, tapping his pen on the table impatiently.

"Don't judge me, okay?" Edie laughed nervously. "So I hooked up with this guy, and after he came, he had, like, a panic attack? He started hyperventilating. Like a full-on panic attack? And then he had to listen to a guided meditation on his phone to calm down."

"*What?*" Peter and Jessa said in unison.

Peter had definitely never heard that before. He tried to think of a scenario where he would need to meditate after coming. Literally the calmest Peter ever felt was during the thirty seconds after he came. In fact, thirty seconds of peace sounded pretty amazing right now, and he made a mental note to text Siobhan and/or Veronica to see about coming tonight. Wait, he was no longer sleeping with Veronica because she'd wanted to be exclusive. Siobhan, then.

"What was wrong with him?" Jessa gasped. Peter rolled his eyes internally at the best-friend-at-the-slumber-party routine.

"I don't know?" Edie said, biting her lip. "I guess he just got really anxious? He hadn't been with anyone since his ex-girlfriend."

"Wow," Jessa said. "What did you do?"

"I just sort of tried to meditate, too? Because then of course *I* was anxious, like I'd done something wrong. But he was totally fine until he came!" Edie dropped her head to the table in shame. She peeked up at them. "Do not put that on TV, my mother would *die*."

"We would never," Jessa soothed, patting Edie's hand while looking at Peter bug-eyed. "I'm so sorry that happened to you. But you're going to feel so much better when you hear mine. Ready?"

Edie sat up and nodded.

"So I went out with this guy who was an agent for C-crowd celebs, maybe B-crowd on a good day, and he took me to this industry party, definitely D-crowd, and then we went back to his place, and he couldn't get hard. But look, it's no worries, I'm supportive. And then he's like 'play with my nipples,' and again, I'm cool, I'm playing with his nipples, and he still can't get hard, so he starts swiping on Tinder *while I'm in bed with him.*"

Edie clutched her throat in horror. "How could that happen to someone as beautiful as you?"

"Please," Jessa said, nonchalantly adjusting her ponytail. "It's swiping culture; it happens to everyone."

"You know all the apps are complete garbage, right?" Peter interrupted. Jessa and Edie paused their tête-à-tête and turned to him. "Not only are the people on them full of shit, but I'm positive a significant percentage are dead."

Jessa rolled her eyes. "Ignore him, Edie. He gets offended by 'men are trash' commentary. Even if it's true."

Peter shrugged. "Statistically it's a fact."

"Like *dead* dead? Like dead-body dead?" Edie asked.

"Look, even if you delete the app, the profile remains. Unless you go deep into the settings to remove it. But most people are too stupid to do that, so I figure half of the people you're swiping on aren't even there. One person dies every twelve seconds in the US—you do the math."

"You've spent a lot of time thinking about this," Jessa said.

"Actually, it didn't take me long at all." He picked up some papers and tapped them efficiently against the table. "So, Edie, let's cut to the chase. Why are you here?"

"What do you mean?"

"Lonely? Always a bridesmaid, never a bride? Don't want to die alone?"

"What?" Edie said, looking confused. "Are you asking if I want to die alone?"

"Sure."

"I mean, of course not?"

"So, you're one of those."

"One of those what?"

"People who think you can avoid the hellscape of human experience through love and marriage."

"Slow down, Pete, your divorce is showing," Jessa interjected.

"I'm confused," Edie said, disregarding the camera completely to look at him. "Is this a trick question? What does 'the hellscape of human experience' have to do with anything?"

"I'm just trying to understand your worldview." Peter kicked back in his chair. "And when people are afraid of dying alone, typically it exposes a lack of fundamental understanding of human experience. What's more alone than death? It's singular."

The tips of Edie Pepper's ears were getting red. "You talk about death a lot, you know that?" she said. "Let me guess, you were a philosophy major back in the day. I know your type—I've definitely dated your type. The philosophy major who thinks Billy Corgan's solo career was underrated. Where'd you go? Yale?"

"Brown. And it was English. And it was."

"Then you should know the phrase *die alone* is hyperbolic. You have a really dark way of looking at things. Who wants to live like that? You don't want someone you love to be with you when you die?"

"To do what?"

"I don't know, comfort you?"

"You've seen too many movies," Peter replied. "Real life is not *The Notebook*."

"Well, this took a turn." Jessa gave Peter a look—he was pressing her too hard. "Why don't you take it down a notch, Nietzsche?"

Peter ignored her. Against his better judgment, he had to admit there was something about Edie Pepper that felt exciting and new. He leaned in, typing and dictating. "Edie Pepper, age thirty-five, appears relatively intelligent, but somehow still believes in fairy tales…" Peter looked up from the laptop and met Edie's gaze. "You know you can get married and still die alone tomorrow. The idea that you have some sort of control over it—over ensuring some perfect person, some soulmate, is going to be there for you in a thoughtful way every time you need them—is ludicrous. It doesn't happen. People are fundamentally selfish."

"Then why do you make this show, if you don't believe in love?" Edie demanded.

"Because they pay me a fuck-ton of money to do it." Peter crossed his arms over his chest and assessed her again. "So, what are you really doing here, Edie Pepper? You told me yourself that you're not a *Key* kind of girl."

Edie's face was almost as red as her sweatshirt. "I'm here because I believe in love!" She stood up and swept her arms around in exasperation. "Really, I couldn't care less about your stupid show, and actually, I'd prefer not to be in a hot tub on national television because that shit is embarrassing and"—she searched for the word—"antifeminist! Maybe coming here was a mistake, but from the moment I saw Charlie again, I just wanted to talk to him and tell him I never forgot him and that, I don't know, I still have so much love for him in my heart. But clearly I'm an idiot. Lauren warned me you'd be full of shit, and here you are, full of shit."

Peter threw his pen on the table, victorious. "Now we're getting somewhere!"

"What?" Edie exclaimed.

"Now that we know you're here for the right reasons, we can talk details." Peter patted her chair. "Sit down."

"You've got to be kidding."

"Sadly, he's not. This is just how he is," Jessa explained. "But luckily I'll be your producer and you'll be working with me most of the time."

"Not entirely true, but sure," Peter said.

"Is this how you do things around here?" Edie asked, slowly sitting back down. "You just mess with me until I get mad and say things I'll regret later?"

"Pretty much," Peter responded.

"He's kidding." Jessa smacked him on the arm again. "Look, Edie, Peter's just cranky. That's his whole personality: cranky. And suspicious. And judgmental."

"I'm waiting for the part where you say, 'and that's what makes him such a great boss and friend,'" Peter interjected. "I am your boss, you know."

"But he's not wrong to push you here," Jessa continued. "After the whole Wyatt Cash thing, we have to be extra cautious. We can't have our show tanked by another person using us for fame, you know?"

"But I would never do that," Edie said. "I don't even want to be famous. I don't brush my hair enough to be famous."

"Obviously, I know that," Jessa said, patting Edie's knee. "But our friend Peter here—he's harder to convince."

"Bottom line: If you join the show, it can't be a stunt," Peter said firmly.

"Now I feel worried that none of this is real," Edie said. "I mean, I know it's not real. But some of it is real, right? Or is it not real at all? When Britton and Murphy got engaged last season, was that real? Or not real?"

"I promise you," Jessa said, hand to heart, "we want to be your friends and help you get everything you want. We believe in your love story."

Edie Pepper did not look convinced.

"Here's the deal." Peter shut his laptop with a snap and leaned forward to look Edie in the eye. "*The Key* is a microcosm that parallels dating in the real world. You encounter all sorts of crazy people in the real world, right? Guys who have to… meditate after sex and so on. And you have to figure out what their intentions are, what they want, what you want, et cetera. *The Key* is the same—there are just cameras along for the ride. Bennett's got to figure out who he can trust and what he wants and what's *real.* That's why millions of people tune in every week—for the tension between what's real and what's not."

"What Peter means is," Jessa took over, "it's as real as you make it. Sure, we've got some gals who will never end up with Bennett, who are just hanging around for some screen time. We all get that. It's a symbiotic relationship—we let them be on our show, and they do things normal people would never do, providing meme-able drama for our audience. But that's just one side of the show. The other is Bennett Charles passionately looking for the woman that will shape the rest of his life. And we think that could be you."

"Does Charlie even want me here?" Edie exclaimed, like all the bad possible outcomes of joining *The Key* had just occurred to her. "Have you even asked him?"

"You'd let that stop you?" Peter asked. "Jessa, call the network. I have an idea for a spinoff—it's called *Alone Forever.*"

"You're hilarious," Edie said dryly.

"Look, we didn't ask him, and we're not going to," Peter replied. "I don't want to put too fine a point on this, but what Wyatt did was lie to millions of people. He went on TV and told the world he was going to find his wife on *The Key* and then, whoops, turns out he wasn't looking for a wife at all. He made everything look fake. Even the stuff that's not. He quite literally shook America's belief in a fairy-tale love story. Our job is to regain America's trust. Make them believe in love again. Rebuild their faith in this process. And the only storylines I'm interested in are the ones that are about true love. And the only way I see this season ending is with a fairy-tale engagement. So, what I'm asking is, do you see yourself on that mountain? And how hard will you fight to get there?"

Edie just stared at him, her mouth opening and closing slowly.

Jessa got up and held Edie by the shoulders. "I wouldn't have brought you here if I didn't think this could work. We just had to make sure you were for real."

"We can help you get everything you've ever wanted. You just have to trust us," Peter added.

Edie looked back and forth between them, her face flushed, her eyes filling with tears. Staring into all of Edie's hope and need suddenly felt uncomfortable. It took a certain amount of delusion to believe in love in the first place. But to believe you could find it on reality TV? That was borderline insane.

"You deserve an epic love story," said Jessa. "Let us give that to you."

Edie wiped her eyes and straightened her spine. "Okay, what happens next?"

Peter gave her his own version of a toothy grin. "We get to work."

TAKE 5 PRODUCTIONS
THE KEY
EDIE PEPPER INTRO PACKAGE [DRAFT FOR EP APPROVAL]
TAPE #47

00:00:00 ESTABLISHING SHOT / CHICAGO

ADAM FOX: How far would you go for true love?

The Key is about finding that one person, a soulmate, who can truly unlock your heart. There are no rules, which is why tonight we came all the way to Chicago to meet the woman who's been here all along, waiting for Bennett to come home.

EDIE / CHILDHOOD BEDROOM / SITTING ON BED WITH STUFFED ANIMALS

EDIE: I'm Edie and I'm here to find love with my high school sweetheart! Again!

EDIE SHOWING YEARBOOK TO CAMERA.

EDIE: Here's Charlie and me our junior year—oh, did you want me to call him Bennett? It's hard—he'll always be Charlie to me. Look, here we are in the production of *Bye Bye Birdie*. He only had one line and he forgot it. How sweet is that?

EDIE AND ALICE PEPPER / MOTHER'S KITCHEN

EDIE: I've known Charlie since forever. Kindergarten. He lived right around the block from here.

ALICE: His mother always had such a hard time with

him. He was always sick and falling over, so this has come as a real surprise.

EDIE: During our senior year we finally started dating. It was magical for both of us. I still remember our first kiss.

ALICE: Edie wore the *ugliest* dress to Homecoming. I warned her, but she did it anyway. Let me find a photo.

00:30:00 EDIE / EDIE'S APARTMENT / SITTING ON COUCH WITH CAT

EDIE: Oh god, I've dated so many people since Charlie. There was a guy who said he was a writer but really wrote undergraduate papers for money. I dated a guy for two months and he never kissed me the entire time, and yes, we were definitely dating. And then there were all the guys who just—poof—disappeared.

But who needs a man when you have a warm cat to cuddle with, right?

CLOSE UP: CAT

B ROLL OF EDIE STARING AT GROUPS OF MEN WISTFULLY

EDIE: But I never gave up on finding love.

EDIE / CHILDHOOD BEDROOM / LOOKING AT OLD PHOTOS

EDIE: And as soon as I saw Charlie again, I knew he's who I'm supposed to be with.

01:00:00 EDIE AND BFF LAUREN / EDIE'S APARTMENT / SITTING ON COUCH

LAUREN: Did I always think Edie and Charlie would end up together? I mean, not really.

EDIE: She's kidding.

EDIE AND ALICE PEPPER / MOTHER'S KITCHEN

EDIE: We never went to prom. I got the stomach flu, and really, he should've gone anyway, with our friends. He had a tuxedo and chipped in on the limo and everything. But he came over and sat on the couch with me. We watched *Steel Magnolias*. And I fell asleep and he still didn't turn it off—he watched the whole thing. He used to say to me "Drink your juice, Shelby!"

ALICE: I don't understand what "adventurer" means. Do "adventurers" have 401Ks?

EDIE AND BFF LAUREN / EDIE'S APARTMENT / SITTING ON COUCH

EDIE: Do you have any advice for me as I embark on this journey?

LAUREN: Well, just be yourself because you are kind and funny and smart and wonderful and we don't have time for any man who doesn't see that, ok? And I love you.

CLOSE UP: EDIE AND BFF LAUREN HUGGING

LAUREN: [whispering] And if Charlie Bennett gives you any <bleep> remind him where he came from. And that I will happily kick his <bleep>. I don't give a <bleep> about his extreme sports <bleep>, I remember his headgear, ok?

EDIE / CHILDHOOD BEDROOM / SURROUNDED BY OLD PHOTOS

EDIE: A lot of time has passed. But I feel like if there's a guy you risk it all for, it's him.

EDIE SKIPPING DOWN CHICAGO STREET

EDIE: I love you, Charlie Bennett!

7

At the end of a long hallway, behind a heavy wooden door meant to evoke the grandeur of California's finest Spanish Colonial estates, there was an artificially moonlit patio and thirteen gorgeous women in a kaleidoscope of formal gowns, sipping champagne and brilliantly smiling/laughing/tossing their hair as they circled like sequined vultures around *Key* suitor Bennett Charles. And at the other end of the hall, thirty feet from that door, *The Key*'s newest arrival was hyperventilating into a paper bag.

"I have dinner reservations," *Key* host Adam Fox said, shoving his Rolex at Jessa in annoyance. "Will she be ready to go, I don't know, before awards season?"

"Edie?" Jessa said, rubbing circles on Edie's back. "You can do this, hon."

Edie continued to puff into the bag, the essence of a Jimmy John's sandwich assaulting her nostrils. The mic pack Velcroed around her waist had begun to sag, pulling with it her Diane von Furstenberg wrap dress, which, despite claiming to be "universally flattering," was clearly not made for chesty gals who were pleasantly round in the middle.

Edie had just assumed the producers would give her something to wear for her big entrance. But apparently contestants wore their own clothes and did their own hair and makeup, so here Edie was with her tits hanging out of a four-hundred-dollar dress she'd purchased on her credit card without even trying it on because Jessa gave her approximately two seconds to choose something before the flight back to LA. Of course Jessa and the Nordstrom salesgirl had assured her it was a fantastic choice, that a "Diane von Furstenberg wrap dress never goes out of style."

Bitches.

"All you need to do is stand up, take a deep breath, and walk through that door," Jessa encouraged. "Everything you've ever wanted is waiting for you on the other side."

Was it? Edie wondered. Because during the past three days of interviews and an assembly line of business operations—the three-hour consultation she'd had with the show's psychologist, the meeting with *The Key*'s lawyer, signing the massive contract and nondisclosure agreement, the STD testing and HPV vaccine, the hurried promotional photo shoot where Jessa had promised her it was no big deal that she was still wearing her UW-Madison sweatshirt, plus the whirlwind twenty-four-hour trip to Chicago to shoot her "intro package"—the fantasy of Charlie Bennett had felt very far away indeed.

How was Edie supposed to know if this was the bravest, most romantic thing she'd ever done, or if she was about to become a total laughingstock every Tuesday night? She stared at Jessa's feet, which were now encased in Edie's very own Birkenstock clogs. Back at the production offices, Jessa had taken one look at the clogs and found them so offensive and "English major-y" that she'd taken off her own suede mules and made

Edie trade. Then she'd arranged Edie's sporadically curled hair around her shoulders and spun her toward the bathroom mirror for a final look. From the boobs up, the dress wasn't too bad. A lot of cleavage, but Edie had a good collarbone and nice skin. They'd smiled at each other in the mirror and Edie had felt warm and excited, like Jessa was her friend and that this was about to be the best night of her life. But then Jessa stepped away, slipped the Birks onto her feet, cuffed her jeans, and somehow instantly looked chic, and suddenly Edie felt unsettled, like she and Jessa were from entirely different planets and there was no way Edie belonged here, not even for a second. It was like her "entrance look" was a metaphor for her entire life. She knew enough to go to Nordstrom and spend an entire car payment on a dress, but she still managed to fuck it up by choosing the wrong thing once she got there.

Edie tried to picture what was waiting on the other side of that door. She could very clearly see the army of women who didn't choose the wrong dress or smudge mascara all over their face mid–panic attack. But what she couldn't see was Charlie. Just when she needed to call upon their unshakable history the most—the backyard campouts where they'd have to pack it in early because he couldn't stop sneezing, or the basement Ping-Pong tournaments that Lauren always won because no one could return the serve she perfected at summer camp when they were twelve—it suddenly all felt hazy and stupid and insignificant.

"I'm not kidding," Adam Fox continued. "This little stunt is already over my contracted hours."

People grow up. They change. They leave.

"Edie, babe," Jessa said. "I know this is scary, but you're fucking fabulous, and Bennett is gonna be thrilled to see you. How could he not be? You've gotta trust me."

Maybe that was the problem. She didn't trust Jessa. But any time Edie questioned something, Jessa was right there to tell her she was "overthinking." Throughout the unbelievably quick trip to Chicago, they'd kept asking her to do things she would never do, like stare longingly into a Wicker Park bar at a pack of dudebros day drinking and watching football for "B-roll." Or how about when they'd wanted to film in her childhood bedroom, and she'd told them it had been converted to a guest room years ago, so they'd gone out and bought what seemed to be an excessive number of stuffed animals to put on the bed and tacked a Britney Spears poster circa 2002 to the wall.

Thank God for Lauren. When the producers suggested they sit on the bed in literal pajamas and giggle about how cute Charlie is (and was) and maybe also braid each other's hair (???) or have a lighthearted pillow fight (!!!), Lauren had laughed right in their faces and said, "Please. I have a career." She did, however, agree to be interviewed after the producers told Edie that she needed her best friend to give her intro package "dimension." Edie clutched Lauren's arm and said "Do-this-for-me-do-this-for-me-do-this-for-me," but then Lauren refused to film with the boxes everywhere (she thought it would make Edie look like a hoarder), so the PAs were sent to haul the boxes to the second bedroom and bring in throw pillows and a couple of lamps and a rug from West Elm (all Edie had to do was post a photo on her Instagram when the show was airing and tag West Elm, #ad #sponsored) and *voilà!* Edie had an apartment.

Later, Lauren's confidence had inspired Edie to refuse when they'd asked her to dance—*literally dance!*—down her street yelling, "I love you, Bennett Charles!" which seemed not only presumptuous (it's not like she'd been *pining* for him since high school) but also completely psychotic. Jessa assured her this was just the sort of exaggeration the show was made of and that it would all make sense in the end when she was standing on a mountain top, engaged to Charlie Bennett. But Edie still hadn't been sold, so eventually they'd compromised on Edie skipping and yelling, "I'm coming for you, Charlie Bennett!" and then they'd filmed that over and over again, with all her neighbors peering out their windows and stopping on the sidewalk to stare while their dogs shat in the grass, until Edie was finally so mortified that she gave the producers one quick "I love you, Charlie Bennett!" just so they could go back inside.

Jessa had this way of soothing her, of working her, that seemed entirely suspect, but that Edie nevertheless succumbed to repeatedly. She was just so goddamn good at it! Edie worried that Jessa was working her now. Preparing to sacrifice her to the reality TV gods. She continued to huff and puff into the bag and desperately wanted to text Lauren, who was quick to assess any situation and provide a reasonable course of action. But Edie's phone was gone, dropped into a Ziploc with her name scrawled on it by a production assistant when they'd landed back in LA, and it was unclear to Edie how much of this current panic was brought on from suddenly being untethered from her entire life, the threat of seeing Charlie again, or simply the speed with which everything had happened.

The first wave of panic set in last night when Edie realized she was actually going to leave her entire life for seven weeks on basically zero notice. Should she have thought about this before? Sure. But had she really believed she was going to be on this show? *Exactly.* But Jessa was always quick with solutions. She'd rubbed Edie's back and signaled to her assistant, Dan, to bring Edie a glass of wine while she hyperventilated on the couch. Who would take care of Nacho Bell Grande? *No problem!* Dan hired a tween who lived in Edie's building (a girl so starstruck by the cameras that she would've worked for a signed headshot of Adam Fox alone) to take care of the cat, check the mail, and generally watch over the apartment while Edie was gone. But how was Edie supposed to leave work for two months? *Easy!*

The Key's lawyer would interface with her company's HR and negotiate Edie's leave. But what in the hell was she going to tell Alice? *Wasn't it obvious?* That Edie would be engaged in less than two months! Jessa called Alice herself and somehow charmed her so thoroughly that Alice dusted off a Chanel suit and even agreed to appear on camera. But—and perhaps most alarming, once thoroughly considered—Edie had absolutely nothing to wear on TV. *No worries!* They'd have plenty of time to shop back in LA, and they'd just make a quick pre-airport pit stop at the Michigan Avenue Nordstrom and pick up something sexy and fabulous for her grand entrance.

So, of course, Edie agreed. And then spent the entire four-hour flight back to Los Angeles working on her outstanding editing projects, passing off what she couldn't get done to her cubicle mate, Jill, transferring the last of her savings into checking to cover next month's rent and bills, and making random arrangements, like canceling her next haircut and becoming increasingly anxious when her laptop was confiscated by a production assistant at LAX. Did they really have to take every single communication device she owned? Wasn't she a full-fledged adult who could both appear on a reality show *and* stay in contact with her friends? But what really pushed Edie over the edge was when they'd finally arrived at the *Key* mansion and she'd caught herself in a full-length mirror and noticed she looked like she was wearing some fancy geometric robe, at least one size too small.

"I don't know, she won't talk to me," Jessa said to someone new.

A pair of designer loafers appeared. Oh, great, they'd brought in the big guns. Edie hadn't seen Peter since their initial interview two and a half days ago. He bent down until his face was level with hers. "How're we feeling, Pepper?"

"Not great, Peter," she yelled into the bag. "Like this is a really bad idea."

"Well, you know, only when we're confronted with death do we ever truly feel alive."

Without thinking, Edie took the Jimmy John's bag off her face and stood up, ready to go off on this morbid motherfucker, but when their eyes met, his were twinkling. He elbowed her in the side. "C'mon, that was hilarious," he said with a smile.

God, he was the worst. Hot-and-cold guys like Peter were the ultimate siren song to Edie's need to please. She wasn't even here for Peter, but somehow his complete detachment and then sudden interest, compounded with his authority over the entire show, made her want him to like her. It didn't help that he was extremely hot. It was like he'd stepped out of a J.Crew catalog from 1994 with this normcore hotness, this sort of restrained masculinity that snuck up on you. His understated, preppy clothes and everyman haircut put you at ease, but then the longer you were around him, suddenly it became impossible to ignore how his green eyes had this very sexy intensity, especially when he took his glasses off. And how thick and touchable his brown hair was. And that clearly he worked out, not in a bulging biceps sort of way, but in that perfectly trim waist in khakis sort of way. Everything he said or did seemed to be tinged with arrogance, and clearly Edie needed a shit-ton of therapy, because even this she found irritatingly attractive.

"Hand over the bag," he said, and reluctantly she did, though her heart was still racing and her hands were shaking. It must be exhausting, keeping up with a man this existential. To his point, she did, however, feel very much alive, though she wasn't going to admit it and wasn't sure she liked it very much. Perhaps an existence dulled by wine and *Real Housewives* was more her speed?

Peter put his hand on her shoulder and pulled her toward him, so he could speak directly into her ear. "Trust me," he said, his breath sending tingles down her back. "This is the best part.

It might feel like the worst part, but right now, the moment before something happens—anything is possible. Anything could happen. It's magic." He pulled back and looked at her seriously. "Do you know what I mean?"

Edie stared at him, trying to assess how he was telling her this, as a friend or as a producer. Because on some level, what he was saying with his minty-fresh breath did make some kind of sense—this was the very last moment before the reckoning of Charlie Bennett, an event seventeen years in the making. What strange twists of fate had to happen to bring each and every one of them here tonight? And if she did believe in magic—at the very least she believed in *romance*, which was its own sort of magic—then what could be more magical than the moment she gathered all her courage and humbly presented herself to Charlie Bennett once again?

"Forget the cameras," Peter whispered in her ear. "You get to choose who you are in this moment. You. And you've just got to roll the dice. Shoot your shot. It's what you came here to do." Peter pulled away from her and they stared at each other for a moment, Edie searching his face and finding, unbelievably, what looked to be a calm certitude, a solid belief in…*her*?

Suddenly she felt electric.

A knowing smile spread across Peter's face, and he pulled her back to him. "Now why are you fucking around like you can't do this? We both know you can handle whatever comes next."

They separated, and suddenly Edie knew he was right. Of course she could do this.

Peter nodded and the energy around them shifted, like it was no longer just the two of them. "It's just one foot in front of the other." He clapped her on the shoulder like they were businessmen making deals on the golf course. "Ted'll be with you the whole time."

From behind a camera, Ted gave Edie a thumbs-up.

"It's the beginning of your love story!" Jessa enthused, shaking Edie by the arms. "And I, for one, am *super* excited." Jessa pulled Edie into a hug, and over Jessa's shoulder, Edie could see Peter walking away. "Just tell him you never stopped thinking about him and that you want to reconnect and see where it goes."

"Let's roll," Peter said to the crew.

Edie took a deep breath and pulled together every ounce of hope and strength and grit she had to put one suede mule in front of the other. She could feel Ted filming her from behind as she walked, and she wondered how her ass looked. Suddenly her right mule slipped, and she stumbled on the uneven stone tile. The crew gasped. Edie broke her fall against the wall, only slightly upsetting a painting of a Tuscan vineyard.

"I'm okay! I'm okay!" she yelled.

"She's okay!" Peter yelled. "Keep going!"

Edie recovered and eventually made it to the heavy wooden door in one piece. She looked behind her at Ted and his camera, at the sound guy following along with his boom mic, and at the rest of the production team at the other end of the hall, Jessa smiling at her with a big thumbs-up, Peter staring at a monitor with his arms crossed and holding his chin in one hand. Edie thought that though this wasn't how she pictured falling in love, it did have its own modern storybook charm. And if she could choose who she wanted to be, Edie wanted to be a woman who loved and was loved in return. Who risked it all.

And so she took a deep breath and pushed open the door to her happy ending.

8

Bennett Charles was in love.

And he'd never been more in love in his entire life.

He attributed the passion coursing through his veins to, sure, the near-constant adoration he was receiving from more than a dozen gorgeous women. And, sure, to his celebrity status and white-glove handling by the producers. And, sure, to the endless steamy make-outs with a revolving door of women that left him jacking off in the shower every night like he was thirteen again. But, if he was being honest, Bennett was high as a kite because there was nothing he loved more than an adventure, and this whole thing—it was a sick ride.

Bennett approached his role as *The Key*'s suitor like he would any of his other escapades: you just had to open your eyes and open your heart and grab it by the balls and ride every fucking inch of that wave until you crashed onto shore. You had to really *live* it. So, every girl he talked to, every date he went on, he was all in. He was open-hearted and enthusiastic, and he'd already found something to love about every single one of the ladies, and *a lot* to love about six or seven of them. They were all attractive, definitely, but hearing their stories, learning about how they'd lived their lives, what they thought about the world around them—it was a beautiful thing, and, man, it really turned him on.

For example, Zo, whose thigh was firmly pressed against his, whose hands were soft and sweet in his, was telling him this story, this amazing story, about being onstage at the American Ballet in New York City in front of hundreds of people and catching her foot on the hem of her costume and falling, her knee popping so loudly when it hit the stage they could hear it four rows back. Two chorus girls in tights had dragged her off the stage. And that was it—at twenty-four years old, she'd reached the end of a twenty-year ballet career. A slow tear rolled down her cheek. For a split second, the tear made Bennett nervous, but then he remembered to wipe it away with his thumb, a look of sweet concern on his face. This was another thing Bennett liked—knowing his role, knowing what he was supposed to do.

In the past, had Bennett been accused of liking only the beginning of things? Yes. And did he love all the initial conversations, first dates, and first kisses of the past three weeks? Also yes. But now, at thirty-five years old, he had a different perspective on what he wanted out of life. He might get off on the adrenaline of all those firsts, but what he wanted now was something that lasted. He'd spent the past thirteen years finding himself, communing with nature, consulting spiritual guides, touching and tasting all the corners of the world. And what he'd come to understand was this: Life was about the relationships you had and the people who loved you. It was the same in every language. And he was a man who'd lived some life, seen some truths, taken some risks, had some heartbreaks, and who, most importantly, knew what he wanted—someone to walk through all the coming days with. And so, he was totally and enthusiastically grateful for this opportunity to say goodbye to all the firsts one by one and ride this experience all the way to the end—to his engagement to the perfect woman, his perfect match, in just seven short weeks.

Zo's hair was falling into her face, and he wanted to kiss her. It seemed like the right time, since the producers were always encouraging him to validate the girls' sharing. He tenderly swept her hair behind her ear before taking her cheek in his palm and pulling her to him. She moaned the tiniest bit as their lips met and, damn, it was sexy. He still wasn't able to completely ignore the cameramen and the sound guys moving around during these intimate moments, or the fact that Zo was twenty-four and he was thirty-five (and really, how was that going to look?), but he willed himself to keep his eyes closed and stay in the moment and kiss her how women like to be kissed, slowly and thoughtfully, with his hand in her hair, and with a sense of control. And without too much sound, because hearing people slurp on TV was the worst. When they finally broke apart, he placed his forehead against hers and smiled.

"That was amazing," he whispered.

"You're amazing," she whispered back.

Out of the corner of his eye, he noticed more bodies had entered the patio, most likely another contestant and her producer ready for time with him, but Bennett didn't want to break the shot just yet. That was another thing that made him a great lead—his years on Instagram had taught him a lot about the camera and making great content.

"Charlie?" a voice said now, raising the hair on the back of his neck. No one had called him Charlie since he was a kid. Bennett pulled away from Zo. An underdressed woman was standing next to Adam Fox and one of the cameramen. The way the patio was lit, Bennett couldn't make out who it was—

a reporter, maybe? Another producer? Someone from the network? But the cameraman was definitely filming her as she approached.

"Charlie," the woman said again as she arrived at the seating area. "Hi."

"Who is that?" Zo whispered, annoyed.

"I don't know," he said slowly.

Bennett tried to keep the confusion off his face. The producers liked to throw little surprises at him, and Bennett wasn't against shock value or serving good content, but he *was* against looking like an asshole. The vibe on the patio was strange—what was he missing?

"It's been a long time!" the woman said, shrugging her shoulders in a dorky but adorable sort of way that for a second seemed vaguely familiar until—*WHAM*—it hit him all at once. Instantly Bennett was filled with the same exact feeling he'd had when he was a white-water rafting guide in the Grand Canyon in 2010 and, in a freak accident, they'd hit a wave just right and this kid, like a five-year-old kid, had flown right out of the raft and was just *gone* for what felt like an eternity. Bennett had frantically scanned the rapids until he caught sight of the orange life vest, and then he'd swum as hard as he fucking could to grab the kid by the arm.

So that was to say: terror. What he was feeling in this moment was terror.

Bennett's skin went prickly around his neck. He stood up and pulled at his tie, trying to breathe. He looked to the camera pointed directly at his face. What the hell was she doing here? They couldn't possibly expect him to date *her*. He tried to speak, but what could he possibly say to an all-grown-up Edie Pepper, who he'd last seen on what was arguably the worst night of his life?

The night that had changed everything.

Seventeen years earlier, Charlie Bennett's mother was determined to throw him a going-away party. She was trying to do something nice for him. Still, her sudden interest in *Lord of the Rings* and throwing a Tolkien-inspired celebration—the card table covered in Middle-earth-themed snacks, the basement rec room transformed into a shire, his friends dressed in Hobbit cosplay—felt awkward and embarrassing because wasn't Charlie being sent away so he could become a different person? Someone who liked nerdy things *less*?

For years, Charlie had done whatever he could to avoid his parents' gaze. It was clear that Bill Bennett thought Charlie was weak and Helen Bennett worried that Charlie was weird, and whenever they paused to assess him, self-improvement projects quickly followed. This time, against all of Charlie's protests, they'd signed him up for a six-week Outward Bound expedition through the Alaskan wilderness. Bill insisted the trip was necessary to "toughen him up" before Charlie arrived at the University of Colorado–Boulder for his freshman year. Charlie, who knew himself to be an indoor kid, was dreading it with every fiber of his being. His flight left the next day.

Edie, however, was spending her summer like a normal person, waitressing at Walker Bros. Original Pancake House, hanging out at the lake with Lauren, and golfing twice a week with her mom. She'd leave for the University of Wisconsin–Madison in August. Even though they'd be on opposite sides of the country, Charlie and Edie were sure their love could survive the distance. And so, after multiple glasses of Legolas lemonade, they'd tiptoed up the basement stairs, snuck past his parents watching *Dateline* on the couch, and slipped into his room to solidify their commitment.

They sat across from each other on the floor, a Yankee candle burning an apple pie flame between them. Edie was dressed as the elf Arwen, complete with poorly fitting rubber elf ears that made it difficult to hear and left her speaking too loudly for the intimate circumstances. Charlie was the ranger Aragorn, and, in addition to the extra-large chain mail shirt he'd purchased last summer at the Renaissance faire, wore his dad's old leather vest, a camouflage poncho he'd found in the basement and sliced up the middle to fashion a traveling cape, and two leather cuffs he'd gotten at Hot Topic that made him feel like a different person entirely. Someone cooler. Someone who wore leather cuffs unironically. Someone like Maroon 5's Adam Levine.

"You're sure your parents won't come in here?" Edie asked, adjusting her velvet cape with nervous hands.

"They think we're in the basement with everyone else," Charlie assured her. "Let's just do it like we planned." He pressed Play on the CD player. The soothing sounds of Enya filled the room.

"Do you remember when we first met?" Edie screamed her lines from *The Fellowship of the Ring*. Charlie waved his hands, motioning for her to keep it down. The candle flickered. "Sorry!" Edie whispered. Then, breathily, "Do you remember when we first met?"

"I thought I had wandered into a dream," Charlie recited.

"Long years have passed. You did not have the cares you carry now. Do you remember what I told you?"

"You said you'd bind yourself to me, forsaking the immortal life of your people."

"And to that I hold. I would rather spend one lifetime with you than face all the ages of this world alone."

At this declaration, a blush covered Charlie's entire body. He dug into his cape and produced a small box. Edie smiled shyly, and Charlie thought she looked very beautiful in her elfin braids.

"You have my heart forever, Edie Pepper," he declared. "I love you."

"I love you!" she shouted. "Forever!"

They exchanged shell promise rings with tribal patterns that they'd picked out at the shop on Central Street that sold incense and statues of dragons. It was time to kiss her, so with his hands clutched firmly in his lap, Charlie leaned forward with his mouth open a little too wide, so that when it finally met hers, it awkwardly engulfed her lips. He was so nervous—he couldn't help it—he started to laugh, and then she started to laugh, and it made him feel better. This was Edie Pepper; he'd known her practically his entire life.

He kissed her again, better this time.

"I brought the instructions," she whispered, picking up a dog-eared *Cosmopolitan* magazine. She began to read aloud. "'Outercourse is a sexy way to be intimate with your man without the risk of going all the way.'"

"Safety first!" he said, jutting a finger into the air. Holy shit, he was embarrassing. He bit the inside of his cheek.

"'First pinch, twist, lick, and blow on the nipple.'"

Edie hesitated before opening her elfin robe. At the sight of her breasts, Charlie felt the wind knock out of him. They were perfect. Perfectly big and round with pink nipples like pencil erasers. He was *thrilled* to finally see them. Sure, he'd seen naked women before on the internet, but something about porn always left him feeling creepy, like he was doing something that wasn't entirely okay. Once he'd walked into his dad's home office—he was just going to print a paper for school—and when he'd woken the computer up, on-screen had been a naked woman on all fours, with a man behind her, pulling her head back by her ponytail to reveal some sort of gag in her mouth. Charlie had immediately gotten uncomfortably hard and returned to his room to masturbate, but after he came, he kept picturing the girl's face and felt guilty, because she had looked wild-eyed, and something inside of him had known this was some fringe version of sex that had little to do with intimacy. But the sexual impulses he felt, like, all the time, were so extreme he sometimes felt he had no control over them at all.

Since he'd kissed Edie for the first time nine months ago on the band bus, they'd made out a lot in his basement. She'd rubbed his dick until he came in his pants, and he'd rubbed her through her jeans in a way that she seemed to like, until finally they'd graduated to his hand up her shirt, squeezing her boobs under her bra, and then rolling around on top of one another and mashing their crotches together through their clothes until he, again, came in his pants. But she seemed to enjoy it, too, though he was much too shy to ask her directly. She would breathe heavily in his ear as he chafed his dick against his jeans until she'd whimper, "Oh, Charlie," and he'd go a little faster until she wrapped her legs around him, holding on tight, until suddenly she would moan and relax against the couch with her eyes closed and a small smile across her face. Then he would know it was over and to kiss her softly all around her face.

"Are you okay?" Edie whispered now. He nodded, so she returned to the magazine. "'Turn him on with your breasts. Cover them in lube and ask him to put his penis between them. Push them together to massage his shaft.'"

"You can do that?" he asked, breathless.

It was unbelievably awkward as they maneuvered into a workable titty-fucking position. The candle was kicked over, and the flame went out as hot wax spilled onto the carpet. When he finally straddled her, his knees resting on her elfin robes, her arms had been pinned to the floor, so she took the cape off entirely. He wasn't sure if he was supposed to take his shirt and vest and cape off, but since he'd always been a T-shirt-on-at-the-pool kind of guy, he left them on. He squirted a pump of Lubriderm between her breasts and began to massage it all over her chest with his eyes bulging out of his head and his dick practically exploding out of his pants.

Finally, he unbuttoned his jeans.

As soon as he placed his dick between her breasts and she pushed them together to sort of bun up his hot dog, he felt like he was going to come. Genuinely, he wanted it to be good for her, too, like the previous times they'd fumbled around with one another, so he tried to go very slowly and think about other things, like what they were even going to eat in the Alaskan woods. Fish? It would be an uncomfortable departure from the Doritos and Bagel Bites he was used to. He tried singing the Bagel Bites jingle in his head to distract himself. *Pizza in the morning, pizza in the evening, pizza at suppertime. When pizza's on a bagel, you can have pizza anytime!* But then he faltered and looked down at her face. Edie was looking directly at his dick jutting toward her chin, and while her expression was somewhat agog, or possibly alarmed, just her looking at his dick for the first time was enough for him to—

"Uh, Charlie—" she said, beginning to sit up.

—shoot an astonishing amount of semen into the air, a glob of which landed directly in Edie's right eye. And while Charlie was collapsing in ecstasy, Edie was yelping at the fire consuming her eyeball and jerking forward, smacking him hard in the face with her skull. Everything went black. He crashed to the floor with a thud, alarming the group of Hobbits in the basement who looked toward the ceiling for a moment before returning their gaze to *Lord of the Rings: The Return of the King* playing on the big-screen TV. Blood poured from Charlie's nose, and he moaned at the pain. Edie struggled out from under him, clutching her eye.

"I'm blind!" she cried, stumbling around the room topless.

"Edie, shh! Are you okay?" he whisper-yelled. He couldn't make out how bad the damage was exactly—he was still catching his breath and seeing stars and trying to angle his head so he didn't choke on the blood that was now rushing down his throat.

"No, I'm not okay!" she whisper-yelled back. "What did you do? What did you *do*? It burns!"

"I'm so sorry! I'm so sorry!" he cried. "Hey, watch out—"

Edie tripped over a discarded Middle-earth staff and crashed head-first into the wall. She crumpled to the carpet, out cold.

The bedroom door flew open. "What the hell's going on in here?" Charlie's dad yelled.

"Charles! My baby!" Charlie's mother rushed over to him as he lay on the carpet with his pants around his ankles. He quickly folded his body into the fetal position and wrapped his traveling cape around him. His mother fell to her knees and took hold of his bloodied face. "Call 911!"

"Now, just calm down, Helen—"

"I will not calm down! Charlie's been attacked! Charlie, what happened?"

"Get out! Get out!" Charlie yelled, desperately trying to skooch away from his mother and get his withering penis back into his pants.

"Hold still, you're getting blood all over the carpet!" Charlie's mom was borderline hysterical now. She had been unusually weepy as his departure approached. "Did you break your nose? Where's the Kleenex?" She yanked open his nightstand and the drawer flew out, spewing an impressive number of condoms and Pokémon cards to the floor. Helen covered her mouth in horror.

"Helen! There's a girl passed out behind the door!" Charlie's dad moved to assist Edie until he realized she was missing her shirt. He shifted his weight from foot to foot, considering, until he settled on ripping items from the closet and throwing them toward her, eyes averted, until Edie lay shrouded in Charlie's graduation gown, a Dungeons & Dragons T-shirt, and two pairs of jeans.

"You have to leave!" Charlie yelled. "Edie? Edie! Are you okay?"

A group of Hobbits appeared in the doorway and watched wide-eyed as Charlie's mom lunged at him with a wad of Kleenex. Charlie rolled across the floor, struggling with his pants along the way.

"My staff!" Gandalf entered the fray to retrieve his walking stick.

"Helen, I really think you should take a look at this girl."

"Bill Bennett, if you don't call 911 right this second—"

"My precious!" Charlie's little brother, Rick, lurched into the room on all fours and began yanking on the promise ring stuck on Charlie's right hand.

"Rick! Knock it off! Cosplay is over, Rick!" Charlie screamed.

"What are you supposed to be?" Charlie's dad asked a new arrival to the doorway.

"I'm a conscientious objector to *Lord of the Rings* due to its patriarchal and misogynistic undertones," Lauren, dressed as Hermione Granger, said. She shrugged. "Really I'm only here to be nice."

Charlie's dad made a face like, *I hear that.*

From the carpet then, a whisper, "Charlie? Charlie? I love you..."

And then everyone turned to a fallen Edie Pepper, who had not only lost her elfin robe but also one of her elfin ears.

The very last image Bennett could recall of Edie Pepper was the bottoms of her chunky Steve Madden sandals as her stretcher was loaded onto an ambulance so she could be screened for a concussion. Before Lauren boarded the ambulance behind her, she'd turned to Charlie on the driveway and shaken her head in weary disappointment. He heard Edie say, "Don't be mad; it's not his fault. It was my idea," and he'd cried more behind the bloody dish towel stuck to his face. Edie was always looking out for him, even though he was a total fucking nightmare. The kind of guy who maimed his girlfriend during foreplay. Then his dad had pushed him into the back seat of his mom's Volvo, also en route to the hospital, to have his nose reset. And from the strong words he overheard their parents hissing at each other from behind his hospital curtain, it appeared he would never see Edie again.

Until now.

The overwhelming guilt and shame he'd felt that night, and in the months after, surged through Bennett as he stood on the *Key* patio with Edie Pepper waiting for him to speak. Bennett had never hated himself more than he did that night, which was saying something, because all throughout high school, he'd hated his pudgy, nerdy, clumsy self a helluva lot. The next morning on the way to the airport, his father had demanded the full story, and Bennett awkwardly tried to explain until his dad said, "Jesus Christ, Charlie, are you telling me you couldn't even fuck her like a man?" And as Bennett had boarded the plane to Alaska with a silver splint taped to his nose and his father's disgusted face burned into his brain, he left with the knowledge that he'd said absolutely nothing to defend Edie, or their love, and his shame had grown deeper.

But then something strange and unexpected happened. Up until this point, Bennett had had zero exposure to the great outdoors except for some family vacations to Door County. He was, and always had been, an indoor kid. His—and presumably everyone else's—expectation was for the Outward Bound trip to be a complete and total disaster. But early into the back-breaking trip, Bennett realized he fucking loved it.

Perhaps it was the magic of arriving in Alaska at the lowest point in his life, desperate for a total escape, but he loved the insane vistas that made him feel small and insignificant and in the presence of something mysterious and majestic. The infinite stars in the night sky—he'd never seen stars like that before. He loved learning to catch salmon in the icy rivers and cook it over a fire. He loved tracking moose in air that was so crisp he'd disregarded doctor's orders and taken the splint off early just so he could feel it rush through his nose more clearly. He loved how moving his body and using his hands shut off the insecurities inside his head. And he loved the brotherhood of guys who didn't ask too many questions about where he'd come from or who he'd been, because they were also on the precipice of becoming men and reinventing themselves too.

Their guide, Jack, had a satellite phone, but it was only for emergencies, so Bennett felt off the hook in terms of contacting Edie. Sure, in the days before the incident he'd promised to write her letters, but now he didn't know what he could possibly say, so he just *didn't*. Instead of focusing on what made him feel like a hopeless, terrible person, he focused on all the things that were making him feel strong—stronger than he ever thought he could be. By the end of the trip, he'd shed twenty pounds, learned that marijuana and exercise eased his anxiety, and felt connected to a group of guys in a way he never had before.

Charlie flew straight from Alaska to the University of Colorado–Boulder and trekked up the stairs to his dorm room with his gear still strapped to his back. He was tired and smelly and sore, but happy—optimistic about who he could become here—and when he reached his room it felt like fate. The festive handmade sign on the door read: BENNETT CHARLES & DAVID SOWINSKI.

How could Bennett ever repay the debt he owed to whatever summer intern had fucked up that sign? As he stood there, it struck him that no one knew him in Boulder, and he could be whoever the hell he wanted to be. It was a complete and total fresh start. And wasn't Bennett an infinitely cooler name than Charles? So when the door swung open to reveal David Sowinski, Charlie shook his hand and introduced himself as Bennett Charles from Illinois by way of Alaska and never, ever looked back.

Had he felt guilty, deleting all of Edie's emails unread during that first term as he found his place in campus life? Sure. But he honestly didn't see how he could reconcile who he'd become, *who he still wanted to become*, with who he'd been. Thinking about her at all made him feel guilty, so he just... *didn't*. Instead, he threw out his fantasy novels and joined a fraternity. His new brothers taught him about weightlifting and protein shakes, IPAs and beer pong, the importance of caring about at least one sport (preferably football or basketball), and, most importantly, how to walk around campus like you owned the place. He got on prescription medications for anxiety, allergies, asthma, and eczema, toned up his body, and quickly changed his major to social geography (the study of people and place), which he was told would offer him the most study abroad opportunities and keep him far from home. He grew out his hair and took out a loan to get a chin implant, and found out that in Colorado, to be cool with the ladies, all a guy really had to do was have a strong jaw, wear good jeans with a tight T-shirt and some Patagonia outerwear, and have basic knowledge of trails good for pointing out constellations and making out. He spent breaks and summers working as a counselor at various camps, eventually receiving certifications in rock climbing and white-water rafting, and he went home infrequently, because though he had changed, sometimes insecurity would boil up in him unexpectedly, like when he dated this really smart girl from the poli sci department who wanted him to talk about his courses, but really, his knowledge was pretty basic because he hardly ever went to class. Who had time to research the food supply in Namibia when you were changing your entire fucking personality? His worst fear was someone getting close enough to pull back the curtain.

Besides, his mom was clingy, and his dad was a real dick.

Looking at Edie now, Bennett didn't know how he was supposed to explain to someone who'd known him *since kindergarten*, who, despite his many faults and food allergies, had always liked him exactly as he was, that Bennett Charles had no interest in exhuming poor, hopeless, Charlie Bennett from the dead, much less parade him around on national television. Did he still feel guilty about how he'd treated Edie? Yes. But an even stronger feeling rose in him now.

And that feeling was self-preservation.

9

Charlie!" Edie Pepper said brightly. "It's me! Edie!" And when Charlie Bennett still looked sorta stupefied, Edie brought an imaginary flute to her lips and reenacted the opening steps of their *Simpsons* marching band routine right there on the *Key* mansion patio. *"Ba-ba-baba-ba-babababa!"* She finished by tossing the air-flute high in the air and twirling her body (with only a slight stumble) before catching the flute again behind her back. Yah! She hadn't done that move in years! Edie leaned forward and gave Charlie's forearm a little shake. "Remember?"

"Edie," he said finally. "What the fuck."

"It's so good to see you! You look great," Edie said, because that's what people said to people they hadn't seen in a long time and because, *girl*, he did. IRL Charlie looked even better than Instagram Charlie. Edie had scrolled and scrolled and scrolled through so many images of the new and improved Charlie Bennett—staring off into the distance sexily, staring straight at the camera sexily, looking confused (but sexily)—that to suddenly be in the presence of this living, breathing, slowly-blinking-and-pulling-at-his-tie Charlie Bennett was maybe the most wonderful, most endearing thing Edie Pepper had ever experienced, and just like that, all her nerves floated away.

Without a filter you could see the texture of his skin and the red splotches spreading across his neck. Without a strategic crop or blurry background, you could drink him in as something more than just a body with washboard abs. Without the likes and comments and follows, Edie saw him as *she* knew him, and it was like having the most delicious secret, because what Edie saw in that moment was not some great adventurer, not some superficial ladies' man. No, what Edie saw was the same sweet, awkward, nervous Charlie Bennett of her childhood, and it reminded her of the boy who'd been too scared to kiss her for the first time, so she'd had to lean over and do it herself. Edie felt such a rush of affection for him that she just wanted to make him feel comfortable, and what better way to do that than to remind him of home?

So, she said, "Hey, how's your mom?"

"Oh," he said. "She died."

"Oh my god!" Edie gasped, clapping a hand over her mouth. "I hadn't heard! I'm so sorry!"

"She didn't die," Charlie said, shaking his head as if to clear it. "I don't know why I just said that." Then he turned and spoke directly into a looming camera. "Can we do that again? That was weird. I don't know what's happening." He turned back to Edie and ran a hand through his curls. "She's totally alive. Wow."

"All right, let's reset," Peter yelled, appearing from behind a large potted palm. "Edie, why don't you go ahead and walk up again."

Edie startled—for a second, she'd totally forgotten she was on a TV show. To her left, the dark portico was full of people and equipment. Lights and cameras and cameramen, sound guys holding boom mics and wearing headphones, producers typing away on their phones or whispering into walkie-talkies, and Peter—*who had been behind a plant*—was now standing in front of her, asking her to walk up again.

"Seriously?"

"Seriously," he said. "And Bennett, you know the rules—don't break to the camera to get out of tough conversations. Verisimilitude is king."

"Fuck off, Peter," Bennett said. "You think you're so fucking clever."

"We've all got jobs to do, man," Peter shrugged. "Mine is making magic every Tuesday night."

"Literally, does anyone care that I have a dinner reservation? Because I'm just wondering if anyone cares," Adam Fox yelled at no one in particular. Then to Peter, "This shit is outside my contracted hours, and you know it."

"Yeah, yeah, okay, let's reset," Peter said, stepping between Edie and Charlie. "Everything's fine." Peter put one hand on Charlie's bicep and the other between his shoulder blades and guided him back to the sofa. Seamlessly, Jessa hooked her arm through Edie's and began to tug. But Edie stayed rooted to the spot. Jessa was talking, but Edie wasn't listening. Because as Peter and Charlie stepped past the coffee table, there on the couch, bathed in a gorgeous, diffused light, was the most elegant, most self-possessed (not to mention *skinniest*) woman Edie had ever seen. She stared off into the distance, shoulders back, head tilted slightly so her dark brown hair cascaded down her back like a Pantene model. Her clavicle looked sharp enough to cut glass. Her lips were Kardashian full, and her dark eyes were shaded by thick, natural brows.

Edie pulled at the wrap of her ill-fitting dress and shifted her weight in the borrowed mules. Slowly, the woman turned her perfectly symmetrical face and they locked eyes. Edie scrambled to place her, mentally scrolling the "Meet the Contestants" webpage she'd memorized on her way to LA when she'd still had her phone and the luxury of scouring the internet like a crazy person. But before Edie could figure out which perfectly perfect contestant she was, the woman's eyes slit, her mouth got snarly, and she lifted her tiny bird wrists into the air and flipped Edie off with both hands.

"Fuck. You. You. Fugly. Bitch," she mouthed with the sort of deliberate girl-on-girl terrorism Edie hadn't experienced since the sixth grade.

MEET THE CONTESTANTS

Zo
24, Retired Ballerina
New York, New York

After spending twenty years training in ballet, Zo is beauty, grace, and confidence personified. Zo spent three seasons as a principal dancer at the prestigious American Ballet in New York City before a knee injury sent her life in a new direction. Now, Zo's looking for her next big love and hopes to find a man who will support her dreams of getting back onstage—or maybe even on the big screen! Her favorite musician is Cardi B. because she "speaks her mind." Zo powers her barre workouts with true crime podcasts, and her favorite serial killer is Ted Bundy!

Bailey
28, Pilates Instructor
Santa Barbara, California

Bailey is a gorgeous and vivacious blonde who loves being active and grew up riding horses on her family's ranch. These days Bailey's into Pilates, yoga, trying out new vegan recipes, bike rides, and sunsets on the beach. Her greatest dream is to become a mother to at least three little ones, and Bailey can't wait to find the perfect man to start a family with! Bailey's favorite holiday is Christmas because she loves decorating the whole house and giving gifts that make her loved ones smile. Bailey's a family girl at heart, but still, she hopes to have an awesome nanny one day so she can travel to Fiji and lie on the beach drinking mai-tais with her super sexy husband.

Max

29, Long-Distance Runner/Track Coach
Kansas City, Missouri

Maybe it's the exercise, maybe it's the protein shakes, but Max glows from the inside out. Max got her start in synchronized swimming and competitive gymnastics and now competes in marathons and Ironman competitions all over the world. Max needs a man who takes initiative and isn't intimidated by the fact she can probably out lift him at the gym. She's a self-starter who knows how to change a tire and has read Suze Orman's *Women and Money* three times. Max says she's never been in love, but she's not worried—she'll know it when she sees it. Because it's not how fast you get to the finish line, but what you learn on the way there.

Aspen

24, NBA Cheerleader
San Antonio, Texas

Aspen's an independent woman looking for a man who doesn't mind holding her purse while she lets her star shine. Aspen's biggest turn-off is jealousy—it's not her fault she works with a bunch of NBA players!—and men who don't like to have fun and be part of the social scene. (Also: men who wear flip-flops.) Her perfect man will be a great Instagram boyfriend with a fantastic career making lots of money because Aspen's love language is gifts—receiving them, that is!—and she loves a man who knows her worth.

Lily

26, Aromatherapist
Portland, Oregon

Some people describe Lily as "too nice," but she knows that those people just need more love in their lives! Lily's passionate about meditation, the healing power of crystals, aromatherapy, and helping others. In her free time, Lily loves hiking the Oregon coast and giving tarot readings to the homeless. Lily's looking for her soulmate and needs a man who's comfortable with PDA, because when Lily's in love, she wants the whole world to know! If she could do anything, Lily would raise penguins in her backyard because they are just so cute.

Marisol
25, Fitness Model
San Diego, California

Marisol's passionate about living a healthy lifestyle and wants to find a man who shares her values. A gym partner would also be great, but Marisol is more than just a pretty face and a slammin' bod—she wants her man to cherish her for who she really is: a kind heart. When the time is right, Marisol wants to tell Bennett about her triumphant 100-pound weight loss journey and see if he can hang with her big Mexican family. Marisol believes you can do anything you set your mind to, and once a year, when she's ready for a splurge, her favorite food is pizza!

McKayla
24, Bartender
Tucson, Arizona

McKayla spends her weekends popping bottles at her favorite clubs, and when the party really needs to get started, she's the first one to dance on the bar. But don't get it twisted: McKayla may be a thrill seeker who's passionate about fun, but she's also a good girl who doesn't kiss on the first date and loves reading British history. According to McKayla, Anne Boleyn got a "raw deal" because the perfect man "always has your back." McKayla's fav celeb is Doja Cat because she's "wild" but "real."

Imani

23, Model

Los Angeles, California

Imani describes herself as sexy and sassy. She's got a lot of opinions, and her perfect man wants to hear them all. Her dream relationship is just like Beyoncé and Jay-Z's iconic collab "'03 Bonnie and Clyde"—that is to say, a total ride or die. As a model, Imani finds herself on the road a lot, but when she's home, she loves to cuddle up on the couch with her man. Her biggest turn-off? Gross feet! Being a model is pretty great, but if Imani had to choose another career, it would be either makeup artist or dolphin trainer, because dolphins are majestic!

Parker

25, Artist / Heiress

Palo Alto, California

Growing up in Palo Alto, Parker always felt like an outsider, even though her family's wealth landed her in the best schools and social circles in Northern California. But really, Parker doesn't care about money or privilege because she is an *artist*. To prove it, she once burned a stack of hundred-dollar bills right in front of the New York Stock Exchange, a clear demonstration that individual wealth cannot change systemic problems. Parker's portraits of snarling women have landed her in the pages of *Artforum* and the *New York Times*. Parker says she needs a man who's not afraid of her Gemini vibes and vintage denture collection.

Emily

28, Humanitarian

Washington, DC

Emily wants to be a force for good. Inspired by Mother Teresa, Greta Thunberg, and Malala Yousafzai, Emily joined the Peace

Corps and spent six years giving back to underserved communities in South America. Now that she's back in the USA, Emily is proud to be a leader of an antiracist book club for white women (you have to dismantle the system from within!) and likes to spend every morning drinking kombucha and reading the *Washington Post*. Emily's looking for a man who shares her dream of a free and equitable society—and who's not scared of her rescue dog, Brad Pittbull!

Bai

29, Violinist

New York, New York

She may have resting bitch face, but Bai's heart is solid gold. Bai loves nothing more than to be swept away by the beauty of classical music, and when she's not wowing audiences as part of the New York Symphony, Bai's wandering the MOMA (her favorite artist is Magritte) or dining out at the city's best restaurants (her favorite food is tuna tartare). The child of immigrants, Bai's always pushed herself to excel and is looking for a man who understands drive, ambition, and making your family proud. Bai's most embarrassing fact? She loves fondue!

Kimberlee

23, Kindergarten Teacher

Denver, Colorado

Kimberlee's looking for her very own Prince Charming and dreams of one day getting married at the most magical place on earth: Disneyland! Kimberlee centers her life around Jesus Christ and wants to marry a man who can lead her and their little ones in faith. Kimberlee loves Hallmark movies, chocolate chip cookies, and the outdoors. But she wants Bennett to know she's not just a "nice girl." Kimberlee may be filled with Christ's love, but she also has a dark side! She hates getting up in the mornings *and* cilantro!

Chantel

28, Lawyer

Washington, DC

Chantel's a small-town girl with big city dreams! Born on the Louisiana bayou, Chantel always knew she wanted to leave the crawfish behind to attend Howard University (with a major in political science) and then Harvard University (law). After a lot of hard work and dedication, Chantel's career as an attorney is soaring, and she's ready to make time to find her perfect man. He brings her coffee every morning and a glass of wine every night. He's career oriented with the kind of smarts that can solve the *New York Times* crossword, even on Sundays! During the week, you can find Chantel stomping Capitol Hill in her designer shoe collection, and on the weekends, stopping by her favorite spa or watching her guilty pleasure, *The Fresh Prince of Bel-Air.*

10

Who's that girl?" Edie asked, stumbling over her mules as Jessa dragged her across the patio.

"What girl?"

"What girl?" Edie gestured incredulously at the second coming of Megan Fox. "That girl!"

"Oh," Jessa said, nonchalant. "That's Zo. Don't worry about her, she's cool. So, you'll just walk up again, same as last time."

"Uh, she doesn't seem cool, Jessa! She's literally flicking me off right this second." Edie craned her neck as she careened along behind Jessa. "She looks like a movie star." Was Zo the NBA cheerleader? The heiress? One of the models? "Is she a model?"

"Ballerina."

Gah. The ballerina with a *favorite serial killer.*

"Oh my god, she's going to kill me, Jessa." Edie gasped. "And that'll be on your conscience *forever.* When she smothers me dead in the middle of the night, you'll have only yourself to blame."

They arrived at the patio doors and Jessa took Edie by the shoulders.

"Listen to me. You just focus on being your fabulous self—"

Across the patio, silhouetted behind the living room windows, was a cluster of blurry bobbleheads peering through the drapes. Edie was going to be *living with them*, these girls who probably would hate her, just for being here! Obviously, Edie knew every single girl in the cast was better than her, but she'd just assumed they'd know it, too—and, well, be nice to her? Leave her alone? But all at once Edie realized it didn't matter if you were a regular person who ate carbs, barely exercised, and bought clothes at the Gap. On *The Key*, everyone was a threat. Behind every pretty pink pout would be some girl ready to cut a bitch because only one woman would emerge from the rubble of her fallen sisters, trudge across their sequined backs, and arrive at Bennett Charles's mountaintop engagement, victorious.

"Holy shit, there are, like, twenty more gorgeous women inside the house, Jessa! Waiting to murder me!"

"Twelve," Jessa said, arranging Edie's hair prettily around her shoulders. "Twelve more women waiting to murder you." Edie snapped her attention back to Jessa, alarmed. "I'm kidding!" Jessa rubbed Edie's arms like a comforting mother. "It's going to be fine. No one's going to murder you. You're adorable; you'll make friends. Let's just reset and then you and Bennett will have your talk, okay? We'll get rid of Zo, you'll have your chat, we'll do some quick product placement, roll into the key ceremony, and then, boom, night's over, and it's time to start thinking about your first date with Bennett!"

With that, Jessa turned and crossed the patio to where Charlie was gesticulating at Peter.

Edie chewed her thumbnail. Charlie did not look happy. Like, *at all*. Charlie's new thirty-five-year-old man voice rang in her ears—*Fuck off, Peter. You think you're so fucking clever*—and a lightning bolt of doubt cracked through the psychotic optimism that had convinced Edie to present herself as a marriage option to a man who was both a stranger and not. It was a little late now, but she had to consider it—what if seeing her again was the absolute last thing Charlie wanted? For the first time, Edie allowed herself to think about all the emails and phone calls that had gone unanswered, about all the years that had passed by without even a Facebook friend request. She'd forgiven him ages ago—they were just a couple of kids, untrained in both foreplay and conflict resolution—and, truly, she'd thought that no matter what, after all these years, he'd be happy to see her, Edie Pepper, his former kindergarten bestie. But what if that wasn't true at all? What if he really didn't want her here? What if her presence was actively ruining this experience for him?

Suddenly Edie felt like the only sensible thing to do was flee.

"It's not you," the camera guy said as he hoisted his camera back to his shoulder. "He hates when they surprise him. The other day they brought in a horse for a Prince Charming promo, and he flipped out. He's nervous like that."

"He's allergic to horses," she said without thinking. Edie turned to the camera guy, but before she could remember his name or get a good look at his face—Ted, that was his name, Ted—he disappeared again behind the camera. Edie knew the crew was strictly forbidden from speaking to the cast, so naturally she understood that she should take Ted's transgression seriously. Some oracle of truth dispensed from the reality TV gods.

Charlie hated surprises. Charlie was just surprised.

A PA rushed over and began frantically shooing her back on set for take 2, and as Edie made her way across the patio, she decided the only way forward was for her to hold this mantra close to her heart. *Charlie hates surprises. Charlie was just surprised.* And when she reached the couch and met his eyes once again, for a second, she almost believed it.

"Edie? Edie Pepper?" Charlie exclaimed. He aimed a torpedo of a smile directly at her heart as he used Zo's miniature thigh to springboard off the couch. "I can't believe it. What are you doing here?"

But in that moment, he seemed so fake to her, like some bad actor on some bad soap opera, and not like the Charlie Bennett she knew at all, or even the Bennett Charles she'd stalked from her living room. The cameras, his seriously white teeth, both their first greeting and now the second—none of it felt real. She'd thought when they saw each other again, it would be effortless. But it was a mess. She had to do something. She had to fix it.

"Yes. It is I, Edie Pepper," she said in a playful announcer voice. "Your high school girlfriend, here to rekindle our love." She shrugged, "I'm sorry, I can't take this seriously. Can we just talk? Say hi like normal people?" She opened her arms to him. "Charlie, it's me! Edie!"

And then the new and improved Charlie Bennett finally smiled a smile that Edie recognized, sheepish, with that one crooked tooth. He stepped forward and enveloped same-old-nothing-special Edie Pepper in a hug. He smelled nothing like she remembered. Her memories were of Play-Doh. Root beer. And, later, too much Drakkar Noir. But now he smelled like a man. Like leather tinged with sweat. Edie melted into his chest, closed her eyes, and savored the feeling of her cheek against his blazered shoulder.

"That's right, Bennett, it's your high school sweetheart, Edie Pepper," Adam Fox boomed, suddenly standing right next to them. "Here all the way from your hometown of Chicago, Illinois, to see if the spark's still there. And, maybe, if you're lucky, the wedlock you two always dreamed of."

Wedlock? Adam Fox *never* brought up wedlock this early in the season!!!

From the couch a peal of laughter.

"What a joke!" Zo seethed. "Nobody's marrying this hog-bodied ho. Get out of my way," she said, shoving Edie with her bony shoulder as she made her way off the patio.

Hog-bodied ho? Edie pulled back from Charlie and without thinking said the first thing that came to mind, a pitch-perfect imitation of bitchiness honed from years of watching reality TV.

"Gladly," Edie said, curling her fingers around Charlie's bicep. "I'll just stay here with my man, winning."

Slowly, Zo pivoted on one foot to face them again. Her lip curled.

"No one's winning anything in that dress, sis."

With that, she walked off the patio, her heels clacking across the tile like gunshots.

Everyone stood silent. Until Jessa starting hooting and rushed across the patio to take Edie in her arms.

"Are you kidding me?" Jessa enthused while Charlie dropped Edie and took two big steps back. "That was *fantastic*."

"Let's cut," Peter yelled. Instantly the crew was in motion. Adjusting lights, moving cameras, Adam Fox walking straight out the door.

"Peter, can I have a word?" Charlie said through gritted teeth.

Jessa smiled at Edie, so big. "I knew you were going to be a natural, and here you are, being a natural." She yelled to Peter, "Peter, wasn't she a natural?"

Peter looked briefly at Edie. "You did great," he said before turning to a guy in a Lakers cap. "Lou, do we have enough coverage on the entrance?"

At a monitor, Lou scrolled through footage. "We can cut something together with this. Add some voiceover. Enough reaction shots for sure."

"Great," Peter said, clapping his hands together. "Let's move on. Edie, Bennett, let's take a seat on the couch and have a little chat."

Edie looked at Charlie looking at Peter, his eyes slit, his shoulders tense, and she was confronted again with the fear that

Charlie Bennett really did not want her here. But from the very first moment she'd laid eyes on him talking to Ryan Seacrest in her living room, Edie believed that the history they shared mattered. That it had built them into the people they were today. The rubber bands on his braces, the papier-mâché volcanoes burping baking soda all over Edie's back porch, that time at the sixth-grade dance when Maddy Morrison humiliated Edie right in front of her crush Tommy Malick and Edie had run out the gymnasium doors and onto the playground to discover Charlie sitting alone on the swings. He'd held her hand and said, "I dunno, Edie, you've always been, like, the coolest girl to me." The first cigarette they'd shared with Lauren on some old train tracks, Charlie losing his fucking mind and digging in his pocket for his inhaler. Their first kiss after the football game senior year. All of it. Fucking *all of it*. Her love, her kindness—*she* had laid the groundwork for Charlie Bennett's transformation into Bennett Charles.

If anyone had a right to be here, it was her.

"Charlie," she whispered, as she approached him. "I just want to talk to you."

He turned to her, grabbing her arm and holding it a little too tightly.

"If you're going to be here," he hissed, "you need to call me Bennett."

TAKE 5 PRODUCTIONS
THE KEY
EPISODE 3 TEASER [DRAFT FOR EP APPROVAL]
TAPE #92

00:00:00 OPENING SEQUENCE

ADAM FOX: Tonight on *The Key*...

EDIE INTERVIEW / PATIO

EDIE: I hope I make some really great friends here.

THE GIRLS PEERING OUT THE WINDOW.

ASPEN: Who is that? Who is he talking to?

THE LIVING ROOM DOORS OPEN DRAMATICALLY. A SILHOUETTE APPEARS.

EDIE: Hi, ladies!

SMASH CUTS OF THE GIRLS GOING CRAZY

IMANI: Who the hell are you?

ZO: She thinks she's going to date Bennett.

MCKAYLA: What the <bleep>. <bleep> no. <bleep> no.

PARKER: I'd like to speak to my lawyer.

MARISOL: We can't add any more girls! We're supposed to be *losing* girls!

ADAM FOX: Ladies, let's just calm down...

BAI: You think you can just come out of nowhere and date Bennett? You don't even know Bennett!

EDIE: I mean, yeah, I do. He was my high school boyfriend.

SOUNDS OF SCREAMING / GLASS BREAKING.

RED WINE SLOWLY DRIPPING DOWN THE STAIRS.

MONTAGE OF GIRLS SOBBING.

BENNETT STORMING DOWN THE HALLWAY/ SHOVING THE CAMERA

BENNETT: Get that <bleeping> camera out of my face.

FADE TO BLACK

1:00:00 ADAM FOX: All that and more, tonight on *The Key*.

11

Bennett Charles was no longer in love.

In fact, as he stood in the dining room, sweating his ass off in front of an army of hostile bachelorettes arranged across a three-tiered riser, Bennett Charles had never been less in love in his entire life. Unless love was an anxious stomach expelling protein farts at a totally unreasonable pace. An hour ago, these girls had been kissing him and using words like *adore* and *smitten* and *wet*, and it'd felt like the last time he'd summited Kilimanjaro—like standing on top of the world, all the possibilities endless because there you were, doing something most people could never do, alive. But now these very same girls were glaring at him like they might rip his arm off and beat him in the dick with it. And there, in the back row, was Edie Pepper. All Bennett could think about was escape.

How in the hell was he going to get off this show without becoming the most hated man in America? The tabloids had *destroyed* Wyatt Cash. The entire *Key* universe turned against him—former contestants gathered to dissect the story on podcasts, gave quotes to magazines, and posted savage memes across their social media platforms.

Exactly what these girls would do to him.

Bennett scratched the back of his neck wildly, like a dog with a sudden itch, before remembering he was on camera. He dropped his hand so quickly it smacked into the side of the faux marble pedestal where thirteen oversized gold keys were displayed in diagonal rows. The pedestal rocked and a single key slid off and fell to the rug. Bennett watched it settle next to his shoe and was once again forced to contend with his skinny ankles that stuck out between the intentionally too-short gray suit pants that Wardrobe had chosen for him, and the shiny loafers with no socks that were not on brand for him at all. Hiking boots. Over-the-ankle hiking boots. That was Bennett Charles.

Bennett stared at the Key to My Heart on the floor, paralyzed by the weight of his sudden rejection and the imminent exposure of Bennett Charles vis-à-vis Charlie Bennett. How was any of this his fault? He didn't invite Edie here—he would *never* invite Edie here—yet the girls' collective rage was aimed directly at him.

"I cancel you! You're canceled!" McKayla, the bartender from Tucson, slurred from the front row. She removed her shoe and threw it across the dining room, where it rebounded off a tripod before a harried production assistant crawled under the cameras' sight lines to retrieve it. McKayla wobbled on her remaining heel and jabbed her finger at the production team. "Canceled!"

That's the other thing the girls were furious about—the abruptly canceled cocktail party. Bennett glared at Peter, who was standing just off camera with his arms crossed over his chest, that same smug look on his face. What a dick. Obviously, he'd been the one to cancel the cocktail party. Another thing that wasn't Bennett's fault! Bennett kept trying to refuse things. Refuse to do the key ceremony, refuse to be filmed talking to Edie, refuse to do interviews, refuse to be Peter's puppet.

While Jessa had lined the girls up on the risers, Bennett had taken back some control and cornered Peter in the kitchen. "You know what I'm going to do when this is all over, Pete?" he'd seethed while Peter leaned against the refrigerator like he didn't have a care in the world. "I'm gonna find your ex-girlfriend, and after I give her the ride of her life, I'm gonna tell her what a pathetic shithead you are."

"Like I told you, she came to us. We didn't go looking for her."

"Don't you have a shred of loyalty, man?"

"C'mon, dawg, calm down." The way he said *dawg*, like he was mocking him. "This is good TV. Think of all the women across America who are going to be so in love with this love story."

"You've got to be kidding. She leaves tonight."

"Definitely not," Peter said, straightening to his full height. He had one fucking inch on Bennett. At most! Asshole. "She stays. We're doing a storyline."

"Then I'll fucking leave," Bennett said, already looking for an exit that wasn't blocked by a camera or lighting rig.

Peter stepped closer to him. "Let's not go down this road, all right? We've already been over your contract. I'm sure you remember you're on the hook for—what is it, three million? Or four?—if you don't complete the season. And, seriously, you don't want me to call Carole Steele, who owns half the media outlets in America—I'm sure you can imagine what she's gonna do if you don't play ball. So, let's just cut the shit. It's you and me, all right?" Peter turned and yelled to a PA. "Can we get a drink over here?" He smiled at Bennett like they were friends. "What do you want?"

"Bourbon," Bennett said despite himself. "And not the cheap shit you give the girls. And a Smartwater."

"Can we get a nice bourbon and a Smartwater over here, please," Peter yelled to a PA. "Listen, I know this feels shitty. I do," he said, turning back to Bennett. "And we don't like to do it this way, either, but it's just how the sausage gets made. And let's keep it in perspective. There are worse things than having a girl you actually know, who you actually trust, looking out for you."

Bennett, through clenched teeth, said, "I don't know her, Peter."

"Of course you do. You've known her your whole life. People don't ever really change."

"What the fuck is that supposed to mean? Is that a threat?"

"What is *what* supposed to mean?" Peter cocked his head and looked at Bennett like he was crazy. "And is what a threat?"

"You think I'm real fucking stupid, don't you?"

"I'm going to need you to be more specific. Because if you're asking if I knew you were a big nerd in high school and changed your name, then get over yourself, Bennett. Everyone was a fucking nerd in high school. You don't think your background check told me that a month ago? Calm down. That's not the story we're trying to tell. Here's your drink."

Bennett took the whiskey and drank it fast. Then he did the same with the water, because chugging Smartwater was better than triggering his asthma in front of this fucking prick. He wiped his mouth with the back of his hand.

It made sense that Peter would've already known at least some of this. Still.

"How am I supposed to trust you when you do shit like this?" Bennett said finally. "I'm not going to let you play me on live television."

"First of all, we're not live—"

"I'm not kidding, Peter. I will slap the shit out of you."

"Bennett, c'mon," Peter said, shaking Bennett lightly by the shoulders. "Why do you think I want you to look like an asshole? How does that help me? I want you to be Prince motherfucking Charming in this motherfucking fairy tale. And to do that, I need you to man up, stop whining, and charm the shit out of the girls for all the housewives, gays, and preteens of America. Can you do that for me?"

Bennett pictured Edie looking at him with those big puppy dog eyes, which normally would've turned him on—he loved that kind of open adoration—but instead just filled him with shame. He was sweating now in places no man should sweat; even his feet felt slide-y in these stupid loafers.

"Why should I?" Bennett said, the reasonable part of him embarrassed by the petulance in his voice.

"Because the entire world is going to love you for it," Peter exclaimed, his eyes shining a little too brightly. "When you treat Edie with the same love and respect you give the rest of the girls, you're gonna look like the sweet, stand-up guy America loves. And when we make her over and send you on your Cinderella fantasy date, you're gonna be like, 'What's that sound?' Oh shit, it's panties dropping all over the world. And when—*eventually*—you send her home because you're different people now, it'll be beautiful and real and nostalgic, and they'll love you even more when you find your wife with whatever interchangeable influencer you choose. So how about you give me some credit—I know how to make good TV. I know how to make you look like a fucking king." Peter paused and took a step back. They locked eyes. "And I also know how to make you look like a real fucking dick. Know what I mean?"

Bennett knew Peter was referencing the incident in the hall when he'd yelled *Get that fucking camera out of my face!* And then, if that wasn't enough, when Bennett had shoved the camera, and also Greg, unfortunately. That one second of footage was enough for Peter to edit Bennett into the kind of guy who yelled and pushed and became unhinged. For the rest of his life, he'd be swearing to everyone he was *not that guy*. He was a *nice guy* with a *bad edit*.

"The girls are already pissed off—if we have a key ceremony, I'm really gonna look like an asshole," Bennett said.

"Nah." Peter clapped Bennett on the shoulder. "Eliminations are just part of it. The women of America don't blame you for that. Want me to send Makeup over for that neck?"

Bennett's skin felt prickly all over. "Is it all red?"

"Yeah."

"Fuck."

It's not like Bennett had been operating under the illusion that Peter had his best interests at heart. Peter was just some know-it-all prick. But before Edie's arrival, Bennett felt at least like they were playing for the same team. But as the makeup artist attempted to calm the Rorschach test blooming across Bennett's neck and chest, it became crystal-clear that no one gave a fuck about his love story. And that any misstep would be used against him. What the hell was he supposed to do? There was no way out. The only way was through. So, Bennett let them powder his neck and guide him back to the living room for the key ceremony.

The girls on the risers were getting restless.

"Bennett didn't want her then and he doesn't want her now," Zo, standing front row center, seethed loudly to two of her minions: Parker, the artist/heiress from Palo Alto, and Aspen, the NBA cheerleader from San Antonio.

"Total fucking bullshit," Parker and Aspen sniffed in agreement.

"That's the tea and it's scalding," Zo pronounced, glaring at him.

The risers trembled with the wiping of eyes and indignant straightening of gowns.

Somehow Bennett thought being on this show was what was going to change everything. He thought he'd come here and pick a wife, and that by virtue of picking someone and that person saying yes on national television, he'd finally be able to give his whole self to another person. But having Edie Pepper on those risers was startling proof that for basically his entire adult life, it had been impossible for Bennett to get close to anyone. Sure, he had lots of friends and followers—he was a great hang. But had he had any relationships, even *one*, like the one he'd had with her?

Bennett sighed and picked up the fallen key. *The Key* was supposed to skyrocket Bennett to book deals and sponsorships and his own adventure-themed TV show. And by committing to one woman on national television, Bennett would also be creating an additional brand, a couple brand, probably even with a couple nickname like Benley (Bennett + Bailey) or Bentel (Bennett + Chantel) or Benani (Bennett + Imani). His entire vision of the future was based on a positive outcome from *The Key*. Bennett and his beautiful wife on the cover of magazines. Bennett and his beautiful wife working with the best comedy writers to create online content in the vein of "just like us!" couples like Chrissy Teigen and John Legend. And then more followers and more content and more followers and more content and more *money money money*.

But as soon as Bennett saw Edie Pepper, he realized it was impossible. Edie knew who he really was, which was no one at all.

Peter strode onto set and clapped his hands like a football coach prepping the team for the big game. "Okay, all right, let's get this thing going." He assessed the girls for a moment. "Edie," he called. "Why don't you go ahead and switch spots with Zo?"

"Excuse me?" Zo screeched.

"I want you two to switch spots," Peter said, pointing to Edie's spot in the third row.

"Sounds great, Peter," Edie called, clapping her hands on various shoulders, crutching her way down the risers.

"There's no way you're getting a key," Zo seethed when Edie landed before her. "They just want a better shot of you crying."

"Maybe," Edie said. "Or maybe they want to hide that dress you're wearing? Sequins. How original."

"You should go home. You're embarrassing yourself."

"Listen up, Hannah Montana. I'm thirty-five years old. I do what I want."

"OMG, I *thought* those were dentures!"

"Yeah, yeah, yeah, save it for the cameras," Peter said, shooing Zo up the risers. Then he strode over to Bennett and leaned in. "Can I talk to you for a second? In the kitchen?"

Jesus Christ, what now? Reluctantly, Bennett placed the Key to My Heart down on the pedestal and followed Peter back into the kitchen.

"Hey, man, relax, you look tense. It's all good." Peter clapped him on the shoulder again. "Can we get another bourbon over here?" he called to a PA. He turned back to Bennett. "I have an idea I want to run by you."

Bennett made a noise in his throat.

"What if we do the key ceremony like usual," Peter continued. The bourbon arrived and he handed it over. "And you choose Edie last, really amp up that tension, and then I'm thinking, what if when she comes up for her key, you give her a little kiss?"

"What the *fuck*, Peter."

"Just hear me out," Peter said, palms up. "Now that we're on the same page that Edie stays, we've got to come together on what that looks like, right? It's a fairy tale. It's gotta *look* like a fairy tale. Right now, it looks like a bad date. You look angry, and what kind of fairy tale is that? But this—a little kiss—that turns it all around. What's more romantic than you kissing her in front of everyone so she knows just how special she really is?"

"There's no kissing at the key ceremony, Peter. Everyone knows that."

"That's exactly what's gonna make it great."

"The other girls will freak out."

"Jessa will deal with them."

"You've got to be kidding me with this." Bennett drank the bourbon down fast, well aware that he was, once again, well and truly fucked.

"Do you trust me?" Peter asked.

"Not at all."

"Fair enough," Peter said. "But I think you should trust me on this. It's not really that big of a deal—you kiss all the girls. Obviously, you should never feel pressured into kissing anyone because, as you know, *The Key* takes consent very seriously. But, look, it's easy. You call her name, you give her a little kiss, and in post we make it into a super romantic moment with swirling cameras and romantic music. You have to picture it—every woman in the world who's ever pined for her ex is just *living* for this moment, where you, Bennett Charles, are every girl's dream."

Bennett stepped closer to Peter. He wasn't Charlie Bennett anymore. He was a guy who'd BASE jumped in India. Who'd rappelled into an active volcano. Who'd jumped out of a helicopter on motherfucking skis. Contract or not, Bennett Charles wasn't intimidated by this prick.

"You need to promise me," he said, looking Peter straight in the eye, "on your honor as a man, that you will never use that footage. From the hall."

Peter gave him the Boy Scouts salute. "On my honor."

And then Bennett was shaking out his arms and legs like an athlete preparing to take the field. He bounced on the balls of his feet, repeating his personal mantra to himself. *Every mountain teaches you something. Every mountain teaches you something.* Some residual soreness from yesterday's pick-up basketball game with the sound guys shot through his left knee, a rude reminder that he was, in fact, thirty-five.

"Let's go."

Peter and Bennett walked out of the kitchen, and Bennett once again took his place next to the podium. He could feel the eyes of all fourteen women boring into him, and a little rivulet of sweat snaked down his back. He ignored it. He was Bennett Motherfucking Charles, and it was time for his speech.

Bennett knit his hands together at the waist and looked at the floor for a moment, as if the gravity of this burden weighed heavily on him. "I believe in this process," he began. He raised his face to the girls, eyes tender. A camera trucked closer. "I believe my wife is in this room tonight. And my commitment to finding her, to building a life together filled with love and adventure—that commitment has never wavered. Buddha reminds us not to rush anything. When the time is right, all will become clear." He took a deep breath and picked up the first Key to My Heart. The teeth dug into the palm of his hand. "Bailey."

Bailey, the Pilates instructor from Santa Barbara, who the girls called Malibu Barbie because she was empirically the most beautiful woman of the bunch, with a ton of blond hair and these big blue eyes and this little nose over full lips, swept down from the risers. Bennett had a major hard-on for Bailey, but he couldn't imagine a girl as perfect as Bailey ever agreeing to marry him. But her eyes were supportive, so maybe he was wrong. He smiled at her gratefully as he took her hands in his.

"Bailey, will you hold this Key to My Heart?"

"Always," Bailey said, smiling in a way that was somehow shy, confident, sexy, and demure all at once. They embraced.

"Zo," Bennett said. After she slinked across the floor to him, he asked, "Zo, will you hold this Key to My Heart?"

"You know I will," Zo responded. And then she placed a hand at the nape of his neck and pulled him to her, planting a seductive kiss on his cheek and whispering, "Send that bitch home," in a way that sent shivers down his spine and almost got him hard.

He continued handing out keys to the girls on Peter's list. Lily, the aromatherapist from Portland with the little yin-yang tattoo on her wrist. Just yesterday, before everything went to shit, they'd been alone for a moment on the group date and Bennett had held that tattoo to his lips. She'd smelled like lavender. Max, the long-distance runner from Kansas City with the purple hair and swole biceps. He could picture her rock climbing in Yosemite with him, and it was hot. Imani, this season's only *real* model, or at least that's what she'd told him repeatedly, referencing the appearance of one-third of her torso in the corner of a Gucci ad as "the time I was in *Vogue*." McKayla, who was always drunk but always fun. Aspen, who'd dry humped him on a pool table. Parker, Emily, Bai, Chantel, and—

Adam Fox appeared and said gravely into the camera, "Ladies, this is the final key of the night."

Bennett took a deep breath.

"Edie," he said.

"What?" Edie and a smattering of indignant girls cried.

"Edie," he said again, tilting his head in a way he knew looked adorable and smiling like, *Come on, get over here, silly*. He could do this. No big thing. He kissed all the girls, all the time. And when this was over, didn't he want to break into acting? He'd start now.

She arrived in front of him. He took her hands in his.

"Edie Pepper," he said, "my oldest friend. Over the years our lives have put miles and oceans between us. But seeing you again, for the first time in a long time, I feel like I'm home." He squeezed her hands. "Edie, will you hold this Key to My Heart?"

"You bet your ass I will," she said. And the way she was looking at him, amused but also like he was really something special—just like that, something inside him relaxed. Suddenly he felt like he could see her, *really* see her, this friend he'd always known. She smiled—that big smile where you could see all her teeth, and he remembered—hadn't she always been like the coolest girl to him? And even though he could feel Greg right on his ass and all the girls holding their breath, Bennett felt ready—happy even. He put his hand to her cheek, leaned in, and kissed her.

WHO IS EDIE PEPPER? 5 THINGS TO KNOW ABOUT BENNETT CHARLES'S EX- GIRLFRIEND
BY LUCY LYONS

Ex-girlfriend alert! *Us Weekly* has learned that Midwestern copywriter Edie Pepper, 35, has joined the competition for Bennett Charles's heart in a surprise entrance during *The Key*'s 22nd season, premiering November 3 on RX.

"I'm so flattered that Edie took time out of her life to reconnect and see if the spark's still there," Bennett said in an exclusive quote to *Us*.

Who is Edie Pepper? Here are five things to know.

1. She's the Oldest Female Contestant in the History of the Franchise

Clocking in at 35 years old, Edie Pepper is by far the most mature woman to ever compete for a Key to My Heart. But is maturity what the extreme sportsman's looking for? Sources tell *Us* that while Bennett claims to be ready for marriage, his wildin' days might not be over just yet.

2. She's Not into Fashion

Edie's official cast photo says it all. Decked out in a red sweatshirt and messy ponytail, clearly Edie's joined the *Key* cast for love and *not* to showcase her sartorial point of view.

3. She's Never Been Married

But don't call Edie a spinster—she just hasn't found the right guy!

On average, women in the US get married at 27.9 years, so at 35 years old, this Bridget Jones isn't too far behind.

4. She Has an Unfair Advantage

Not just high school sweethearts, these two lovebirds have known each other since kindergarten! Bennett tells *Us*, "Seeing Edie again was like a warm hug from home. I've been traveling for so long—it's been years since I've had that feeling. Like I'm right where I'm supposed to be."

5. She's Looking for Her Soulmate

According to her cast bio, Edie "loves to laugh" and is looking for someone she can "trust." Will that be Bennett? Sources tell *Us* Bennett's "falling in love" with "multiple women." Fingers crossed Edie doesn't get her heart broken for good!

12

The first thing Peter Kennedy saw when his alarm went off at four thirty a.m. was a lightly snoring Siobhan. She was lying on her stomach, her dark hair fanned over her smooth brown shoulder, his white Frette sheet draped across her waist. She was very beautiful, Siobhan. A model. Last night he'd texted her when he left production around eleven. He'd walked into his ocean-view condo in Malibu a little before twelve, taken a shower in his white marble bathroom, wandered around his perfect midcentury living room, with the crisp leather couches and minimalist art that the interior designer had picked out and installed, eaten a banana in his pristine chef's kitchen, and then dug up his old Chicago album and put it on the turntable. He stood at the window, watching the waves, brooding over the sad state of music today—you really weren't going to get full brass out of Post Malone—occasionally lip syncing along with the big moments—*Just say you'll love me for the rest of your life/I got a lot of love and I don't want to let gooooo*—before settling again, watching the waves, until one fifteen, when Siobhan had finally arrived, tipsy from an industry party, and they'd had disappointing sex until two.

He didn't know what was wrong with him. He just felt... unsettled. Out of sorts. Like there was something jumpy inside of him that kept surging against his chest. Siobhan had been drunk and performative. She'd had her hands wound through her dark hair, tossing her head around and moaning as she rode him, stretching out her torso so her small breasts were flattened against her chest and he could count her ribs. He'd held her hip bones in his hands as she bounced, and the unsettled feeling had surged. It was so strange, like he wanted, just for a second, to jump out the window, let the waves carry him away. And then he was so grossed out by his own bullshit that he knew he was never going to come, so he flipped her over, wrapped his hands around her shoulders, and pushed deep inside her the way she liked, pulsing against her g-spot until she came hard against him.

Almost immediately she said, "You—"

"I'm good," he said, rolling away.

Now Peter stared at the soft hair covering the hollow place between her neck and shoulder and had an impulse to press his face into it and burrow into her. Lately he could feel that Siobhan was on the verge of *wanting more*. She'd gotten very riled up last week about a random sore throat he'd had, imploring him to go to the doctor and then DoorDashing him chicken soup that he found in his lobby long after it'd arrived because, obviously, he'd gone to work. Peter had thought about cutting it off then, but he despised the idea that maybe he was just some remote, cold person. He reached his hand out to touch her now, but as much as he willed himself to do it, his hand just hovered over her back, so eventually he got up and put on his running clothes instead.

As his feet beat the pavement down to the beach, he thought about Julie, even though he was beyond tired of thinking about Julie, and hated thinking that everything came back to Julie, that his own seemingly permanent disillusionment and hard-heartedness were caused by and all about Julie. He'd met Julie when he was still a struggling writer, and she was just starting her career as an agent. He'd pursued her hard, like an infatuated idiot, which he supposed he was. He was just taken by her. She was spunky and savvy and ballsy and knew exactly what she wanted and spoke her mind and seemed to know her place in the world in a way he didn't.

When she'd finally accepted him into her bed, the gratitude he'd felt was, frankly, ridiculous. But that was the dynamic between them. Julie was to be adored; Peter was to be grateful. And as Julie quickly rose through the ranks as an agent, the more industry parties they had to attend. She'd get mean-drunk off vodka tonics, and in the car on the way home, talk shit about everyone, particularly him. She'd complain about something he'd said to someone she didn't think he should've said it to, or, conversely, berate him for not talking to some bigshot producer with the authority to hire him onto a new prestige drama. He began to regard her determination as unpleasant and supercilious, and when she'd sense his unease, she'd make sure to remind him that he was lucky to even be there.

Why did they get married?

Why did anyone get married? They were thirty. It was time.

Obviously, it had been Julie's decision to get divorced.

The real turning point had been when Julie signed an emerging starlet who, under Julie's tutelage, became very, very famous very, very quickly. Suddenly the parties Julie attended included the likes of Brad Pitt, and Peter supposed that's when Julie began to regard him as a starter husband. There he was, a reality TV showrunner, the absolute lowest of the low on the Hollywood echelon.

He supposed they were both disappointed in how he'd turned out.

So, she'd left him. They'd been married long enough that it was either have a baby or get divorced, so they got divorced. Her lawyer emailed Peter an exit package with such a sizable payout that it was the first time he truly understood Julie's regard for him as some sort of talentless hack. He also felt really fucking stupid for not being more aware of just how much money Julie was making, and would continue to make, and wondered why he'd been the one to make the down payment on the Palisades house if Julie was sitting on cash like this. But *of course* she was—her starlet was signing multimillion-dollar deals every day. He just hadn't been paying attention because he'd been traveling around the world manufacturing love stories, goddammit.

Peter thought about not accepting the package. About preserving some of his dignity and just walking away with what he'd come in with. And then, alternatively, demanding an audit of their marital assets, because what the fuck else did he not know? Julie would never have offered this kind of money unless there was more to be had. (Now he understood why her business manager had done their taxes for years.) Ultimately, at the urging of his sister, Elizabeth (the only person Peter ever discussed anything remotely close to feelings with), he signed the papers, bought the condo in Malibu, had the interior designer furnish it, and went to Fiji for a week, where, in an uncharacteristically expressive move, he threw his wedding ring off a cliff and watched it plop into the ocean. Then, in a more Peteresque fashion, he agonized for the rest of the week over the possibility of a sea turtle or some rare fish choking to death on it.

When he returned to LA, he never saw Julie again, aside for her name printed relentlessly in the trades. And then the tabloids once she started dating the newest iteration of Batman.

Already, at five, the sun was hot. Peter took off his shirt and tucked it into the waistband of his shorts. His feet dug through the sand at a steady pace as the waves continued to roll in. He was thirty-nine years old and tanned and trim and had all his hair and could fuck models if he wanted, but what did he know about love? Only that it was bullshit and hurt like hell and, paradoxically, probably the only thing that really mattered. Unfortunately, in the way of most divorced people, Peter still believed in love very deeply—he just found it impossible to accept in any form other than the romantic ideal he held in his mind. What he wanted—a partnership like Barack and Michelle's—was likely impossible. He was difficult, both exceedingly average and annoyingly exceptional. He was too old—he should've picked someone smart and kind back in college, before the big bad world got hold of them, because, *god*, the women in LA. Who could muster the energy to create something real when everything was an illusion?

And now Peter circled back to his essential problem, the root of his unsettling: how to make Bennett Charles fall in love with Edie Pepper.

That kiss last night—that kiss was definitely a start.

During his years at *The Key*, Peter had stood watch over thousands of make-outs. Watching two good-looking people dry hump for the cameras had become as mundane as an episode of *Wheel of Fortune*. But watching Edie Pepper and Bennett Charles's kiss was something else entirely. What he thought would be a light peck had turned out to be much, much more. Bennett urging her to open her mouth to his, which she did, eagerly. The way Bennett slowed down the pace of the kiss, as if to savor it. The way she dug her nails into the nape of his neck as he bit her bottom lip, and the way she smiled against him when he released it. The way he threaded his hands into her hair and the tiny pauses where they'd open their eyes at the same time and glance at each other and smile before starting all over again.

At first Peter was so astounded he didn't really understand what he was seeing.

And then it hit him—*chemistry*. Edie Pepper and Bennett Charles had chemistry.

But there was something else. Something more.

Connection.

One glance at the wild-eyed girls on the risers and Peter knew that this was undoubtedly true. Sure, it was generally understood that you don't kiss the suitor at the key ceremony—it was *disrespectful to the process*. But Peter could see it wasn't just that. The women were seeing exactly what he was seeing, and they were terrified. The natural order of things had been upended, and almost instantly, the girls had dissolved into hysterics. They'd screamed and sobbed. Kimberlee, one of the ones who was eliminated, even collapsed, at which point Jessa rushed in the on-set medical team and they'd gotten great shots of Kimberlee breathing into an oxygen mask while the other girls clutched each other in horror.

In reality TV, the hardest thing to produce was authenticity. Which was why producers constantly lied to the contestants and manipulated them and tricked them into a false sense of security before pulling the rug out from under them once again. So when Edie and Bennett had finally pulled apart, her cheeks flushed pink and Bennett smiling in a way Peter had never seen him smile, sort of unguarded and goofy—Peter knew then, with absolute certainty, that they did in fact have a show, possibly even a great fucking show, one that Carole Steele and millions of people would love. Peter could see the entire season—the most dramatic season ever—laid out right in front of him. All he had to do was push the pieces forward.

So why wasn't he happy?

TAKE 5 PRODUCTIONS
THE KEY
EPISODE 4 TEASER [DRAFT FOR EP APPROVAL]
TAPE #202

00:00:00 OPENING SEQUENCE

ADAM FOX: Tonight on *The Key*...

A MOTORCYCLE FLIES DIRECTLY AT THE CAMERA.

ADAM FOX: Bennett's on the road to love. But with so many amazing women, who holds the key to his heart?

THE MOTORCYCLE PULLS UP IN FRONT OF THE MANSION. BENNETT REMOVES HIS HELMET, SHAKES OUT HIS HAIR.

ADAM FOX: Will it be Zo? The ballerina with an insatiable zest for life?

ZO MOUNTS THE BIKE. SHE WAVES AT THE GIRLS AS THEY RIDE OFF INTO THE SUNSET.

ADAM FOX: Or will it be Aspen, the NBA cheerleader from Texas who's never been in love?

BENNETT AND ASPEN LOUNGE ON A YACHT DRINKING CHAMPAGNE.

BENNETT: What's your favorite color?

ASPEN: What's yours?

BENNETT: I asked you first.

ASPEN: I asked you second!

BENNETT: Blue.

ASPEN: Mine too!

BENNETT: No way! What's your favorite food?

ASPEN: What's yours?

BENNETT: My mom's lasagna.

ASPEN: Mine too!

BENNETT: No way!

BENNETT AND ASPEN MAKE OUT.

ADAM FOX: Or what about Bailey, the gorgeous Pilates instructor from Santa Barbara with a heart of gold?

BENNETT AND BAILEY ROCK CLIMB. SHE'S A NATURAL. WHEN THEY REACH THE TOP, THEY KISS.

BENNETT: You're perfect.

BAILEY: No, you are.

ADAM FOX: Or Max, the long-distance runner from Kansas City who shares Bennett's passion for competition?

BENNETT AND MAX WATCH FOOTBALL. AFTER AN EXCITING PLAY, THEY JUMP IN THE AIR AND BUMP CHESTS, SPILLING BEER EVERYWHERE.

ADAM FOX: Or will our newest bachelorette,

Bennett's high school sweetheart, Edie, unlock his heart?

THE GIRLS SURROUND BENNETT ON THE SOFA. HE PLAYS A GUITAR AND SINGS.

BENNETT: *I won't let your head hit the bed, without my hand behind it.*

EDIE AND ZO JOCKEY FOR POSITION ON THE COUCH. ZO SHOVES HER AND EDIE FALLS TO THE FLOOR. BENNETT DOESN'T NOTICE.

ADAM FOX: Whose heart will be broken for good?

MONTAGE OF GIRLS SOBBING IN FORMAL WEAR.

ADAM FOX: And who will be left to pick up the pieces alone?

SOMEONE FAINTS AT THE KEY CEREMONY.

1:00:00 ADAM FOX: All that and more, tonight on *The Key*.

13

Peter!" Jessa called from the craft services truck. "You're late!"

"It's seven fifteen. My call time is eight," he replied, climbing out of the back seat of the Lincoln Navigator. *Key* staff were everywhere—unloading cases from vans, hauling equipment, erecting lighting rigs around a beach volleyball court where, in just about an hour, eight gorgeous women were set to prance around in bikinis and maybe even hit a volleyball, all for the love of one complete douchebag.

What more could America want?

"I've been waiting for you. I've got a case of sabotage for you to investigate!" Jessa said wryly as she handed him a cup of coffee. "Mushroom coffee imported from Finland, one Splenda, just the way you like. Let's go." She pushed him toward the clubhouse.

In addition to outlining the quid pro quo with the Beach Club (at least two clear shots of the Beach Club's signage to air prominently during the episode, one talking head with the lead describing the luxe surroundings, and first right of refusal on any *Key*-produced nuptials), the production notes also helpfully quoted GOOP's review of the location, deeming it the "go-to destination for luxury beach weddings made to impress out-of-towners." As they stepped through the clubhouse doors, Peter couldn't help but agree with the assessment. The Beach Club's Malibu-rustic décor had the exact je ne sais quoi every fishtail-braided bride could ask for. An entire wall of glass facing the ocean. Thick farmhouse beams crossing the ceiling. Plank floors burnished to a soft gray, as if they'd been weathered by the sea itself. Reclaimed-wood dining tables attended by a variety of flea market chairs. White linens, white candles, white china, various frondery, and driftwood waiting on a sideboard for a slew of unemployed actors in tuxedos to arrive and set and fill and clear for another #marriedmybestfriend jubilee.

Peter sighed. The Beach Club's ambience was not dissimilar to the wedding he'd had at a ranch in Santa Barbara eight years ago, except Julie would've never allowed the driftwood. She'd spent $20K on floral alone.

Now the space was quickly converting from *Martha Stewart Weddings* into *Key* production control. Monitors were being set up to stream feeds from the cameras on the ground. Producers were working on laptops or pacing around, consulting iPads and calling out orders on walkie-talkies. Typically, Peter liked to post up in the command center and own the story from a global perspective—develop characters, find plot beats, identify vulnerabilities, and radio them to the producers on the ground or the PAs logging footage in the corner. But with Carole Steele still breathing down his neck—he was fielding texts and calls from Carole and her emissaries all day every day—Peter was more focused than ever on overseeing every single part of the show. Today he'd be on the ground, right next to the action.

Jessa led him out a glass door and onto a large deck.

"Look," she said, pointing toward the ocean.

Peter shielded his eyes with his hand and spotted a man surfing an impressive wave. A drone swung perilously overhead. "Is that Bennett?" he asked.

"No, it's Taylor Swift," Jessa said. "Of course it's Bennett!"

"Just what can't he do," Peter said dryly. "They'd better not lose that drone. We're already over on the equipment budget, and I'm not buying another."

"Shut up, they won't," Jessa said. Bennett wiped out and the drone swooped higher in the sky. "It's gonna look great. I just came up with it this morning. He's going to surf some sick waves—three-hundred-and-sixty-degree drone footage—and then we'll get him running on the beach with his surfboard under his arm, some straight-up *Baywatch*-type shit. Slo-mo of him shaking out his hair. Oil up his chest. The whole thing. You're gonna love it."

"I already love it."

"Good. You *should* love it."

"Is this the sabotage? I don't get it."

"No, this is just a bonus. C'mon." Jessa led Peter down a staircase to the beach. "I'm glad you're finally letting Edie go on a date, by the way."

"It's been less than a week." He trudged through the sand behind Jessa. Suddenly Peter wished he wasn't the kind of guy who walked on the beach in a button-down, jeans, and Prada loafers. The grips and camera ops were all in T-shirts, shorts, baseball caps, sneakers, and flip-flops. He sighed. Sometimes being a person with very little chill was a real pain in the ass. Jessa, of course, was perfectly dressed in a tank top, cropped wide-leg jeans, and Birkenstocks, her ponytail swinging and lips bright pink.

"A week in that house is like a lifetime," she said.

"It's better this way. Builds tension."

"Except you risk him getting caught up. He's really into Bailey right now."

"He's into everyone. He's a pig in shit. How's she seem today?"

"You're about to find out."

"How ominous," Peter said with a raised brow. "By the way, I read through the notes in the car. The storylines look weak. Carole's pushing for fully developed plot lines—do we even have a real feud between the girls yet?"

"I knew you'd say that," Jessa said, glancing over her shoulder with a smirk. "Which is why I spiced things up."

They arrived at a row of thatched-roof changing huts. Jessa rapped on the door of the middle one.

"Edie?" she called.

"Yeah?" came a shaky voice from inside the hut.

"I brought Peter so we can get to the bottom of this. Can we see your suit?"

The door opened and a hand poked out, clutching a wad of fabric. Jessa took it and held it up for inspection. Shredded strips of Lycra blew in the breeze like miniature car wash ribbons.

"Jesus," he said. "What the fuck happened?"

"From what we've pieced together, sometime between breakfast and when the girls started changing, someone got into her bag and Freddy Kruegered Edie's tankini."

Jessa winked, and Peter closed his eyes for a moment, reminding himself not to yell. Clearly, Jessa had no intention of clearing her hijinks with him this season.

"Hey, guys?" called the voice from inside the hut. "You know, I'm not really the kind of girl who runs around in a swimsuit on national television. Maybe this is a sign? Maybe I should just go on the next date instead? Is there, like, a spelling bee? Or a hot-wing-eating contest?"

"Don't be ridiculous. Of course you're that kind of girl!" Jessa yelled toward the hut. "And you cannot miss out on this time with Bennett. Trust me—things move fast around here. Outta sight, outta mind."

"Agreed!" Peter yelled toward the hut. He decided he might as well give Jessa exactly what she wanted, a no-nonsense showrunner investigating the case. "Do we know who did it?"

"Parker reported that Zo and Aspen missed breakfast. So right now, they're our prime suspects."

"Who's producing them? Have they been notified?" he said, pulling at his collar. It was hot already.

"Working on it." Jessa lassoed the shredded tankini through the air. "I thought you might want to talk to them. The girls. We can't have contestants damaging other people's property."

"Of course," he agreed. "Edie," he yelled at the hut, "I want you to know we take this sort of thing very seriously. Guerrilla warfare is against the ethos of *The Key*."

Jessa gave him a thumbs-up. "Not to mention the code of conduct."

"Not to mention to code of conduct," he yelled toward the hut.

"I appreciate you saying that, Peter, but, you know, the girls really seem to hate me—"

"They don't hate you," Jessa interjected. "They feel threatened and they're lashing out. That's what girls do."

"I mean, is it?" Edie yelled from the hut. "Because I would never do this shit!"

Jessa opened her mouth, but Peter held up a hand. "Of course you wouldn't," he said. "Because you're an adult. So, look, let me apologize on behalf of *The Key*, and you can trust that I'm going to take this seriously. I'll circle back when I have more information, okay?" Peter made some notes in his phone and shot a couple photos of the shredded swimsuit. "In the meantime, what about the date?" he asked Jessa.

"Two steps ahead of you, Captain," Jessa said. "I already got her a new swimsuit from lost and found. I washed it—by hand,

I might add—and dried it under the hand dryer, the whole time thinking, *This is so hip. Reduce, reuse, recycle, zero plastic, zero waste*—Edie's like our very own no-fast-fashion upcycle warrior. It's so zeitgeist I'm literally dead over it. Edie, come out, let us see how it looks!"

"Never!" Edie yelled from the hut. "Literally no one has ever looked worse in a swimsuit than I do right this second."

"Oh, stop," Jessa said. "No one likes how they look in a swimsuit. Let us see!"

"Gigi Hadid. That other Hadid. Any Kardashian. The Jenners, too. Cardi B. Jennifer Aniston. Jennifer Lopez. Lizzo. There are all sorts of people who like how they look in a swimsuit. But I am not one of them!"

"A swimsuit body is just a body with a swimsuit on it," Peter added helpfully.

Jessa rolled her eyes. "Edie, you don't need to look like Gigi Hadid. You just need to look like yourself. That's the only person Bennett wants to see."

"Lies!" Edie yelled from the hut. "Do you promise not to laugh?"

"Of course we promise," Peter said. "You're our number one girl."

The door to the changing hut creaked open, and Edie Pepper stepped out onto the sand. Instantly, Peter's face flashed with alarm. He didn't know much about fashion, but over the years he'd seen *a lot* of girls in bikinis and he knew that this—*this was not it*. The suit was faded purple with fuchsia hibiscus flowers and green and yellow palm fronds strewn every which way. A flimsy purple skirt was attached to the waist and hung toward her crotch in a ruffled V, giving the whole thing a bizarre tropical ice dancer flair. And not only was the suit itself abjectly ridiculous, but it also very clearly did not fit her. It looked old and saggy, like the elastic had lost its sap, and frankly he worried about it even staying on during the volleyball game.

Then he realized it would make great TV if it fell off.

Peter had to hand it to her—Jessa was really hitting her stride this season.

"See," he said with a reassuring smile. "You look great."

Edie looked at him like he was insane. "While I'm happy to concede this bathing costume is basically an outward expression of my very soul—which, as you may have guessed, is a cross between Bette Midler in *The First Wives Club* and Bette Midler in *Hocus Pocus*—I also know I look really fucking dumb. I'm not blind."

"I think it's a totally nineties-inspired VSCO-girl realness moment, and I am *feeling it*," Jessa said with authority. She reached over and hiked a fallen strap back onto Edie's shoulder.

"Jessa, you are the only person on the planet who could wear this swimsuit and make it look good. Related: I hate you." Edie crossed her arms over her chest. "There's no way I'm wearing this on camera."

"Don't be crazy—" Jessa began before Peter cut her off. If Jessa's tactics were working, Edie would already be down on the beach with the other girls. He could tell by the look on Edie's face that tough love wasn't the way to go. But what was? Flattery? Sure, but also something else.

"No, what you're going to do," he said, stepping toward her and looking her intensely in the eyes, "is close your eyes. Do it." She looked at him skeptically, but he was not deterred. "Do it," he said again firmly. And she did. "Now, I want you to think about the way Bennett kissed you. And not just think about it—I want you to focus on it until you can feel his hands in your hair. Do it." Peter watched her. Nothing much for a moment, but then her cheeks flushed, and a small smile played at her lips. "Good," he said. He stepped closer, spoke softly in her ear, like they were sharing a secret. "I saw the way he kissed you. I haven't seen him kiss anyone like that. And you know what I thought? I swear to God I thought, *That's what love looks like.*" Her eyes popped open, and they locked gazes. They stared at each other until out of nowhere Peter became very aware of her body, soft and curvy and full, and just how close he was standing to it. He'd noticed, sure, that Edie was charming in her girl-next-door sort of way. But this stupid swimsuit was loose enough that he couldn't help but notice just how round her breasts were and—with a truly colossal amount of surprise—that he would very much like to push her back into the changing hut, and kiss her until she never thought about Bennett Charles ever again.

Where the hell had *that* come from?

"So, are you going to let some bitchy girls get in the way of taking what's yours?" Peter heard Jessa say. He swallowed hard and took a big step back. "This is *your* love story," Jessa continued. "You've just got to go out there and *write it.*"

Peter was suddenly very hot, and he started fanning himself with his button-down. For all his years at *The Key*, he'd been careful. Never too familiar with the girls. He didn't even allow himself to think about them or their lives in any other context than *the show*. How many girls had he stood next to in bikinis? Never a problem.

"Now go make those hoes eat it on the volleyball court!" Jessa added, triumphant.

Then Edie and Jessa were hugging, and Edie was saying, "But I'm not even good at sports," until finally she was trotting off toward the water where Lou had the rest of the girls gathered on the sand, posing for a camera sliding back and forth along a track. Of course, Peter understood this storyline, this low-key humiliation. They watched her for a moment.

"They're gonna eat her alive," Peter said.

Jessa cocked her head. "Is that a problem?"

"Not necessarily." Peter sighed. First an inexplicable moment of attraction and now a crisis of conscience brought on by the presence of a normal person on set. Regular girls weren't even his thing! Unless, maybe, sometimes they were? "How'd you pull this off?"

"You know I have my ways." Jessa gave him a smirk and adjusted her ponytail. "Anyway, it wasn't hard. Picked up the granny suit at the Salvation Army last night and sliced hers up this morning during breakfast. Zo was just in the bathroom. You know the drill. Barbie flu."

"You're going to hell, you know that?"

"Am I?" she looked at him quizzically.

"I don't know." He shrugged. "It's a little mean, don't you think?"

"Since when do you care about mean?"

Since when, indeed. Down on the beach Edie was piling her hair on top of her head with one hand and fanning her chest with the other. She looked over her shoulder and caught his eye. Smiled. Peter's heartburn surged and he fished a roll of Tums out of his pocket, feeling—and not for the first time—just a little bit terrified of Edie Pepper.

14

Edie Pepper was standing in a semicircle of possible wives, still daydreaming about that key ceremony kiss and digging a wad of swimsuit out of her buttocks, when she had the peculiar sensation of being watched. She froze, her hand still lodged in her butt crack, and slowly looked over her shoulder. Lo and behold, there was Ted, down on one knee in the sand, adjusting the lens of a camera pointed directly at her ass.

"Ted," she hissed. "Knock it off!"

Edie flapped her hand to shoo Ted away until she accidentally spanked Aspen, the NBA cheerleader from San Antonio, hard on her bare and impressively firm derriere.

"Don't break a nail, sis," Aspen said, her eyes slit.

"Sorry! I just didn't want him filming my ass."

Aspen laughed. "What makes you think he's filming *your* ass?"

Edie took a good look at Aspen's butt. It looked like it had been drawn by some pervert at Pixar, with impossibly round cheeks offset by a gleaming white thong that ran between her legs and up her backside to her shoulders, where the spandex then split into two white bands that ran down the front of her body like suspenders. Side boob, under boob, all the boob really, except for where the fabric skimmed over impossibly tiny nipples. The swimsuit continued in taut strips over her flat stomach before joining again in a tiny V at Aspen's crotch.

Where was her pussy? *Where was her pussy?* was all Edie could think. Seriously, where the fuck was it? A swimsuit like that would literally slice Edie's labia in two, leaving her spilled out the sides like the two folds of skin hanging off Jack Nicholson's neck in *Something's Gotta Give*. Edie scanned the rest of the girls and was dumbfounded by the utopian display of demure vaginas.

"Girl, what are you wearing?" Aspen asked, peering at her.

"I was just about to ask you the same thing," Edie said, attempting a bitchy sneer. "I've got dental floss bigger than that contraption."

"Shocking. Since everything about you is"—Aspen measured with her hands—"*bigger.*" She mugged for the camera before holding one hand to the sky and inspecting her manicure in the sunlight. Her long, petal-pink nails were filed into sharp points.

"Actually, my real swimsuit was mysteriously sliced and diced this morning," Edie said. "You wouldn't happen to know anything about that, now would you, Edward Scissorhands?"

Aspen raised one perfectly arched brow. "What's Edward Scissorhands? Like a band?"

Edie clutched her throat in horror.

Max, the long-distance runner from Kansas City, leaned forward to join the conversation.

"No shit?" she asked, her lavender hair glinting in the sunlight.

"Shit," Edie said ruefully.

So far Edie hadn't spent much time with any of the girls. They mostly treated her like a pariah and avoided her, leaving Edie wandering the *Key* mansion while they went on dates, bored out of her mind and wondering what the fuck she was doing there. Her roommate, Parker, the artist/heiress from Palo Alto, spent the time between dates scrawling lipstick portraits of Bennett—and his girlfriends—across torn pages of the *LA Times*. Obviously, Edie supported any woman making a political statement, but when her own face appeared on their bedroom wall drawn over the headline EARTH TO HIT CRITICAL GLOBAL WARMING THRESHOLD BY EARLY 2030S, it made it somewhat difficult to fantasize about getting married and having Bennett's babies.

But from what Edie could tell, Max seemed like one of the normal ones. Today she was the only other girl in a one-piece, though Max's was a sleek Ivy Park x Adidas with the hips cut practically to her armpits. Her body was *sick*. The other girls were thin. Some were *enhanced*. But Max looked strong, like you could bounce quarters off her thighs. "You don't happen to know anyone who might have a vendetta against me?" Edie asked Max, making eyes toward Aspen. "Who might want to make me look stupid?"

"What? Me?" Aspen seemed genuinely surprised. "You think I cut up your swimsuit?"

"Or maybe your BFF Zo?" Edie offered.

"Why would we do that?" Aspen asked with confusion.

"Maybe because you're mad I'm here? Because you're worried I'll steal Bennett away from you?"

Aspen studied Edie's face before leaning in for a conspiratorial whisper. "Babe, chill out. That shit's for the cameras. Nobody touched your swimsuit. But keep an eye on Bennett, okay? You seem like a nice person. I've got a couple weeks on you and, *trust*, the guy's a mess."

But before Edie could process this information, a field producer bounded across the beach with the enthusiasm of a golden retriever set loose upon the sand. "Okay, okay, smiles up, big, big, let's go! I want to see teeth! I want to see smizing! I want to see enthusiasm!" He paused and put a hand to his ear, listening to his headset. "Here comes Adam!"

Everyone turned to watch Adam Fox and his entourage make their way down the beach. A woman dusted his face with powder while another handed him a set of cue cards he briefly glanced at before shoving them back at her. He settled on his mark in front of the girls. As the cameras got into place, Edie hoisted her boobs back into what was left of her swimsuit's cups. There was no time to obsess over what she was wearing or Aspen's hot take, only time to embrace the moment. Edie Pepper was finally on her very first *Key* date!

"Rolling," the director yelled.

"Speeding," the sound guy responded.

And then Adam Fox softened his face and began. "It's week five, and connections are forming…" he recited to the camera.

Watching Adam Fox make the kind of speech Edie had seen him make a zillion times before was wild. On TV, his energy was all neutered father figure, earnestly doling out advice and making sweeping declarations about the power of love. But in real life he was a pompous egomaniac who easily flew off the handle. Knowing this was sort of sad, similar to the feeling Edie got when a Michael Jackson song came on the radio and her first instinct was to dance.

"—and it's getting harder and harder for Bennett to say goodbye to these amazing women, but he has to stay strong if he's going to find out who holds the key to his heart." Adam Fox paused. "Time. Time to make and strengthen connections is so precious, which is why it's more important than ever for the women to emerge victorious from today's date and win that exclusive one-on-one time with Bennett at a private concert featuring...*Meghan Trainor*!"

As if on cue, the girls squealed like a gaggle of tweens about to meet their favorite TikToker, jumping up and down and practically knocking themselves over with their bouncing bosoms. Edie was so shocked by their sudden outburst it took her a minute to catch up. "Yay!" she yelled finally, jumping a few beats too late, clutching her ragged swimsuit to her chest. "Yay?" she said again, looking around at the semicircle of girls who'd already composed themselves. Zo rolled her eyes so hard she almost fell over. From across the circle, Bailey gave Edie a sympathetic smile.

"Cut!" the director yelled.

"That was really great, Adam, really great," the field producer said to Adam Fox's departing back as he slogged back through the sand toward the clubhouse. "Reset for Bennett!" the producer yelled, and the girls were hustled into a new formation facing down a long length of beach. "Cue Bennett!"

And then, just like a dream, down the beach, Bennett Charles emerged. He was hard to take in fully, between the cameraman running backward down the beach in front of him, the PA grasping the cameraman's T-shirt, guiding him across the sand, and the drone swinging around overhead. But from what Edie could tell, Bennett was jogging across the sand with a surfboard tucked under one arm. His wetsuit was unzipped to the waist, with the top dangling sexily behind him, and his pecs and abs were glimmering in the sun, like a real-life Dylan McKay.

"Hanging out on beaches all over the world is one of my favorite things to do," Bennett began after he'd reviewed his cue cards, been sprayed down with oil, and settled in front of the girls. "So today, I thought we'd have some fun in the sun with a friendly game of beach volleyball. And today's MVP, well, she's not only going to get a Key to My Heart, but also a very special surprise from me." And then, with a twinkle in his eye, Bennett Charles shook out his sun-kissed curls. Droplets of saltwater flew through the air, and when one hit Edie's bare chest, she knew instantly—*lovestruck*—that nothing would stop her from winning this game.

15

On the south side of the beach volleyball court, Team Edie prepared for battle. Max, applying strips of blue zinc from forehead to chin in a *Braveheart*-inspired declaration of war. Bailey, gathering her lush locks into a high ponytail and double knotting her string bikini. Lily, contorted on the sand in lizard pose, stretching her hip flexors. And a newly energized Edie, shadowboxing Ted's camera while bellowing, "The power of love courses through my veins!"

Max gathered the team. "Okay, we want to win this thing and score that extra time with Bennett, amirite?"

"Right!"

"And you know what's gonna get us there?"

Unfortunately, the girls did not know what would get them there.

"Focus and communication!" Max yelled.

"Focus and communication!" the girls yelled back.

"Let's talk strengths," Max continued. "In addition to being a decorated runner, I'm also proficient in most sports, including speed skating, lacrosse, discus, and bowling. A little beach volleyball is no problem for me. What about you guys?"

"I was on the volleyball team in high school," Lily offered, tying her hair in braids.

"Excellent. Bailey?"

"I grew up in Santa Barbara," Bailey said with a smile. Her teeth were perfect. "All we did was play volleyball. And ride horses. My pony was named Teapot and she had these gorgeous freckles on her flank—"

"Awesome. Edie?"

Edie, who'd been scanning the beach for Charlie, snapped to attention. "Um, no idea?"

"Like, you've never played volleyball?" Lily asked. "Or you've never played *beach* volleyball?"

Edie shrugged. "I was an indoor kid?"

"You poor thing," Bailey said, squeezing Edie's arm.

Max windmilled her arms through the air. "Okay, all right, now that we know where we're weak, we can work around it. Most errors on the court come from being in the wrong place at the wrong time. Edie, we'll keep you next to me. I'll take seventy percent of strikes, you thirty. And remember, it's timing over technique."

Edie felt like she had questions, but the field producer bounded over and started shooing them toward the net. "Let's go, let's go, we're losing light!"

"Hands in!" Max cried, and they each put a hand in the middle. "On three: Jump! Set! Spike! Win!"

"Jump! Set! Spike! Win!" they cried, and Edie, who'd never been on a sports team a single day in her life, was both jostled by the amount of screaming required and oddly energized by the pursuit of a shared goal. Suddenly she found herself making hooting noises, punching the air with one arm and holding up her swimsuit with the other.

As the girls arranged themselves across the sand and the crew got into position, Bennett Charles, freshly changed into a pair of tight blue swim trunks with a silver whistle dangling from his neck, strutted onto the beach with his producers and made his way to the lifeguard's chair looming over mid-court. As Edie took her place at the net, she tried to catch his eye—if there was anyone who'd appreciate this swimsuit, it was Charlie.

He'd always loved a good costume.

He climbed the wooden ladder, mounted his perch, and with his hands on his hips, appraised the scene below. His gaze finally landed on Edie, and for a second, his face flashed with surprise, like he'd forgotten she was there, before transforming into amusement as he took in her look. He jutted his chin and hollered, "Lookin' good, Pepper!"

"Aww, he's sweet," Zo said, arriving at the other side of the net. "'Cause you look like Tonya Harding washed up on a beach in Tampa." She adjusted the hips of her bikini—her thigh gap was more like a thigh highway. "Not that I've been to Tampa. I wouldn't be caught dead in Florida."

"Ma'am," Edie said, turning to Zo. "I hope you'll forgive us when we don't invite you to the wedding."

"Please. The only way you're getting married is if you show up on some TLC show and marry a dude who's never seen your face." Zo blew a kiss to Charlie. He made a show of catching it midair and pressing it to his heart. She turned back to Edie with a smirk. "Actually, I love that journey for you."

And with that, Zo caught a volleyball from a PA and stalked toward the serving line.

What a bitch! Edie turned around quickly—two could play this walk-off-haughtily game—and instantly crashed into Ted and his camera. Down she went, landing soundly on her ass in the sand.

"Medical!" Peter yelled, jogging across the sand to Edie. "Are you okay?" he asked, hinged at the hips to assess the situation.

"Do you need a doctor?" She shook her head, and he slung his arms under her armpits and hoisted her back to her feet. "Good as new," he pronounced. As Peter trotted off the court, sand exploding around his loafers with each footfall, Bennett Charles brought his whistle to his lips and gave it one sharp blow.

"Let the game begin!" he cried.

Zo threw the volleyball high in the air and served it with impressive strength, speed, and accuracy at Edie's crotch. When it hit her, she emitted a guttural "Oof" and was felled to the sand once more.

"That's one!" Zo cheered.

Max pulled a fetaled Edie to her feet. "Fall down seven times, get up eight," she said, brushing Edie off.

Zo launched another ball directly at Edie, but this time Bailey yelled, "Mine!" and Edie jumped out of the way. Bailey set the ball to Max, who rose high into the air and, with an impressive roar, slammed it back over the net.

"Yes! Yes! Yes!" Max yelled, rewarding each member of the team with a chest bump.

From the lifeguard stand, Bennett continued to enthusiastically blow his whistle.

The game continued unevenly—one minute the girls were crashing into each other and totally missing the ball, and the next they were crushing epic volleys that had Bennett Charles on the edge of his seat. Lily's ankle bracelet played a veritable symphony as she ran across the court while Bennett yelled from the lifeguard chair, "Go, Lily! Go, Lily! Go!" until she tripped and crashed hard, catching a faceful of sand, and the chimes were silenced once again. After a long volley, Zo set McKayla for a spike that she crushed over the net, catching Bailey on the ass with a resounding *thwack*. Immediately, Bennett flew down from his perch, his face full of concern as he stared at the splotch on her left butt cheek. Edie was stunned when he pulled

Bailey in for a hug and stroked her hair, like she was some precious treasure, right in front of everyone. Zo continued to serve the ball directly at Edie while Max did her best to volunteer as tribute, running and diving all over the court until her blue zinc was smeared all over her face, arms, and chest. But clearly Bennett didn't mind, because during the break they talked strategy, miming various plays together, and Edie noticed him licking his lips as he gave Max a fist bump. And after almost every single volley, Aspen darted to wherever the ball landed and slowly bent over to retrieve it, her lovely lady lumps waggling for Bennett and the cameras. Once he even applauded. From the sidelines, Adam Fox, who'd been called out from the clubhouse to interview the girls in faux ESPN mini segments, held a small electric fan to his face and muttered, "This show used to have some class. Now we might as well be on Bravo."

When Parker lost a diamond earring, a time-out was called and a search mounted with PAs and low-level producers digging around on their hands and knees in the sand until, miraculously, it was found. But then Jessa thought Bennett should be the one to find it, so he stopped doing pushups and knelt on the beach, his abs glistening, and on cue, pulled the earring from the sand, offering it to the sky like some swole Indiana Jones. Parker flew into his arms and covered his face with kisses. Edie put a hand over her mouth to stifle her outrage.

"No one ever said it was gonna be easy," Jessa said, materializing at Edie's side.

"I'm getting my ass kicked all over this beach in Dorothy Zbornak's swimsuit," Edie complained. "And he hasn't even talked to me once."

"You've got to push yourself to stand out."

"I'm not going to bend over and shake my ass at him, Jessa."

"Of course not. But you gotta do whatever *Edie Pepper* would do to get her man."

Jessa winked and handed Edie the volleyball.

As Jessa walked away, Edie wondered, what *would* Edie Pepper do to get her man? It's not like any previous strategies had worked. Isn't that how she'd ended up on *The Key* in the first place? And she had no clue what she'd done to inspire Charlie's key ceremony kiss—it just sort of *happened.* Jessa was constantly chirping *Just be yourself* at her, but had there ever been a time when just being herself had actually worked?

It was Edie's turn to serve and everyone was waiting, so finally she gritted her teeth, said a little prayer to Oprah, and threw the volleyball straight up in the air. It levitated in the sky for a moment before dropping lower, lower, until Edie raised her fist—*THWACK!*—and sent it careening straight into a camera.

"Whoa!" Peter shouted as a couple of grips in backward caps and cargo shorts lunged to save the gear.

"Sorry!" Edie yelled, mortified. "Sorry!"

The shrill trumpet of Bennett's whistle rang through the air and Edie shielded her eyes from the sun to look up at him.

"Nice one, Pepper!" he yelled from his tower.

"You suck at this," Zo taunted when they faced off again at the net.

"You suck at life," Edie retorted, before finding it within herself to dive for a ball, which she missed. The saggy crotch of her swimsuit dragged through the sand, pulling a castle's worth into her nether regions.

"At least I don't have crabs," Zo said, pointing at the sand pouring from Edie's crotch as she struggled to her feet. "You've got a natural habitat down there."

Finally, they were tied at game point. Max called a time-out and gathered the team in a huddle.

"You guys are doing awesome, okay?" she said, assessing her bedraggled team. Edie, grumpy in her sagging granny suit. Lily, her hair sticking out from her braids in tangled clumps.

Bailey, somehow still put together, if a touch flushed. "Just fucking awesome." A thought occurred to her, and Max stood up quickly, knocking Ted and his camera back a few steps. "Has it been a dirty game? Yes. But here's what I always say: The plan never survives first contact with the enemy. All we need now is one great play and this thing is O-V-E-R, over. And the one-on-one time is *ours*."

While Max outlined the strategy for the final play, Edie watched Peter interview Charlie a few feet away.

"Do you like when the women fight over you?" Peter asked.

"Do I like it when the women fight over me?" Bennett parroted back to the camera. "Hmm…let me think about it…*Yes.*" He smiled easily. And then glanced over at Edie, his hands resting on his hip bones. Peter followed his gaze, his hands shoved in the back pockets of his jeans. She stared at the two of them staring at her, the hard-bodied Bennett Charles and the hard-boiled Peter Kennedy, not paying attention to a word Max was saying.

"Edie," Max said, snapping her fingers in front of Edie's face. "Did you catch that?"

"Oh, yeah, of course," Edie said. She gave the team a reassuring smile. "Got it."

"For Bennett!" Max yelled.

But while her teammates rushed the court, Edie stood on the sidelines watching Charlie stride away from Peter and, unbelievably, straight into Zo's crotch. Paralyzed, Edie stared as Zo jetéd into his arms, wrapping her legs around his waist and pressing her vagina into his six-pack. He cupped her tiny bikinied butt, and she threw back her gorgeous bobblehead, laughing. Then, as the camera circled, Zo brushed back the sweaty curls from his forehead, placed her hand on the back of his neck, and pulled him to her, kissing him right in front of everyone.

A strange noise gargled in Edie's throat.

"Having fun?" Peter asked, appearing at Edie's side.

"Oh, yeah, this is a great fucking time, Peter," Edie spat. Her entire body vibrated with the uncomfortable realization that her super-special-made-for-TV-kiss, the beacon of hope that had kept her going through every stage of this humiliating day, was maybe not so special after all. "Super glad I left my entire life behind to watch Bennett remove Zo's spleen with his tongue." Edie angrily dusted off her sandy butt. "But you know what I really love? Having a camera up my ass while I keep falling on it. I'm thirty-five, Peter. I get sore from *sleeping*. I'm not going to be able to walk tomorrow. But I guess that's not a problem since Bennett Charles/Charlie Bennett—whoever the fuck he is—forgot I even exist."

"Fair enough," Peter said, arms crossed and rocking casually on his heels.

She glared at him.

"Have you thought about, I dunno, spraining your ankle? That might get his attention."

"Are you being serious?"

"Maybe, maybe not. Just spitballing here." Peter paused like he was thinking it over. Across the beach, Bennett put Zo down and gave her a little pat on the butt as she trotted back across the court. Peter turned to face Edie. "Here's the thing. You're here for the right reasons. But the right reasons on *The Key* are just... *a framing device*. Most people don't take it so seriously. That's your problem. That's why you're not having fun."

Edie slit her eyes at Peter. "My problem?" she said through clenched teeth. "Maybe the *show's* the problem, Peter. Maybe the *show's* why I'm not having fun."

"Exactly!" he said, jabbing his finger in the air like a professor whose pupil finally arrived at the correct answer. "The show's the show. It's got a format, and you either accept it or you don't. Edie, who finds love this way? It's absurd. You've put yourself in an absurd situation. What you need to do now is connect to the ridiculousness of it all. Have a little fun."

Edie dug a wad of swimsuit out of her butt. "Me agreeing to wear this swimsuit on national television wasn't absurd enough for you?"

"No, it was." Peter laughed.

She glared at him again.

"C'mon," he said, shaking her arm to snap her out of it. "Honestly, I didn't think this whole thing was gonna work. But you've surprised me. And I can admit when I'm wrong. Even if I hate to be wrong." When she didn't soften, he slung his arm over her shoulders and gestured to the *Key* world before them. "Edie, look around you. You're like an actual person in a sea of interchangeable sponconners, and really, I like that about you. Who cares if you fall on your ass and your swimsuit is ugly? America's gonna love you for it. Because that's exactly what America would do if she were here. If there's one thing America's good at, it's falling short of her ideals."

Edie couldn't help herself; she started laughing. "Are you seriously invoking 'America' right now?"

Peter laughed. "Yes, but as a metaphor. Look, Edie, you're like the Paul Rudd of *The Key*. An adorable everywoman. But an exceptional one. Someone we can root for."

Edie turned to him. Peter always seemed totally in control, moving through the *Key* world with a restrained swagger that was clearly dangerous. Guys who were brash and authoritative, but also sweet and funny, were total sociopaths, and Edie knew she shouldn't trust him. Seriously, if she'd seen Peter on a dating app, with his East Coast prep good looks, Ivy League pedigree, and big job, she would've thought he was a bot and immediately swiped left. Still, she found herself relaxing whenever he was around. There was this vibe between them, like they were the only adults in the room, and for that reason, Edie *did* trust Peter, and felt like he was the one who would take care of her through this insane experience.

"I have to admit—you're good," she said. "Maybe even better than Jessa."

"That's why they pay me the big bucks." He grinned. "But, seriously, Edie, I think you're great. You're smart and funny and irreverent, and I like you a lot. But it's not me you have to show. It's him." Peter pointed at Bennett looming over the volleyball court, the sun illuminating him from behind like Zeus himself, alight once again on the lifeguard chair. "And right now, you're fading into the background. Get out there and make your mark. Don't take no for an answer." They locked eyes. "If you want to win this, then you have to go out there and show Bennett why you're the girl he's going to marry."

And just like that, Edie was running back onto the court. She still had all these uncomfortable feelings—confusion, annoyance, embarrassment, doubt—but none of them felt like how she *wanted* to feel, which was happy, fun, chosen, *loved*, so she decided to embrace the optimism that had brought her to *The Key* in the first place. Of course, Charlie was distracted—*The Key* was a fucking circus! A smorgasbord of naked women!—but Peter was right, if she lost her shit every time Charlie talked to another girl, she'd never get what she wanted, which was Edie and Charlie back in love, their life together about to begin.

"Just do it like we said, and they won't expect a thing," Max whispered when Edie arrived at the net. "I'll set you. You hit the ball over the net. That's all you have to do. Make a fist and hit the ball over the net. Game over."

"Wait, *what*?" Edie said, but already Max had a hand between Edie's shoulder blades and was shoving her to the net where, once again, she came face-to-face with Zo.

"Just so you know, it's going to be me and Bailey at the end," Zo said, her voice dripping with faux concern. "I just don't want you to be blindsided. Peter gave us contracts a week ago that guaranteed it." Zo adjusted the clip at the center of her chest holding her bikini top together and laughed deliciously when Edie's jaw dropped. "Don't tell me you actually thought you were going to be more than a one-episode sideshow? Please."

And then the ball was in the air. Edie stood paralyzed in the sand. Not since Brian had Edie whiplashed so quickly from love and hope to doubt and despair. Contracts? For the end? Edie scanned the beach and found Peter standing with Jessa at mid-court. He was holding his chin in his hand and staring at her, brow furrowed. She was so stupid, always so fucking stupid. Suddenly she could see herself as she really was—thirty-five years old and throwing herself around the beach in some Value Village swimsuit, ever the fool, chasing a volleyball for some man who did not want her.

"Edie!" Max screamed.

Edie snapped to attention just in time to see the ball flying directly toward her. All the anger and confusion and desire and shame and hope and embarrassment of the last week surged through her, and she balled her right hand into a fist and jumped. "Fuck you!" she screamed at Zo as she flew through the air and smashed the ball over the net and directly into Zo's tits, which, upon impact, immediately popped free from their tiny restraint. Instantly Bennett was on his feet, blowing his whistle.

The ball boomeranged from Zo's chest back into the air with impressive speed. Edie, who never did anything halfway, crashed into the net, which held for a second before—*SNAP*—and then Edie was falling with the webbing wrapping around her as she plunged toward the sand. The ball slammed into the net pole and began to ricochet toward an oblivious Bennett Charles, who, like a horny tween, was straining to get a better look at Zo's tits.

"Bennett! Watch out!" Peter yelled.

SMACK!

When the ball struck him in the face, Bennett was wholly unprepared. Instantly he was falling—*BANG CRASH BOOM PLOP*—six feet down to the sand.

"*Bennett!*" the beach shrieked.

"She's killed him! That stupid bitch killed Bennett Charles!" McKayla wailed as Edie took her final repose on top of Zo, her face nestling perfectly between the ballerina's breasts.

And then everything went blissfully black.

TAKE 5 PRODUCTIONS
THE KEY
BENNETT CHARLES AMBULANCE TEASER [DRAFT FOR EP APPROVAL]
TAPE #207

00:00:00	AN AMBULANCE SCREECHES THROUGH THE CITY
	IN VOICEOVER:
	BAILEY: . . . there was just so much blood . . .
	PARKER: . . . one more inch and he'd be gone . . .
	MCKAYLA: . . . scared? More like terrified. His face was perfect . . .
	MAX: . . . these are the moments where you realize what's important in life . . .
	ZO: . . . this is all *her* fault . . .
	LILY: . . . my mind is focused on healing energy . . .
	ASPEN: . . . I can't picture my life without Bennett! Don't ask me to! . . .
	EDIE: . . . is he okay? Is he okay? Is he okay??? . . .
	HOSPITAL SOUNDS, BEEPING MACHINES, ETC.
	FADE TO BLACK
	ADAM FOX IN FRONT OF THE KEY MANSION
00:30:00	ADAM FOX: All that and more, tonight on *The Key*.

To: Carole Steele
From: Peter Kennedy
Subject: Quick Update

Hi Carole,

Hope you're well.

Just wanted to loop you in on a small mishap we had in the field today. Bennett fell during a group date and sustained some minor injuries, but otherwise I can assure you he is fine and that, as they say, the show will go on. The doctor is patching him up as we speak.

We're in contact with legal and will send a full report to Stacey once the risk assessment is complete.

Let me know if you'd like to hop on a call, but I can assure you that everything's under control here.

Best,
Peter
Sent from my iPhone

16

"What-the-fuck-what-the-fuck-what-the-fuck!" Peter yelled. "How could you let this happen?"

"Me?" Jessa yelled back. "How could *I* let this happen?"

"I knew this girl would ruin everything!" Peter kicked the vending machine and then hopped around the hospital corridor on one foot, his Prada loafer not designed to withstand such outbursts. "Fuck! This is why you can't put regular people on the show, Jessa. You can't have earnest love seekers all up in their feelings. How many times have I told you—"

"Peter, calm down."

"Calm down? *Calm down?* Our lead is lying in a hospital bed with his face smashed in. His *face,* Jessa. What do you think this show is about? It's about *his face.*"

"And also his abs—"

Peter stopped hopping. "Do you know how many people work on this show?" he demanded. Before she could answer, he continued, "Two hundred and fifty-three people. But *of course* you don't know that. You're not the showrunner. You can make jokes and laugh it up while I worry about the two hundred and fifty-three people who are about to lose their jobs."

"Seriously, Peter, stop. No one's losing their jobs." Jessa swiped her debit card through the vending machine PIN pad. "Let's just get you a Coke and—"

"Sugar makes me anxious!" Peter said, throwing his arms in the air in exasperation. "You *know* that. Seriously, do you ever listen to me?"

"When you say something interesting," Jessa muttered, still facing the vending machine. She took a deep breath and turned to him with a soothing smile. "Have you eaten anything today? Exactly. So we'll just get you a Coke—you love a Coke. Why don't you just sit down for a second? And then we'll come up with a plan."

Peter looked around the hospital corridor vaguely before collapsing in a plastic chair outside Bennett's hospital room. He held his head in his hands and stared at the faux wood floor. "We're losing control of this thing, Jessa," Peter said quietly. "Every time I think we've righted the ship, dealt with Wyatt Cash, found a new lead, placated the network, it all falls apart again."

Jessa handed him the drink and sat down in a chair on the other side of the door. She sighed. "Accidents happen. And he's gonna be fine. It could've happened with or without Edie. It's not her fault."

"Isn't it?" Peter gulped down some of the Coke. The effervescence instantly insulted his reflux.

"Besides," Jessa continued, "Bennett's rugged. That's, like, his whole thing. Think of it like an action movie. What if we got him an eye patch or something? That would be hot."

"This isn't *Die Hard*, Jessa. Pretty sure our target audience isn't trying to fuck a guy in an eye patch." Peter chugged the rest of the Coke and threw the bottle toward the recycling. It hit the rim and bounced one, two, three times, before hitting the floor and rolling down the hallway. "You should leave this godforsaken town. Trust me, you'll be happier."

"I'm not unhappy," Jessa said. "And, newsflash, the women of America can still get wet over a guy with some facial lacerations. Our target audience basically had their sexual awakening to *Game of Thrones*. And it's the entire reason I watch *Jack Ryan*. I have no idea what's happening on that show. But when John Krasinski is all tormented and then an assassin pops out of the bushes and Jack's polo shirt gets tight because he's not just a guy with a PhD anymore, he's a counterterrorist machine? Bitch, I'm here for it."

"Who would've thought Jim Halpert could carry an action show."

"It's hot, trust me."

"Yeah, yeah," Peter said, getting up to retrieve the Coke bottle. "Where is she now?"

"Edie? Max and Bailey took her to the cafeteria for some tea." Before Peter could react, Jessa added, "Don't worry, Amy and Dan are with them. No one will escape."

Peter tossed the bottle into the recycling. "Is she going to pull it together?"

"Of course she is."

"I think that's optimistic."

"Nah, we'll get her there." Jessa paused. "You should talk to her, though. You guys have a thing."

"We don't have a thing."

"She trusts you."

"Well." He paused. "She shouldn't."

"Besides, he's going to take her to the end, all on his own. You just wait."

Peter guffawed. "You're insane."

"You don't understand Bennett," Jessa said, casually scrolling Twitter. "Really, he's just a chunky kid who's never felt loved.

She adores him in just the way he needs. Unconditionally." Jessa shrugged. "It's not that deep."

Peter stopped pacing and looked at her. Unbelievable. For all her wins this season, Jessa still completely misunderstood the fundamentals. "If people were smart enough to choose the people who adored them unconditionally, Jessa," he said, "we wouldn't have a show at all."

A stern-looking nurse in pink scrubs and a name badge that read "Yolanda, Nurse Supervisor," approached. "I've seen a lot, but an entire waiting room filled with cameramen and girls in bikinis? It's like an episode of *Love Island* out there." She crossed her arms over her chest and peered at them through bifocals perched at the end of her nose. "What show is this anyway?"

Jessa jumped up. "You watch *Love Island*? I love that! *Love Island* is sort of a trashier version of our show. This is *The Key*."

"Never heard of it."

"Are you serious?" Peter exclaimed, eyes widening.

Nurse Yolanda shrugged and walked back to the nurses' station, calling over her shoulder, "Best get those cameras out of my waiting room."

"We're on it!" Jessa said with a big thumbs-up.

Peter sighed dramatically, blowing a great gust of air out of puffed cheeks. "You've got to be kidding me. We're getting replaced by *Love Island* in the fifty-five-plus demo?" He collapsed in the chair again and massaged the muscles at the base of his neck. "Truly unbelievable."

"We don't need the entire crew," Jessa said, poking at her phone and thinking out loud. "I'll have Chuck bring the vans around. But the girls should stay—what if we get a chance to shoot with them? Maybe we should get them some robes or something. Oh my god, let's get them hospital gowns, that would be hilarious." She waggled her brows at Peter.

"If we lose the fifty-five-plus demo, our ratings will be in the toilet."

"They'll probably let us bring one camera in, so let's keep Greg..."

"Jessa." Peter looked at her seriously. "I know you think I'm just some high-strung asshole who worries too much. But you don't get it. This season, this could end my career. You'll be fine, but me—Carole Steele is going to ruin me. And then what? I'm going to be some high-strung asshole who failed at some shit he didn't want to do anyway?"

Jessa looked up from her phone. "Then why does it matter?"

She really wasn't hearing him. "You're really not hearing me. Everything is fucked. We've got an injured suitor. We've got hysterical contestants. We've got insurance liabilities and a completely fucked production schedule, which continues to fuck our already fucked budget. Not to mention this impossible love story. It's an *impossible* love story. How the fuck are we supposed to get Bennett Charles to propose to this girl on a mountaintop in five weeks when in her very first week in the field, she derails the entire show and breaks his fucking face?"

"God, Peter!" Jessa yelled. "We made amazing TV today! That game was *insane*. Not only do we have endless slo-mo of gorgeous girls in bikinis tearing each other apart, we've got Zo's bare tits, ambulances and paramedics, sobbing contestants, a bleeding Bennett Charles, and you won't shut the fuck up about Carole Steele and insurance liabilities? Who are you? The Peter Kennedy I know would've already been plotting our next move by now." Jessa took a breath and softened her tone. She put a hand on his shoulder. "Honestly, I'm worried about you, P. You haven't been acting like yourself. I can't figure it out. Is it Wyatt? Because that whole thing is behind us, and we have our show. This is it. Last week the nerdiest girl in school got kissed by the most popular guy in school and all the mean girls went crazy.

And then today, the most popular guy in school fell off a lifeguard tower, and this little brush with death made everyone realize that it's more than just a crush—*they are in love with him*—so what happens next, huh? This is *literally* the most dramatic season ever, and I want to know where the hell Peter Kennedy is, because he's supposed to be my partner in all of this."

Peter sighed. He picked at a smear of Bennett Charles's blood on his jeans. Peter and Jessa *were* a team. And everything she was saying was right. He was a story guy—he'd *always* been a story guy—so why was he acting like such an administrator? Peter thought about how he couldn't come with Siobhan riding him, and then for some reason, his mind pulled back into his spotless apartment with the ocean lurking, dark and roiling like an abyss. Wasn't there a time when he would have loved this? But he couldn't shake the feeling that what they were doing was wrong—and not wrong in any clear way that he could understand or parse. Like, wrong how? Morally wrong? But since when? Had Peter grown a conscience? But why?

Peter ran a hand through his hair and tugged at the ends to bring himself back to the moment. He tried to explain. "Listen, I know you're right. I do. It's just—"

The door to Bennett's hospital room opened and a doctor so attractive he looked like an actor on a Netflix show stepped into the hall. Peter and Jessa jumped to their feet.

"How is he?" Peter demanded.

"Dr. Kang," the doctor said, shaking their hands. "The patient"—he referred to his iPad—"Charles Bennett, confirmed I could speak with you. It's a broken nose. Apparently, he broke it in his teens—reinjury can be common. At this point everything looks superficial; we've reset it. He shouldn't need surgery."

"That's great news!" Jessa said, enthusiastically shaking Peter's bicep. "See, P, everything's going to be okay."

"But what about his face?" Peter asked. "He's the star of our show. When can he start filming again?"

"It's swollen, but that will go down with time. Ice packs, ibuprofen, rest."

Peter's phone began pinging loudly and repeatedly. He dug it out from his pocket as the doctor continued. "Possibly his orbital sphere will bruise as the blood makes its way from the site of injury—"

"Fuck!" Peter yelled. "The tabloids have it!" He shoved the phone at Jessa. "How do the tabloids have it?" Peter scanned the Google alert—

KEY STAR BENNETT CHARLES SEVERELY INJURED IN "FREAK ACCIDENT"

KEY SUITOR HOSPITALIZED IN LOS ANGELES

THE KEY'S BENNETT CHARLES IN "EMERGENCY SURGERY"

KEY STAR SUFFERS "EXTREME" FACIAL INJURY

BENNETT CHARLES GRAVELY INJURED ON SET— IS THIS THE END OF _THE KEY_?

"Oh my god," Peter groaned, scanning the articles. "'This isn't the first time showrunner Peter Kennedy has been in hot water,'" he read aloud. "Blah, blah, blah, Wyatt Cash—see, Jessa! I told you—"

And then his phone started ringing. *Carole Steele, New York, New York.* Peter's eyes went wild and instantly he threw the phone down the hallway. It skidded across the floor and came to rest under the nurses' station, where Yolanda looked up from a chart and glared before kicking it back out again. It settled in the middle of the corridor, blinking and flashing and vibrating.

"Sir, do you need a Xanax?" Dr. Kang asked. "Because I'm going to need you to calm down. This is a center of healing."

"He definitely needs a Xanax," Jessa said.

"I was being facetious," Dr. Kang said.

"I was perfectly fine before she"—Peter pointed at Jessa—"gave me that Coke."

Dr. Kang assessed Peter. "At this point I should make it clear we don't allow illegal drugs on hospital grounds. I will call security."

"Coca-Cola," Jessa clarified, shoving Peter through the door of Bennett's room. "Thank you so much, Doctor. I'll make sure he behaves himself, and we'll be out of your hair in no time. But while I have you here, is there someone I can talk to about taking maybe just one camera into our patient's room? Maybe you can help with that? Just for a minute? I'm sure you can imagine how documenting our star's injury would be an important part of documenting his journey. We'll be quick."

"You'd have to go down to hospital administration, but they're unlikely to approve. We just had a Housewife in last week for a vaginoplasty, and they put the kibosh on that before the very first Kegel. Cedars is better for that sort of thing—the doctors think they're celebrities. It's embarrassing, really." Dr. Kang looked Jessa up and down and then smiled a smile that had clearly worked for him many times before. "But how about you take in one camera, we'll keep it between us, and when you're done, we go for a drink?"

Jessa looked Dr. Kang up and down and smiled a smile that had clearly worked for her many times before. "After today, I'm going to need at least three." She leaned in. "And I'm definitely into recreational Viagra, so don't forget the samples."

WYATT CASH TALKS BENNETT CHARLES'S "MAJOR" ON-SET INJURY

Added by E!NewsNow

2.3 million views / cc

[RYAN SEACREST]
Hey guys, I'm Ryan Seacrest, and this is *E! News Now*. According to reports, *Key* star Bennett Charles was rushed into emergency surgery Thursday afternoon. Sources *say* the extreme sports adventurer was filming in Malibu when, in a "freak accident," he took a fall so severe it might just end the season.

[INTRO CREDITS]

[RYAN SEACREST]
We've got *The Key*'s very own Wyatt Cash in the studio. Hey, Wyatt.

[WYATT CASH]
Well butter my butt and call me a biscuit, Ryan, I am *shook*.

[RYAN SEACREST]
I think we all are, Wyatt. What have you heard about Bennett's condition?

[WYATT CASH]
Sorry to say it ain't good, Ryan, it ain't good. Word on the street is Bennett Charles fell right on his face. And now he's looking less like one of those Hemsworth brochachos and more like a slice of Mamaw's blueberry pie.

[RYAN SEACREST]
Ouch! The network says: "Reports of an accident on *The Key* are wildly overblown. While this is by far *The Key*'s most dramatic season ever—premiering November 3rd on RX—this

specific incident was a minor mishap and filming will resume as scheduled this week."

[WYATT CASH]
As a son of Jesus, I believe in miracles. But even Kris Jenner takes time off when she gets her face done. I bet you a nickel the next time we see Bennett Charles is when Billy Eichner plays him on Ryan Murphy's *American Horror Story: The Key*.

[RYAN SEACREST]
I hope you're wrong, Wyatt. Bennett Charles, we wish you well! Wyatt, can we talk about your own painful exit from the show? How are you doing?

[WYATT CASH]
That's mighty kind of you, Ryan. Being forced out of the closet on the front page of the tabloids—I wouldn't wish that on anyone. But I am blessed. Never before have I been able to live my truth and now that I am, I promise never to lie to America again. Which is why I'm starring in Hulu's brand-new reality dating show for gay men: *COCKBLOCKERS*! In a house of twenty-five men, who will get rocked? And who will get COCKBLOCKED?

[RYAN SEACREST]
That's great, Wyatt. Why are Mandy Moore and other celebrity moms eating their placentas? Find out right after this.

17

Seriously?" Bennett shouted. "You're laughing? You think this is funny?"

Well, sorry, but it *was* funny. After Jessa pushed Peter through the door of Bennett's hospital room and he saw Bennett lying there, looking pathetic in a faded hospital gown with a silver splint taped across his nose and a rash consuming his neck, his hair all flat and sad, suddenly Bennett didn't look like Extreme Sports Prince Charming anymore. He looked like an aging frat boy who'd landed himself in the hospital after cracking his face open during some sort of Sunday Funday keg-stand nostalgia bullshit in Mark's or Nick's or Steve's garage, and all at once it struck Peter as funny—*so fucking funny!*—that he had elevated this douchebag to national prominence and was giving himself a fucking ulcer over getting him engaged, this idiot who Peter would never give the time of day to in real life, except—*except!*—this *was* real life, which Bennett had reminded him, crossing his forearms (with the stupid lotus tattoo and the bracelets in string and bead) petulantly across his chest, "This is my fucking life, Peter, like my actual fucking life," and then they'd stared at each other in silence for a moment until Peter burst out laughing. Guffawing, really. The whole thing just suddenly struck him as absurd. Like when Bennett Charles had fallen from that lifeguard chair, *Peter* had been the one to cradle Bennett's head in his lap and press Lily's gauzy sarong to his face to stanch the bleeding. While Jessa had paced through the sand and yelled at the 911 operator, *Peter* had been the one to notice the tears escaping from Bennett's eyes and to not only wipe them away with his thumb, but to yell at everyone to back up so they wouldn't see. While Edie and the rest of the girls sobbed, while the cameramen circled, while they all waited the slow sixteen minutes for the paramedics to arrive, *Peter* had been the one to lightly stroke Bennett's forehead. *Peter* had been the one to risk his own life sitting on a tiny bench seat while the ambulance screeched around corners. Peter's life was now completely intertwined with this fucking guy's, and he was quickly realizing that he was more invested in Bennett's future happiness than his own. And the fact that he—*Peter! Peter Kennedy!*—spent the days, hours, minutes, seconds of his life writing love stories when he couldn't even come while fucking a model—*a model!*—well, sorry, it *was* funny.

"You're such a dick," Bennett accused. "Where's my phone? Give me my phone."

Peter held up a hand—just a minute, he was pulling it together. But then he looked back at Bennett, a felled giant, and lost it all over again. A beach volleyball game had landed Mr. Extreme Sports in the hospital. A beach volleyball game he hadn't even played in! And it was already front-page news on all the tabloid sites in America. And Carole Steele was going to—what was it she'd said?—oh, yes, *stab Peter to death with her Louboutin.*

"I'm done with this shit. I'm not even kidding. I want off this fucking show."

"Me too," Peter said, straightening. He strode to Bennett's bedside and took his meaty palm in his own; they were brothers now. "Yes. Let's quit. Why not? Let's quit before they ruin us. We'll leave." He threw the blanket off Bennett's legs.

"Have you lost your mind?" Bennett snatched the blanket back. "What the fuck is wrong with you?"

"What? This is the best idea I've had in weeks!" Peter paced around, all the possibilities rushing through his body. "We'll just walk away. You go back to Colorado or Chicago or wherever the hell you came from, and I'll go to—I don't know, who cares? And you can tell me how to do it, how to become a whole other person." He stopped pacing and peered at Bennett. "For real, how does one become"—he made exaggerated air quotes—"'Bennett Charles'?"

"You think this is some sort of joke?" Bennett's entire body was turning red except for his white knuckles, which were clenching the top of his blanket.

"I'm serious," Peter implored. "Listen, I never cared about the whole Bennett Charles thing. Who cares if you invented a douchebag, because it works for you, right? Honestly, I'll probably invent some sad asshole writing shitty poetry by a shitty lake and spend the rest of my life alone."

"Give. Me. My. Fucking. Phone," Bennett seethed.

"I don't have your fucking phone!" Peter yelled.

They stared at each other.

"I don't even have *my* phone," Peter said with a shrug. He took his glasses off and rubbed his eyes. He sighed. "Look, Carole Steele brought Edie here, not me. I've always been on your side."

"On my side?" Bennett yelled. "On *my* side?" And perhaps because he was so used to cameras documenting his every move, Bennett Charles did something only seen on TV—he started ripping the various hospital accoutrements from his body. Except the splint across his nose was really taped on there good, so it was more like he was picking at a stubborn price tag rather than dramatically flinging it off. "Fuck you, Pete. You don't give a shit about anyone other than yourself."

Peter put a hand to his heart, as if he'd been greatly wounded. But really, he was sort of wounded. Had they finally arrived at the crux of it? Was Peter Kennedy a selfish asshole who used people and did not give a fuck about Bennett Charles? (If anything, he actively disliked him.) Was that it? Was that the root of Peter's unsettling? Or was it something worse? Like somewhere along the line, had he developed something akin to a conscience, and it was ruining his ability to carpe diem every single opportunity that was being shoved in his face?

The splint refused to budge, and eventually Bennett stopped flailing and collapsed back onto the bed. "Show's over. I'm hurt. I won't film anymore." His face sagged in an exhaustion so comical, Peter couldn't help but start laughing all over again.

"You're not that hurt." He choked with laughter. "You fell off a lifeguard chair, not El Capitan."

"I am in pain!" Bennett roared as the door opened and Jessa stepped in. She held out Peter's phone.

"It won't stop. Carole. I think you'd better answer it."

Instantly Peter stopped laughing and his heart began to race. There was no escaping Carole Steele. He could throw his iPhone into the ocean and change his name to something stupid like Conner or Cooper or Colton, and still, one day she'd find him, most likely sitting on an Adirondack chair with a fishing pole in one hand and a faded Tolstoy in the other (who was he kidding; he wasn't going to write), and though he'd be aware of the death knell of her stilettos clacking against the old wooden dock as she approached for his final humiliation, he'd still find himself surprised when she placed a manicured hand on his shoulder and leaned down to whisper *I'm so glad I fired you* before she heaved him into the lake—Adirondack, Tolstoy, and all. And as he sunk into the murky depths, the very last thing he would see would be the *Us Weekly* Carole held above her head like John Cusack's boombox in *Say Anything*, with the extravagant Italian wedding of his ex-wife Julie and the new Batman across a two-page spread.

Except maybe this was finally it, he thought as his heart continued to beat *thunka-thunka-thunka* against his chest. If he collapsed right now, it would all be over. What was it Jessa had said? Why does it matter? It mattered because, actually, he didn't want to spend the rest of his life growing a beard and staring at waterfowl while he rolled his failures over in his mind like some sad sack character in a Franzen novel. He had more agency than that. He had dreams about who he was going to be—ideally a series creator of a prestige drama with a wife who made him a better person, plus probably some kids and a dog—but he kept failing and failing again until here he was, about to have a heart attack on the set of a tanking reality show, and when his obituary ran in the *Hollywood Reporter*, it would say that even though he was just thirty-nine years old and an avid runner/intermittent vegan, the stress of this job had killed him.

How could he accept that?

Peter held out his hand. If he couldn't escape and he couldn't keel over and die, then he'd just have to take this fucking call.

"Put it on speaker, Pete, I've got some things to say to Carole," Bennett called from the bed, flexing his biceps with a renewed sense of authority.

Peter looked at him, his face smirking under that silver splint, and instantly Peter was prepared to feed Bennett Charles into a meat grinder and turn the crank himself if it meant getting what he wanted—skyrocketing ratings, an Emmy, a shot at developing his own show based on his own ideas. But then, just for a moment, an image of Edie Pepper in that saggy floral swimsuit crossed his mind and he felt something strange.

Guilt? Shame? Or, God forbid, *attraction*? Peter had been in LA for so long, he'd forgotten what it was like to be around someone so guileless. When Jessa put Edie in that ridiculous swimsuit, he'd been shocked to find himself not only hot with temptation, but also protective, like he didn't want to edit her into some laughingstock. And when Edie'd thrown herself all over that volleyball court, he'd been surprised to find himself amused, but in a warm way, like she'd unlocked some secret place inside of him that remembered how to laugh and have fun. And when they'd stood together on the sand, surveying the *Key* world before them, he'd been astonished to find himself meaning what he said. She *was* smart and funny and irreverent. And—*what the fuck*—he *did* sort of like her. Not enough to throw away his career. But enough to know that whatever he did to Bennett right now, he was also doing to her.

But then the phone hit his palm and Edie was gone.

"This is Peter," he said, voice confident, heart rate already falling as he seized back control and hit the Speaker button.

"I have Carole for you. Please hold."

Silence. Peter, Jessa, and Bennett stared at the phone, watching the seconds tick by until finally at 7:52—

"Peter, you stupid, arrogant prick."

"Hi, Carole," Peter said. "Great to hear from you. I've got Bennett with me."

"Fantastic. Go ahead and kick each other in the balls. I'll wait."

"I'm not sure what you've heard, but I can assure you—"

"Cut the shit, Peter. I already know Humpty Dumpty fell off the wall. Tegan's been putting out this PR nightmare for you for over an hour. What the hell's wrong with you? This isn't rocket science. All you need to do is put Bennett Charles on a mountain top, set up the cameras, and get him engaged to Edie Pepper. That's it! But instead—"

"Engaged to Edie Pepper?" Bennett surged up like Frankenstein's monster. He jumped out of bed and tore off his gown and flung it at Peter, who found himself momentarily shrouded in the strong scent of laundry detergent and Bennett's particular musk. "Are you people insane?" Bennett yelled, flailing around the room in just his tight blue swim trunks. "Look at this shit," he yelled, scratching wildly at his inflamed Adam's apple. "I'm *fucking allergic* to Edie Pepper!"

"We're prepared to resume," Peter said, removing the hospital gown from his head. "However, as you may have noticed, Bennett's experiencing some hesitation—"

"Aww, is Benny-Wenny in his feelings?" Carole singsonged before turning her tone icy. "Listen up, you ungrateful turd. I don't care if kissing Edie Pepper shrivels your balls into tiny little pecans and makes you sneeze so powerfully you shoot them out your nose. This is *my* show. And if you think I'm going to let you derail *my* show with *your* feelings, then you're even stupider than you look."

Bennett's eyes went wide.

"Not to worry," Peter said, locking eyes with Bennett. "I've explained to Bennett the terms of his contract and advised him that he needs to think about his future. Being engaged to his high school sweetheart for six months will be worth everything that comes next. All the possible spin-offs, the book deals, the eventual collab with REI on a line of trekking gear. I can assure you; he gets it." Bennett opened his mouth, but before he could say anything, Jessa clambered over the bed and clamped a hand over his mouth. "We're on the same page, Carole."

"We better be. Shooting resumes tomorrow."

And with that, Carole Steele hung up.

Jessa took her hand off Bennett's mouth, and for a second, Peter thought Bennett was going to slug him. And, maybe, just maybe, Bennett's fist smashing into Peter's face might feel great.

Like some sort of visceral *Fight Club* release, an explosion of pain blooming through his cheekbone, nose, eye, and how alive would he be then, right here, right now, with his neck snapping back and his head hitting the wall before he fell to the floor? But then Bennett shook his head—some passing look of disbelief and then something like resignation—and he sat down on the bed, his head in his hands. "You people are insane," he said quietly. "You can't just decide who someone gets engaged to. You're not God."

"But don't you see?" A bolt of energy shot through Peter, and he waved his arms around like one of those wacky inflatable guys outside a used car lot. "I am."

18

I'm not perfect!" Bailey protested while, honestly, looking pretty perfect.

After the disastrous group date, a distraught Edie had been deposited by the producers in an empty hospital cafeteria to wait out the crisis with Max and Bailey. A sound guy had given Edie his Nike windbreaker to put on over her stupid swimsuit, and she had zipped it to her chin to distract from the fact that it barely covered her ass. Bailey, however, never went to the beach without accoutrements and was once again beautiful, appropriate, *covered* in a simple caftan, her face spritzed with Evian facial mist.

"Bailey, look, I love you, but you don't get it because this would never happen to you!" Edie said with total certainty. After two hours in the cafeteria, Edie now knew that Bailey had been raised on a ranch in Santa Barbara with her parents, retired Olympic athletes Natalia (badminton) and Frank (triathlon), and her older brother Reynolds (sport climbing). She was also kind, supportive, and patient. Combined with her beauty and

Bennett's clear interest in her, she really should be vomitous. In fact, Edie would hate Bailey if she didn't like her so much.

"*I* break people's noses," Edie continued. "Because *I'm* a total nightmare. *You* are not. *You* would never break someone's nose."

"I broke a nose once," Max interjected from the aisle where she'd been doing various calisthenics to ease her boredom. Even Max had packed a pair of track pants. She cartwheeled into a handstand and continued upside down. "Went for a header and took out number twelve's nose. It's all part of the game, Pepper."

"Max," Edie said, deadpan. "He wasn't even playing."

"Bennett's an athlete!" Max propelled herself to her feet and then slid into the splits. "He knows scrapes and bruises. I'm telling you, he's fine."

"And you're fine, too," Bailey added.

But Edie knew none of this was *fine*. Not only had she embarrassed herself every single second she'd been on *The Key*, but she also knew that even if Charlie Bennett was a whole new person, scrapes and bruises were definitely *not* his thing. She'd seen his face when his head was propped on Peter's lap in the sand. She knew that face—despair, self-pity, a total commitment to the tragedy of the experience. *That* was Charlie Bennett.

For an instant, seeing the real Charlie had been a comfort. Like Edie knew exactly who he was and exactly what she should do. How many times had Edie picked Charlie up with her pep talks and reasoned perspective? But then he'd been put into that ambulance, and she was left to wonder, once again, what exactly she was doing here.

When Edie barreled her way onto *The Key*, she'd understood that at some point Charlie Bennett had become this new person: Bennett Charles. But honestly, she didn't think it would matter all that much. She *knew* him. She'd *always* known him. Sure, there were all these external changes—the glow-up, the extreme sports, the influencer status—but didn't all of that just make him a hotter version of himself? Edie couldn't help it—she was a child of Oprah. Self-improvement and living your best life were concepts she'd metabolized wholeheartedly. Wasn't getting better each year a totally normal thing to do? Sitting in the cafeteria now, though, Edie felt like she'd missed something major—like, not only did she really not understand the internal changes that had driven Charlie's metamorphosis into Bennett Charles, but she had also never even considered them. Like, did he even read Tolkien anymore?

Edie thought again about their key ceremony kiss. It had felt so romantic, after all these years, to be kissed like that by him. He was a much better kisser than he'd been when they were younger. She remembered him being more awkward then, their teeth clanking together. The key ceremony kiss, though—that kiss had made her feel wanted, desired, like she was exactly where she was supposed to be.

But now she couldn't stop thinking about how, when he'd leaned in, she'd noticed he was wearing makeup. It hadn't been blended well at his hairline, and some had smeared on his collar. Everything felt slippery, like too many possibilities were playing out at once: He was Charlie Bennett, pitiful in the sand. He was Bennett Charles, muscular, with this deep man voice, who knew how to kiss. He was Charlie Bennett, the boy she'd always known. And Bennett Charles, a total stranger.

Edie looked at Bailey and Max. After Zo's incredible bitchiness on the patio that first night, Edie had assumed the other girls would hate her just as viciously, but Bailey and Max had taken care of her all day. They'd welcomed her onto their volleyball team and tried their best to make up for her lack of skills. They'd kept her company at the hospital and let her rehash the accident over and over again. Edie's heart warmed a bit. If there was a silver lining to all this embarrassment, it was definitely making friends.

Edie double-checked that there were no cameras around before she took a deep breath and leaned in closer to Bailey. "The last time I broke his nose," she said conspiratorially, "he didn't speak to me for seventeen years."

"Now *that's* interesting," Max said, finally taking a seat at the table. "Tell us more."

Edie waved her hand. "It's stupid—it was an accident. Still my fault, though, just like earlier. It was his going-away party and we were making out and we got sort of tangled up together and my head hit his nose. But anyway, after that we went to college, and I never heard from him again."

"Wait, why not?" Max asked.

"I don't know!" Edie said. "He just, like, *disappeared*. It was awful. And I was really hurt because even then I'd thought about us spending the rest of our lives together, you know? He was my *boyfriend*."

"Ghosting is for pussies," Max declared.

"Oh my god, I've never even thought about it that way." Edie's jaw dropped. "My first ghosting…"

"It's so weird to me that you've known each other forever," Max said. "I don't know why—people know each other. But you just seem like you're from two totally different worlds. You're really down to earth. He's…I mean, he's Hollywood, right?"

"What was he like in high school?" Bailey asked. Her face took on a dreamy look and she ran her fingers through the ends of her long blond hair. "I bet he was homecoming king, a soccer star, National Honor Society…"

Max guffawed. "Please. Bennett's a lot of things. National Honor Society he is not."

"Actually, he was pretty nerdy in high school," Edie admitted. "He wasn't my boyfriend until senior year. The rest of the time we were just friends. But we did everything together. We were in the marching band. He was sweet. And rashy. He always had rashes."

"Checks out," Max said. "I've diagnosed him with psoriasis a million times in my head."

Bailey smacked her on the arm, laughing. "Be nice."

"I know you guys think I'm blowing this out of proportion," Edie said, "but just hear me out: I think maybe I shouldn't have come here. Because, in what world does the same bad thing happen *twice*? I break his nose and he never speaks to me again. And then seventeen years later, I show up and break his nose *again*?"

To Edie's dismay, Max started laughing. "I think it's pretty hilarious, actually."

Edie gave her a look.

"It sounds like fate to me," Bailey chimed in. "Sort of romantic! Like a chance to handle it differently or something?"

The dreamy part of Edie wanted to agree with Bailey and say it was fate. Except Edie preferred when coincidence supported the romantic narrative she'd already cooked up in her head and didn't involve her injuring anyone. And there was something else bothering Edie. Like she was beginning to understand why Lauren had told her not to come here in the first place.

"I think maybe I just made this completely insane, psychotically impulsive decision to come here because I wanted this one thing so badly. To be loved. No matter the cost." What was it Peter had said? *The show's the show. It's got a format, and you either accept it or you don't.* How could she not have known better? A TV show? To find love? Really? *Most people don't take it so seriously.* She covered her face with her hands. "This is mortifying."

Max leaned over and pulled Edie's hands from her face.

"Pepper, come on," she said, her face full of compassion and love. "How do you think any of us ended up here? No one thought this through. We *all* just want to be loved."

Edie was thunderstruck. It seemed impossible that could be true. Cool, strong, smart, independent Max and Bailey—

every man's dream—wanted love just as badly as Edie did? Edie struggled to accept the idea that her romantic rivals, who were just so much better than her, could be fueled by a similar desperation.

"I've been looking for my true love forever," Bailey said with a little sigh. "But you would not believe how many men out there are just not very...*nice*?"

"Even in Santa Barbara?" Max asked.

"They're probably even worse there! They're all unemployed trust-fund surfers. And such know-it-alls! They lecture you about composting. As if I don't know about composting!"

Edie put her hand on Bailey's shoulder. "I've dated these men." They all laughed. "But you? You could marry *anyone*. I bet you could marry Alexander Skarsgård if you wanted to." Mentioning marriage suddenly reminded Edie of something else. "Wait. On the court, right before the accident, Zo told me something. She said Peter gave you a contract guaranteeing you a spot at the end."

"A contract?" Bailey looked genuinely confused.

"That's what she said—Peter gave you both contracts guaranteeing you spots at the end. And then she said I was just a one-episode sideshow."

"That's mean!" Bailey exclaimed. "You're not a sideshow. You're fabulous."

"And the way you've been playing this, Pepper, you're definitely gonna be on at least *two* episodes," Max joked.

"Is it true, though?" Edie pressed.

"Of course not!" Bailey said. "I think I've spoken to Peter maybe one time, and it was way back during casting. He talks to you way more than the rest of us. And I don't think Bennett would let Peter decide who's at the end anyway. Do you? Bennett's looking for his true love. I think it's important and real for him." Her face softened, as if her dream wedding was playing out in her mind's eye. "True love's gonna find its way—that's what I believe. No dumb volleyball game's gonna stop it. You just wait and see."

They all thought about that for a moment, but before Edie could decide if she agreed—true love had become seriously confusing—the door opened, and Jessa strode in with a bottle of craft services rosé and a stack of plastic cups.

"Edie Pepper, are you a graduate of the Bethenny Frankel School for Girls, or what? Way to snag that screentime, bitch! What a group date debut!"

Edie stood up quickly. "Oh my god, Jessa, is he okay?"

Jessa set the cups on the table and unscrewed the wine. "Please. He's fine. Never better." She poured. "If anything, you did him a favor. His nose needed more character. Before he was like, whatever handsome. But now he'll have gravitas!"

Edie pulled the windbreaker's hood over her head and folded herself over the table. "Oh my god, I hate myself. Can I go home? Please? Jessa, please get me a ticket home."

"You can't quit now. We haven't even started traveling yet!" Max exclaimed. She turned to Jessa. "We're going to Everest, right? Base camp? I brought my winter gear."

"I'll never tell," Jessa said. "But the travel location is great. A can't-miss."

Edie lifted her head an inch from the table. "Great. Maybe I can accidentally knock him off a mountain this time. Yodelay hee hoo, oh no, she killed him!"

"The ratings would skyrocket," Jessa said, passing around the wine. "Peter'd be thrilled."

Edie dropped her head dramatically back onto the table—*thunk*.

"We need you," Bailey said, rubbing Edie's back like a mother. "What if we go to New York? Who's going to take me to the Olive Garden in Times Square? You promised. You said,

'Bailey, the people watching is insane, and I know you don't eat bread, but at Olive Garden, you will.'"

"Besides," Jessa said. "I already know how we're going to fix this."

Edie sat up slowly, ever the optimist. "You do?"

"I do." Jessa smirked. "We're going to change the narrative entirely. Out with the old, in with the new." She raised her glass to toast. "It's time for a makeover."

"Eeeeeeee!" Bailey squealed, spilling her wine, and Edie's, all over the table.

To: Jessa Johnson; J. Daniel Peterman
From: Peter Kennedy
Subject: Makeover Montage / Cinderella Fantasy Date

Jessa/Daniel,

Thanks for the hard work shuffling the schedule so we can get Edie's makeover and Cinderella fantasy date together this week. I realize it's no small task.

Dan, I asked you to think outside the box and deliver a makeover proposal that puts Edie's strength and determination front and center, and I think you've achieved that. It's approved to shoot tomorrow. (I doubt there's money to license the song, but feel free to ask Jeremy. If not, I'm sure he can get you some AI-generated workout beats.)

Jessa, I asked you to give me a Cinderella date that was both fresh *and* nostalgic and I love what you've come up with. It's approved to shoot Monday.

Also, we need everyone off the Bennett injury story. Jessa, work with Tegan in PR and book him on one of the infotainment shows. Or *Us/People*. But I want at least a two-page spread—no sidebar or web-only bullshit. America needs to see he's the virile stud they know and love.

Keep up the good work.
P

TAKE 5 PRODUCTIONS
THE KEY
EDIE PEPPER MAKEOVER
[PROPOSAL BY J. DANIEL PETERMAN]

MAKEOVER MONTAGE

INT: OLD SCHOOL BOXING GYM – DAY

Punching bags on rusty chains, smelly mats, a fraying American flag pinned to the wall—you gotta want it to train here. You gotta claw your way to the top.

A spotlight flicks on with a BUZZ. There's a WOMAN in the middle of the ring. Her hoodie's pulled low. Her body's wilted like a bolt's been loosened, sinking her head, shoulders, and arms toward the floor. But if you look closer you can see it in the clench of her fist—grit.

MUSIC UP: "LOSE YOURSELF" BY EMINEM

EMINEM
Look, if you had, one shot,
one opportunity,
to seize everything you ever wanted,
in one moment,
would you capture it?
Or just let it slip?

Metal doors CLANG. Footsteps POP. A TEAM enters, striding side by side, superheroes with blow-dryers, clothing racks, and medical equipment.

The WOMAN looks up. It's EDIE.

QUICK CUTS:

... EDIE runs on the beach; she's struggling. The DATING COACH yells—

DATING COACH
No pain! No pain!

... EDIE's laid out on a weightlifting bench. Waxing strips are stuck all over her face. Hands appear and rip them off. EDIE moans.

... in the locker room, A HAIRSTYLIST shows EDIE how to dry her hair.

HAIRSTYLIST
She's never going to get it.

DATING COACH
She's got to.

... back on the beach, EDIE trips and falls.

... EDIE stares straight ahead, struggling to keep a glowing Crest 3DWhitestrips Blue Light™ LED teeth whitener in her mouth, as a syringe enters the frame. It punctures her brow.

... a very full glass of green juice. EDIE refuses to drink it.

DATING COACH
You want to get married?

EDIE chugs.

... EDIE collapses in the sand. And then finds it within herself to start crawling.

DATING COACH
That's it! That's it!

. . . the DATING COACH holds up a tiny thong and giant pair of Spanx. EDIE chooses the Spanx. The TEAM cheers.

. . . EDIE applies her own lipstick. The TEAM cheers.

. . . the DATING COACH shows EDIE how to toss her hair and smile. EDIE masters it. The TEAM cheers.

. . . the HAIRSTYLIST and MAKEUP ARTIST put the finishing touches on EDIE's hair and face. She's never looked this beautiful.

. . . EDIE back in the ring, twirling in a variety of fairy-tale ball gowns.

. . . LAST SHOT: brand-new, super gorgeous EDIE steps in front of a mirror. A promotional photo of the CONTESTANTS is stuck in the corner. EDIE picks it up, crumples it, throws it over her shoulder.

She smiles.

Her teeth are blinding.

19

Edie Pepper could not fucking breathe, her Spanx were so tight. And she was so hot, sweat had begun to pool between her boobs and threatened to overwhelm the armpits of the one-size-too-small, floor-length, strapless Victoria Beckham gown that had taken two sets of hands to zip. Yesterday, when she'd tried it on, Edie had been very intimidated by the slit that went all the way up her thigh like Angelina Jolie's dress at the Oscars. But now, as she flapped the hem through the air like a deranged flamenco dancer, she was beyond grateful for the breeze circulating around her boiler room of a crotch.

"Give me a hint?" Edie pleaded. "You know I hate surprises."

"Can't, won't, sorry," Jessa said with a devilish smile. She motioned for Edie to lift her arms and patted her armpits dry with a towel. "Now get in the limo. You don't want to be late for the biggest night of your life."

A chauffeur opened the limo door, and after one last hug from Jessa, Edie attempted to follow her cameraman, Ted, into the back seat. But her gown was so tight she couldn't bend. As soon as her butt hit the seat, the gown's seams contracted and hissed. Afraid everything was about to snap, Edie slid down the leather until she was horizontal, with her shoulders propped on the seat and her legs jutting akimbo into the limo's expanse.

"And, Edie"—Jessa leaned in through the open door—"I mean it. You look stunning. *Stunning.*" And with that the door snapped shut and Jessa was gone.

"Wait, are you not coming?" Edie asked. But the limo was already moving slowly down the *Key* mansion's long driveway. This was fine. Wasn't this how Lady Gaga traveled to the Grammys? No problem. Edie strained to peek out the window at the sister wives that production had gathered on the lawn to wave her off. Who knew all Edie needed was a dedicated team of celebrity stylists, makeup artists, estheticians, dermatologists, colorists, nutritionists, and personal trainers to look like she belonged with the beautiful people of reality TV? When Edie saw her gorgeous self for the first time, she suddenly understood why all these women felt innately entitled to Bennett Charles. *This must be what it feels like to have never had a pimple*, she'd thought. *Bulletproof.*

"Just the two of us?" Edie asked Ted. It was weird. Typically Jessa or another producer accompanied Edie everywhere she went.

Ted shrugged. Edie sighed. No matter how many times she'd tried to work her charms on Ted, he'd never spoken to her again—just that one time, the first night on the patio. She wasn't sure if she could even picture his face. Ted was the camera, and the camera was Ted. Edie glanced around the limo. Black leather seats; a little bar with an ice bucket and crystal decanters of booze; a tinted panel concealing the driver. It all felt very retro. And also poignant, like Edie was harkening back to a simpler time, before she knew the pursuit of love included things like dick pics and the Marvel Universe.

The limo slowed and the door across from her opened. An out-of-breath Peter Kennedy slid in. For a millisecond she felt electric. Thrilled to see him, and thrilled for him to see just how beautiful she was now.

But then Edie Pepper remembered she hated Peter Kennedy.

The last time she'd seen Peter, he'd been cradling Charlie's head in his lap. Then, through her tears, she'd watched his departing back as he got into the ambulance behind the stretcher. And that was it. Days passed. She'd been poked and prodded and cinched and squeezed, and every time a door opened, she'd expected to see him there. But he never came. She'd thought they were friends! Or something *like* friends! But he never checked on her, not even once. And every day he didn't come, the grudge Edie nursed became deeper and more complicated.

"Hey," he said, lightly panting like he'd run to catch up. He noticed Edie starfished across the floor and raised a brow. "How's it going?"

"I can't sit in this dress," she said, staring straight ahead as the limo started moving again. "It's too tight."

"Ah." Peter nodded. "Well. Sorry about that. I can let Wardrobe know if it's a problem."

Edie slit her eyes. "If you want to be concerned about something, perhaps you could've popped by when they were waxing my asshole, because let me tell you, *that* was a treat." She looked out the window. "At this point, I think I can handle the dress."

"Waxed your asshole?" Peter sounded impressed. "That definitely wasn't in the production notes."

He grinned. She glared.

Hating Peter felt exactly right, even if Edie didn't totally understand why. There were the surface reasons, of course. He'd gotten her to wear that stupid swimsuit. He'd made her play volleyball. He'd told her she was smart and funny and irreverent and that all she needed to do was show Charlie and he'd want to marry her. He'd hyped her up—and then she'd hit the ball that ricocheted off Zo's tits and into Charlie's face. And, of course, there were also Zo's accusations about the contracts and the final two. Maybe Peter hadn't given out contracts, as Bailey had said, but now Edie knew Peter *could* give out contracts. The possibilities of what Peter *could* do to ensure whatever outcome he wanted suddenly seemed endless.

Still, there was something else. Something more. Something harder to put her finger on, something that nagged and hurt like rejection.

"Are you producing this date?" she asked.

"Nah," he said, fanning himself with the fabric of his shirt. "I just thought it'd be nice for us to catch up on the way over."

Edie stared out the window.

Peter gestured to Ted. "Hey, man, you can relax. We don't need this on camera."

Ted put the camera on the seat next to him. He had a nice face. Like somebody's dad.

"So," Peter said, turning back to Edie, "you look fantastic."

But the way he said it, with this singsongy lilt, the way he drew out *fantastic. So! You look fan-tasssssssss-tic!*

She turned to him. "Do I?"

"Of course."

"Then why do I feel like that's not what you mean?"

Peter shrugged. "I mean, sure, generally I'm against the erasure of individuality in pursuit of a homogenous Instagram aesthetic that appropriates features from various ethnic groups and serves to perpetuate impossible beauty standards for women already oppressed by a patriarchal society. But for you I'll make an exception. You look very attractive." He smiled at her, and he was infuriatingly handsome. "See? I'm a feminist. Intersectional, even. Don't forget I went to Brown."

"Wow, I'm so glad the Ivy League stopped by to mansplain beauty to me. I feel so confident and ready for this date now, thanks!" Suddenly, in the face of Peter's judgment, lying prone across the back seat of a limo felt intensely embarrassing. Fuck the dress. Edie shimmied up the seat, so she was at his level. Jessa had told her specifically that Peter was all about the makeover! "I'm confused," she said, her voice thick with sarcasm. "Isn't this what you wanted? For me to be beautiful enough for Bennett Charles?"

But as soon as the words were out of her mouth, she regretted them. During the entire makeover process, she'd tried to keep herself sort of detached, like it was just one of those funny things that happened when you went on reality TV. But now the truth hung in the air between them. Because didn't becoming beautiful matter a helluva lot? Wasn't being beautiful the final step to getting everything she wanted? A sick feeling of mortification at her own shallow ideals swelled in her stomach and pressed against her Spanx.

"C'mon, you know that's not what I meant," Peter said while Edie tried to fold an arm over her chest. Suddenly the gown, the makeup, the hair—all of it seemed like an outward symbol of her ridiculousness, her try-hardness, her childishness. But every way she placed her arm only accentuated her cleavage more and she could feel Peter noticing. She gave up and they caught eyes. "I'm just saying *personally*, I don't need you to look like everyone else," he continued. "I liked how you looked before. Like a real person. But *empirically*, you look great." He smiled, and his unchecked arrogance was infuriating.

"Whatever." Edie shifted onto one hip to stare out the window again. The limo was exiting the highway and gliding down the palm-lined streets of Beverly Hills.

Peter sighed. He dug around his pocket and produced some Tums. For a moment, the only sound was the pop of the Tums against his molars.

Finally, the masticating concluded. "Look, I'm sorry. Clearly, I've said all the wrong things. Sometimes I act smart when I'm nervous. It's a problem. You look beautiful. You do."

She looked at him again and his face was sweet and kind, except everything about him was suspect now. He'd gotten into the limo knowing she would care if he thought she looked pretty. How could she not? So much money and time had been spent on this, like she was some sort of *Trading Spaces* forty-eight-hour project. And she'd gone along with it because she'd wanted to be beautiful. And then she *was* beautiful. And then he'd made her feel stupid on the biggest night of her life. Why?

"Why are you here, Peter?" she demanded.

"Should I not be here?" His head cocked. "This is my show, you know."

"Exactly. It's your show. So tell me what you want. You don't need to manipulate me. I'm a big girl, I can take it."

"Is it so hard to believe I just wanted to see how you're doing?"

Edie glared at him.

"Jeez, all right," he said, hands up in surrender. "But I'm not here to manipulate you. Wait, when did I manipulate you?"

"Oh, I dunno, how about when you got me to wear that stupid swimsuit and made me play sports on TV?"

He made a face. "That was manipulation? I thought I was facilitating your eventual marriage to Bennett Charles."

She didn't say anything.

Peter sighed dramatically. "Okay, look," he began after a moment. "This is actually a good segue into what I've been thinking about. About what I want. What you want. What Bennett wants. And I think we're aligned. But then..." He struggled to find the words. "But then I worry something's off. And that it's gonna blow up in our faces."

"I have no idea what you're talking about."

"It's just this whole situation—"

"What 'situation'?"

"You know, this situation." He paused. "It's a crisis of conscience, maybe. Honestly, I blame you. I'm not normally like this." He massaged the muscles at the base of his neck before dropping his hand and looking at her again, something beseeching in his eyes. "It's just that you're not like the other girls, Edie. It's fucking me up a bit. You actually want something. What? Love? And I'm just not sure I can give that to you. The other girls, they'll be fine. To them, fawning over Bennett is just an occupational hazard. A first step toward hawking tummy tea to tweens on Instagram. They're not girls who will get seriously hurt; they've got whole other lives. But you—if this doesn't work out, will it crush you?"

A hot fire of indignation sparked inside Edie, obliterating all her previous insecurity. It was one thing for Edie to think she wasn't good enough. It was entirely another for stupid Peter Kennedy to think it.

"You don't think I can do this," she said, laughing at the absurdity of it all. "You came here because you don't think Bennett Charles could fall in love with someone as average as me."

"That's not what I'm saying—"

"That's absolutely what you're saying, with the added bonus of making sure I know I'm not pretty enough to sell garbage on Instagram. Except, fuck you, I don't want to sell shit on Instagram, and also, I *do* have a whole life outside of this. And you know who's about to be a part of that life? Charlie Bennett. Because unlike you, he gets me."

And then, in a moment of perfect synchronicity, the limousine pulled up in front of a gleaming Spanish-style building and there, standing under a spotlight at the top of a white staircase, stood a tuxedoed Bennett Charles. As the limo slid to a stop, he smiled his perfect smile, with that one crooked tooth, and waved, hand down by his hip, adorably shy. Why would Edie ever let Peter distract her? This was her big night, her chance to seize everything she'd ever wanted. Was she going to capture it? Or let it slip?

"Now if you'll excuse me, it's time for me to fall in love."

Edie pulled at the door handle, but it wouldn't budge. Getting desperate, she kicked at it with one stiletto until the door suddenly swung open.

Out Edie Pepper rolled, already swept off her feet.

20

Bennett Charles was done with love.

Unfortunately, the weight of this decision—plus his status as a reality TV hostage—made the slow trek up the stairs to this Beverly Hills high school even more harrowing than his final ascent of Kilimanjaro, and on that day, the northeast anti–trade winds had gone berserk and there had been a palpable fear that what had started as a simple climb had somehow turned into a slick tightrope between life and death. Tonight, however, the air was a perfect LA seventy-two with a pleasant breeze and almost no humidity. Still, his feet were like lead, and he was just destroying the pits of his Hugo Boss tuxedo.

The toe of Bennett's patent leather loafer nicked the top step and he stumbled onto the summit. Fuck these stupid shoes and their slick soles! Bennett sighed and smoothed his jacket, looking down at the spot where Edie's limo was set to arrive. It's not like there was anything *wrong* with Edie. She was a good person. But he just couldn't see how he could date Edie, love Edie, and continue living his life as Bennett. For a second, he thought he could try. When he'd kissed her at the key ceremony, he'd felt something, a door opening, maybe, a path to merging his identities, possibly, and he'd felt centered in a way he hadn't for years. But then the volleyball date. The volleyball date solidified there was no way Edie fit into the future Bennett envisioned for himself. How was that his fault? Sure, he'd been distracted by the other girls, but why'd she have to go and break his nose? *Again?*

Unfortunately, he knew it wasn't that simple. It pained him to admit it, but he knew he'd been showing off. Performing for the cameras. Strutting around and letting all the attention fill up the emptiness inside. Somehow walking, talking, and existing miles away from both Charlie Bennett *and* Bennett Charles in this weird hubristic space where he was almost an entirely new person. A meathead douche high on adoration, gawking at some girl's tits until a volleyball smashed him in the head.

Pain shot through his sinuses and Bennett pressed the pads of his fingers to either side of his nose, pressing the edges of the white butterfly strip that just this morning had replaced his silver splint. Last night, after a long day of production when he'd valiantly gone horseback riding and line dancing and licked salt off McKayla's neck before tossing back three shots of tequila in an American Southwest–themed date, Jessa'd hopped in the production van. He was still pulling the straw out of his hair from the literal roll in the hay when she smiled with something like friendship and said, *Trust me, don't worry. Tomorrow you go out with Edie. She got a makeover. You're going to die, she looks so good.*

He'd lain in bed that night, rolling his options over in his mind. If there was one thing the past decade of adventure had taught him, it was that the only way to survive an expedition was with a firm grip on your emotions, decisiveness in times of peril, and a plan. Finally, he arrived at a three-point strategy for getting out of *The Key* alive. (1) Forget every mushy vision of the future. (2) Refuse to be manipulated. (3) Focus on survival.

All he had to do was survive the next four weeks.

And then, if there was truly no other option, he'd spend the next six months engaged to Edie Pepper until his contract ran out and they no longer owned where he could go, who he could talk to, and what future deals he could make. He'd disappear into the Himalayas until it all blew over.

A production assistant swept his shoulders with a lint brush and Bennett startled. Then a guy from sound appeared, said something about his mic. Bennett held his arms out and the dude shoved his hands into Bennett's jacket and probed around for the cord. His head brushed against Bennett's chest, and it exacerbated the feeling of hopeless isolation in Bennett's heart. For a moment Bennett considered pulling him in for a hug, resting his chin on the guy's head and breathing in his shampoo, just to feel something that wasn't this. But then the mic issue was resolved, and the guy jogged back to the production van, a lighting engineer flicked on a spotlight, and there he was, Bennett Charles, at the top of the steps, alone.

The limousine pulled up to the curb. Bennett took a deep breath, put a smile on his face, and waved like a good boyfriend. All he had to do was lead her into the high school for the re-creation of the senior prom they'd never attended because Edie'd had the flu, deliver a romantic speech, and then kiss her, visualizing the big moment that would usher in the next commercial break. And then he could go home. At least for the night.

A PA who'd once brought Bennett an Imodium after an ice cream in the park date popped out of the driver's seat, dressed like a chauffeur. The cameras swirled into place as he trotted to the passenger door. He took hold of the handle and waited for the signal from Lou, who was grinding a piece of Nicorette and watching the monitor with one arm in the air like *wait for it... wait for it...* until finally Lou pointed at the PA—*go! go!*

go!—and the limo door swung open for the big reveal. Out Edie Pepper tumbled onto the parkway.

Oh, shit!

Instinctively, Bennett made a move to fly down the stairs, but the AD shooed him back with a clipboard. "Are you okay?" Bennett yelled, craning his neck as the PA and a newly materialized Peter Kennedy hauled her up from the ground.

"I'm fantastic!" she called, snapping her sexy black gown back into place. She floofed her blond waves around her shoulders. Then, as if remembering something, she struck a pose. Shoulders back, hands at the hips, one bronzed leg cutting through the slit in her dress. Blood dribbled from her exposed knee.

"Medical!" Peter yelled, waving to the producers on the sidelines.

A dude with a first aid box ran over and knelt in front of Edie. As he dabbed her knee with gauze, she held her pose and smiled. Bennett smiled back, unsure. It was strange looking at this new Edie Pepper. It was like he was seeing her for the very first time, this beautiful woman, except he did know her, didn't he? He'd always known her. If he thought about it, he could visualize the spatter of freckles on the back of her neck that he'd stared at when he sat behind her in middle school art. Or the scar in the shape of a triangle on her shoulder from that time when they were six and she rode her bicycle straight into the chain link fence at the edge of the blacktop because she'd forgotten how to brake.

Bennett watched as Peter whispered something in her ear. A dark look crossed her face, and she wrenched her leg away from an incoming Band-Aid. She said something Bennett couldn't hear and then shoved her elbow straight into Peter's gut. *What the—* Peter stumbled back a couple of feet until his ass hit the limo's trunk. Bennett strained to see what was happening, but now Jessa, Medical, Lou, and a bunch of other production people were in the way. Why the hell was Edie assaulting the showrunner right before their big one-on-one date?

Suddenly a great rush of hope filled Bennett's heart as a possibility he'd never considered filled his mind. Maybe he wasn't alone after all. Maybe, just maybe, Edie was a victim, too. Peter had insisted that she'd come to them, that she'd been the one to force her way onto the show. But Peter was a known liar. And from the looks of it, Edie knew that, too. Maybe what really happened was they'd dug through Bennett's past and found the yearbook with Bennett and Edie in matching band uniforms on the cover of the Clubs page. He could picture the photo in his mind, right down to the dorky epaulets at their shoulders and the tall red plumes on top of their caps. All at once it made sense that they'd gone looking for her. Lured her here. Made her promises, just like they'd made him promises.

Then another idea crossed Bennett's mind. What if, just like him, Edie wasn't the same person she'd been seventeen years ago? What if the whole volleyball thing was just some weird coincidence and in real life, Edie was totally successful and loving and kind, a great dresser and a good cook—all the things that were on his wife list after all? Had he even talked to her, really talked to her, since she'd been here? *The Key* was this pressure cooker of women and five-minute conversations meant to hang a lifetime on. It left him dizzy and confused and relying on snap judgments and base instincts. But here was someone he knew was a good person. Why was he so willing to remember her as a loser anyway?

Hadn't she always been like the coolest girl to him?

Bennett searched the crowd, suddenly desperate to meet Edie's eyes and share this new understanding that, just like when they were kids protecting each other on the playground, they were once again allies. When she finally emerged, the emotion he felt was quick and overwhelming. It wasn't just that she was beautiful, though that helped, of course. It was also this new understanding that maybe, just maybe, someone might have his back—that someone might actually care about him, the *real* him—that sparked Bennett's own brilliant smile. And even when Lou hopped around waving his Lakers cap like *go back! go back!* so the shot could be reset and they could do it all over again, Edie kept moving. She made her way up the stairs, and when the heel of her strappy sandal slipped and she stumbled onto the top step, he was right there to catch her.

"I got you," Bennett said, pulling her into a hug that made him want to cry with relief.

She wrapped her arms around him, too. "Thanks, friend."

As soon as Bennett Charles and Edie Pepper walked hand-in-corsaged-hand through the doors of the Beverly Hills high school, ghosts were everywhere. It didn't matter that this wasn't the high school they'd attended almost twenty years ago. One look down the long hallway evoked the din of changing classes, the reverb of slamming locker doors, and even the slouchy specter of Bennett's long-term nemesis Tommy Malick, all low-slung homeboy jeans, feigned punches, and wet gleeks. A trophy case commending the Beverly Hills football players, National Merit Scholars, and elastic-faced theater kids raised from the dead the entire Midwestern cast of the 1999 New Trier production of *Fiddler on the Roof.* And all at once that old tech anxiety began brewing in Bennett's stomach and he looked at Edie, wondering if she was thinking about *Fiddler*, too. Her face was in profile as she stared down the hall, and it was almost like there were two Edies—this beautiful woman in the sexy black dress, and the sixteen-year-old girl who'd danced in her long brown skirt with Tevye's daughters. Bennett used to light her brighter than the rest of the cast because he'd been madly in love with her for at least a year. "A girl without a dowry can't be so particular. You want hair, marry a monkey!" That was one of her big lines, and it always got a laugh. The way she'd said it—*marry a monkey!*—out of the side of her mouth, like she was Joan Rivers or something.

Bennett's cheeks got hot. Jesus, the pull of his former self was strong. But Bennett Charles wasn't a chubby nerd running lights anymore—he was the leading man.

He squeezed Edie's hand. "C'mon, I have a surprise for you."

"What is it?" she asked, the soft dreaminess in her face sliding away.

"It's a surprise!"

"You know I hate surprises."

Did he know that? "Not this one," he said, scattering the ghosts as he pulled her toward the double doors leading to the gym. Cameramen rushed to keep up.

"Is it twenty women in bikinis poised to rip each other's hair out in a kiddie pool of Jell-O?"

He stopped and looked at her seriously. "People are starving all over the world, Edith. You think I'd waste Jell-O? I'm not a monster."

She looked up at him through thick lashes and smiled a very cute half smile, a little bit amused, a little bit *I got your number*. "It better not be an obstacle course," she continued. "Because this dress wouldn't survive that. I don't know if you noticed, but I had a little trouble getting out of the limo."

"Did you? To me, you were the picture of elegance." Then, in his best George Clooney, he took her cheek in his hand, dropped his voice to a husky whisper, and looked into her eyes. "Don't be nervous. You're perfect. This night is perfect."

A blush crept across her cheeks, and she bit the corner of her lip. He thought about kissing her but decided not to blow his wad before they even got through the doors.

"C'mon." He started pulling her down the hall again.

"Basketball? And you get to break my nose this time?"

"A nose as cute as that? I would never."

"I'm really sorry about that, by the way."

"Don't be. I know what I'm getting into with you, Pepper. It wouldn't be foreplay if someone didn't break their nose."

Her mouth fell open, and for a second his stomach dropped. Why did he always say the wrong thing? But then the loudest laugh—a guffaw really—escaped her lips before she clamped a hand over her mouth, and then they were both doubled over, and he was laughing harder than he'd laughed in a long time. What a fucking crazy thing to say on mic with the cameras right fucking there! But now Bennett understood it was exactly the right thing to say, it was exactly what they needed to acknowledge their past and move on to the future, and all at once he realized that none of it mattered. No one knew what they were talking about; it was their own inside thing, and then he understood how stupid it was that he'd been carrying the weight of this one mortification for almost twenty years and countless satisfied sexual partners later. And—*poof*—just like that, Bennett Charles let it go. It was silly and funny, and he was safe. They smiled at each other.

They started walking again, the double doors looming until finally he reached for the handle. He looked at her, feeling mischievous and excited, about to surprise a beautiful girl with something he knew she was going to love.

"Ready?"

She grabbed his arm. "Is it Beyoncé? Because you have to tell me if it's Beyoncé. I will pee my pants."

"It's not Beyoncé," he said, a bit deflated. Did she really think he had access to Beyoncé? He wasn't *that* famous. "But I promise, you're going to love it." And with that, he pushed open the door and they walked into another world. Well, a gymnasium outfitted by *Key* production to look like another world, like the sort of gorgeous high school prom seen only on TV or in the movies. White globes in a variety of sizes and brilliance were suspended from the rafters, blanketing the entire room in a sort of avant-garde celestial moonscape. Gauzy white fabric covered the cinder-block walls, and there, on an accordioned stage right under the raised basketball hoop, was the real surprise: the Goo Goo Dolls launching into the opening riff of "Slide."

"Shut. Up!" Edie exclaimed, grabbing his hand and dragging him toward the stage.

She immediately started dancing, right in front of Johnny Rzeznik, somehow totally unselfconscious, just moving her body and smiling and laughing. And somehow just by being near her, watching her express joy like it was the most natural thing in the world, he was able to let the wave of music take over until they were both dancing, not worried about the camera on the crane gliding around overhead and capturing all his terrible white-guy dance moves, just moving his body and singing along with her, *What you feel is what you are, and what you are is beautiful...*

The Goo Goo Dolls transitioned into "Iris," a song that always felt super romantic to Bennett, like it touched something true inside of him, the music cracking open some hidden well of feeling, and immediately he wanted to touch her, to hold her, so he pulled Edie to him and wrapped his arms around her until their bodies were pressed together and he could tuck his face down into her neck and breathe her in.

...'cause I know that you feel me somehow...

"This is unbelievable," she whispered as they moved together.

The music built into a dramatic swell, lifting him up until he could almost see every single one of his dreams coming true, and then dropping out again to the lone guitar in what he could only take in as some sort of metaphor for solitude—*I just want you to know who I am.* It was like every single moment of Bennett's life had brought him to this moment, to this realization that, *yes*, Bennett Charles *did* want to be known, and while he understood, of course, that it was impossible that he could suddenly be in love, the lights, the music, the girl—it all felt like a peak experience, like something straight out of a movie, and that, *that*, is when he kissed her.

After having their portrait taken in front of a balloon backdrop and touring a classroom filled with posters highlighting their high school days, Bennett and Edie were escorted up three flights of stairs to their final shooting location—an intimate candlelit rooftop, where they were now drinking champagne and enjoying the twinkling lights of the city below while he regaled her with stories of his travels.

"On the bike trip across the Middle East, I was gone for six months. Riding every day, camping every night."

"It sounds amazing," she said before polishing off her champagne.

"There's nothing like traveling and losing yourself in a new culture. But it can get lonely, you know? Like during the day, I felt like I could do anything, but at night, you're lying on the ground in the middle of the desert, staring up at the stars, and you feel very small. It's a weird sense of accomplishment mixed with total insignificance." He paused and sighed thoughtfully. "I guess that's how I ended up here."

She nodded and signaled to Jessa for more champagne. For a moment he felt like there was a weird gulf between them. Was she bored? But then Jessa came over and refilled their glasses and Edie smiled at him, a little elastic, a little drunk, with that sort of toothy smile she'd always had, and for some reason, it reminded him of playing Monopoly on her back porch. And then, between the memories and the champagne, he felt warm and schmoopy all over again.

"Do you remember when we first met?" he asked.

"Hmm..." She looked up at the sky. "One of my earliest memories of you is at Lauren's birthday party. We were, like, five? Six? I don't have kids—I'm not good with ages—but remember it was a roller-skating party? And you didn't know how to skate, so one of the moms was teaching you on the carpet?" She was looking at him merrily now. Something like fear pricked the back of his neck. The cameras pushed in. "Like while everyone else was going around in circles on the rink, you were on the carpet by the tables—"

"No, I mean literally the very first time we met, like the first time you said, *Hi, I'm Edie,* and I said, *Hi, I'm*—"

"—and right when we came back to sing 'Happy Birthday'"—she was laughing now, pretty uncontrollably actually—"Mrs. Wasserman came around the corner with the most beautiful birthday cake, with these gorgeous piped roses, and somehow you roller-skated right into it, like with your arms directly planted into Lauren's cake. *Smash!*"

Bennett clenched his jaw. This was not the memory he would've chosen to play out on national television. He tried to smile—*ha-ha, what an idiot, fun!*—but he felt pinched, like he wanted to tip the stupid table over and watch the votives with their artificial flames explode against the concrete. Why would she bring this up? Was she trying to humiliate him? But why would she do that? He was being crazy. He was being a guy who was so insecure he couldn't handle being the butt of a joke. Well, ha-fucking-ha, yes he could.

"Oh man," he laughed. "I don't remember that! Are you sure that was me?"

"Oh, it was definitely you," she said. "I remember thinking, *Charlie Bennett, he is fucking fun.*"

"That is not what you thought."

"Of course that's what I thought! I was like, this kid knows how to have a good time. Skate into a cake today, what sort of shit will he get up to tomorrow? Lauren—she was the one who cried. But somebody's dad went and bought Twinkies and it was fine." Edie started laughing again and shaking her head at the memory. "God, we were a bunch of nerds."

"You still talk to Lauren?"

Edie nodded. "Every day. She thought it was insane I was coming here. She says marriage is oppression." Edie put her champagne down and looked at him, her face suddenly serious. "Do you think marriage is oppression?"

"Wow. That's an intense thing to say." Of course Lauren would say something psychotic like that, and for a second, Bennett wasn't sure if he'd always disliked Lauren or if he disliked Lauren because Lauren disliked him. But what he did know was that this was an opportunity for him to deliver one of the marriage speeches the producers went crazy for. "I've wanted to get married my entire life," he said, taking her hand. "I want the whole thing, you know? The partnership. Where my wife is the first person I want to talk to in the morning and the last person I want to talk to at night. And we have a couple of kids and a big Christmas tree and a dog and probably more like a Land Rover than a van, but you get me—soccer practices and birthdays, and when they're old enough, adventures, like the whole family riding camels across the Sahara. And my wife, she's the center of it all." He looked at her, and what was that? Some mistiness in her eyes? "What could be better than that?"

"Nothing could be better than that."

"I remember the *very* first time we met," he said. "It was in the cafeteria."

"Oh my god, the allergy table!" Edie exclaimed. "I completely forgot about the allergy table. It had a sign! With a dancing peanut! What'd it say?" Edie thought about it for a second. "It said something silly."

"'It's Cool to be Peanut-Free,'" he supplied.

She clapped her hands with joy. "That's *exactly* right."

"You were wearing red overalls," he continued, suddenly able to see five-year-old Edie and her messy blond hair like it was yesterday. "You had a *Babysitters Club* book stuck in the front pocket."

"What can I say?" She crinkled her nose. "I was an early reader."

Suddenly the past, all the things they knew about each other, didn't seem so scary. They were just kids. Bennett thought about his five-year-old self in that cafeteria. He'd had a Care Bears lunchbox. He'd really loved it, with its happy rainbow and bouncing bears floating along clouds of hearts and stars. That is, until his dad had told him it was "super gay." Thinking about it now, Bennett couldn't help but marvel at how all these little moments, they just came together, one by one, until suddenly you're thirty-five years old and you've spent your entire adult life making sure everybody knows how tough you are. That you can easily bench 150 pounds. That you can swipe right and be having sex within the hour. That you haven't cried in fifteen years.

"You were walking by, and you had the hot lunch," he continued. "And I was so jealous. I *never* got hot lunch."

"Because Helen was looking out for you."

"Because Helen was looking out for me," he agreed. "But you asked me why I was sitting by myself. And I said they made me sit there. Because everybody's PB&Js could kill me." It seemed so ridiculous now, he couldn't help but laugh. He took her hand in his. "You threw away your lunch so you could sit with me."

"Of course I did." She placed her hand on top of his and stared straight into his eyes with a soft smile on her face. "You had Cool Ranch Doritos."

He laughed. The moon was bright, casting everything in a soft, magical glow. He looked to her again, continued more seriously. "I never forgot that, you know."

"You never knew what a great kid you were. I'm pretty sure I loved you from the very beginning," she said, looking at him like she could really see him, both the five-year-old version *and* the man he was and maybe could be. All at once he realized something he thought he already knew, except perhaps he'd only known it as an idea before. It wasn't the Instagram followers or jumping out of planes or climbing mountains or even having twenty gorgeous women fighting to marry you—it was simply the people in your life that made you happy, that gave you everything you needed.

In one fluid motion he was up from his seat and kneeling before her. Not a proposal, but perhaps a sort of nod to their future. He put his hand in her hair and pulled her to him, kissing her, Edie Pepper, this girl who'd always been kind to him. He kissed her tentatively at first, different from the way he kissed the other girls, more Charlie Bennett than Bennett Charles.

Because maybe, for the first time, his whole heart was in it.

TAKE 5 PRODUCTIONS
THE KEY
OTF INTERVIEW: BENNETT CHARLES PROM
TAPE #382

00:00:00 PRODUCER 1: He should go out with Bailey next.

PRODUCER 2: Bailey?

PRODUCER 1: Yeah. Bailey.

PRODUCER 2: But that doesn't make sense. We're already set with Zo for tomorrow. Why would we give him Bailey? He's rated Bailey #1 every single week.

PRODUCER 1: Last time I checked this was still my show.

PRODUCER 2: Oh Jesus Christ, Peter, you're starting that again? I don't even get to have an opinion?

PRODUCER 1: Sure, you do. But you're wrong. And I know that's a bummer, but it's Bailey next.

00:00:30 PRODUCER 2: But that doesn't make sense! We've got him right where we want him—falling in love with Edie. Why would we risk that by bringing in the girl he's been obsessed with for weeks? We need to keep Bailey away from him for as long as possible so when they do finally go out, it's too late. Have you forgotten the plan? It's Bennett gets engaged to Edie.

PRODUCER 1: Bench Zo. Here he comes.

BENNETT: Hooooooooleeeeeeeee shit.

PRODUCER 1: A good night, huh?

PRODUCER 2: Are we rolling?

BENNETT: The best fucking night, you guys. Wow.

PRODUCER 2: OK, B., you know the drill—straight to the camera.

BENNETT: I mean, I admit it, I doubted you—I thought you were fucking with me—but I'm man enough to admit when I'm wrong—

PRODUCER 2: Ok, to the camera though—

BENNETT: Peter, I know we haven't always seen eye to eye, but I just had, it's hard to describe . . . I had a spiritual experience. Like, I broke through some real emotional barriers. And I just—I just want to thank you, alright? You're not a bad guy. I get it now. Wow.

PRODUCER 2: Oh my god.

BENNETT: Can we fast-forward to the end? I think this is it! I think Edie's The One!

PRODUCER 1: That's the byte. Let's wrap.

21

It was almost one a.m. by the time Edie Pepper descended the long staircase in her gown and heels and tottered over to the limo where Peter Kennedy was waiting. Most of production had already packed up and gone—Bennett Charles had been shoved into a van and ferried back to the mansion fifteen minutes ago—and it was just the two of them now, Peter and Edie, facing off under the streetlight. Peter held back a smile as she evaluated the black blazer he'd shrugged on over his oxford and the livery cap he'd placed at a jaunty angle on his head. He had his line all ready to go.

"Budget cuts," he said with a grin.

It took her a second, but then she laughed.

Peter swept open the door to the back seat with a chivalrous bow. "M'lady."

"You're gonna drive this thing?" Edie peered at him. "Do you even know how to drive?"

"Of course I know how to drive!"

"I've only ever seen you ferried around in the back of a Navigator in big sunglasses, like you're Lindsay Lohan or something."

"Pepper, you wound me. My sunglasses are appropriately sized. Now get in the car." He placed a hand on her warm back and ushered her toward the back seat.

"Aren't you the big, important showrunner?" she protested. "Don't you have other shit to do?"

He did, in fact, have other shit to do. And there were a million people paid to deal with things like driving contestants around, so Peter was free to deal with the shit he had to do. But for some reason, while he stood on the sidelines watching Edie on the monitors, he couldn't stop thinking about the hurt way she'd looked at him just before she fell out of the limo. Not to mention the pointed anger that had powered that punch to his gut. And as he'd brooded, watching Bennett hold Edie in his arms, suddenly Peter felt deeply unsettled. And because Peter didn't like to sit in a feeling for too long, and because he orchestrated over-the-top gestures for a living, this funny little chauffeur moment was almost instinctual in its conception. It hadn't been difficult to come up with. Or execute. Frankly, it was no big deal. Just Peter utilizing his talents to make things right between them, totally detached from feeling.

"Here I am, trying to do a nice thing, letting everyone leave early, and you insult me. I'll have you know I'm an excellent driver." He prepared to close the door behind her. "As long as we don't make any right turns, we'll be fine."

"Oh no," she said, struggling to get back out. "No way. If I'm dying tonight, I'll stare death in the face. I'm sitting up front with you."

"Fair enough." Peter trotted around and opened the passenger door.

"Why are you being so nice all of a sudden?" She looked around at the deserted street. "And where are the cameras? Where's Ted?"

"I'm always nice," he said, wounded.

"Sure you are, Mr. I-Went-to-Brown-and-Your-Beauty-Isn't-Intersectional."

"Still not over that?"

"Not quite."

"Have I mentioned how lovely you look tonight, Pepper? Everyone thinks so—"

"You're making it worse. Just get in the car."

But the way she said it—*just get in the car*—was like she was amused, and then his own misgivings—like the lingering confusion over why he'd gotten into that limo with her earlier, or why he'd insisted on Bailey for the next date when a decision like that clearly undermined everything they were working toward, or the way Jessa had looked at him when he announced he was going to drive Edie back to the mansion himself—faded away as Edie slid into the front seat and her dress split open, exposing her bare legs. Peter tried not to stare and instead closed the door behind her, running around to the other side, where he was immediately stabbed to death by the daggers Jessa was glaring at him from the top of the staircase. He tipped his cap to her and got in the car.

It took Peter a second to locate the ignition (fine, it had been years since he'd driven himself anywhere) and then he spent a stupid amount of time tweaking the mirrors because it felt like something Seth Rogen or John Krasinski would do when a cute girl was watching.

Finally, he turned the key. "Last chance to call an Uber."

"I don't even have a phone. You took it, remember?"

"Right," he said with a shrug. "Stuck with me, then."

Peter plunged the limo into drive, and they began making their way down the moonlit streets of Beverly Hills. While he hunched over the steering wheel, an unconvinced Edie flipped down the visor and felt around. Popped open the glove compartment and rifled through the registration papers, fast-food napkins, and breath mints. Knocked on the console, as if expecting a secret compartment to reveal itself.

"For real. Where'd you hide the cameras?"

"No cameras," he said, keeping his hands at ten and two and his eyes on the road. Now that the limo was in motion, the reality of his romcom-inspired gesture was hitting him. It would be a big problem if he crashed the limo. Fuck, he realized somewhat belatedly, eventually he'd have to get on the 405!

"You forget I'm a founding member of the Lady Dicks, Chicago's premier feminist true crime detective club. I've completed enough Hunt a Killer boxes to know everything's a play. What gives?"

"In fact, I haven't forgotten the Lady Dicks. Your description of the seven-layer dip is seared into my memory."

"Don't be judgy. You'd love a Midwestern potluck. So much cheese."

"I'm lactose intolerant."

"You would be."

He tore his eyes from the road and caught her smirking. "Savage," he said, shaking his head. They laughed.

"Seriously, Peter," she said, relaxing against the seat, "what's going on? You drive me home and I reveal my deepest, darkest secrets in some sort of hidden camera footage? And then you're free to go to the Chateau Marmont and smoke a doobie with Leonardo DiCaprio or whatever you Hollywood types do after work?"

He raised his brows. "'Smoke a doobie?' I didn't know you had that in you."

She smacked him in the arm.

"Careful, I'm driving!" They reached a stoplight and he turned to her. "Is it so hard to believe that I just wanted to do something nice for you?"

"Only you would categorize 'nice' as putting my life at risk when you clearly don't know how to drive." They stared at each other for a moment before Edie ripped the chauffeur cap from his head. "You can't fool me, Peter," she said, inspecting the cap for electronics. "Really? No cameras?"

"Really. No cameras."

"Well, in that case," she said, placing the cap on her head, "do you mind if I unzip this dress? I cannot fucking breathe."

"Whatever you need to do, my friend."

Peter watched through the corner of his eye as Edie edged the zipper down her back. When the light turned green, he turned his focus back to the road. Edie relaxed against the seat and closed her eyes with a sort of dreamy look on her face. The chauffeur cap slid down her forehead.

He cleared his throat. "You hungry?"

Her eyes popped open. "Oh my god, I'm starving. Why don't you people let a girl eat? It's very rude to put a plate of food in front of a person and then be like, talk about your feelings, but do not, no matter what, touch this chicken piccata."

"You'll thank me later when there's not a gif of you chomping into a cheeseburger all over the internet."

"For the right cheeseburger, it'd be worth it."

"There's one of those Taco Bells with the margaritas not too far from here. What do you think? *Yo quiero Nachos Bell Grande?*"

She was delighted by his reference to the Taco Bell ads of the late nineties. "That's my cat's name," she said, surprised. "Nacho Bell Grande."

"I know that's your cat's name, Pepper. That's why I suggested it. I do, in fact, listen when you talk."

She looked at him and he could feel the energy shifting from lighthearted truce into something more complex. "Tell me the truth," she said finally, her brow furrowed as much as her new Botox would allow. "After the whole volleyball thing—why'd you ignore me for three days and make me feel like you were mad at me, and then show up right before my one-on-one to make me feel shitty about a makeover that *you* supposedly wanted?"

"Edie. I'm the showrunner. I don't—*I can't*—produce individual contestants—"

"Oh, I know. You've mentioned the showrunner thing many times. It's very impressive." She flopped back in her seat, annoyed. "Except for some reason you were around a million times before, egging me on, giving me speeches about fighting for love, and then when something terrible happened, and you could've actually helped me, you let it be all my fault."

"Edie, c'mon." Without thinking he took one hand off the wheel and placed it on her leg, intending a sort of brotherly pat, but finding instead her thigh hot and bare and smooth. Suddenly Peter became aware of himself touching her, knowing he should *not* be touching her, except it felt surprisingly great to be touching her, and quickly he pulled his hand away. His heart was beating fast, and he was overcome by the need for the situation to be resolved, so he rocketed the limo over a curb and into a CVS parking lot.

"Look, Edie, what I was trying to tell you before, you're not like the other girls—"

"This again? Peter! I get it! You've already made the 'Edie isn't as good as the other girls' thing abundantly clear!"

"Will you just listen for a second!" he yelled.

She looked at him, wide-eyed.

Why the fuck was he yelling? Why did everything feel so fraught this season? What was he even doing here, driving around in the show's prop limo in the middle of the night with a contestant when he should be at home in bed reading or fucking Siobhan? She stared at him, waiting for him to speak.

"Look, I'm sorry," he said, finally landing on the only thing there really was to say. He was surprised to find himself actually meaning it. "I acted like a jerk. What I keep trying to say, and clearly keep saying all wrong, is that you're someone I could know in real life or something. You're like, a real person, and while I like that a lot, in the context of this show, it's changed things in a way that I find confusing, and sometimes, I'm a little slow to catch up. All right?" He paused. He was crossing all sorts of lines he knew better than to cross. Still, he kept going. "I'm sorry. I am. I should've checked on you after the volleyball game and before the makeover to make sure it was what you wanted. It wasn't my intention to make you feel stupid. If anything, earlier, I just wanted you to know that you don't need to change. Like, at all. I wanted to make sure you were okay. But I did it all wrong and it was shitty and I'm sorry."

She looked at him, her face inscrutable for the longest time, until he couldn't stand it.

"Edie, seriously! What more do you want? I stole a limo for you! I apologized! I want to take you to Taco Bell, which I realize isn't Nobu, but it's almost two in the morning and we both have to work tomorrow—"

"I'm going to provisionally accept this apology with the understanding that one"—she counted on her fingers—"you're not going to make me look or feel stupid again; two, you're going to stop disappearing because it makes it impossible to trust you; and three, in addition to the Nachos Bell Grande, I'm also going to need at least two Doritos Locos tacos. I'm not a ninety-pound vegan, and I don't want you to treat me like one."

Peter smiled. "Deal." He turned the key in the ignition, and it was only when he was steering the limousine *thunk thunk scrape* over a concrete parking divider that he remembered Carole Steele and the hospital strong-arming they'd just given Bennett, and for a split second while the limo descended, Peter wondered if he should mention the whole *You're going to propose to Edie or we're going to ruin your life* thing. But that would be insane. She would flip out. Never speak to him again. No, clearly the better plan was to continue manipulating everyone in the name of entertainment.

Fuck.

"One of everything!" Peter announced to the cashier, like he was Daddy Warbucks showing little orphan Annie the world.

The Taco Bell cashier stared at him, her sparkly purple eyelids stalled at a bored half-mast.

"God, Peter, don't be so embarrassing." Edie nudged him out of the way with her hip. "Don't mind him," she said to the cashier. "He's the type of person who drinks coffee made out of mushrooms. Can you believe that? Mushrooms! But you're from LA, of course you've seen it all." Edie and the cashier exchanged a look before Edie turned back to him. "You got guardrails, or should I really just order everything?"

Peter was about to explain that mushroom coffee was chock full of health benefits and also *delicious*, but then he realized he didn't want to be the annoying partial vegan with acid reflux issues who special-ordered his mushroom brew from Finland right now.

"Nope," he said. "Shoot your best shot, Pepper."

"I like your attitude, Kennedy. Now give me your credit card."

Peter dug out his wallet and handed over his AMEX.

"Don't forget the margaritas," he said, even though the thought of a margarita made his esophagus burn.

"You say you know me, but then think I could forget the margaritas." Edie shook her head before turning back to the cashier.

Peter dug a handful of Tums out of his pocket and walked through the empty restaurant to a plastic booth in the corner. He brushed the seats and table off with paper napkins, wondering how she knew about the mushroom coffee. Jessa? So they'd been talking about him. Great. Another fucking thing to be anxious about. He sat down. He needed to relax. Ever since he'd steered the limo over that parking divider, he'd been grossly overcompensating for the tightrope of lies he found himself on. But were they lies, exactly? Or completely normal, behind-the-scenes machinations *The Key* was built on? Edie walked toward him in a playful Jessica Rabbit slink, pointing one leg and then the other in her sexy black gown. She had a full tray, and his credit card was tucked into her cleavage.

"I got you margaritas *and* a Mountain Dew," she said mischievously, setting the tray on the table. "Just to see if your brain would explode."

"How thoughtful."

"I said to Sandra, 'Sandra, if it's neon green and full of sugar, he wants it.'" She handed him a plastic cup and straw. "Do the Dew, Peter," she laughed before sliding into the other side of the booth.

"I'm definitely going to regret this tomorrow, aren't I?"

"Probably. But we'll have fun tonight."

So, she was having fun. Peter relaxed a bit.

"Okay, I got us a bunch of stuff to share," Edie continued. "Doritos Locos, Nachos Bell Grande, Crunchwrap Supreme, extra margaritas because Sandra says liquor's done at three—"

"What the hell is a Crunchwrap Supreme?"

"You're thinking about it too hard, Peter. Trust me, as soon as all that trans fat hits your tongue, serotonin's gonna flood your brain and you're gonna be on your knees thanking me."

Out of nowhere, an image of Peter on his knees with his head up her dress, thanking her, came to mind. He choked on his Mountain Dew.

"Are you okay?"

"Great," he sputtered, trying to recover himself. "What flavor is this anyway? What do they call it?"

"I'm not sure. Original flavor? Mountain Dew flavor? Let me taste it." Edie took the plastic cup, and he watched her wrap her lips around the straw. "Mmm...it tastes exactly like what sunshine would taste like if it were caffeinated and bubbled and poured into a glass. It's perfection."

"While I appreciate your thoughtfulness," he said, unwrapping a taco, "I think I'll stick to the margarita."

"Suit yourself." She shrugged.

Peter took a sip of the margarita and held himself back from exhaling a stream of fire as the acid hit his throat. Maybe Jessa was right—maybe it was time to see a doctor. Most likely it was an ulcer that was going to explode one day and kill him. Maybe tonight. Peter looked at Edie, happily munching on a taco, and had the strange thought that if he died eating junk food with her, maybe it wouldn't be the worst way to go.

"So," he said, throwing caution to the wind and squirting fire sauce on his dinner. "Tonight seemed to go well."

"It was great," she said, pulling a chip from their Nachos Bell Grande.

"It was great? That's all you have to say? Do you know how long it took the set designers to hang those balloons?"

"I thought you wanted me to save all my reactions for the cameras?"

"I just wanted to know if you're in *looooooooove*," he singsonged.

She paused, taco mid-mouth, and stared at him.

"What?" he asked.

She stared.

"What? Why are you giving me such a hard time?"

She put down her taco and fixed him with a steady gaze. "Because you deserve it."

"I thought we made up."

"You hate being wrong, don't you?"

"In what way?"

"Well, you were pretty certain Bennett could never fall for a girl like me, and I think it's pretty clear after tonight that he does like me and that you were wrong." She took her straw out of her empty margarita and placed it triumphantly in a new one.

"Hmm..." Peter said, sucking down the rest of his drink. Even if his throat was on fire, he wanted to keep up with her. "Not exactly. Maybe I thought that at the beginning, but I changed my mind a while ago. It was you who wasn't so sure."

Edie harumphed. "Me? Please. I've always known what Charlie and I have."

"You said Charlie."

"So?"

Peter shrugged. "I'm just saying—Charlie isn't Bennett."

"Oh, whatever," she said, tossing a crumpled wrapper at him. "You're insufferable. Bennett, Charlie, they both like me now."

Peter laughed. "That they do."

They were silent for a moment, and then Edie looked at him seriously. "Tell me the truth. Did you just want me on the show so you could make me look like an idiot?"

Her gray eyes looked very pretty under the fluorescent lights. He could lie, of course. But what was the point? He already had too many secrets.

"Edie, I'm a reality TV producer. Of course I did." He put down his margarita. "But it isn't like that anymore. If anything, you make the show seem sort of idiotic, not you."

"I'm sure you say that to all the girls," she said laughing, swatting him on the wrist.

"I don't, actually. Just you. You're special."

"Stop saying that!" she exclaimed. "When you say 'special,' you mean 'weird' or 'quirky,' and all I've ever wanted my entire life was just to be like everyone else."

"Really?" he said, curious. "Why?"

She laughed. "I don't even know anymore!" She twisted her mass of hair up into a bun and secured it with the straight end of a plastic fork. "I blame my parents. They were old when they had me and never paid much attention, and I just felt like if I could be a cheerleader or homecoming queen, it would make everything okay." She covered her face with her hands. "Which is, like, intensely embarrassing now, being here, after an extreme makeover. Like, I'm a full adult person, doing the same shit over and over again, expecting different results."

He thought about it for a moment. "I've only ever wanted to be exceptional."

She looked at him like he was crazy. "Aren't you?"

"Definitely not."

"I'd hate to know what you think unexceptional is." She pursed her lips, finishing her margarita. "You seem pretty exceptional to me."

"I do?"

"Peter, you run marathons and helm one of the biggest shows on network television. What more do you want?"

Peter stared at her, dumbfounded. He'd never felt like a successful person. He was divorced. He'd given up on his dream to be a writer. He barely called his parents or made time for his friends. When she started laughing, his own ridiculousness made him laugh, too. He didn't even care that they were being loud and obnoxious, and suddenly Peter had a strange feeling like he was seeing her for the first time. Her sort-of-too-big smile radiated this unmitigated joy that was not only beautiful but looked like something Peter himself had never been unselfconscious enough to experience.

But he wanted to.

"This is nice," she said, gesturing vaguely at the restaurant, their table, him. "It's the first time I've felt like my actual self in a while."

"It is nice," he said, staring at her for long enough that he got uncomfortable and decided he needed to do something else. He started organizing the Taco Bell detritus back onto the tray.

"Oh my god, this song." She pointed to the speaker attached to the ceiling. "I *love* this song."

Peter stopped and listened. Phil Collins. "Sussudio." "Phil and I are birthday buddies."

"What does that mean?"

"It means we share a birthday."

"Stop it."

"It's true. January thirtieth. When I was in college, I used to throw him a birthday party every year."

"You threw Phil Collins a birthday party? But not yourself? Do they even allow parties at Brown?"

He laughed. "Only if they're for Phil Collins."

"Did you get Phil a cake?"

"Of course. With 'Happy Birthday, Phil!' on it. And, you know, eighties costumes, Genesis blasting from the speakers, that sort of thing."

"I'm confused," she said, leaning over the table to peer at him. "'Cause that sounds awesome. Peter Kennedy, are you trying to tell me that at one point in time, you were..." She paused dramatically. *"Fun?"*

"Oh, I'm fucking fun," he said. And then—perhaps because the margaritas had hit him just right—he wanted to prove to her just how fun he was. He jumped up, caught the beat, and started dancing right next to their table, shaking his ass and lip synching all the big notes. She watched bug-eyed until he dragged her up from the booth, and then they were both breaking it down, right in the middle of Taco Bell.

"What the hell is a Sussudio anyway?" she asked, mid-sprinkler.

"I think it's the girl's name?" he said, doing his best running man. "But I've never met a Sussudio so it's hard to know."

"Google it!"

He watched her do the robot. "How are you single? You're a total catch."

"Shut up!"

"Don't you want to ask why I'm single?" he asked, adding imaginary apples to an imaginary shopping cart.

"Nope. Checks out."

He laughed and took her hand and spun her around. Her black gown was halfway unzipped, and the hem swirled in the air as she whirled. He pulled her to him until they were most definitely dancing together, sometimes touching, sometimes pulling away just for the delight of coming back together again.

It felt like the most fun he'd had in years. And when the song ended, and their bodies were pressed together, and she was looking up at him with her lips softly parted—for a moment he thought he might kiss her.

"Does this mean we're friends now?" she asked finally. She took a step back.

He could feel his face morph from the exuberance he'd felt just a second ago to something softer, a little hurt. Yes. Friendship. Friendship was the only option. Or, well, not even an option—he shouldn't be friends with her. He shouldn't be *anything* with her. Fuck, was he drunk?

"Friends," he said, putting a palm up for a high-five. "What else would we be?" He shook his head, trying to clear it. "I'll call an Uber."

22

Edie floated into the *Key* mansion on a cloud of dopamine.

How many of her thirty-five years had she wasted feeling not good enough? Not pretty enough, not thin enough, not cute and sweet and adorable enough? But after tonight, Edie Pepper was *done* with all that. Suddenly *anything* was possible. She was beautiful! Gorgeous! Sexy! The star of her very own romcom! She was *magic*. Everything seemed to sparkle as Edie twirled around the foyer on numb toes—so what if the fairy-tale stilettos *were* sort of excruciating? An entire night spent in Bennett's arms!

And then, strangely... *Peter's*?

Edie was too exhausted to think about that now. She was determined to stay in her dreamy haze for as long as possible. It didn't matter if teams of people had orchestrated every single romantic moment. Or that she was supposed to call Charlie "Bennett." Or that absolutely nothing like this had ever—or would ever—happen to her again. Because right now Edie understood why girls all over the world were obsessed with Cinderella. Going to the ball felt fucking great.

Edie skipped up the stairs on her maimed feet to the room she'd been sharing with Max since they'd become besties after the volleyball game. Max's previous roommate, Kimberlee, had been eliminated the night Edie arrived. It felt so long ago now, like everything had changed and would change again. Edie opened the bedroom door and a dart whizzed past her head.

"Oh, shit, sorry!" Max called from her bed.

The weirdest thing about the *Key* mansion was that it was actually somebody's home, leased to production twice a year—a sort of showbiz Airbnb. Max and Edie had the tween boy room, sports themed, with Lakers bedding, beanbag chairs in the shape of baseballs, framed jerseys, and a dartboard on the back of the door. Max loved shooting darts from her bed and kept a cup of missiles on her nightstand.

Edie pulled the dart out of the carpet. "What are you doing up?"

"Couldn't sleep," Max said, taking the dart from Edie. "Probably because I was too excited to hear about your super-special-fantasy-one-on-one date! Squee!"

"Liar." Edie laughed. She shut the door and flopped onto her bed. One of her extensions stabbed her skull. She wriggled a pillow underneath her head. "But I'm thrilled you're up because obviously I'm dying to talk about it."

"Obviously." Max turned on her side to give Edie her full attention. "So, let's hear it. Was it everything you ever wanted?"

"And more," Edie said dreamily. And then she launched into a no-detail-too-small play by play—the Goo Goo Dolls, the dancing, the portraits, the champagne, the *kissing*. But as she described Bennett Charles on his knees, holding her face in his hands, kissing her until she thought she might rip his clothes off right then and there, suddenly Edie realized she was being insensitive. "Max, my god. I'm being an asshole." Edie sat up. "I've never dated the same guy as my friends before—do you even want to hear this?"

"Edie," Max said, shaking her head. "It's fine. Obviously, I'm a lesbian."

"Wait, *what*?" Edie jumped up. She grabbed her pillow and hit Max with it. "You're a lesbian? This whole time? My best friend in the whole entire world is a lesbian! I can't believe you didn't tell me."

But Max was laughing too hard to speak. Tears were forming in the corners of her eyes as she fended off Edie's pillow assault.

"That's the first time I've said it out loud!" Max marveled. "I thought I was bi. Or pan. Or sapio. But Bennett's sealed the deal. I've been thinking about it all night. I'm definitely a lesbian."

"Oh my god." Edie dropped the pillow and enveloped Max in a hug. "I'm so happy for you."

Luckily Max had a bottle of cocktail party pinot squirreled away in the closet. They sat on the floor between their beds and passed it back and forth while Max revealed everything. Her mom, an ardent Christian and die-hard *Key* fan, had nominated her for the show.

"At first, I was annoyed. But then I figured, why not? I'd torn my meniscus and couldn't compete for six months. And it seemed like maybe Bennett and I had a lot in common—sports, camping, whatever—so why not give it a shot? It felt like a win-win: Sharon gets to tell her friends I'm straight; I give men one last shot. But I have to tell you, and I've thought about it *a lot*." Max took Edie's hands in hers and gave her a serious look. "Men are *awful*."

Edie nodded vigorously. "They *are* awful!"

"Have you listened to Bennett talk?" Max continued. "Like really listened? I'm pretty sure I've never heard him say *anything* that wasn't directly about him."

"He's not that bad," Edie protested. "I think he's cute. And the way he talks about the world—I never thought I wanted to ride a camel across the Sahara. But now, maybe I do!"

"I should've done *The Challenge.*" Max took a swig of the wine. "I would've killed on *The Challenge.*"

This night was truly wild. Edie couldn't get over it. Max was a lesbian and Edie was a full-grown woman dating her high school boyfriend on TV. But, ugh, now that Max pointed it out, it *was* sort of impossible to ignore just how much Bennett talked about himself—about his travels, his wellness, his future plans—and just how little he asked her about herself, her life, her goals. Her plan had been to ignore it! Focus on the green flags, not the red ones. But as the glow began to fade, Edie wondered about its origins. Was the euphoria she was experiencing because of Bennett? Or something else? And then there was that other thing she was trying to avoid. That inexplicable moment at Taco Bell where—*just for a second*—Peter had looked like he might kiss her. She didn't want to think about it because if she *did* think about it, she'd have to wonder if she'd done the absolute stupidest thing she could ever do and developed a crush on the *showrunner*, a man so far out of her league he might as well be Idris Elba while she was, well, *herself*, Edie Pepper, a normal person. But what *was* that? His hands on the small of her back, Edie gazing up into his face and finding a relaxed, happy version of Peter, pulling her closer, the length of their bodies touching.

"Max, can I tell you the weirdest thing? You have to promise that you won't tell anyone."

"Pinky swear."

"Okay, look, I know I can be delusional," Edie began as they joined pinkies, "but after the prom, Peter was there. With a limo. To drive me home."

"By himself?" she asked, curious.

Edie nodded. "And then we went to Taco Bell and ate nachos and sort of had the best time? It's so weird. I don't know what to make of it."

"I do." Max scoffed like it was the most obvious thing in the world. "He likes you."

"Oh my god, he does *not*."

"This makes me like Peter more. He's got taste. Who knew?"

"Max, be serious. Look at him. He's gorgeous. He's rich. Jessa says he dates *models*. He's the *showrunner*. He can't like *me*."

"So?" Max shrugged. "You're gorgeous. Maybe not rich, but you're employed. And you're funny and smart and kind, and honestly, he'd be lucky to go out with you. You're a catch."

"I'm drunk." Edie took another swig of wine. "I'm doing that thing where I fantasize things into being that aren't there. That's how I ended up on this show in the first place! I'm here to get engaged to *Bennett*."

"You don't seem that drunk." Max pursed her lips in thought. "Here's what I think: Besides making new friends, the best part about being here—about being away from our whole lives—is that it's *clarifying*. And here's what I know for sure." She paused dramatically. "Bennett's an idiot."

They burst out laughing. Bennett *was* sort of an idiot. But wasn't he also adorable? And wasn't his idiocy just insecurity weaseling its way out? It was charming. When they were talking about how they first met, Edie could tell he was nervous that she might say something that might not fit into this whole world he was building. And she just wanted to tell him, *Charlie, you're fine, it's all fine.* But she didn't even have to because he'd recovered, all on his own. And then they'd had that moment of connection over the kindergarten cafeteria, and it was a moment you couldn't really even explain to someone else. It was just this *knowing*.

But then something occurred to Edie.

"Wait, does this mean you're leaving the show?" she asked, a little hysterical. Edie crawled over to Max's side of the room and plopped down beside her. "Because I don't want you to leave. I need you here." She hooked her arm through Max's and laid her head on Max's shoulder.

"Please." Max laid her head on top of Edie's. "I'm going on whatever the big trip is. I've come all this way, and Bennett Charles owes me an adventure."

"You know, my best friend Lauren, she might be perfect for you," Edie began.

"Pepper, don't do that thing where you try to set me up with the only other lesbian you know."

"She's pretty great though." Edie elbowed Max in the side. "Just sayin'."

TAKE 5 PRODUCTIONS
THE KEY
ZO SNEAKS INTO BENNETT'S ROOM
TAPE #412

00:00:00 THE MIDDLE OF THE NIGHT. A KNOCK AT THE DOOR.

ZO: I'll never stop fighting for Bennett's heart.

THE DOOR OPENS. BENNETT BLINKING, CONFUSED, IN HIS UNDERWEAR.

ZO: Can I come in?

ZO AND BENNETT ON THE BED. SHE SLITHERS ALL OVER HIM.

ZO: I had to see you.

BENNETT: Mmm...

ZO: I couldn't stand it anymore, knowing you were with *her*.

BENNETT: Trust the process. Believe in us.

ZO HOLDS HIS FACE IN HER HANDS.

ZO: I'm falling in love with you.

He doesn't say anything for a moment.

BENNETT: I think I'm falling in love with you, too.

THEY MAKE OUT. IT'S STEAMY.

BENNETT: You have to trust the process. I know it's hard, but everything will become clear.

ZO: That's not the only thing that's hard.

ZO STARTS KISSING HIM ALL OVER.

BENNETT: You should go. People will be mad.

ZO'S HAND WANDERS INTO BLACK BOX TERRITORY.

ZO: You don't want me to stay?

BENNETT MOANS. THE CAMERA BACKS OUT OF THE ROOM. BENNETT MOANS AGAIN.

23

The final eight girls—Edie, Bailey, Max, Lily, Zo, Aspen, Parker, and McKayla—were back on the risers, waiting for Bennett to arrive so the key ceremony could begin. It struck Edie that with their bodies angled toward center just so, their hands clasped at the waists of their plunging gowns, they looked like a choir. Edie watched McKayla slide a hand down the front of her dress and hoist a boob back into place. Well, maybe a slutty choir. And if this were *Glee*, this would be the moment when they'd all burst into Ariana Grande's

Break up with your girlfriend
Yeah yeah, 'cause I'm bored

More tongue-in-cheek musical numbers—that's what the show needed. Just thinking about suggesting it to Peter made Edie smile.

"Who do you think's going home tonight?" Bailey whispered, looking particularly elegant in an off-the-shoulder cobalt gown that highlighted her blond hair, blue eyes, and tanned skin.

Max and Lily turned from their spots in the front row. Max also looked amazing in a sleek black jumpsuit, her lavender hair blown into a pompadour, and Lily was serving ethereal beauty in a cream maxi dress with her long hair parted down the middle, framing the adorable spray of freckles across her nose. As part of her makeover, Edie had been gifted a new wardrobe, and tonight she'd chosen an asymmetrical Norma Kamali dress that ruched from her right shoulder down to her left calf like a chic five-hundred-dollar toga.

"Definitely not us," Max said.

They nodded. Definitely not them.

"I hope it's Zo," Bailey said.

They gasped—Bailey *never* talked shit about the other girls. Zo was clearly this season's villain, but Edie was under the impression that when the cameras were off, Bailey actually liked Zo. They did yoga together. Shared chia seeds.

"Why? What's up with Zo?" Edie asked, but before Bailey could answer, the doors opened, and Bennett and Peter strode in. Bennett looked stupid handsome in his slim-cut gray suit, that intense key ceremony look in his eyes. Peter was more relaxed in chinos cuffed over white high-top Converse and a soft navy sweater. He had his hands shoved in his back pockets, pulling the sweater tight against his lean runner's bod. When he caught her eye, he smiled.

"She was in Bennett's room last night," Bailey whispered, dragging Edie's attention away from Peter's chest. "She didn't come back 'til this morning. McKayla saw her walk of shame right through the kitchen."

The girls gasped again.

"It's not like Zo owes us anything," Bailey continued. "But it's totally against the rules, you know? And she told Aspen how *adventurous* he was." She leaned in to whisper. "She was talking about sex!"

Jaws dropped. Sex on *The Key* wasn't totally unheard of, but it *was* totally scandalous. The sort of thing that made the season promos and was teased every single week until the climax. (Literally.) They collectively turned to look at Zo. Her tiny body was Saran-wrapped in a nude-illusion gown studded with Swarovski crystals. She twinkled her fingers at Bennett.

Bailey wiped a burgeoning tear from her eye. "Yesterday we were in the hot tub, and everything was perfect and special and…he said he was falling in love with me."

Edie put her arm around Bailey. The stages of love on *The Key* were: crazy about you, falling for you, falling in love, and *in love*. It made sense that Charlie would already be falling in love with Bailey—who wouldn't fall in love with Bailey? Still, the fact that he'd said it to her and not to Edie made her feel sort of sick.

"Oh, honey, don't cry, your lash is going to fall off," Lily said.

"It just makes me feel weird about Bennett," Bailey said, wiping her eyes. "And then if you start thinking about any of it too much…"

Edie knew *exactly* what Bailey meant. She supposed it was inevitable that the euphoria of prom night would fade—no one could live in peak romance every moment of every day—but as it had ebbed, all sorts of questions and thoughts and feelings had risen to take its place. And she found if she considered any of them, it was a quick spiral back into *what the fuck was she doing here?* Charlie was on dates with other women—apparently sleeping with them and saying he was in love with them—while she'd sat around for a week pondering their *connection*. Truly, it was better not to think. Because if she thought about any of it—Bennett Charles making out with other girls, which one of her friends she'd have to crush to win his heart, how Alice was going to react to Edie dry humping on TV, or the very secret way Edie was constantly scanning the set for Peter—it all fell apart.

"Rolling," the lead camera op yelled.

"Speeding," the sound guy responded.

The ceremony began.

"When I started this journey, I'd been traveling the globe for years," Bennett began. Edie turned to look at him standing next to that stupid pedestal of keys. "And I'd begun to think my match didn't exist." *Surely he wouldn't sleep with Zo*, Edie thought. Not when Edie was here. Not when Bailey was here. "I said to myself, where is she? Nigeria? Tanzania? Bangkok? Amsterdam? London? Tennessee? But I'd already checked those places and didn't find her." Edie studied Charlie's face—sort of generically handsome, like an idea of handsome, rather than a distinct person she knew or understood. Suddenly the pomp and circumstance, the keys, the girls, the solemn name calling, and one man anointing them one by one felt very, very wrong. "But now I think everything is exactly as it should be because she's right here, right now, in this room tonight." Their eyes met, and for the first time, picturing a life with Charlie seemed impossible. "What an incredible feeling."

24

The hot topic of conversation as the cast boarded the plane to Scotland was: where in the world was Bennett Charles? Because no one had seen him at the gate. And he certainly wasn't crammed into coach with the six remaining contestants and the production crew. And he wasn't with Peter and Jessa in business, either—Aspen had already snuck around the curtain to check. Without their phones, social media, or even a book to distract them, the girls were obsessed. *Where was Bennett?*

"Maybe he's on a different flight?" McKayla posited.

"You fucking think?" Zo huffed.

Edie, however, wasn't thinking about Charlie at all because she'd not only scored an entire row to herself at the back of the plane, but also an *Us Weekly* from a flight attendant.

"I don't know how you can read that stuff," a voice from above said once they'd reached cruising altitude. "I can't get through the first page without my face melting off from the heat of my own superiority."

Edie looked up and there was Peter leaning against the empty seat across the aisle.

"While I appreciate the attempt at self-awareness," she said, "I don't believe for a second you're not interested in Demi Lovato's new collab with Fabletics."

Peter laughed. "Just don't let the boss catch you with contraband. I heard he's a real dick."

"The worst," she agreed. "But I swear to god, Peter, if you confiscate this magazine, I will pop the emergency hatch and sail off into the atmosphere."

"Well, we can't have that." Peter moved out of the aisle so the flight attendant and her drink cart could get through. "You might as well tell me what it says about the show." He plopped down in the empty seat across from Edie. The space was too small for his long legs and Edie watched as he folded, crossed, and shifted his body around, trying to make it work.

"You gonna be okay? Coach life isn't for everyone."

Peter settled on pressing his knees into the seatback with his spine straight and his feet flat on the floor. He clapped his palms on his thighs and looked around, nodding as he took in the glory of coach. "I think I can handle it. I'm tougher than I look, Pepper."

"Are you, though?"

"What's the litmus? Bennett Charles? 'Cause I have it on good authority he's not as tough as he looks. And that authority is me."

"Who breaks their nose at a volleyball game they're not even playing in?"

"Edie," Peter said seriously. "I've been telling Jessa that for weeks."

They smiled at each other until the vibe shifted from an innocent pleasure at being together into an uncomfortable awareness of that pleasure. Edie looked away first, flipping the magazine to "Wyatt Cash is 'Thrilled' for Bennett Charles, Reveals Top *Key* Picks" before handing it across the aisle.

"Spoiler alert: Bailey, Zo, and Aspen are the frontrunners for the extreme sportsman's heart."

"Well," Peter said with a conspiratorial look, "*US Weekly* hasn't met you yet." He gave the sidebar a once-over before tossing the magazine back to her. "It's amazing what they'll report. When I worked on *Survivor*, a contestant broke his tooth in half, spit it out, kept playing, and no one would pick it up. The story, not the tooth. But if a *Key* girl walks into a Starbucks, everyone goes nuts."

"Tabloids are all about fantasy, Peter. No one wants to read about a toothless guy who hasn't showered in a month. Not when there's Gwyneth Paltrow's seaweed cleanse or JLo's strength routine or Zendaya's Oscars outfit."

"Don't forget Bennett's weightlifting manifesto," Peter added. "I'm sure that's a fascinating read. Lots of tips on how to boil chicken. Where to buy cargo shorts. And, oh, how to craft an entire personality around stanning Bear Grylls."

"Tell me how you really feel."

"He's *your* boyfriend."

Edie looked away.

Was Bennett Charles her boyfriend?

The cabin lights dimmed. After a moment, Peter said he'd better head back to his seat, that she should sleep, long flight. But then the flight attendant appeared and offered them a nightcap, and next thing you know, Peter was sipping bourbon with a blanket smoothed over his legs, his shoes were off, and the toe of one Converse was sticking into the aisle the tiniest bit. Edie was cozy, too, with her hair piled on the top of her head and an eye mask strapped across her forehead. She had her UW-Madison hoodie on. Her armrests were up, and her legs were tucked onto the seat next to her as she leaned toward him.

They'd been asking each other the most ridiculous questions—favorite Backstreet Boy (Brian), best iteration of a potato (a tie between french fries and mashed)—and their shared hot takes were really making her laugh.

"Okay, I've got a good one," Edie said, pointing her bourbon at him. "What's the best Tom Hanks movie?"

"Oh, that *is* a good one."

"Lotta choices."

"Lotta choices," he agreed. "And a lotta *good* choices, which you can't say about every actor. Canonical choices. *Philadelphia. A League of Their Own. Cast Away. Sleepless in Seattle. Forrest Gump.* You know there's a coalition of people who hate *Forrest Gump*? It's not a cool film to like these days."

"Are you going with *Gump*?"

"Calm down, Pepper, I haven't made my selection yet." Peter aped a series of thinking poses—stroking a nonexistent beard, taking his glasses off and holding them to the light, rubbing them on his sweater, putting them back on. "You want just one movie or top five?"

"Just one."

"You're tough, Pepper, you're tough. This is the legendary Tom Hanks we're talking about." Finally, Peter clapped his hands together. "Okay! I've scoured my internal IMDB, and I feel confident in my answer. Ready?"

"I've been ready," she said, casually polishing off her bourbon.

"Big."

Edie froze. "Are you serious?"

"Houston, do we have a problem?" he asked. "That was an *Apollo 13* reference, by the way. You're welcome."

"No problem," she said. She just really couldn't believe he'd said *Big*. When Edie asked this question as her icebreaker on dating apps, she was always looking for a guy who said *Big*.

Or *The Money Pit*. Or *Toy Story*. *You've Got Mail.* Or even *The Post*, because a journalist with principles was a very sexy thing. But all the time it was just *Saving Private Ryan*, *Saving Private Ryan*. To Edie, *Saving Private Ryan* indicated this macho sense that emotion could only be expressed if a man was pushed to his absolute limit. But Edie's worldview was not about staring straight at the worst of humanity—war and death, brotherhood and love only in the face of war and death. Essentially what Edie wanted was Tom Hanks himself—or at least what he embodied to her—reaching out and touching all the possibilities of human experience from a place of good humor and an idealistic certainty that everything would work out in the end.

"It's just that *Big* is the perfect answer." She shrugged, nonchalant.

"Pew, pew, pew!" Peter said, shooting dorky lasers in the air with his fingers. "I knew it. It's that piano scene. And the trampoline he's got in the middle of that Tribeca loft. And how complicated adults make things when kids just *get it*. And it's sweet, but not too sweet. Just the right amount of sweet."

"Peter, that's exactly right," Edie said, astounded by this meeting of minds. "You know, you can tell a lot about a person from their favorite Tom Hanks film."

"Oh yeah? What can you tell about me?"

She smiled. "That you're sweet, but not too sweet. Just the right amount of sweet."

He threw an airline pillow at her.

"*Big* makes sense for you, though. It's a love story, but a platonic one." She put the pillow behind her head and stared into the darkened cabin. "About a boy who gets in over his head, but he's got the love of his best friend, he's got the love of his mother waiting for him back home, so when it counts, he can see what he's made of." She leveled her gaze back to Peter. "None of that romantic love stuff you don't believe in."

"First of all, wrong. There's a very creepy love story between Tom Hanks as twelve-year-old Josh and Elizabeth Perkins as thirtysomething toy exec Susan. Second, when did I say that about love?"

"Oh, I don't know. Maybe that time you gave me a speech about dead people on Tinder."

He scoffed. Then winced.

He took his glasses off and rubbed his face with both hands.

"Are you getting me?" He peeked at her through his fingers. "Don't get me."

"Too late." She cocked her head at him. "What's the deal with you, anyway? You were married?"

"I was married," Peter confirmed, dropping his hands. He put his glasses back on and took the little red straw out of his bourbon, twisting it around his finger until the skin went white. "For six years. Julie. It didn't end well. Well, I guess it did for her. She's with someone else now."

"I'm sorry."

"Yeah. Well." He drank the rest of his bourbon.

"You can have feelings, you know. I won't tell."

"Promise?" he said with a grin. He looked down at his tray table and sighed. "I think I'm just realizing how much I shut down after my divorce—how much I threw myself into work so I wouldn't have to think about it. And I was angry, you know? Just the maddest producer of love stories in the world." He looked out the window, and then back at her. His eyes were sad, and Edie felt very aware of his physical presence. If she reached her hand across the aisle, she could touch him. "I don't feel great about that," he continued. "I've been thinking about my past, about love. Maybe it's time for me to change." He noticed how she was folded up into herself, listening to him intently, with her arms pulled into her sweatshirt and her hood up. "You cold?"

"A little."

"Take my blanket."

"Oh, I have one in the overhead bin. I just have to get up and get it."

"This one's already unwrapped." He stood and fluttered his blanket over her, wrapping her up in his nice Peter-y smell. He sat back down. "But what about you? Weren't you with someone before this?"

"Brian," she said.

Edie sighed. The one thing she *had* been letting herself think about—finally—was Brian. About how there'd been red flags, starting with the fact that he'd only been separated from his wife for two months when they'd met. And how separated was he? He'd been living in the basement. Edie wasn't an idiot; she knew from the beginning that everything with Brian was high-risk. But she'd just wanted it so badly. And so she'd steamrolled ahead until she got her heart broken. And then Charlie Bennett had been on TV.

"I think maybe I'm the opposite of you," Edie said. "When Brian and I broke up, I threw myself back out there immediately. All the apps. All the dates. And then the first chance I got, I flung myself all the way to Los Angeles."

Edie shut her eyes and pulled the blanket closer. The breakup with Brian had always been about more than just Brian. But it was a hard thing to admit, because wanting Brian, wanting Charlie, wanting love...if she really thought about it, she could find her desire for a partner deeply embarrassing. Because her desire for love coupled with the persistent absence of love always brought Edie back to the painful conclusion that it must be her—that there must be something wrong with *her*.

"I've always just wanted this very simple thing, you know?" The intimacy of the darkened cabin made it easy for her to tell him the truth of it. "Love. And I just don't understand why I can't have it."

"Maybe because it's not simple at all," he said. His eyes were green with little flecks of gold. "Maybe love isn't this thing we stumble into one day. Maybe you have to wait for it. And maybe that's what makes it special."

25

When Edie Pepper imagined herself on *The Key*, she was always bathed in a gorgeous, diffused light, sliding a Tiffany rock onto a perfectly manicured finger. Not sitting around all day at some theater in Scotland with her sister wives, not only still single but also unbelievably bored, her nails chewed to bits.

"My feet hurt," Edie proclaimed into the ether, just to say *something*, do *something*.

"That's because for once your shoes don't look like they were made for a gnome," Zo said, rising from a downward dog. "Those Birkenstocks make me ill."

"This is where I get confused." Edie struggled to sit up on the gear cart she'd been sprawled across for the last hour. "I thought Birkenstocks were in? Don't the cool kids wear them?"

"You're not a cool kid."

"Point taken. But just wait till you're thirty-five. Plantar fasciitis sneaks up on a bitch."

"News flash: I'm a ballerina." Zo pirouetted across the floor to prove it. She landed near the craft services table. "I know about feet."

"Then why are you always wearing stilettos!" Edie demanded. "They're bad for you!"

"Because I'm five-two, and unlike you, I care if I look like a troll on TV." Zo picked at the food trays. "What do you do anyway?"

"Like, my job?"

"Yes, like your job."

"I'm a copywriter."

Zo curled her lip. "Gross."

Edie laughed. "Yeah, I guess it is sort of gross. Not the sort of thing dreams are made of."

"Too bad, so sad."

Edie let out a dramatic sigh. "Seriously, when are they going to be done?"

They turned to stare at Bennett and Bailey, who were learning a traditional Scottish fling on the other side of the theater. Bennett had the hem of his kilt tucked into his waistband, and his bare butt had been on display for at least ten minutes. The first time he'd pulled this trick—literally this morning, walking down Victoria Street with his string of girlfriends on the Edinburgh group date—it had been sort of funny. But now that they'd been filming for *hours*, it seemed decidedly not funny at all. The day felt interminable because they were constantly stopping for little one-on-one scenes. The Scottish fling with Bailey. Bennett feeding Max a hog roll. Watching Bennett and Zo get sorted into Hogwarts houses at a coffee shop where J. K. Rowling wrote parts of *Harry Potter*. (Zo was a Slytherin, obviously.) And now, with nothing to read, nothing to do, and no way to leave, Edie was so bored she could scream.

"Jealous?" Zo asked, nodding at the happy couple.

Edie considered. "Not really? Maybe. I don't know." She looked at Zo. "You?"

"I don't get jealous." Zo popped a cherry tomato into her mouth. "Bennett can get on this train or not. Either way I'm going."

"Going where?"

"To the top."

"The top of where?"

"Oh my god, Edie, are you brain damaged?" Zo dropped a carrot back on the tray in disgust. "I didn't spend twenty years of my life dancing twelve hours a day, living off string cheese and almonds, not to *be someone*. Maybe I can't dance professionally, but I'm still a star."

"I love that."

"Don't make fun of me."

"I'm not making fun of you!" Edie joined Zo at the table. If anyone had what it took, it was Zo. "I'm serious—I think you're fierce. How old are you anyway? Twenty-five?"

"Twenty-four."

"Exactly. When I was twenty-four, I was wasting my time at dead-end jobs and having way too many Samantha Jones–inspired one-night stands that never—*ever*—turned out like Sam promised." Edie shuddered at the memory. "I admire the way you know what you want. And that you're not afraid to go get it."

"Who's Samantha Jones?"

Edie's entire life flashed before her eyes.

"I'm kidding. We had *Sex and the City* in preschool, Grandma. But just so we're clear"—Zo pointed a celery stick at Edie—"I don't need you to admire me."

"Of course you don't." But for the first time Edie wondered if Zo *did* care about her opinion. "Don't be so defensive. It's not always a competition."

"Wrong. *The Key*, Hollywood, ballet—it's all the same. There's only one spot at the top, and everyone wants it. And the people with heart will do *anything* to get it."

Maybe at the beginning Edie believed that, but now? Edie spent more time hanging out and laughing with the other contestants than she ever did with Charlie. "That sounds like some real 'clear eyes, full hearts, can't lose' bullshit to me," Edie said. "Don't you think it's more complicated than that?"

"Maybe you need more ambition." Zo crossed her arms over her chest and looked at Edie thoughtfully. "You could do more, you know. I've seen you on the monitors. You're good on camera. There's something charming about you. Not hot, but charming."

"Zo," Edie paused dramatically. "Are we becoming *friends*?"

"No."

"We're definitely friends." Edie slung an arm around Zo's tiny shoulders. "And since we're besties now, I think I should tell you that there are a lot of rumors about just how far you'd go to get engaged to Bennett."

Zo shrugged her off. "I've never lied about why I'm here."

"So it's true?"

"What?"

"You know what I mean…"

"Actually, I don't."

"God," Edie said, exasperated. "I heard that you"—she made a circle out of one hand and stabbed it with a finger as she stage-whispered—"*fucked him*."

"Oh, you did, did you?" Zo threw her head back and laughed. "Well, I'll tell you a secret. We didn't fuck because he came, like, the second I touched his dick."

Edie gasped. "Shut. Up."

Zo smirked. "It's true."

But before Edie could process this revelation against her own sexual knowledge of Charlie Bennett, Aspen and Max scuttled around the lighting equipment and joined them.

"You guys," Aspen whispered, "check this out!" Max pulled a bottle of Scotch from behind her back. "I got that hot camera guy, Derek, to buy it for us!"

The production rules were clear: no day drinking. But from the moment they'd landed in Scotland, Peter had been MIA, and now what they'd all suspected had been confirmed: Bennett Charles was getting frisky with contestants. While this information wasn't exactly shocking, it definitely exacerbated all the uncomfortable feelings Edie had been trying her hardest to keep at bay. She'd come to *The Key* to fall in love and get engaged. But as the days went on, picturing herself on that mountaintop was becoming more and more difficult. It was uncomfortable to admit, but Edie wanted to be engaged to Bennett the most when Charlie was still alive and well in her imagination. Not charging around a historic city with his ass out.

Edie grabbed the bottle of Scotch. Sometimes shit was just so complex, there was no other choice but to drink.

By the time the girls arrived at their final shooting location, a twilight cruise down the River Forth, they were lit. Especially Edie, who'd drank enough Scotch to kill a small child. Still, she valiantly clutched the gangplank and struggled toward the boat in her cocktail attire, only catching her heel in the metal ramp and nearly pitching into the icy water one time.

"Let's keep it together, Peps," Jessa said, dragging Edie onto the deck.

"I love you, Jessa." Edie took Jessa's face in her hands and peppered her cheek with kisses. "You're like a real friend, you know? But where's Peter? Why isn't he here? I miss him. He's never around, and that's stupid." Edie noticed the lipstick smeared on Jessa's cheek and rubbed it with her thumb before noticing the stars and the moonlit water. "Look at this!" She swept her arms at the vista and twirled. "I'm the king of the world!"

Jessa grabbed Edie by the arm before she twirled right off the boat.

"Water. You need water."

For most of the cocktail party, Edie was relegated to the back of the cabin, being forced to hydrate by a rotating cast of PA babysitters. She was feeling very philosophical by the time Jessa's number two, Dan, came to visit.

"What *is* love?" Edie asked him. She had her high heel hanging off one toe. She swung it in arcs through the air until it fell off. "Baby, don't hurt me." She fell against Dan, laughing uncontrollably. "No more."

"Big *Night at the Roxbury* fan?" Dan asked, propping her back up.

"Is that where that's from?" she asked, amazed. "That shit is fucking *profound*." She got serious and pulled Dan by his shirt so they could speak with their faces inches apart. "But, seriously, Dan. What *is* love? Do you think Bennett Charles *loves* me?" She let go of Dan and jabbed her straw into the side of her mouth to gulp some water. "'Cause I think he loves Bailey."

"How does that make you feel?" Dan asked, smoothing his shirt.

Edie narrowed her eyes. "Don't psychologize me, Dan. What are you, twenty-five? You haven't even seen what the world has in store for you. The hellscape." Something occurred to her. "Aw, Dan, the hellscape of human experience. You know who said that to me once? Peter. He's funny, right?"

But before Dan could answer, Jessa arrived to take Edie for her one-on-one time with Bennett. Jessa brushed the hair off her face, wiped the mascara from under her eyes, and hoisted Edie from the couch. Hand in hand, Jessa led Edie to the deck, and there was Bennett, magnificent in his red plaid kilt, dark suit jacket and tie, bare legs, and shoes with no socks. All at once Edie knew this was the moment to attempt the patented *Key* move she'd seen the other girls execute flawlessly. She ran at him full speed and jumped into his arms, almost knocking both of them overboard.

"Are you having fun in Scotland?" he asked once they were settled on a bench at the edge of the boat. He rested his handsome face on his knuckles and fixed her with a loving gaze.

"Where'd you get this chin?" she asked him, sticking her pointer finger against the cleft in his jaw. "Was it always there? I don't remember this chin."

He chuckled awkwardly and removed her hand. "What was your favorite part of the day?"

"Right now, obviously," she drawled. "Being with *youuuuu*."

So what if he'd ejaculated on Zo? They could still make this work. Suddenly, this was the most hilarious thing Edie had ever thought *ever*, and she laughed and laughed until she couldn't breathe. After way too long, her laughter dissipated and she leaned back against the leather bench, content. But then she noticed Bennett looking at her like she was crazy and suddenly realized she was very, very drunk. Edie straightened up and wiped her eyes, knit her brow, and pressed her lips together in a serious way. She was a serious person discussing her serious future.

"How are you feeling about going back to Chicago for the lock-in?" Bennett started again. But now Edie was craning her neck around Ted and his camera, trying to get a look at the production people gathered under a small awning. Peter? No Peter. Peter? No Peter. "Edie?"

"Hmm?" Edie turned back to him. "Chicago." She nodded. "Home. E.T. phone home."

"Edie," he hissed under his breath. "What the fuck." He smiled at the cameras. And then scratched at his neck until red slashes appeared.

What were they talking about? Edie dug what was left of her nails into her palm and brought herself back to the moment. Oh, shit, the lock-in. The *overnight date*. Whatever contestants survived this week's key ceremony would leave Scotland and eventually meet up in their hometowns to reunite with their families and spend a whole night off camera. Locked in. No keys. Edie tried to picture being in her apartment with Bennett Charles, and it seemed totally bizarre. Somehow the spaces between their childhood and now, their *Key* prom and now, kept shifting and widening until everything felt unreal. How many possible ways their lives could've played out. She could've never come here at all, just watched *The Key* on her couch like a normal person. Or what if they'd never broken up? Instead, they could've been married with two adorable kids they took to soccer practice in a minivan. Or what if Edie was by herself again? Would that really be the worst thing? Being here—she didn't always feel connected to Charlie, but she was starting to feel connected to this version of herself that was confident, fun, and a good friend. Maybe that was enough?

"How are *you* feeling about the lock-in?" she finally managed.

Bennett gazed into the sky. "For us, it's a lot more than just a trip to meet the parents, huh?" he said, launching into one of his speeches. "But I think everything that has kept me from home, those worries, those pressures—it's all disappeared now that you're here. I don't feel afraid anymore, which is wild.

A guy like me who takes on crazy experiences every single day shouldn't be scared to go home. But I think for years I thought I could only be one thing. Strong or weak. But you—you help me be my whole self. You always have." He stared into her eyes. "And, you know, I really love that about you."

Before Edie could wonder where *I really love that about you* fell on the *Key* stages of love, he was kissing her, pressing his mouth against hers with a fervor that made her heart race. He pulled her onto his lap, and her dress hiked up her thighs. From some faraway place, Edie observed that she was just a body reacting to his kiss, to his strong hands pressing against her back. Or maybe she was just a boat, floating, no captain, no oar, just going wherever the current led.

When they pulled apart, they smiled at each other goofily, like they'd done something special. She pulled back to look at him.

"Bennett Charles," she said, feeling flirty, "what's the best Tom Hanks movie?"

"Easy," he said with a shrug. *"Saving Private Ryan."*

An answer so upsetting, Edie instantly felt nauseous. Awkwardly she dismounted Bennett's lap and landed hard on the bench, her stomach churning. Was she going to throw up? A camera pushed in. If so, where? Edie scanned the deck for an exit, and, of course, that's when she saw him. Peter. Standing next to a life preserver, one arm crossed over his chest, the other holding his chin in his hand as he stared at her.

"Fuuuuuuuuuuuck," Edie said.

And then she leaned over the railing and hurled.

The night Zo was eliminated, shit really hit the fan.

Perhaps it was the pressure of the impending lock-ins. Or the Scotch everyone (except an extremely hungover Edie) drank on the way to the key ceremony on the shore of Loch Lomond. But when Adam Fox appeared, framed in a panorama of glassy water and rolling hills, and said—

"Ladies, the final key of the night."

And Bennett Charles slowly raised his eyes from the grass and said—

"Aspen."

—Zo completely lost her shit.

Instantly she started screaming. Like a sea witch emerging from the loch itself, Zo released a series of high-pitched staccato shrieks, her head thrown back, dark hair whipping in the wind. Everyone—Bennett, the girls, production—gaped at her, shocked such a heinous sound could come from such a tiny woman. Until, suddenly, like a plug pulled from a socket, Zo's jaw clamped shut, and the loch was silent once again.

"I swear to god I won't stay if you don't want me to," Aspen begged, bravely reaching a hand toward Zo.

"This is not how this ends, you pre-ejaculating piece of shit," Zo hissed, and with the preternatural grace of an enraged prima ballerina, Zo lunged across the grass toward Bennett.

"Oh my god," Edie said, grabbing Max's arm. Zo's hands were Wolverined in the air like she was going to claw his eyes out. "She's going to kill him."

Bennett scanned the premises as if looking for an exit—across from him, an infantry of bachelorettes; on both sides, clusters of production people under pop-up tents; behind him, the loch. Edie watched three separate cameramen and their attending PAs dart across the grass to keep up with Zo. A drone shot across the sky. At the production tent, Jessa held Peter back. And that's when Edie realized she was watching a master at work. Of course Zo wasn't going to walk off set with her head held high. She wanted an exit that would leave everyone talking.

"Bennett!" Peter yelled as Zo closed in. "Run!"

Finally, Bennett started to run, darting back and forth across the grass like a wide receiver, occasionally spinning into a fake-out and heading in the opposite direction. But Zo was both fast and undeterred. Anticipating his strategy, she kept up with his maneuvering until finally they arrived at a stalemate, crouched like tigers in the grass, waiting for the right moment to strike.

"Listen, Zo," Bennett pleaded, his hands up in surrender. "It's not you, it's me—"

"Aaaaaaaarghhhhhhh!" she screeched as she lunged. But at the very last second, Bennett dodged, and Zo flew past him, down a little hill, straight into the lake.

"Zo!" Aspen screamed, lurching across the grass in her stilettos. When she reached the water, Aspen didn't hesitate before wading in after her.

"Oh no, her dress!" Bailey cried as they watched Aspen sway for a moment on her six-inch heels before falling ass-first into the water.

"You're going to regret this, Bennett Charles!" Zo snarled, her gown hanging off her in a wet sheet. Zo started wrestling with her mic pack and stood to look Bennett in the eyes. "And to think I loved you," she spat, enunciating every word with the snarl of a seasoned soap star.

"She. Is. *Magnificent*," Max declared.

Bennett collapsed in the grass, pulling his tie and fanning himself with his shirt. Red splotches crept up his neck and he began to wheeze. Bailey and a cameraman fell to their knees at his side. "It's so hard," he croaked. "Being loved this much."

"Oh, babe," Bailey said, pulling him to her bosom. "I know it is."

AMID ALLEGATIONS OF "TOXIC ENVIRONMENT," *THE KEY* PREMIERES TO LOWEST RATINGS IN SERIES HISTORY, SHOWRUNNER WEIGHS IN

BY LUCY LYONS

Most dramatic season ever? So far audiences don't think so. Only 5 million viewers tuned in to watch extreme sportsman Bennett Charles make his debut as *The Key*'s twenty-second suitor, but showrunner Peter Kennedy says he's not worried.

"If anything, we were expecting this," Kennedy told *Us*. "America needs a chance to get to know Bennett and—just like the twenty gorgeous women vying for his heart—we know they're going to fall head over heels in love."

The relatively unknown philanthropist stepped into *The Key*'s lead role after photos surfaced of previous suitor Wyatt Cash at a gay bar in Miami, effectively outing the fan favorite from both the closet and the competition. Petitions for Cash to remain on the show with an all-male cast were ignored, even as criticism over *The Key*'s heteronormative agenda continued to plague the series.

Is America ready for a LGBTQIA+ season of *The Key*? "That's something we're working toward and a season I want to see," Kennedy said. "At the end of the day, *The Key* is focused on telling compelling stories about compelling people and that's why we've remained a ratings juggernaut for almost twenty years."

Also affecting ratings, complaints about a too-white cast and allegations about the show's "toxic environment." Speaking on the condition of anonymity, an eliminated contestant told *Us* the pressure to be sexual is commonplace.

"They make you do things you would *never* do," she said. "No one told me that I had to sleep with Bennett Charles to stay on the show. But it was, like, *implied*."

Multiple sources confirm *Key* producers use the lure of fame to convince contestants to do anything from parade around in lingerie to make late-night off-camera visits to the suitor's bedroom.

"Sleeping with Bennett Charles was the worst mistake of my life," the contestant continued. "And I want the women of America to know he only cares about being famous. He'll pick whoever the producers tell him to. The whole thing is fake. And degrading. And toxic."

When asked about the allegations of toxicity on *The Key*, Kennedy said, "We are aware of these statements and take them very seriously. A commitment to not only consent, but enthusiastic and clear-minded consent, is at the heart of *The Key*."

Feminist watchdog groups have called for a total boycott, but despite the premiere's low ratings, *The Key* continues to lead Tuesday night, winning in the ever-important 18–49 demo.

The Key airs on RX Tuesdays at 8 p.m. ET.

26

Peter Kennedy was in love.

Or falling in love?

He had no idea, but either way, he wasn't happy about it.

For years, Peter had been certain that *falling in love* was purely a narrative device *The Key* used to keep multiple contestants on the hook and the show moving forward. But now, as he was being consumed by all these *feelings*, he'd developed a begrudging appreciation for the nuance. Surely, he couldn't be *in love* with Edie Pepper. They'd only met six weeks ago! She was a contestant! But when he tried to pick it apart, pinpoint the origin of all these bizarre mushy feelings, he was irritated to find that just like the torment of his acid reflux, somehow they seemed to have always just *been there*, lighting him on fire from the inside out.

(The irony of his heartburn evolving from medical issue to metaphor—well, it was almost too twee to bear.)

Agonizing over the stages of love quickly led to agonizing over his failed marriage. Peter had been certain that his divorce was this terrible thing that happened to him without his consent. But now he was forced to wonder how he could've picked someone so clearly *wrong* for him. Julie did not like him. In fact, upon reflection, Julie's desire to both shame him *and* mold him seemed to be the spark that brought them together. At the beginning, he supposed, there was something exciting about it. And surely he'd "loved" her then, but over time, as her disdain for him became impossible to ignore, he tried not to think about his feelings for Julie at all. They were married. What was there to think about? So he'd completely detached, thrown himself into work, until she'd put them out of their misery. And he'd taken this epic failure as evidence that love, marriage, a family—none of it was meant for him. He wasn't husband material. He wasn't even boyfriend material.

But, what if, with the right person, *he was*?

A terrifying thought.

Peter skulled his beer and let the glass hit the bar with a thud.

"Jesus Christ, Peter," Jessa complained, wiping spatter from her iPad. It was tradition that before the lock-ins, there was always a hotel bar takeover. For one night, the moratorium on fraternization was suspended, and the hometown contestant, all the traveling producers, directors, PAs, cameramen, lighting, and sound guys gathered to drink and sing karaoke. The lead, of course, was always sequestered at another hotel. Peter had hoped to fly ahead to Kansas City for Max's date and skip Edie's entirely, but somehow he'd still ended up in Chicago, in the same room as the woman he was desperately trying to avoid. "Knock it off with the grumpy old man bit. We've got work to do."

Yeah, they did. Never before had *The Key* begun airing while *The Key* was still filming. Wyatt Cash and the delayed production schedule had forced the parallel paths, and when Peter agreed to it months ago, he'd been so focused on saving the show he hadn't thought through the implications. But now the pressure of shitty ratings and bad press on top of dragging this bloated production over the finish line—it was like a powder keg waiting to explode. Normally Peter would have time to coach the lead on the right moment to declare his love—the full *I love you*—and lay the foundation for the last-second cold feet drama and fantasy engagement. But instead, in addition to the twelve-hour shoot days, Peter was doing press, dropping spoilers on surprise podcast visits, and signing onto Zoom calls with the marketing team back in LA to yell about fixing whatever the fuck the problem was with the marketing mix because whenever Peter opened his phone to the tabloid sites, Bennett's goddamned love story was two or three scrolls down the page.

"I'm going to bed," he announced.

Jessa looked up from her notes. "You can't. It's not good for morale."

Peter made a sound in his throat, an annoyed *uch*, before frowning and ordering another beer. He glanced at Edie. She was laughing at something Lou was saying. Her cheeks were flushed a pretty pink, which irritated Peter even more. He'd come to notice that he loved when she had her hair up like this, all messy and cute. It felt more like *her* than the glam Barbie-tron Jessa had created. He'd even come to love her stupid red sweatshirt with the strutting badger that she wore on planes. And her too-loud laugh that he used to find embarrassing broke him open now, especially when he was the cause of it. And her penchant for bad music and chemically laden foods. And how smart and funny and vulnerable she was. And how she showed him the world in a new way. And how he felt when he was with her. Fuck fuck fuck *fuck*, *FUCK*, Peter Kennedy was crazy about, falling in love with, maybe *in love* with Edie Pepper.

"Seriously, I'm going to bed," he told Jessa as soon as he saw Edie heading their way.

"Not till we go over the schedule for tomorrow. We've got a tight schedule, and there's the whole thing with the band."

Peter stood just as Edie arrived.

"You guys work too hard," she said with that big smile. "Put the iPads away, I heard there's going to be karaoke."

Peter couldn't help himself. "If we didn't work so hard, how would all your dreams come true? How else would you end up engaged to the King Douche himself?"

Edie cocked her head. "What's that supposed to mean?"

"Nothing." Peter gathered his phone and room key from the bar. "I'm calling it a night."

"Why does he say shit like that?" Edie asked Jessa. Then, to his departing back, "Why do you say shit like that?"

He turned. "Like what?"

"Oh, I don't know," she said. "Just the shit you say that's clearly meant to make me feel stupid."

"I'm not making you feel stupid." Peter caught his reflection in the mirror over the bar. He looked like a smug asshole. He shouldn't be baiting her. Why was he baiting her? "Maybe liking Bennett Charles is making you feel stupid."

"Peter, what the hell?" Jessa interjected.

"Who said I liked him?"

An image of Edie straddling Bennett in Scotland—*right in front of the cameras!*—crossed Peter's mind and he was righteous all over again. "You're still here, aren't you?"

"Oh, I'm sorry, did you want me to go?" Edie challenged. "Is that why you've been ignoring me? Because you haven't spoken to me in days, Peter. But here you are now, the night before the lock-in, ready to share your opinion. So, let's hear it. Let it all out. 'Cause I really don't see your point."

There was a reasonable part of him that knew he should shut up, that knew he was not only putting the show at risk, but also exposing himself in a way that was better left concealed.

But there was an even bigger part of him that was hurt by her blatant disregard for their…whatever it was. *Connection.* And who wanted her to know it.

"Just saying, you looked pretty happy when he had his tongue down your throat in Edinburgh."

"Peter!" Jessa exclaimed.

Edie stepped toward him until they were face-to-face, two prizefighters ready to knock each other out. "Are you serious right now?" she hissed. "You're gonna come at me with some slut-shaming nonsense over a show that *you* produce? Who made your repressed, cranky ass the moral compass of *The Key*? At least I'm out here. At least I'm *trying*. Which is more than I can say for you, someone who thinks love is some unattainable mirage because he's too scared to let someone actually know him. Well, *I* know you, Peter. And the truth is, you have some good moments, but overall, you suck."

And with that, Edie turned on her heel and walked out of the bar.

"Dude." Jessa gaped at him. "What the *fuck*?"

Peter threw his arms in the air.

Exhaled an angry sigh.

Rubbed his face with both hands and scratched his scalp until his hair was standing on end.

Of course Edie was right. Of course he was a hypocritical asshole who'd set her up to fall in love with Bennett and then got mad when she did. And *of course* he was scared to let someone know him, because, just like she said, he had some good moments, but overall, he was a mess. The kind of person who equated being in love with feeling like shit. And if he loved her, which he thought maybe he did, why was he acting like this?

Peter took off through the lounge. Right as he turned the corner to the elevators, he saw her getting on.

"I'm sorry—" he said, jumping in after her.

"Save it," Edie said, pounding the button for the eleventh floor. "We have, what? A week and a half left? Then we never have to see each other again." She gestured at the closing doors. "You can go. You're super good at that." He didn't move. "Oh, good, you're gonna stay. Why would I care? I don't care."

"Well, I care!" Peter yelled before he could stop himself. Seeing her cold like this made him feel wild and desperate. "If you haven't noticed, I care so fucking much it's literally ruining my life!"

"Oh my god," she said, rolling her eyes. "Poor Peter."

He stepped in front of her so she'd have to look at him. "Edie," he pleaded. "I'm sorry."

"Great, apology accepted." She stepped to the other side of the elevator. "So let's just drop it, okay?"

He knew he should drop it. Let her get off the elevator and then ride back down to his room and check his email. Except that's not what he wanted to do anymore. It was like on that plane to Scotland—all at once this dream of domestic life came back to him and he could picture them together, not in his Malibu condo, but maybe somewhere in the hills, or Topanga Canyon—they could get one of those *Selling Sunset* agents to find them a place, she'd love that, and he'd make BBQ chicken and corn on the cob and they'd eat on the deck, butter running down their chins. And maybe they'd have a couple of kids—he could already tell she'd be an amazing mom from the way she listened so deeply to everything the other girls said to her, and by how much their feelings mattered to her—and it was this vision of their life together that ruined everything about his current workaholic bachelor situation, not to mention made every single LA girl seem completely wrong for him. Now, when he fell asleep next to his glowing laptop, with that stupid little snow globe of the Chicago skyline she'd given him when they met sitting on his hotel nightstand, he felt sad because all he wanted to do was fall asleep next to her.

"Trust me, I wish I could," he said, a little manic. "It would make everything easier if I could drop it. 'Cause, you know, I'm just over here dismantling everything I've built over the past ten years because of you."

Edie stared at the doors, unimpressed. "What are you even talking about, Peter?"

"Edie, Jesus Christ, don't you get it? I'm crazy about you! When we're not together, all I do is think about you. I watch footage of you, which, as I'm saying this out loud, I realize sounds completely creepy. But sometimes I'm watching you and you seem so into Bennett that it makes me fucking crazy and I can't figure out how you actually feel because whatever it is between us feels so *real,* but then, there you are, making out with Bennett, which is just like—" He was pacing around the tiny space now, his hands on either side of his head, mimicking an explosion. "And you deserve so much better. You're so smart and funny and kind and I like you so much and every time I'm with you, I just want to be with you more, so yeah, I leave! Because this is insane! It's a really bad idea! But you know that video with Janet Jackson in that bone vest, 'like a moth to the flame, burned by the fire?' That's the situation here."

The words tumbled out of him with no planning or discretion, just a ramble of adoration he wished he'd crafted and rehearsed into the sort of epic romcom declaration that Edie deserved. But it wasn't his fault! He wasn't some practiced Prince Charming. He was just some guy. But wasn't there also something great about that? Maybe he didn't have to be anything other than just some guy who was learning what real love was now that it was right in front of him. He stopped pacing and looked at her.

"Edie," he said, not sure how far he was willing to go until the words were out of his mouth. "I'm falling in love with you."

Slowly, she turned to face him. Her eyes were wide.

"What did you just say?"

"I said *I'm falling in love with you.* And I don't know if you're into me or Bennett but"—Peter threw his hands in the air—"I hope it's me, Edie. I don't even care if it makes me a dick. It *cannot* be him."

They stared at each other.

What the hell was he doing? He was telling a contestant that he was in some sort of love with her? He hadn't said the word *love* to anyone since Julie, and he had intended never to say it to anyone again. And Edie was in the final four, for chrissakes! But it suddenly occurred to Peter that he didn't care. Right this second, he didn't care about his career or the show or what anyone would think. All he cared about was her. And telling her he was in some kind of love with her couldn't be worse than not telling her. Well, actually, it could. But the bottom line was that he didn't care. He kept waiting for his heartburn to surge, but it didn't. And, strangely, even though that speech had been totally out of character, inside he felt calm, like all the moments of his life had led him here, to this moment.

Edie put both hands over her face and inhaled slowly. When she dropped them, her pretty gray eyes were wet, and her face had lost that hardness. She looked like how she looked on the plane, like she was wide open to him.

Slowly he reached his hand toward her.

"Edie," he said softly, tracing his finger down the side of her arm. "Please."

And, just like that, she was in his arms. When he kissed her, there was no caution or apprehension or any of the tentativeness that comes with a first kiss, just an explosion of everything he'd ever wanted, and then pretended he didn't want, and then was starting to accept that he wanted more than anything in the world. He wrapped his arms around her and kissed her, Edie, who kissed him back with the kind of passion he couldn't remember ever experiencing in his life, her lips on his, his hand up the back of her shirt, her nails cutting exquisitely into the back of his neck—

The elevator ground to a halt. Someone cleared their throat. Peter and Edie pulled apart. In the doorway was a silver-haired couple, the woman clutching her pocketbook to her chest in alarm. "Get a room," the man said, guiding his wife onto the elevator.

"Thank you," Peter said. He reached out and straightened Edie's shirt. "Negotiations are ongoing."

Edie stifled a laugh and stepped off the elevator. Peter watched her go, not sure if he should follow.

The doors started closing.

Was that it?

Could that be it?

Finally, Edie looked over her shoulder.

"You coming?" she challenged.

A lifetime of cross-country had Peter out of that elevator like he was Tom Cruise in *Mission Impossible*. He grabbed her hand, and they sprinted down the hall like a couple of fugitives. Until he realized he had no idea where he was going, and she laughed and pulled him the other way. When they reached her door, he pulled her to him again, sliding his hand to the nape of her neck before kissing her slowly, more deliberately than he had before, luxuriating in every second of it.

"God, Peter, who knew you could kiss like this?" she said, a little breathless.

He tried to come up with something witty but just blushed and got shy.

Edie took her keycard out of her pocket and dipped it into the electronic lock. It flashed red. She tried again. Red. One more time. Red.

"Shit." She turned to him. "Is this a sign? You sure we should do this?"

"Not at all." He paused. "All I know is I've never wanted anyone the way I want you right now."

And then that too-big smile that made him believe in all the fucking fairy tales broke across her face. He took the keycard and with one swipe unlocked the door.

Peter was doing his best to savor every second of this experience—Edie pressed against the wall, gasping into his ear as he bit her neck—but he was also losing himself entirely as he followed her lead. Edie sliding her hands into his back pockets and pressing his cock directly into her crotch. Edie winding her fingers into the waistband of his jeans. Edie pulling his shirt over his head.

"All this time you've been keeping a six-pack under wraps," she teased, throwing his shirt on the floor and placing her fingertips on his stomach. "Not bad, Peter, not bad."

"Fortunately for you," he said, moving her from the wall to the bed, "I'm not the kind of guy who needs relentless adoration of his sick muscles."

"Well, I am that kind of guy," she said with a grin. "So get to it."

Peter laughed. She lifted her arms, inviting him to take her shirt off, and quickly he obliged. He kissed her again and didn't waste any time unhooking her bra and throwing it into the void. He moved his hands and his mouth to her breasts, which he'd thought about in the shower just this morning, and which were even more fantastic in real life.

"You're beautiful," he murmured.

"You say that to all the girls," she joked.

"Don't do that," Peter said, pulling back and looking at her intently. "Just you."

For a second, emotion flickered across her face, and she looked like she might cry, and he felt unsure, like he'd said the wrong thing, but then she pulled him to her again, her hands strong and insistent, and they pushed up the bed, her fingers at the waistband of his jeans as he unbuttoned hers. He pulled her pants down past her hips and then inelegantly used his foot to try to get them the rest of the way off. When they got stuck at her ankles, he grumbled against her lips, "What the hell?"

"My skinniest jeans," she said with a laugh.

Peter pushed himself to the end of the bed and removed one leg, then the other, and tossed her pants to the floor. He kissed both her knees before lying down next to her again, running his hand over every square inch of her ass and thighs until her hips were moving every time he got close. He peeled off her underwear and she threw her leg over his hip, opening herself to him, and when he finally touched her, moving his fingers up and down, pausing at her clit, then up and down again, she gasped and bit his neck, hard. He slid his fingers inside of her and she was warm and wet, and his cock was hard against his jeans. He stroked her and kissed her and stroked her more, Edie Pepper, this woman who was upending everything he thought he knew about love.

"I'm going to come if you keep doing that," she whispered.

"I want you to," he said, pressing his face into the hollow of her neck and breathing her in.

And then he was moving his hand against her faster and she was moving in a rhythm against him and saying his name and moaning. He took her nipple in his mouth and right as he bit it, he felt her come against him.

"Peter," she gasped finally, breathing hard.

They laid there for a moment, staring at each other, and he thought about how disconcerting it was to have all his emotions right up at the surface like this. How he felt so warm toward her and wanted to make her come like this all the time. He brushed her hair off her face and a filament of a thought about the show and *what in the hell was he going to do about the show* floated through his mind, but then she was tugging his pants off and then her mouth was around his cock and he had no more thoughts about anything other than the sensation, like he was flying, until she asked if he had any condoms.

"Right," he said, pushing up from the bed. He found his pants and then his wallet, where he retrieved a condom, and when he returned, Edie was under the covers waiting for him, her hair loose around her shoulders, a mischievous grin on her face.

"What?" he said.

"Nothing."

"Tell me."

"I'm just trying to remember what you said in the elevator," she said, twirling a lock of her hair like some winsome coquette. "What was it again?"

"About Janet Jackson?" he asked. "I remember the name of the song, by the way. 'That's the Way Love Goes.'"

"I know the name of the song, Peter. It's peak MTV. I'm talking about the other part."

"Hmm," he said, sliding in next to her. "About when I watched footage of you? Standard protocol. The EP watches all the rough cuts."

She kicked him in the shin. "The other part!"

"Oh," he said, kissing her collarbone, nibbling her neck. "When I said I was falling in love with you?"

She pulled all her hair in front of her face and nodded. "Say it again," she said, wrinkling her nose.

"Edie Pepper," he said. "I'm falling in love with you."

And then they were kissing, and he was putting the condom on and she was on top of him and he was inside of her and they were moving together and it was nothing like the random hook-ups Peter had had over the past few years. It was like he'd completely forgotten sex could be like this, because surely at some point, he'd known. She felt so good riding him that he said, "If you keep doing that, I'm going to come," and she said, "I want you to," and then they were moving together faster until he came and she did, too, a few seconds later.

After a moment, he sat up and wrapped his arms around her, burying his face in her chest, breathing hard. She wound her fingers through his hair and held him to her. He listened to her heart beating while she held him, and he felt his breath slow as he relaxed into her softness. She hadn't said it, but Peter felt certain she was falling in love with him, too. Because it was clear to him that what they had between them was, well, *everything*.

Then all at once, the *everythingness* of the everything took his breath away.

"You okay?" she asked, smoothing his hair back and kissing his forehead. "Do you need a guided meditation to calm down?"

And then they were both laughing and Peter was hiding his face from her and doing his best to ignore the pounding in his chest because, holy fuck, what had he done?

And what the hell was he going to do now?

27

When Edie woke up, Peter was gone.

In his place, a note:

BACK TO WORK. TALK SOON.

—P

A topless and wild-haired Edie shot up in bed, clutching the sheet to her chest in a mostly symbolic display of modesty considering she was, once again, alone. She snatched the hotel stationery off the pillow where Peter's head should've been. Edie considered the five staccato words over and over again before finally letting her fingers go limp. She watched as the note fluttered back down to the bed where just last night Peter had touched every inch of her body. Oh god. Edie covered her face with her hands. Her cheeks were hot with an old, unknowable shame, this thrumming, subterranean knowledge that there was something fundamentally wrong with her. And that Peter had seen it and then left.

Edie looked at the note once more, praying the words had shifted into something more optimistic, like *Went for coffee, back soon, let's get married! Love love love love love, Peter.* But the note—*a fucking note!*—kept screaming at her in all caps—*of course Peter was the sort of deranged person who wrote in all caps!*—that he had, once again, disappeared.

Peter Kennedy had gone BACK TO WORK.

Edie collapsed on the bed, holding the note to her chest in the exact same spot where just hours ago she'd held Peter. After they'd thoroughly exhausted themselves pawing at each other like teenagers—well, like teenagers who were good at sex—Peter had sat up and nuzzled into Edie's chest in a way that made her feel almost maternal toward him, like he was some precious thing she wanted to love and protect. She'd run her fingers through his hair, and his arms had been wrapped tightly around her waist. He had an adorable spray of freckles across his shoulders. Peter was frecklier than she imagined, Edie remembered, smiling at the thought, because wasn't intimacy astonishing? Back at the bar, Peter had just been Peter. Grumpy, aloof, arrogant Peter, who half the time Edie was sure she hated. But now she knew the sounds he made when he came. It turned her on so much—Peter exposed like that, Peter's grip on the universe relaxed like that, Peter's hands digging into her ass like that—that she'd finished *twice*. The memory now felt so embarrassing that her eyes stung, and she rubbed them until her cheeks bloomed with last night's mascara.

Another memory, a teensy, tiny, little nothing of a moment she'd planned to ignore, came to her now. She'd had her lips pressed to his shoulder, to those freckles she'd never seen before but were all of a sudden *hers*, when out of nowhere, she sensed that something had changed. His shoulders had tensed. He took a sharp inhale. And then he stopped breathing entirely.

She'd held her breath, too, waiting for what came next.

When they were on the elevator and Peter had said he was falling in love with her, instantly it'd felt like this sharp, inevitable truth. But then also like some dreamy fantasy untethered from real life, where Edie was a contestant on *The Key* and Peter was some Hollywood hotshot on the brink of his most dramatic season ever. But then, everything with Peter was like that. One second Edie thought he was too serious and cold and that it was pointless to even try to be friends with him. They'd never understand each other—she was messy and impulsive and out there, and he was judgmental and shut down and dated models. But then he could also be warm and playful and sweet, and say incisive things like "Maybe love isn't just this thing we stumble into one day. Maybe you have to wait for it. And maybe that's what makes it special," with his green eyes boring into her like everything she'd ever wanted was right there in front of her because the only person who truly understood her was him.

And then, once again, she was left trying to reconcile her shifting ideas about Peter.

He was almost aggressively cynical. And his entire supercilious nature was extremely annoying, not to mention manipulative in the way that it activated her need to please. He had this particular way of watching everything around him, his face blank and withholding, that Edie sort of resented, or at the very least thought was borderline rude. But when Edie said something that caught him by surprise, that tickled him just right, his smile would break across his face, totally unguarded and almost sheepish at his own delight, and Edie found that there was nothing she loved more than making Peter smile. It felt like they were sharing a secret, like she was the only one who could reach him like that.

So she'd believed him when he said he was "falling in love" with her. Honestly, at first those words didn't sound like him—too cheesy, too juvenile. But now it made sense. Falling in love included an escape hatch. It was some murky pre-love stage that prompted hope for the future but allowed for backpedaling. It expressed an interest, a desire, without certainty.

Except what Edie wanted at this point in her life was certainty—she wanted the whole thing.

Still, there was no time to think critically when his hands were in her hair, when his lips were on hers. The heat of his body, the smell of him—it was like some wonderful drug she'd wanted to inject directly into her veins. The unbridled way that he'd kissed her, like he wasn't this tightly wound neurotic at all, but this solid man full of passion and mystery. Of course, throughout her life, Edie'd had all sorts of daydreams about what she wanted sex to be like that rarely came true. But with Peter, every moment had felt like exactly what she wanted. Exciting, but also tender and sweet, the power between them constantly shifting. One moment he was in control, channeling his Peterish intensity into making her come, and then she was, touching and licking him slowly until all that cold bravado was stripped away and he was at her mercy. Edie thought perhaps this negotiation surprised them both, except clearly that was the only way it could be between them. She'd loved the assured way he'd handled her body, both confident but also listening and watching for her responses. And she'd loved when she was on top of him, how he wasn't like intense Peter at all, but this soft, open version, looking at her like he was in awe.

After, when her lips were pressed against those freckles, when Peter's breathing had stopped and everything became still between them, Edie knew two things for sure.

One: Edie Pepper did not love Bennett Charles *or* Charlie Bennett. Frankly, as soon as Peter looked at her with those plaintive green eyes and slid one finger slowly down her arm, Bennett Charles had evaporated from Edie's consciousness as quickly as he'd arrived two months ago. It was clear that whatever feelings she thought she had for Charlie were just a product of the past or fanciful dreams of the future, neither of which had much to do with the present or who Edie was at this moment, which was a thirty-five-year-old woman who, sure, was impulsive and perhaps a little needy, but who was also—and this was becoming clearer to herself every day—smart, capable, good-natured, loving, and very much deserving of love.

Two: Cracking the door open to the reality of what Peter and Edie had done would bury them in a landslide of problems. Any initial thoughts Edie had about if and how and when they would escape *The Key* without Peter getting fired, without hurting Charlie, or without becoming media spectacles themselves were instantly complicated and overwhelming and not romantic at all. And who wanted to deal with that? Especially when Edie was still dreamy under the dawning reality that not only was Peter Kennedy falling in love with her, but that maybe she was also falling in love with Peter Kennedy. That for all his complications and arrogance, it was his arms she wanted around her, his kiss on her lips, his words in her ear.

So instead of asking Peter what was wrong, or acknowledging that things weren't simple, Edie had made a joke.

"Do you need a guided meditation to calm down?"

And he'd laughed. And then he'd squeezed her once more before shifting her off of him and walking into the bathroom. And when he returned, he held her just like he was supposed to, but it seemed sort of stiff and disconnected, like some part of him was lost to her, like they were strangers all over again. Eventually his breathing got deeper and he'd rolled over, leaving her to stare at those freckles, no longer a sweet symbol of intimacy because, somehow, Edie knew that if she ran her fingers across them, he would flinch.

Falling in love.

All the years Edie had watched *The Key*, *falling in love* seemed like such a valid declaration. A pit stop on the way to everything she'd ever wanted.

But now she understood it for what it was.

Bullshit.

Then, a knock at the door.

He was back!

Edie sprang from the bed, wrapping the white duvet around her body like a sarong. She was just steps from the door when the duvet, still tucked tightly under one corner of the mattress, jerked back, and Edie stumbled to the floor.

The knocking continued.

"Just a sec!" Edie cried, untangling herself and, in the process, discovering last night's thong trapped between the sheets. Shit! There were her jeans in a slutty pile on the floor. Her bra splatted across the desk lamp. Where in the hell was her shirt? Quickly, Edie abandoned hope of reuniting with her clothes and ran to the bathroom for the hotel robe. She shrugged it on, ran back to the door, thought better of it, ran back to the bathroom for a speedy gargle of Listerine, tried to fix her hair and rub the mascara off her cheeks, gave up, and then, breathless with anticipation, ran back to the door and threw it open.

"Good lord, what happened to you?" Jessa asked, breezing past Edie with her ponytail swinging. "You're not even dressed! Chop-chop, girl, we're got places to be!"

Edie stared at her dumbfounded.

And then it hit her.

The lock-in.

"We've got a full day," Jessa said, stepping over the duvet and plopping down on the bed. Edie grimaced, wondering if she should mention the sex that had taken place right where Jessa was sitting.

"First some B-roll of my favorite lovebirds, Edie and Bennett, roaming around the most romantic city in all of the

Midwest," Jessa said, poking at her iPad. "Then I have something very special planned for you, something nostalgic that you're gonna *love*. But don't ask—it's a surprise. Then off to Mama Pepper's for a little 'meet the parents' moment and some engagement talk—" Edie gasped, and Jessa looked up. "I know, I'm excited too! And then the very best part, the lock-in. Super-special, off-camera time for you and Bennett to say whatever needs to be said and then make it official with your hot naked bods." Jessa wagged her brows suggestively at Edie.

Slowly and then all at once, Edie understood that BACK TO WORK literally meant Peter had gone BACK TO WORK producing the show. And that the corollary to BACK TO WORK was Edie as one of Bennett's final contestants, Edie as one of Bennett's options for marriage, Edie locked in a room with Bennett all night long. But Peter couldn't possibly think that Edie should go on the lock-in like nothing had happened. Right? Edie was typically up for a lot, but there was no scenario in which she went from naked in a bed with Peter Kennedy to her mother's kitchen table with Bennett Charles.

"Seriously, what's with you?" Jessa snapped her fingers in front of Edie's face. "Are you hungover or something? We don't have much time."

"Jessa..."

Edie sat down next to Jessa. She bit her knuckle, trying to figure out what made sense. *The Key* was Peter's realm, and maybe Edie should let him chart the way forward. Except, there was no way Jessa would've come here unless Peter told her to.

"Do you need to shower, or should I get you some flip-flops so you can go on this date as the guy from *The Big Lebowski*?"

Edie looked up at Jessa and nodded. And then kept nodding. Until she was nodding like an evil villain on the verge of a grand plan.

"I need to shower," she said. "Let me shower, and I'll meet you in the lobby in forty-five minutes."

"Thirty minutes," Jessa said, consulting her iPad. "We'll do your makeup in the van."

"Thirty minutes," Edie agreed, standing up and guiding Jessa to the door. But then it occurred to her—it was still early. What if Peter just hadn't seen Jessa yet? What if he was on his way to talk to Jessa, to tell her he was falling in love with Edie and that they needed to devise a plan for extrication? Wouldn't Edie be jumping to conclusions if she didn't at least ask?

"By the way," she said, trying her best to sound nonchalant, "have you seen Peter?"

"Peter?" Jessa said, picking lint out of Edie's hair. "He went running."

"Running? When did he go running? And, like, where?"

Jessa made a face. "Girl, I don't know, he went running. Around. That's what he does when he's in a mood."

"Uh-huh."

So, Peter was in a mood. Well. Edie would show Peter a *mood*.

"If you see him," Edie said, taking Jessa's hands and squeezing them like she was a beatific bride and Jessa was her glowing bridesmaid and, together, they were full of wonder at the day to come. "Can you please let him know that I cannot thank him enough for everything he's done to make my wildest dreams come true, which is, just a reminder, *getting engaged to Bennett Charles*. I cannot wait to give Bennett *all of me*. Know what I mean?"

"Aw, that's fantastic, babe." Jessa pulled Edie in for a hug. "But don't give Peter too much credit. I've always known you and Bennett belong together."

Edie laughed. And then started plotting her escape.

EXCLUSIVE: *KEY* PRODUCTION HALTS AFTER FAN FAVE EXITS DAYS BEFORE FINALE

BY LUCY LYONS

Alexa, play "We Are Never Ever Getting Back Together" by Taylor Swift! *US Weekly* has learned that fan favorite Edie Pepper has left *The Key* just days before the finale, when sources tell *Us* she was a shoo-in for an engagement.

What went wrong between the extreme sportsman and his high school sweetheart? It appears Charles's flagrant womanizing and bad-boy behavior played a big part. Rumors have dogged Charles for weeks, with former contestants coming forward to expose *The Key*'s "toxic environment," even alleging Charles's enthusiasm for physical attention contributed to a slew of sexual dalliances and subsequent breakups that left many of the women feeling used.

"He hooked up with absolutely everyone," a former contestant tells *Us*. "It was insane. I wasn't ready to sleep with him and, surprise, surprise, the next day I was going home."

"I think Edie knew him better than any of us," another contestant says. "I'm not surprised to hear she left. She knows what a liar he is."

According to Charles, it's not that simple. In an Instagram post this week, Charles captioned a pic of the ocean with a ray of light breaking through a cloudy sky: "Even the worst storms will pass, and the sun will shine again." He went on to thank his fans for their continued support, adding, "My intention, since day one, has been to find the woman I'm going to spend the rest of my life with. My heart breaks to know that people I care about have been hurt in the process. I look forward to the day I can make it right."

For her part, Edie Pepper captured the hearts of Key fans immediately and quickly emerged as an icon for single women everywhere. What is it about Pepper that resonates? Noted Key podcaster Julia Pitman says Pepper is a feminist face for a series stuck in a patriarchal past. "She's messy, she's imperfect, she says what she thinks, and she's the ripe old age of thirty-five. That's to say, she's just like us," Pitman says. "And when we see someone who's not twenty-two or a size zero believing she's worthy of finding love, well, that's powerful television."

So, what's next for Edie Pepper? In addition to fan accounts on Instagram and Twitter, celebs like Reese Witherspoon, Mindy Kaling, and Amy Schumer have shown their support for Pepper by signing a petition for the Midwestern copywriter to step in as next season's lead.

The Key airs on RX Tuesdays at 8 p.m. ET.

28

Wait, wait, wait, wait, wait," Lauren said as she sped down Lake Shore Drive. She flicked her eyes to the rearview mirror, just in case a *Key* production van had emerged hot on their tail. "You're telling me you went on this stupid show to fall in love with Charlie Bennett, but instead you *banged the showrunner*?"

"That's exactly what I'm telling you, Lauren." Edie clutched the door handle. "And, worst of all, I think I might really be falling for him."

Lauren made an appalled squawk before careening the Prius across two lanes of traffic. A horn blared. Good lord, Edie thought her escape from the hotel had been harrowing, but Lauren's *2 Fast 2 Furious* driving was almost worse than the frantic packing, tiptoeing down eleven flights of stairs with her massive suitcase thumping down each step, and then cowering under the front desk to dial Lauren's number on the receptionist's iPhone.

"Seriously, I *cannot* with you right now." Lauren flung the Prius down the ramp for Irving Park and the car began speeding west. "Who don't you love, Edie? You love everyone. Here's a thought: Stop loving people."

"Lauren!" Edie exclaimed, alarmed by both the Prius's last-second dodge around a group of commuters and the brazen assessment of her love life. "You can't be judgy right now. *We are in crisis.* You can judge me all you want later, but right now, you need to be supportive."

"I *am* being supportive. I came as soon as you called, didn't I? *Laureeeeeeeeeeennnn, saaaaaaaavvvvve me*," she mimicked. "And here I am, saving you. I should be at work."

"And I love you for it, but you don't have to kill us in the process!" They swerved around a double-parked Amazon truck. "Seriously, Lo, slow down! They're not *literally* after us." Edie looked out the back window. "At least, I don't think they are."

The Prius staggered to a halt and Lauren faced Edie.

"You know I love you. I support you always. You know that. But you have to admit this is crazy. Even for you."

"Which part?"

"All. Of. It."

Edie looked out the window and pouted. A new Pilates studio had moved in next to her favorite coffee shop. Maybe now she could finally get into a sustainable exercise routine. She could do Pilates every day before work. Bailey was always talking about how great Pilates was, even tempting Edie with claims that you spent a lot of the class lying down. Anyway, Edie could do Pilates, and then stop at the coffee shop for a chai latte because she was the new and improved Hollywood version of Edie who wouldn't touch a white chocolate mocha with a ten-foot pole, and then hop on the train to work, where she'd attend meetings about web content for health insurance companies with an optimistic attitude and then return to her desk, happy to churn out blog posts about oral health for millennials. And she'd become more active on LinkedIn. Attend women's networking events. Focus on her career until everyone could see just how successful she was and that she didn't need a husband or children. And she'd get some cool hobbies. Maybe something hipster-y, like tinsmithing. Volunteer at a nursing home. Take up sailing and throw around words like *starboard* and *land, ho!* and meet all sorts of cool new friends who'd celebrate her as a single woman because life at sea waits for no man.

But then thinking about overhauling her life this way felt so upsetting that the adrenaline from her big *Key* escape drained from her body. Sure, Edie could reinvent herself. Again. Except all that searching and trying and scrambling didn't feel true anymore. It felt exhausting. And ridiculous.

"Do you really love him?" Lauren asked. "'Cause he sounds like sort of a dick."

"He's just from Connecticut." Edie started to cry thinking about Peter. "But once you get to know him"—she sniffled—"he's, like, super sensitive and funny and smart and great at sex. And it's the worst, because maybe I love him in an actual, *real* way, and he left me anyway, and I'm sorry—I know I've made a mess of everything and you shouldn't have to take care of me. I'm a full adult person."

"Fuck." Lauren exhaled, finally accepting the gravity of the situation. She steered the Prius into a Walgreens parking lot and threw it into park. "It's gonna be okay," she said, softer now. She wiped a tear off Edie's cheek. "We've been through worse. Remember when I was dumped by Evil Janine?"

"You were so devastated you went back to eating meat just to spite her." Edie hiccupped. "We went to Bavette's for filets and I forgot my wallet and you had to pay, like, four hundred dollars for that meal and I don't think I ever paid you back." Edie cried even harder. "I'm really sorry about that. I'll Venmo you as soon as we get home." Edie threw her hands in the air, exasperated by the universe's vendetta against her. "But I don't even have my *phone*—"

"It's cool—"

"That was shitty of me. I'm going to be better, Lauren, I promise. But that night, when you threw up because you hadn't eaten meat in two years, I held your hair back. I did that."

"Of course you did."

Edie wiped her tears with the back of her hand. "When I realized he was gone, I thought, I should just go on the lock-in anyway, you know? Like, rub his nose in it, make him jealous, make him see how desirable I am, how much Bennett wants me. But I just couldn't. In some weird way I understood that the only person that would hurt is me."

"Yes, bitch!" Lauren applauded. "That's growth! That's maturity!"

"And maybe it would've hurt Charlie, too, you know?" Edie shrugged. "I mean, I'm not delusional—I don't think 'Bennett Charles' has all his hopes and dreams wrapped up in me. But using him to make Peter jealous? I'm not a monster."

"What's the deal with Charlie anyway? What's he like?"

"He's sweet. And hot." Edie thought about it. "But this new version of him needs a lot of attention. He's got this frantic vibe that he tries to hide, but you can always feel it, like, right there."

"So, he's exactly the same."

Lauren smirked, and they cracked up.

"I guess so." Edie shook her head. "Honestly, it's always made me feel very loving toward him. I just want to be like, 'Chill out, it's cool. I got you.'"

"You've always had a lot of empathy for idiots," Lauren agreed.

"Being on reality TV is sociopathic." Edie looked at her best friend seriously. "I'm not kidding. It's literally insane."

"I know."

"Not to mention *producing* it."

"Awful."

"But why would he leave like that, Lauren?" Edie dug around in the glove compartment for a Kleenex. She found an old Taco Bell napkin and let out a strangled cry. The universe was relentless. She blew her nose. "That's what doesn't make sense. Why would he tell me he's falling in love with me and then just disappear?"

"I mean, I don't know him, Edie. What do *you* think?"

Edie chewed her lip. "Maybe he didn't know what to do about the show-slash-his-career?" she offered finally. "Maybe he was scared?"

"Fear's a very real motivator," Lauren agreed. "It's how you ended up on this stupid show in the first place."

"What do you mean?"

"I mean, you got dumped by Brian and you got scared you'd be alone forever, so you grabbed onto the first thing you saw, and now here we are."

Edie's eyes got big. It's not that this assessment didn't ring true, but the ease with which Lauren declared it was a shock. "If you knew all that," Edie said, crossing her arms over her chest, defensive, "why didn't you tell me not to go?"

"Oh my god. *I did.* I texted you the number to my therapist's office."

"So you think I'm stupid for going? And that this is all my fault?"

"Of course I don't think that."

"You don't?"

"Edie, I think it's inspiring the way you go after what you want. But, you know, you take big swings. And sometimes they're big misses. And that's okay, too. But I think you need to understand that this time, it's bigger than you. You're all over the internet—"

But Edie was in her own world.

"The thing is, I don't understand how dating is the one thing you're supposed to do over and over again and keep expecting different results. It's terrible. You get your heart broken, or you sleep with someone, and they disappear before you even open your eyes, and you're expected to pick yourself up and dust yourself off. How am I supposed to keep doing this?"

Lauren shrugged. "Maybe you're not."

"What does that mean?"

"I dunno. I'm just saying—I see you struggling for answers to something that seems sort of unanswerable. I think sometimes people get lucky and they find what they're looking for. Sometimes people get married and spend their lives miserable. Some people find a lot of fulfillment in their careers, or through helping others, or gardening or cooking or art, and so maybe a partner isn't the most important thing to them. There are all sorts of ways to be a person, and none of them is less valid than another. I think what you, Edie Pepper, are supposed to do is figure out how to be happy. How to love yourself. And maybe take the pressure off, pull the release valve on this one thing for a minute."

Edie sighed. Everything was terrible. Except Lauren. Lauren was never terrible.

"So, am I just supposed to not want things?" she asked in a small voice. She looked down at her hands, embarrassed. "And then I'll be happy?"

"Edie, my love, you can want *everything*. You just can't hate yourself because you don't have it yet." Lauren tugged on Edie's ponytail affectionately. "You're gonna be okay. Lemme just run in and get some supplies. And then we'll go home and turn on Bravo."

"Only my truest soulmate would know what I need right now is Doritos and Erika Jayne." Edie put her palm over her heart. "I love you."

"I love you, too." Lauren got out of the car. But then she paused and leaned back through the open door. "But no more reality shows, okay? Like, this is it."

"This is it," Edie agreed, nodding vigorously. "This is it."

TAKE 5 PRODUCTIONS
THE KEY
EPISODE 9 TEASER [DRAFT FOR EP APPROVAL]
TAPE #592

00:00:00 OPENING SEQUENCE

ADAM FOX: Tonight on *The Key*...

BENNETT CHARLES HOLDS HIS HEAD IN HIS HANDS AND SOBS.

ADAM FOX: Finding the key to your heart is never easy.

BENNETT PUSHES THE CAMERA AWAY AND LEAVES THE ROOM.

BENNETT: ... I can't, I can't...

THE CAMERA JOSTLES, TRYING TO KEEP UP WITH A FLEEING BENNETT.

ADAM FOX CHASES BENNETT DOWN A CITY STREET.

ADAM FOX: Bennett! Bennett, wait up!

LONGSHOT OF BENNETT AND ADAM IN AN ALLEY. BENNETT IS HUNCHED OVER; THE PAIN IS TOO GREAT.

ADAM FOX: Can you tell me what's going on, man?

BENNETT: She left, dude, she left. I don't know why, but she left.

BENNETT MOANS, MOMENTARILY BLOWING OUT THE MIC.

ADAM FOX: Edie?

BENNETT: She didn't even leave a note. She didn't say anything, she just left. I don't know what I did. What did I do?

ADAM FOX: If Edie Pepper holds the key to your heart, then you have to do whatever it takes to get her back.

A LONG PAUSE.

BENNETT STRAIGHTENS UP.

FADE TO BLACK

1:00:00 ADAM FOX: All that and more, tonight on *The Key*.

29

Peter Kennedy trudged up the stairs to Edie Pepper's apartment, the apology he knew he was going to have to make stuck in his throat like one of those Key to My Heart–shaped cookies craft services would inevitably trot out at the finale. Peter hated those fucking cookies. So dry. So predictable. So Instagrammable.

Yes, he'd made some mistakes. He could admit that. For one, he'd underestimated Edie's need to be butterfly-kissed at dawn. And he should've called for extra security; Peter knew better than to let key players out of his sight. And when he was hunched over in the lobby adjusting his laces and Jessa said in a voice from above, "What the hell happened last night?" he shouldn't have wavered. He should've told her then that they were changing course.

Honestly, he thought he had more time.

Still, Peter had the feeling that what he considered his fault and what Edie considered his fault were two different things. Why was he an asshole for taking a minute to figure things out? And why was she *not* an asshole for fleeing the set like this was some episode of *Prison Break*? Now the press was circling, Carole Steele was on the warpath, and an entire day spent not in production was costing them hundreds of thousands of dollars and creating a cascade of logistical problems for the already overwhelmed production team to solve. And what about Peter's own bruised feelings—did she not even think about how her little escapade would affect him? Not to mention his complete and total infuriation at having any feelings at all! And the terror that periodically rushed up his spine like a spider, reminding him that he was really close to the worst-case scenario, a total PR shitstorm where Peter himself ended up on the cover of *People*.

To be clear, it's not like Peter *wanted* Edie to go on the lock-in with Bennett. Peter didn't want Edie to do *anything* with Bennett, except perhaps say goodbye to Bennett, dramatically and in front of the cameras.

What he wanted was a second to think through his options.

The bottom line was that this entire drama could be traced back to the fact that he was a producer, Edie was a contestant, and they were stuck in the middle of the most dramatic season ever. And as much as Peter would like to make some grand gesture and grab Edie by the hand and run off into the night, this was real life, where Peter had significant responsibilities to every single person who worked on *The Key*, plus the network, the audience, the advertisers, the various prongs of industry driven by each season—the podcasts, the merch, the live traveling tour—and even Bennett Charles, who Peter certainly fucking hated, but who Peter had dragged into this mess and who would, unfortunately, have to be the public face of it.

Peter rounded the corner of the stairwell. Framed in a doorway was his runaway, beautiful in baggy sweatpants and a T-shirt that read BRUNCH SO HARD. Her hair was wild in a way that reminded him of how she'd looked in bed, and instantly he was filled with regret. For a moment it was clear he should've ignored his thrumming anxiety and desperate need for escape and instead turned to her and woken her up by running his hands all over her body and sliding his tongue inside her until she moaned. And then Peter thought he might take the steps two at a time until they were tearing each other's clothes off right next to what appeared to be an umbrella stand in the shape of a frog. But then another woman stepped into the frame, her face set in a best-friend-kicks-terrible-boyfriend-in-the-balls sort of way, and Peter was once again reminded that real life so rarely had anything to do with the movies.

He paused on the landing. "Hey," he offered.

"Hey." Her smile was suspect. All lips, no teeth.

They stared at each other, neither of them willing to speak first. Peter stuffed his hands in the back pockets of his jeans and kept his face impassive. He knew his assessment of this entire situation and subsequent actions were fueled by that secret, hurt place inside of him, but knowing that and being prepared to make different choices were two very different things.

"Well," she said. "Are you coming in?"

Edie's Chicago apartment was charming in a way that Peter's Malibu condo decidedly was not. Weeks ago, before he knew this woman would change the course of his life, Peter had seen glimpses of it in the background of Edie's intro package and hadn't thought much about it at all. But standing here now, with the radiators clanking and Edie's cat tiptoeing between his legs, Peter was surprised by how drawn he was to the place, to the vintage crown molding, the hardwood floors, the big windows overlooking the tree-lined street, the cozy blue couch that looked perfect for an entire day reading.

"I like your apartment," he said. He knelt to scratch the cat. The cat purred and lifted its chin.

"Oh. Yeah. It's sort of a mess." Edie gestured vaguely. "I moved in right before the show." She pointed. "There's still an entire room filled with boxes."

Peter straightened. "You must be Lauren," he said to the woman standing sentry at the doorway to a long hall. He tried smiling his best smile to distract from the flood of worry that not only was this reunion going to be a three-way dialogue with the best friend, but the best friend was also a journalist.

"Hi, Peter," Lauren said tersely.

"We're off the record, right?" He tried to keep his tone cute.

Lauren rolled her eyes. "I write about politics. And education. Not everyone thinks Hollywood is the most important thing in the world."

He nodded. "Fair enough."

Lauren gave Edie a look. "I'll be listening from the kitchen if you need me."

Peter was relieved to see her go. "She's tough." He smiled at Edie, ready to make nice, but the hurt and disappointment on her face made him sick with regret, and then he was annoyed all over again.

"Remember when we first met?" she said finally, twisting the cord from the blinds around her finger. "And you accused me of being the type of person who was, how did you put it, 'trying to escape the hellscape of human experience through love and marriage'?"

"Vaguely."

"When I saw you coming up the stairs, that popped into my mind. And I thought, how could I be with someone who thinks there's no escape from the hellscape of human experience? Or that the human experience is a hellscape in the first place?" She shrugged. "You know what Oprah says: When people show you who they are, believe them."

Peter gritted his teeth rather than correct her. Oprah didn't say that; it was Maya Angelou. Oprah just said it on TV.

"Can we be nice, please?" he said.

"I am being nice."

"Okay."

They stared at each other.

"I'm really mad at you, you know."

"I can tell." Peter sighed and took a step toward her. "But don't you think this is just a misunderstanding?" he offered. "That if you really think about it, there are all these outside factors—the show, whatever. But without them, everything would be fine? We'd be happy?"

"In what way?"

"In the way that obviously I didn't want you to go on an overnight date with Bennett and that I want us to be together."

Edie threw her hands in the air. "How is that obvious, Peter?"

"How does everything that happened last night not make it obvious?"

"You left! I woke up and poof, you were gone!" She crossed the room toward him, her gray eyes angry. "And then Jessa shows up to get me ready for my lock-in. You do the math—it's literally *not* obvious at all."

"Edie, come on. I just wanted a second to figure out how to handle things." Peter took off his glasses and pressed the heel of his hand to his eye. "You forget I have to deal with an entire show. I can't just drop everything."

"How could I forget that, Peter?" she yelled. "And am *I* not part of the show? Isn't it your literal job to make sure *I'm* okay?"

"You don't get it!" he yelled back. "To run something like this, you have to be willing to piss people off. To hurt feelings. You think the CEO of Starbucks doesn't know his plastic cups are suffocating the planet? That sea turtles have them stuck on their heads like fucking party hats? But to lead an organization like that, you've got to be willing to say, fuck the turtles, what my board wants is plastic cups, and I serve at the pleasure of the board. It's the same here—I don't want to be concerned about the narrative, but it's literally *my job* to think about this from all angles. You're already all over the tabloids—"

"Wait, *what*?"

"I'm handling it. The important thing is, of course *in theory* I want to run off together, but you don't get what that means *in practice*. Do you want paparazzi staked out in front of your apartment? Do you want me to get sued by an entire television network? Do you want the narrative to get so out of control that all of a sudden you've got Bennett Charles giving interviews about how you used him, lied to him, cheated on him?" Peter held his hands up. "I get it—it's not like that—but it doesn't matter what it's like. What matters is who's in control of the story, and right now, thanks to your little escape routine, it's not us."

"Oh, I'm sorry," Edie said, her tone saccharine. "I'm so sorry that being abandoned by a man who may or may not love me is triggering for me." She slit her eyes. "I see now it was inconvenient for you."

"I didn't abandon you! I left because I needed to figure out what we were going to do!"

"Exactly!" Edie pointed a finger at him, victorious. "That's not how relationships work, Peter. *You* don't leave and decide what's going to happen next. *We* decide *together* what's going to happen next."

For a second, Peter felt like he'd been slugged. He'd never once considered that perhaps he should get her input on how they should proceed. And then, all at once, he realized that at no point when he was lying there losing his mind did he ever think, even for a second, that he could turn to her and ask what to do. Or even just seek comfort in her arms. This knowledge, that Peter had no idea how to actually be a partner to anyone, took his breath away.

"I just... I just..." Edie wiped a tear with the back of her hand. "I just don't understand why you have to be so disappointing," she said finally.

The truth of that statement was almost too much to bear. Without thinking, Peter struck back. "Maybe because I'm an actual fucking person, Edie, not just some idea you made up in your head. And maybe if you'd drop the romcom bullshit and meet me here in the real world, we could work it out."

Edie took a step back like she'd been slapped. Immediately he was filled with regret.

"Edie—"

Peter's phone began to ring. He fished it out of his pocket. Carole Steele. Fuck. "Just give me a second." Peter braced himself for whatever came next. "Hi, Carole."

"Peter, I look at you and I think, 'How in the hell did men ever rule the world?' you're so fucking stupid."

"Good to hear from you, Carole," Peter said flatly. He paced the living room. "I'm happy to report we're close to getting today's drama worked out."

"I'm so glad to hear it. Except it's just like a man to take credit for a woman's work."

Peter's stomach dropped—what in the hell was Carole talking about? Sweat pricked his neck and his ears started to ring, like the tinny sound of trumpets, far away but increasing. He paced past the coffee table. Beneath a sweating glass of water was a yearbook, flopped open to a spread of senior portraits. One in particular—one Peter was all too familiar with by now—was framed in a thick, hand-drawn, heart. Suddenly, Peter was struck by the fact that Edie never explicitly said she was falling in love with him, too. And that, perhaps, he'd just decided that she was.

"Once it became clear you couldn't bring this over the finish line, I stepped in," Carole continued. "So why don't you meet me outside. We'll have a little chat."

Suddenly Peter couldn't breathe. Carole Steele was here? In Chicago?

The sound of trumpets was rising, louder now, and Edie was at the window. There was a whoosh of air as Lauren rushed to join her. Drums. Cymbals. Flutes. The cacophony came closer and closer until he understood what Carole had done.

She'd taken over.

30

Advancing en masse down Edie Pepper's quiet Roscoe Village street was, quite unbelievably, a marching band. Strutting five across, the band members' feet struck the pavement with military precision, each step sending shockwaves through the plumes in their caps. White-gloved hands thrust trumpets, trombones, flutes, and piccolos into the air in synchronized choreography. And there, leading the charge with the enthused high steps of an aging band teacher, was Bennett Charles and his bass drum—*BONG BONG BONG*—charting the tempo like a heartbeat.

"You've got to be kidding me," Lauren sighed. "The nightmare continues."

Cameramen jogged on the sidewalk, pausing to grab shots of the procession before taking off again to find new vantage points. A drone swooped across the sky. And standing on the small patch of grass that was Edie's front yard was Jessa and a regal-looking woman in a navy sheath dress cinched to her slim body. A Birkin was hooked over her right arm, and the soles of her nude pumps were a telltale red. As she leaned toward Jessa, her blond bob fell from her face and revealed a slight curl in her lip, almost a sneer, like with one wrong word she might snap.

Edie had never seen anyone so exquisitely terrifying in her entire life.

Then Peter was behind her, enveloping Edie in his perfect Peter-y smell, all pine and sandalwood and leather, as he leaned to look out the window. The way he was standing, with one hand flat against the glass and his body pressed against her, she could easily turn and fold into him, let him wrap his arms around her until the trumpets and the cymbals faded into nothing. How nice it would be to pretend like he'd never left, like they'd never fought at all. But then Edie remembered—*maybe because I'm an actual person, not just an idea you made up in your head*—and she was gutted all over again. Both by the ease with which he'd been so mean, and by the gross, incisive truth of it.

Peter groaned and pulled away.

"What are they playing?" Lauren asked. "NSYNC?"

"Backstreet Boys," Peter and Edie said in unison. "I Want It That Way."

The anger came in hot. "Why do you know that?" Edie accused. "Did you do this?"

"Me?" He looked at her like she was crazy. "You think I came here to work things out and was like, you know what might help? Bennett Charles and a marching band?"

"Oh, right, I'm crazy for thinking a man who plans stunts for a living should know why there's a fucking parade outside my front door!"

"Peter," Lauren mediated. "Maybe you didn't bring them, but you must know what's going on."

Peter sighed.

"Peter!" Edie demanded, feeling more frantic with every passing second. She'd left *The Key*. She was no longer a person on TV. Except here *The Key* was again. "What the hell is this?"

Peter put his head in his hands. "It's the lock-in."

Edie's jaw dropped.

"They brought it anyway." Peter collapsed on the couch and held his head in his hands. "Carole Steele is out there. The president of the network." He took Edie's hand and looked up at her, imploring. "I mean this in the nicest possible way, but I don't think you understand what it means to have the president of a television network on your front lawn. When I say she can destroy us, what I mean is, she can destroy us in ways you can't even imagine. Think hundreds of thousands of bots charged with ensuring every person in America knows your name. She's scary, Edie. She plays nice at first, dangles incentives in front of your face like some fairy godmother—but if she doesn't get what she wants, she will not hesitate to ruin you. Edie, are you listening to me?"

Abruptly the music stopped, and the apartment was pitched into silence.

Then, the static of a megaphone ignited. "Edie! Edie Pepper!" Bennett Charles called. *"You're the key to my heart, Edie Pepper!"*

The part of Edie that was watching her life spin out of control from a rational, detached distance was feeling very loved by how quickly Lauren and Peter put aside their low-key hostility to take up their mantles as best friend/possible boyfriend and devise a plan.

"She's got to break up with him," Lauren said.

"Right now, in front of the cameras," Peter agreed.

Then, before Edie could change her clothes or her mind, all three of them were thundering single file down the stairs and out the front door.

But the part of Edie that was right here, right now—the part that was vividly aware of the cameras and her saggy bra and Charlie Bennett frantically waving hello and the scary New York lady striding toward them—that part was completely and totally about to lose her shit. A sound guy appeared with a lavalier mic and Edie lifted her shirt so he could attach the pack to the waistband of her sweats while Bennett banged his drum—*BONG BONG BONG*—and the band started up again. It was almost deafening at street level.

"I can't do this," she yelled to Peter.

Peter placed his body between Edie and the rapidly approaching Carole Steele.

"Edie, when I met you, I thought this show was going to chew you up and spit you out. But I was wrong. So wrong. From day one you've been completely yourself, and that's why America loves you."

His face was serious, but his green eyes were kind. Edie noted that he'd said, "and that's why *America* loves you" and not "that's why *I* love you." Did he love her or not? And what did "America" have to do with anything anyway? Since when did "America" give a shit about Edie Pepper? Despite these questions, she did feel a wave of comfort. Peter was capable, efficient, experienced—all sorts of things Edie felt like she wasn't at all—and, despite everything, she felt like she should trust him. He knew what they should do next.

"This is it," he continued. "Your last chance to tell your story the way *you* want to tell it."

But Edie had never wanted to tell a story. What she'd wanted was to fall in love. It was clear now that at some point she should've stopped and considered the repercussions of putting her life on television. But before, when it was just an idea—a fantasy—she'd never imagined there would be anything she wouldn't want to scream from the rooftops. Now, of course, there was Peter. And Charlie. And the need to have this conversation in private.

"Tell him you don't love him. Tell him it's over. But do it big, like Zo. You see your neighbor in the window?" Peter pointed. "And that photog with the big lens down the street? Do it big so they can put it on the internet before Carole or anyone else can change the narrative. We'll figure out the rest later. I promise."

Edie looked from Peter's intense face to Charlie's merry one as he marched in circles in his band uniform. From a distance, he looked like the sweet boy she remembered. A breeze rustled the trees and leaves swirled across the sidewalk. Everything smelled crisp, like fall, and all at once she could see them there, senior year, playing their instruments at halftime, and then later on the bus, their first kiss. It was a lifetime ago. But also like some fundamental part of her that she should honor and protect. Maybe Charlie Bennett wasn't her One True Love, but what she understood about him, didn't she understand it because they were the same? A couple of insecure dreamers wanting something so badly they'd risk anything to get it?

Edie wiped her eyes. "I don't want to hurt Charlie," she told Peter. "I don't want to embarrass him."

His eyes went wide. "Are you serious right now? That's where you're at? You can't possibly have actual feelings for him, do you? Edie?"

"Peter, so glad you could join us," Carole Steele called.

"Edie," Peter said, sharp. "I get that so far this hasn't been great, but doesn't anything I said last night matter to you?"

"I don't know what it means, Peter," she said, shaking her head. "It feels like you're not sure. Like you want me on this sinking ship with you, but like maybe you're also gonna leave me there."

"Edie, I would never—"

"And this must be our little Midwestern firecracker, Edie Pepper," Carole said, so close now Edie could smell her expensive perfume. "Trying her best to blow up my show."

"Edie, if you feel any love for me at all, you will do this," Peter said, a little frantic. "There's no other way. Go, now." He gave her a little push toward the street before turning to face Carole himself. "We're all ready to go, Carole. And I think you're going to like what you see."

The sun was blinding as Edie stepped off the curb and into the sort of romcom fantasy she'd dreamed of her entire life. Except now Edie understood that sweeping romantic gestures—the over-the-top fantasy dates, the trumpets, the tubas, the Goo Goo Dolls, the perfect Hollywood kiss—they were all just smoke and mirrors, like small, unsatisfying orgasms that barely delayed the inevitable plunge back to reality. Moments that lasted were sharing the truth of yourself in the back of a darkened plane, or laughing over Nachos Bell Grande, or the kind of sex where you came twice, long and hard, or even just, simply, the desire to work things out after a fight. Edie looked over at Peter, his hand on Carole's back, guiding her across the lawn, out of the cameras' line of sight, his head tilted toward her, working her the same way Edie had seen him work countless people before, and she understood that when he'd accused her of being caught up in a fantasy, he hadn't been wrong. But for so long, all she'd wanted was to get married, and, really, any man would do.

But not anymore.

31

After almost twenty years of freedom, Bennett Charles was right back where he started: bound by the shackles of a high school band uniform. He stared at the pageantry in the mirror, first at the red and white jacket with the epaulets at the shoulders and the gold buttons running down the chest that should've been too tight, but when he'd windmilled his arms, stretched his chest, and then his triceps, bending and pulling his elbow behind his head, not one seam protested—just another reminder that every second he remained on this show, he was losing inches *and* gains. Conversely, the red polyester bibbers were too tight against his anxious stomach, and the subsequent flatulence was just another lure to the ghost of Charlie Bennett, who he could feel hovering—a shadow, a specter, a body-snatcher, ever present when Bennett was vulnerable or weak.

A PA knocked on the bathroom door.

Reluctantly, Bennett slid on his white gloves and placed the pièce de resistance—the white shako with its towering red plume—upon his head.

And there he was.

Charlie Bennett.

First thing this morning, they'd sequestered Bennett in a hotel conference room.

Something was wrong. No one would tell him anything. He knew it was bad. Still, it couldn't be *that* bad.

But then Carole Steele walked in.

She was the same as Bennett remembered—tight dress, towering heels, that particular air of derision—and any confidence Bennett might have left evaporated as she sat down.

"Edie's gone," Carole announced.

It took him a second to process. Edie was gone? Bennett frantically racked his brain, scrolling through a whirlwind of dates and time zones to the last time he'd seen her. Okay, it was on the boat in Scotland. She'd been drunk. And, sure, a little crazy. But all the girls were, like, *a lot* right now. Managing their feelings was a full-time job. Wasn't that what was so special about Edie? Once they'd gotten used to each other again, their relationship felt like it had when they were kids. Uncomplicated and steady. So, why would she have left?

Wasn't Edie his North Star in a sea of starlets?

"Uh, where did she go?" Bennett started to feel sick. Chicago was the place he felt the most insecure. He did not want to be here without her. He looked at his watch. "We're supposed to start filming the lock-in in an hour."

"If we knew where she was, it would make things simpler." Carole crossed her arms over her chest. "But as it stands now, it looks like you and me, we've got a big problem on our hands."

Bennett wasn't sure he could deal with any more problems. The past two months had almost killed him. At the beginning,

The Key was like this epic party where he was living every man's dream, with twenty gorgeous women panting for him day and night. But then Edie showed up and all at once it was no longer just silly dates and making out with hotties—every single thing he said or did became some commentary on who he was, Bennett Charles or Charlie Bennett. Still, despite all the machinations, Bennett had believed he could make it out of here intact. And maybe even in love.

But then, like some cosmic wake-up call, that volleyball had smacked him right in the fucking face. He'd broken his nose (again), and this part of himself, the Charlie Bennett of it all, crept closer. He hadn't wanted to take Edie to the prom, but then spending time with her had felt warm and something like home. He'd been easily swept up in the music, the dancing, the kissing, the nostalgia. The way Jessa hopped around and enthusiastically hugged him on breaks, so excited that Bennett and Edie were connecting, just like she knew they would, because they had all this history between them. It had felt great, hadn't it? To not only find in Edie something that felt like love, but also to stop fighting, to give everyone what they wanted?

But after the prom, production had him going out with two to three girls *a day*, cycling through encounters so quickly it made his head spin. He had no emotional clarity at all. When he was with Edie, he loved Edie. When he was with Bailey, he loved Bailey. When he was with Zo, he loved Zo. Or at least *wanted* her. No one understood the pressure. At cocktail parties, the women would argue about who got to talk to him—literally pulling him by the arms like Stretch Armstrong. On the nights before *Key* ceremonies, he couldn't sleep, and his stomach would be in knots. The tears, the hate, *the physical assault* he had to bear as he let them go, one by one.

But, *finally*, a light at the end of the tunnel—the lock-ins.

Just days ago, he'd been in Santa Barbara for Bailey's lock-in. They'd ridden horses at sunset. Cooked vegan enchiladas with her mom. Played pickleball on the home court with her dad. Made s'mores by the firepit and kissed under the stars. Every moment there felt right. She was beautiful and patient and sweet, and they talked about *everything*. And then, when the cameras were finally gone and they were cuddling in bed together, he didn't even try to sleep with her, even though he really fucking wanted to, because Bailey wasn't just one of the four remaining contestants, she was one in a million. Bennett wasn't even sure if Bailey would say yes. But he *was* sure that the reason he'd endured all this trauma was to find The One. And she was it.

Now it struck Bennett that maybe Edie leaving wasn't a problem.

Maybe Edie leaving was an *opportunity*.

"Is it the worst thing if Edie is gone?" he began, trying to sound nonchalant. Production had never stopped pushing the "Bennett gets engaged to Edie" storyline, and even though he loved Edie, he knew now it was more friendship than romance. Could they have a life together? Probably a great one. She was a solid, steady choice. But Bailey, that's who he was crazy for. "Because I've been meaning to talk to you about Bailey. Maybe it's okay—"

"No, it's not fucking *okay*," Carole seethed.

Carole pulled a MacBook out of her bag. She proceeded to unveil a PowerPoint deck synthesizing the latest press, social media chatter, data, and metrics. Quickly it became clear that without even trying, Edie had captured the hearts of all the gals and gays in America. Fan accounts, trending tweets, tabloid articles, TikTok tutorials ("Get Edie Pepper's No-Look Look in 5 Minutes or Less!"), media mentions, and soaring ratings. *Next slide.* Even her gifs and memes were adorable.

Next slide. His were mockery. Bennett crying. Bennett with a bloodied nose. Bennett tripping off his motorcycle. *Next slide.* The Q Score that measured his brand appeal had tanked. *Next slide.* The countless tweets that made him out to be, on a good day, a callous player, and on a bad one, borderline #MeToo. *Next slide, next slide, next slide.*

Peter had told Bennett that there'd been a lot of gossip and social media chatter after Zo left—they'd had him put out that statement on Instagram (well, they'd had him provide his login info so they could put out that statement on his Instagram)—but the sheer amount of hate was *staggering*.

Instead of a tough, sexy mountain man, he was pathetic. And everyone knew it. A very old fear washed over him. No one liked him. No one had *ever* liked him.

"Do you understand what I just showed you?" Carole asked.

He nodded.

"No. You don't." Carole leaned forward and looked him dead in the eye. "We gave you an entire television show, millions of eyeballs, and a PR machine, and you still managed to fuck it up with your dumb ideas and dirty dick. You shit the bed. Because you were certain you knew better." She sat back and crossed her legs, one elegant stiletto casually arcing through the air. "You handed the show to Edie Pepper." She snapped the laptop shut. "Do you get it now? *She's* the one America is obsessed with. *She's* the star. You made yourself *irrelevant.*"

Bennett thought he might vomit. Just a second ago he thought he might walk out of here with Bailey and that all his wildest dreams could come true. But now, the idea of rejoining the real world as the most hated man in America was nauseating.

"So, Bennett, tell me, because I'd love to know," Carole said now. "How are we going to have a finale when no one gives a shit about you or your love story?" She placed her claws on his forearm and snapped him to attention. "I would hate for you to end up on that mountaintop, all alone, because no one will have you."

He looked in her eyes and understood, maybe for the first time, that from the moment he'd walked into the RX offices, they'd owned him. He should've been smarter. Interrogated their power and the risks. But he'd been certain he deserved not only a hot wife, but internet adoration, because wasn't he special? Hadn't he done every single thing in his power to make himself so? But now the truth could not be denied.

He was a fool.

"What do you want me to do?" he asked finally.

"Get Edie back, of course!" Carole exclaimed. "Ask her to marry you! Declare your love and slide a rock—that I paid for—onto her finger! What you do after that, I don't really care. But you're not leaving until you give America what they want. A happy fucking ending."

Bennett Charles was in love.

Truly, madly, deeply in love with his high school—and America's!—sweetheart Edie Pepper.

Or at the very least, he was determined to look like he was.

Edie was standing on her front lawn now with Peter and an all-grown-up Lauren Wasserman while a sound guy adjusted her mic. They would get engaged and do a press tour and he would love her for the incredible friend that she was. Bennett sliced his mallet through the air and the band started up again. So what if he was wearing this stupid uniform or being manipulated into getting engaged to Edie Pepper? He was going to sack it up and do whatever it took to come out of this alive. Bennett Charles was going to war, and this stupid band uniform was just camouflage. He banged his drum, each strike announcing to the world that BENNETT CHARLES LOVES EDIE AND DEFINITELY NOT BAILEY.

Finally, Edie approached. Two color guards rushed up and removed the massive drum from his chest and carted it off like ants with a crumb. He removed his shako and ran a sexy hand through his curls before propping the cap against his hip. She stood before him looking sort of disheveled in sweats and hair that definitely needed to be brushed. Now he understood that the internet would love her coming out here with no makeup, just being herself on TV. *Relatable!* the captions would scream.

"Hey, Charlie."

He smiled. At the end of the day, wasn't Edie the safest choice? He didn't even know if Bailey loved him. And if he couldn't count on Edie Pepper to love him, really, he couldn't count on anything at all.

"Edie," he began, tossing his cap aside and taking her hands in his own. "From the moment I met you, I knew our lives would be woven together forever. In the words of our favorite band, the Backstreet Boys, 'You are my fire. My one desire.'"

"Right," Edie said, clearly uncomfortable. She glanced over her shoulder at Lauren, who was faux gagging on the sidewalk. God, Lauren could be such a bitch.

"You remember, right?" He signaled to the band. They lifted their instruments to the sky and the street was blasted with music once again.

"Of course, I remember!" she yelled over the sound. She waved her arms to get the band to stop. "But that was a long time ago. Things are different now—"

Bennett fell to his knees. Clutched her hands.

"I don't know why you left," he said, staring deeply into her eyes. They'd told him she was mad about Zo. That he'd *disrespected* her by sleeping with Zo. "But you've got to come back. I'll do anything to make it right. Anything. I'm nothing without you."

"Well, that's definitely not true." She tried to step away, but his grip was strong.

"I'm sorry," he pleaded, covering her hands with kisses. "I made a mistake. Zo was a mistake. I know you're mad, but we can't lose thirty years of connection over a mistake. I was confused. I took it too far. But, Edie, I—"

But before he could finish, she dropped to her knees in front of him. She put her hands over the microphones attached to their collars. "You've got to let this go." She pressed her lips together and looked at him significantly, something he was supposed to understand. "I don't want to embarrass you, but it's over, Charlie. I'm not coming back."

His eyes searched her face for a clue. He could feel Carole and the cameras boring into him. "But why?" he squeaked finally.

"For one, you don't love me—"

"Don't say that, you can't say that—"

"—I'm not what you want, Charlie. I've never been what you want! You didn't even want me here—"

Bennett jerked back, eyes wild. "Did Peter say that?" Bennett scanned the set, looking for that piece of shit traitor Peter Kennedy. "Because, Edie, you know Peter can't be trusted. He's been manipulating both of us, this whole time."

Edie peered at him. "What are you talking about, Charlie?"

"I saw you come out with him. Just now. Whatever he told you, it's not true, okay?"

Her brow furrowed, and for the first time he wondered what she knew versus what he knew versus what Production and America knew. He'd come on this show for an adventure. And now every bad decision, every fucking humiliation, would haunt him forever.

Redemption—*respect*—depended on Edie Pepper.

"Tell me the truth," she said.

"You have to believe me." He reached behind her and unplugged her mic pack before doing the same to his own. This was his moment to get his future back on track. "Yes, I was surprised when you showed up," he whispered. "Maybe I was a little, I don't know, *scared*. Because I was this different person, and you were *you*. But, Edie, any deal Peter and I made, or Carole and I made, or whatever, it's all just symbolic, okay? It doesn't mean anything. It never did." He gave her a look, like *let's talk about this off camera*, but she shook her head and dug her fingernails into his forearm, insistent. He sighed and ran a hand through his hair again, finally landing on absolutely the wrong thing to say. "Edie," he said, staring right into her eyes. "I would've always chosen you. Even if they didn't make me."

TAKE 5 PRODUCTIONS
THE KEY
OTF INTERVIEW: BENNETT CHARLES / CHICAGO
LOCK-IN DATE
TAPE #902

00:00:00 BENNETT CHARLES CLUTCHES HIS BASS DRUM.

THE PLUME IN HIS CAP QUAKES WITH EVERY SOB.

32

"The good news is, you're an icon for single women everywhere," Lauren said over FaceTime. Because Lauren was an adult, she was hard at work making a beautiful vegetarian paella.

Edie, however, was standing at her fridge with her nose deep in some old takeout. "This pad thai smells awful." She'd been locked in her apartment for three and a half days. Ordering Grubhub again seemed impossible.

"Why didn't you have groceries delivered like I told you?"

Edie rolled her eyes. Who could cook at a time like this? She tossed the pad thai in the trash and slid to the floor. Besides, she'd deleted all the apps except Grubhub and FaceTime off this old iPad she'd dug out of a moving box. *The Key* still had her phone and her computer, so as soon as she plugged the iPad in, the notifications exploded. Texts, emails, Hinge, Bumble, Tinder, The League, WhatsApp, Facebook Messenger, Twitter, Instagram. Edie stared in horror as even Brian Heart Emoji flashed a series of brief communiques—

I'm sorry.

I made a mistake.

I love you.

EDIE. CALL ME.

Lauren threw chopped peppers into a sauté pan. "Why don't you bring me dinner?" Edie begged. "You know I'm too depressed to eat a vegetable alone."

"I'm not having my picture on TMZ again."

"You got a lot of ladies in your DMs from that."

Lauren gave Edie a look. "The last thing I need is some random Instagram girlfriend."

"I don't know, what if she's nice?"

"Edie, is this you believing in love again?"

"Definitely not. I hate love." Edie stood up and walked to the window. "The paparazzi never leave to go pee. Isn't that amazing?"

"Sure," Lauren agreed. "You know, you're gonna have a lot of career opportunities from this. You could be an influencer. Or start a podcast. After the volleyball date aired, your followers went through the roof. Over 900K on Insta now—way more than Charlie."

"It's so weird," Edie said, peeking out the curtain. "What do you think it's about?"

"I think it's about you being a cool fucking person."

"Be serious, please."

"I am being serious." Lauren slid her paella in the oven and plopped down in front of the TV. She picked up the remote. "Like I said, according to most of the internet, you're an icon for single women everywhere. You're basically Charlize Theron. Or Selena Gomez."

Edie didn't feel like Charlize Theron. She didn't feel beautiful or powerful or strong. She felt bloated and hungover. And like her hair smelled. And like her tear ducts were on fire from three days of sobbing after having her heart ripped out and stomped on by a stupid Prada loafer.

"Do you think he had feelings for me? Like, for real?" Edie asked for the twelve thousandth time. She walked past the immense floral arrangement Carole Steele had sent. The card had been blank, except for Carole's name and phone number. Edie arrived at the bedroom and crawled into bed, pulling the comforter up to her chin. "Or that he used me, strung me along to make sure I stayed for the finale?"

"I think he was probably just doing his job and things got complicated."

"Yeah," Edie said, the tears starting up again.

"But, Edie, it doesn't matter what I think. It matters what *you* think. What *you* believe to be true about Peter."

Edie thought about the last time she'd seen Peter. She'd been furious, storming down the street with Lauren running to keep up. She made it to the front door. He'd stopped her.

"Edie!"

She turned on him. "You're making him pick me? Are you fucking serious, Peter? Was I always just some joke to you?"

He shook his head furiously. "It's not like that," he pleaded. "Let me explain."

Except she didn't fucking care anymore. "Don't bother. This entire thing was a mistake, and I really don't fucking care anymore!"

He pushed Ted and a boom mic back with his forearm and leaned toward her to whisper. "Edie, please listen to me. I haven't been trying to hurt you. This is all just—"

"Words, Peter," she'd spat. "Nothing you say means anything. Anything at all."

Since then, she'd gone back and forth about what it meant.

"Oh my god!" Lauren shrieked suddenly.

"What?" Edie said, a pillow over her head, no energy left to care. Maybe she'd take a hot bath, put on some Adele, and cry.

"Peter! He's on TV!"

Edie shot up, dislodging Nacho Bell Grande, who yowled and fled for the kitchen. "Where?" she screeched, running for the living room. "What channel?"

"E!" Lauren yelled from the bed, where Edie had abandoned the iPad.

Edie snatched up the remote and swore as it slid around the apps before finally landing on Hulu, which, of course, was its own mess trying to navigate to live TV. For a split second Edie felt vindicated for all the years she'd continued paying for live TV. See! It *was* necessary. Finally she found E!, pressed Select, and the screen went dark—Come on! *Come on!*—before flickering to life, and there was Peter Kennedy, back in her living room, with Ryan Seacrest.

The first thing she thought: He was so handsome. She'd almost forgotten just how handsome he was, because Peter's handsome was a sort of low-key, normcore handsome. Or maybe it was just that even though she hated him to death, she felt so much love just seeing his face again, hearing his voice, watching the way he held the back of his neck with one hand and cast his eyes to the ground as he listened, and then the slow smile and cute way he nodded before responding. It all filled her with such resounding emotion, she had to grope her way to the floor.

"We're thrilled, Ryan, that you're enjoying this season as much as we are," Peter said, looking and sounding just like his competent, Peter-y self. "Every season we want to give America the most dramatic season ever, but this, *this* is really it."

"The internet can't stop talking about Edie Pepper," Seacrest said. "What is it about her that women relate to so much?"

"Well, I'd never presume to speak for the women of America." Peter and Seacrest exchanged a chuckle. "But I couldn't be less surprised by how our audience is responding to Edie." Edie scooched closer to the screen. Either she was imagining things or Peter changed when he said her name. He was suddenly blinking a lot. Clenching his jaw. Like he might...*cry*?

"Edie's the most extraordinary person I've ever met."

"And you know JLo!" Seacrest joked.

Peter laughed. "Well, I met JLo one time," he demurred. "Edie has everything a man could want in a partner. She's kind, she's smart, she's funny, and she's beautiful, and I've never met anyone more willing to love with their whole heart." He took a breath. "*The Key*'s not an easy process. Lots of hearts get broken along the way. But Edie's taught us what it means to be present and really show up for your life. And how to treat the people you love." He paused and looked directly at the camera. "And, personally, I hope she's in my life forever."

Seacrest squinted. "Your life? Or Bennett's?"

"Oh. Bennett's." Peter cleared his throat. "And like, all of our lives generally. America's lives."

"What can you tell us about the finale?" Seacrest asked. "Will Edie be back?"

"C'mon, Ryan, you know I'm not going to tell you anything about the finale. Other than *The Key* airs Tuesdays at eight p.m. on RX."

Peter and Ryan shook hands, and as Ryan introduced the next segment, Edie lay down on the floor and stared at the ceiling. Holy shit. Had Peter Kennedy, Hollywood hotshot and showrunner of *The Key*, just appeared on national television and declared his love for her? Or at least walked right up to the edge of it? Sure, he'd left himself some plausible deniability, but he'd literally just said to the entire world that he wanted her, Edie Pepper, in his life *forever*. *Holy fucking shit.* She should forgive him. They could work it out. Why couldn't they work it out? Because he was neurotic. Impossible. Rigid. Because he produced her, manipulated her, abandoned her. Except, didn't he come back? Didn't he try?

Peter wasn't perfect. But neither was she. And maybe it took two decades of bad dates, Bennett Charles, and even the return of Brian Heart Emoji for Edie to realize that love was never going to be as pretty or simple as some movie montage. But it was sincere, complex, and *hers*.

And she wanted it, warts and all.

Edie sat up and turned off the TV. Someone was screaming.

Lauren!

Edie ran back to the bedroom and scooped up the iPad. Lauren was jumping around her kitchen. "Holy shit!" she squealed. "Are we going to forgive him? I mean, clearly he needs therapy, but like, I see what you mean, there's something vulnerable and authentic at the center. I thought he was gonna cry!"

"I know!" Edie started to cry herself. "So, we think he loves me? And I should forgive him? What do I do—do I tell him I love him? Because I think I do, Lolo. Like, it's been a mess. And it looks *nothing* like I expected. But seeing him right now, it's like my heart might explode. He's difficult. He checks out when he's scared. But I've never in my life had a man believe in me like he does. It's like he looks at me, and he sees something special. He calms me. And maybe I open him up. And, I mean, I know he didn't want me to get engaged to Charlie. But everything just got so out of control… Fuck, I don't even have his phone number! And, let's be honest, he's *so* out of my league. But I've never been so sure. It's a mess, but it's real. But I don't even have his phone number! How is that possible? I've had his dick in my mouth, but I don't have his phone number!"

"Let's be honest, it wouldn't be the first time."

Edie and Lauren both doubled over, they were laughing so hard. Truly, best friends were the greatest love of all.

"Lauren! Get serious. What am I gonna do?"

"The flowers! Call the number on the flowers!"

Edie gasped.

"Lauren Marie Wasserman, are you suggesting that I go back on *The Key* and pretend I want to get engaged to Charlie Bennett, but really hunt down Peter and proclaim my love for him in my very own over-the-top romantic gesture? When just twenty minutes ago you called reality TV 'a scourge on modern feminism' and said that if I had any sense, I would stop watching it completely and get a better hobby, like composting or competitive Scrabble?"

"Bitch, shut up. Even I believe in true love *sometimes*."

Ten hours later, Edie Pepper was on a plane to Switzerland.

33

"Edie's back."

Peter looked up from the press release he was writing about his permanent departure from *The Key*—a fantastic eight years, millions of viewers, honored to have been part of moments that shaped not only reality TV, but television history—to Jessa standing in the conference room door waiting for him to respond. Edie was back? Peter glanced at the clock. The mountaintop engagement was scheduled to begin in thirty-five minutes. He sat back and waited. Whatever this was, it wasn't good.

"Carole didn't want me to tell you until the last minute."

And there it was. Carole. Carole didn't want *me* to tell *you*. Fuck. Peter took a closer look at Jessa. She wasn't wearing any lipstick. Her sleek ponytail was replaced by a messy bun on top of her head. Sneakers instead of heels. And then he almost laughed. How many times had he walked past a mirror and caught sight of himself with that exact same expression? Like some burnt-out, sad-sack producer, carrying the weight of a show that had brought in $97 million in ad revenue last year?

"Who knows she's here?" he asked, holding on to hope that if no one knew, he could still stop it.

"A lot of people know, Peter."

Peter sighed and pushed his laptop aside. After the marching band debacle, he'd grabbed the first PA he saw and told them to fast-track Edie's phone and computer from the LA offices back to her apartment so Peter—now en route to Los Angeles—could contact her before his flight to Switzerland. He'd emailed her, texted her, checked his phone constantly, but she never responded. So five hours before he boarded the plane for the finale, a Hail Mary: Peter went to the E! studios and did the Seacrest interview, hoping she'd see it, hoping she'd understand just how much he regretted all the ways he'd hurt her. Still nothing. More days passed and now they were minutes away from the final key ceremony. And Edie was back.

Unfortunately, he wasn't stupid enough to think she was back for him.

"What's she doing here, Jessa?" he asked, understanding now that they'd gotten her back together with Bennett behind his back. "Are you going to fill me in on the plan? Last I heard I was still the showrunner."

Jessa sat down across from him. "She's here to get engaged to Bennett."

Peter's heart sank. "She can't be."

"She is."

Peter leaned across the table and stared Jessa down. "She told you that directly? That's what she said? That's what she wants?"

"Peter," Jessa said, softly now, like a best friend delivering hard news. "She's already in the dress."

Peter sat back, took his glasses off, and set them on the table. She couldn't possibly want to get engaged to Bennett. He exhaled a rush of air before crushing his face with both hands, mashing his cheeks together, and rubbing his eyes until little white specks floated across his vision.

He'd tried so hard to throw himself back into work, to box up all his emotions and focus on getting the job done. For two days he'd locked himself in this conference room and focused on organizing his files for his successor. Still, sometimes without warning, he'd been scared he was about to lose it. A clip of her smiling that big smile. Or on the plane, when the in-flight movie options included *Cast Away*, *Forrest Gump*, and *Catch Me If You Can*. His sister kept texting him, *Peter, come home. You can stay with us for a while, it will be good for you.* And when he was alone in his room at night with nothing but time to think.

She was actually going to go through with it. "So that's why you want me on the helicopter," he said finally, putting his glasses back on. "You're neutering me? On my own fucking show?"

"Peter, I'm sorry," Jessa said, looking tortured, but not really tortured enough, in Peter's opinion. "We both know this is your last season. I can't piss Carole off. I've got my own career to think about." She took her hair down and then twisted it back up again. "And somebody's got to think about *The Key*."

Peter laughed. He'd spent almost his entire professional life thinking about *The Key*. "So, what, you're a double agent? My protégé turned mastermind?"

"Peter, c'mon. It's not like that."

"Oh, yeah? What's it like?"

"You lost your shit over this girl, Peter. I'm sorry, but that's facts."

"Oh, fuck off," he said, more venom than he knew he had rising to the surface. "You've been waiting for the right moment to push me out. Congratulations."

"You're an asshole, you know that?"

"Yeah, I fucking do!"

They stared at each other.

Peter ran his hands through his hair and yanked at the ends before dropping his hands uselessly in his lap. "I'm sorry," he said. "That was fucked-up. Obviously, you're not wrong."

"Obviously," Jessa said. "Don't put your shit on me, Peter. We've been friends a long time, and I don't deserve it."

"You're right," he said, chastened. "You don't."

"And while you've been making a mess, I've been cleaning it up."

He nodded. Jessa was doing what she had to do. She was taking control of production. Jessa was getting it done.

"So, look, this is what's going to happen," she continued. "You're gonna leave it alone. You're gonna get on the helicopter, you're gonna direct the sky shots, and then, when it's a wrap, you're gonna get on the first flight outta here, go home, and pull yourself together."

Peter hated this plan. He glanced at the clock. Twenty-seven minutes to the finale. He'd already given up so much to ensure this season got over the finish line. Maybe it was time to accept it—Edie didn't want him. From the very beginning she'd come here to get engaged to Bennett Charles, and didn't Peter promise her that? Maybe, after all he'd put her through, the only thing to do now was get out of the way.

Jessa reached across the table and took his hand.

"I'm sorry. I know you liked her."

Peter stared at the useless printer sitting at the end of the table. Despite two days of visits from the Alpina Gstaad's IT department, the printer continued to flash error messages in German and had never, not once, spit out a single call sheet.

"Does everyone know?"

"I don't think so. No one important, at least."

And then she squeezed his hand before getting up and walking out.

Edie was about to get engaged and Peter was going to have to watch the whole thing play out from a helicopter in the sky. He stood up, grabbed the printer off the table and shook it, hard. Suddenly the printer roared to life, ground its gears, and delivered two days' worth of pages onto the floor.

Edie had been trying to get to Peter for two days now. But from the moment she stepped off the plane, she'd been a hostage. Three random producers and two security guys had met her at the airport and refused to answer any of her questions during the two-hour drive to the Alpina Gstaad, the luxurious Swiss resort where she'd be imprisoned. They escorted her straight to her room, where both the TV and phone had been removed. When her luggage showed up, the iPad she'd stowed in a sweater was gone. Still, Edie didn't really start to worry about her plan until she opened her door at two a.m. and there was a security guard popping his gum on the other side.

What was her plan exactly? Fly to Switzerland, find Peter. That was it. Unfortunately, she hadn't accounted for the whole prisoner thing. Or that Peter wouldn't be around during her interviews, dress fittings, and B-roll shoots featuring Edie strolling the snowy grounds, draped in a scarf so long it wrapped around her neck three times and *still* dangled past her knees. Every time she was out of her room, Edie frantically scanned the lobby, the restaurant, the ballroom, for Peter. Once she pretended to be confused by the bathroom signage and found herself hissing, "Peter? Peter?" by some fancy urinals.

"Where's Peter?" Edie asked Jessa casually. "Shouldn't he be here?"

"Peter's doing press in LA."

But Edie knew Peter wasn't in LA. He was here, at the Alpina Gstaad. She could feel him in the efficiency of the production schedule, in the way everyone waited for the lighting to be just right before taking the shot, and in the carafe of mushroom coffee she'd spotted on the craft services table that no one in their right mind would drink but him.

When she woke up on the morning of the finale and still hadn't found him, Edie really started to get nervous. Everyone kept hugging her and congratulating her, as if it were a given that she would get engaged to Bennett Charles today. Typically, the finale was built upon the suitor making a tortured choice between *two* contestants. But when Edie asked what had happened to Lily, Max, and Bailey, no one would tell her anything about the lock-ins or if any of her friends were here now. None of this was working out like she'd hoped, and when she approached Jessa about calling the whole thing off, Jessa said, "Oh, hell no, you're not Julia Roberts. You don't get to pull the *Runaway Bride* thing more than once," and then she'd dragged Edie off to get her makeup done.

For six hours she was plucked, painted, glued, brushed, curled, and cinched. And when they brought her to a full-length mirror for the big reveal, she had to admit she looked gorgeous. The gown, a seven-thousand-dollar white Marchesa with a sequined bodice and feathered skirt, was the most luxe dress Edie had ever seen, much less worn. Her extension-laden hair flowed down her back in gorgeous waves. Diamond earrings dangled from her ears. Delicate Jimmy Choo strappy sandals adorned her feet. The overall effect was stunning.

And completely bridal.

Jessa approached with a lush white fur coat. She draped it over Edie's shoulders like she was some glorious snow princess from Narnia.

"Jessa, seriously, I can't do this."

"Of course you can." Jessa bared her teeth and pointed for Edie to do the same. She checked for errant lipstick. "All your dreams are about to come true."

"You have to listen to me," Edie insisted. "I don't want to marry Bennett."

Jessa laughed and floofed Edie's hair. "Who said anything about marrying Bennett? It's only an engagement." Jessa considered Edie in the mirror for a long moment before taking her by the shoulders and spinning her around. "Look, I don't care if you turn down his proposal. Carole won't like it, but she'll deal. I don't hate a feminist, I-choose-me moment." Jessa arranged Edie's hair around her shoulders. "Bailey's here. Did you know that? She looks beautiful, too. Like a bride."

"Bailey?"

"It's so weird, but it seems like she really loves him, don't you think?" Jessa cocked her head and was quiet for a moment. But then she smiled wide. "Okay! Let's go!"

Peter shrugged on his Burberry peacoat and walked through the lobby, past a tuxedoed Bennett Charles in the final stages of mic check, through the massive kitchen and out the back door of the hotel. Snow crunched under his loafers as he followed Ted across the lawn and into the waiting helicopter.

The helicopter lurched into the sky with the door wide open. Peter closed his eyes. Ted couldn't film with the door closed, and as freezing cold air whooshed into the cabin, Peter waited for his anxiety to take over. They rose higher. Peter opened his eyes. Apparently, his heart was too broken to bother scaring the shit out of him. He leaned over and looked out the window.

The view was spectacular. The ground blanketed in fresh snow. The towering fir trees all dusted in white. The mountains rising into the sky, dwarfing the hotel's turrets below. Typically, natural beauty like this would make Peter think about God—whatever God was—and he'd remember that he was just some minuscule part of some great big universe, and he'd feel centered in a way, understand that everything in his life both mattered and didn't. But now, the grandeur only clarified that he was a real fucking idiot who'd majorly bungled his shot at being a decent person during his limited time on earth. Maybe that was dramatic, but now it seemed clear that Peter had spent literal years of his life prioritizing his career. Happily taking advantage of people, with very little reflection on his own culpability or intentions. He'd ignored his family because he'd been ashamed and couldn't handle seeing the disappointment on their faces. And now that he finally understood all that really mattered was who you loved and how you loved them, it was too late. He was stuck in a helicopter while the love of his life was about to get engaged to the biggest douchebag of all time.

Ted handed him an iPad.

"That'll pick up visual from below," Ted said into his headphone's mic. He pointed to a button on-screen. "Press that and you'll get the feed up here as well."

Peter nodded.

"She's coming out now."

Ted took up his camera. The copilot double-checked Ted's safety harness. With a thumbs-up, Ted was kneeling on the floor of the helicopter, shooting the scene below.

Peter sighed and looked at the iPad, at the split screen of Edie. First, Ted's long shot: Edie in a blur of white, moving up the mountain on Adam Fox's arm. Now, of course, Peter regretted all the wedding tropes they trotted out for finales. In the close-up from the ground, her face looked emotional in a way Peter couldn't quite parse but made his entire body singe with regret. She reached Bennett in the middle of a circle of glowing candlelight. She took his hands.

Peter's heart pounded. He attempted to shift his brain back into work mode and come up with some instructions for Ted to improve the shot, but the shot was perfect. Ted didn't need Peter to tell him how to do his job. Ted had been with *The Key* for as long as Peter had. He was the best camera op they had. Out of nowhere, tears stung Peter's eyes. He was going to miss Ted. He was going to miss all these people and all that they'd made together. It wasn't perfect, and some of it was actually sort of fucked-up, but this show had been everything to him.

"It's been great working with you these past eight years, Ted," Peter said, trying to keep his tone casual. "Probably my opinion won't count for much soon, but if I can ever help, recommend you to someone, I know you were thinking about a move to film—I'd be happy to."

"You going somewhere, Pete?" Ted said from behind the camera.

"Yeah, well..." Peter said. "You know how it goes. All things come to an end, right?"

"That they do." Ted was quiet for a moment. "A lot of shit people in Hollywood. Always thought you did a good job. You're solid. Fair. I always liked that about you."

"And here I thought everyone thought I was an asshole."

"Oh, they do."

They both laughed before falling silent again, contemplating the scene below.

"How many people you think we've seen come through here?" Ted asked.

"On the show? Hundreds. Including casting? Thousands."

"All these people looking for love," Ted mused. "And the funny thing is, in all these years, this is the first time I've ever seen *The Key* deliver. Too bad the man she loves isn't down there." Ted pulled away from the camera and looked at Peter. "Sort of ruins the moment, don't you think?"

Peter's eyes went wide as he took in Ted's meaning.

Of course, Ted would've noticed something going on between Peter and Edie. Ted was always there, a fly on the wall. It was literally his job. Peter's face went red when he realized how many times Ted had probably watched Peter stare at Edie holding hands with Bennett, or kissing Bennett, or laughing with Bennett, Peter frowning on the sidelines like an angsty, lovesick teen.

On the iPad, Bennett was talking but there was no audio. It was clearly a speech, a declaration of love that Peter himself should be making. And all at once, that part of Peter that believed in love very deeply, that believed in Edie, that understood it was now or never, burst to the surface. He had to do something.

"She does love me, right?" Peter said, standing up as best he could in the tiny space. "That's what you're saying?"

"Jeez, Pete," Ted said from behind the camera. "For a smart guy, you can be pretty dense."

"Well, you could've mentioned it before we got on the fucking helicopter!"

With adrenaline coursing through his veins, Peter leaned into the cockpit and told the pilots to let him the fuck out.

"What the hell you talkin' 'bout, mate?" the pilot said in a thick British accent. "We can't 'let you out.' This is a helicopter."

"Yeah, I know what it is," Peter said, suddenly exhilarated. "Can you land?"

"Look at the trees—if you wanna land, we gotta go back."

"No time for that." Peter looked around. The door was already open. "You got a ladder, a parachute or something?"

The copilot cracked up. "Nobody told me we was flyin' James Bond." He made eyes at the pilot. "We got James Bond here."

Peter flicked his eyes to the iPad. Bennett looked dangerously close to getting down on one knee. "Fly over there!" Peter pointed toward engagement rock. "Fly above them. Until the snow swirls around and fucks up the shot."

The pilots looked at each other, skeptical.

"Yeah, those aren't our instructions, mate. The girl was clear—stay far enough away they can't hear the copter."

"Well, I don't give a shit," Peter declared. "*I'm* the showrunner and *I'm* in charge of this entire production."

"That's true," Ted said. "He's the showrunner."

Grumbling, the pilot turned the helicopter and flew lower—*WHOOSH WHOOSH WHOOSH*—toward engagement rock. Peter looked to the iPad, at Edie and Bennett now looking up at the sky.

"Give me the ladder," Peter demanded. "I'm getting out."

"You're gonna break your legs, mate," the copilot said. "But if you insist."

The copilot lifted a seat cushion and removed a metal chain ladder from a compartment below. He motioned Ted out of the way, and the helicopter's feed cut off as Ted took a seat. The copilot attached one end of the ladder to bolted hooks on the helicopter's floor and then threw the whole thing out the door where it flew like a kite in the wind.

The copilot took Peter by the shoulders. "Don't let go, mate."

Peter swallowed hard. Took off his jacket. Rolled his shoulders three times. And then he began his descent.

"Before you came back into my life, I was adrift," Bennett said as he held Edie's hands. He rubbed his thumb back and forth across her skin. The cameras circled. "I knew there was more in this world meant for me. And then you, Edie Pepper, showed up, my oldest friend. You made me strong. You made me loyal. You showed me who I could be: a husband."

Over his shoulder, Edie watched a helicopter approaching. Strange, it kept getting closer until Bennett's words were swallowed in its roar. Everyone turned to look.

"Cut, cut, cut!" Jessa yelled. "Who's got ears on the helicopter?" She spun in a little circle in the snow. "Somebody tell them they're way too close! It's fucking the shot!"

Edie took the deafening *WHOOSH WHOOSH WHOOSH* that would kill their mics as an opportunity to talk to Charlie for real. She grabbed the lapels of his tuxedo and yanked him in.

"Charlie!" she screamed. "Don't propose to me! Do you hear me? You can't, you don't love me!"

He grimaced. "You're my choice, Edie."

"Oh my god!" She shook him back and forth, trying to knock some sense into him. "Knock it off! I adore you, Charlie, I always have. But we're friends! Don't you want to choose Bailey?"

"I can't choose Bailey," he yelled back, the façade finally cracking. "They told me I can't. It's you they want. *Everyone* wants *you*. And, Edie, maybe you think I'm an idiot, but I really think you're the only person I can get through this with. I know that now. You may be the only person who's ever really gotten me, you know?"

"But that's not true! Bailey loves you! She told us she was falling in love with you."

He looked away. "Bailey will find her happy ending." He looked back at Edie and gave her a smile that was clearly forced. "We'll make it work. America will love us."

"You'd rather propose to me because you think people will like you for it?" Edie said incredulously. "Charlie, that's insane."

"I never said I was a good person." He shook his head and looked incredibly sad. "I've got a long way to go, all right? Of course, I love Bailey. She's incredible. But you don't understand what it's been like—no one cares about how I feel or what I want. I've walked every step of this *alone*. The whole world hates me. When she sees what the world's been saying about me, Bailey will hate me. Please don't hate me, too."

Edie looked at him, at this man she'd known since kindergarten. He looked more like Charlie Bennett now than when she'd arrived. He was thinner, rashier, and his mannerisms were smaller, more humble. He was scared and anxious, just like he'd always been. And all at once, she realized her greatest gift, since they were five years old, had been believing in him.

She pulled him into a hug. Shut her eyes and held him to her.

"I believe in you, Charlie," she said into his ear. "I always have. Do what's in your heart. It's the only way."

When she opened her eyes, a ladder was dangling out of the helicopter. What the hell? Then something was coming out of the door. A foot? A shoe?

A Prada loafer.

Immediately, Edie released Bennett and started running, her strappy sandals slipping in the snow. Peter! Edie fell to her knees but quickly got up again, running toward the ladder hurtling through the sky. And then there was Peter in midair, slowly inching his way down.

"Oh my god, *Peter*! Be careful!"

A gust of wind picked up the ladder and flung it to the right. Peter rode the wave, flying back and forth on a pendulum before the ladder stabilized again. He lifted a foot to take another step down. Another gust of wind. And as the ladder twisted and jerked, Peter lost his balance. One leg stabbed through the empty space between the rungs. His grip slipped, and with one leg still tangled, he slid.

Edie watched with one hand over her mouth in horror.

Ted hung out of the helicopter, trying to steady the ladder while Peter extracted his leg. Cameramen appeared on either side of Edie. Peter looked down. There was still a good twelve feet between him and the ground.

He jumped.

"Peter!" Edie screamed.

In slow motion, Peter Kennedy fell through the air. Finally, he hit the snow and began to roll down the mountain in just his jeans and gray cashmere sweater.

Edie took off, the snow deeper now. She hiked her feathered skirt to her knees and kept wading in, the fur coat dragging behind.

"Peter? Peter! Are you okay?"

She fell to her knees at his side.

Peter laid in the snow, laughing his ass off.

"Did you see that?" he said, grabbing her hand. "I've never been that extreme in my life!"

For a second Edie was speechless. But then, there was the man she loved, who she'd flown across the world for, spent days searching for, who could've died trying to get to her, there he was with snow in his hair, his cheeks bright red, laughing, and then Edie was laughing, too, brushing the snow off him, covering his face with kisses, so relieved he was okay.

"It was super extreme," she agreed, the thrum of the helicopter fading into the distance.

Peter sat up. "You look beautiful," he said, taking her cheek in his cold palm. "And I know I've been awful, but I love you, Edie, I really do. And here's the deal: I'm gonna quit this job. And I'm gonna go to therapy. And I know I've got some learning to do about what it means to be in a relationship. But I'll learn. I'm a quick learner. And I'm not going anywhere, okay? I'm here. And this is exactly where I want to be. With you."

Edie started crying. Big, heaving sobs that she didn't quite expect and definitely couldn't control. She put her hands over her face. "Don't look at me," she squeaked.

Peter got to his knees and held her. Finally, her breathing slowed, and she could look at him again.

"I thought you were 'falling in love with me,'" she said, squinting at him like a detective. Her face was streaked with mascara and one false eyelash was askew. "And now you say you 'love' me? Are you sure? How do you know?"

Peter rubbed the mascara with his thumb. "Well, if you must know, I've spent some significant time over the last few days thinking about what love actually means. Somehow, I found myself circling every single *Key* cliché I'd ever heard—love comes when you least expect it, nothing made sense until I met you, I can't imagine my life without you, you make me a better person—and I realized all of it is how I feel about you." He shrugged. "I admit it's very embarrassing to be a walking cliché, but here we are."

"Peter." Edie was smiling the biggest smile she'd ever smiled in her whole life. "That's beautiful."

"It's cheesy." He laughed and pulled the wonky eyelash from her eye. "But that's what you do to me, Pepper. You crack me wide open." And then he kissed her, a long slow kiss that left her breathless.

"Peter, I love you, too," she said, her forehead pressed against his. "I'm sorry I didn't say it sooner."

"Pretty sure I didn't deserve it sooner."

Peter helped her up and they stood together in the snow and took in what was left of engagement rock. Candles tipped over, blown out. Jessa yelling into a walkie-talkie. A PA leading Bennett off set. The production crew staring, dumbfounded.

"You're gonna be in so much trouble," Edie said, amused.

"And it's one hundred percent your fault." And then they were laughing again, and he was kissing her, and she was kissing him, and they were falling back down in the snow, Peter burying his arms in her fur coat, Edie pushing her face into his neck, breathing him in.

"Listen," he said, pulling back to look at her. "I know you were planning to get engaged today, so that's a disappointment."

Edie rolled her eyes. "Obviously I wasn't. I've been looking for you."

He smiled, brushing the hair off her face before continuing, more serious this time. "And I want to ask you to marry me. But not here, all right? Not like this. When it's you and me. No cameras, no bullshit."

"Definitely," she agreed, on the verge of tears all over again. "I mean, your mom might hate me. We don't even know."

Peter slapped a palm to his forehead. "That's right! You haven't even met my family. And she probably will hate you. She's a real shrew." He dodged Edie's slap.

"My mom's going to love every single thing about you," she said. "I'm not sure I'll be able to stand it."

"Don't worry. She'll like me less when I'm unemployed." He took Edie's coat between his fingers. "By the way, is this real fur?"

"I have no idea. They just put it on me."

"C'mon, Pepper," Peter said, pulling her out of the snow. "We gotta get you on camera saying how beautiful you feel in this faux fur."

"Is it faux, though?"

"No idea. But trust me, you don't want the PETA people after you. We'll have enough problems when I'm sued by the network. Will you still love me when I'm penniless?"

"For richer or poorer."

He smiled and kissed her again, the kind of kiss that made Edie want to tear his clothes off.

"Seriously, can we get out of here?" she demanded when they pulled apart. "I cannot feel my feet."

Peter looked at her shoes. "Who wears strappy sandals on a mountain? I expected more of you, Pepper. A practical Birkenstock at the very least."

"All right, Mr. Designer Loafers. Just for that, you're gonna carry me down the mountain."

"May I remind you that I just fell out of a helicopter? Surely, I've cracked at least three ribs. I'll carry you to engagement rock, but that's it. Then you walk."

"Fair enough."

And then Peter scooped her up, like a bride crossing the threshold, and they made their way through the snow toward the Alpina Gstaad.

"Let's get the hell out of Switzerland," he said.

"Oh my god, yes. But can we do that? Can we just leave?"

"Why not? Let's go to Paris for a few days."

Edie looked at him agog. "Peter, are you serious? 'Cause I love you already. My whole heart might explode if we go to Paris."

"Then Paris it is."

"You're gonna have to get me a phone, though. I've got to call Lauren. And I can't be in love in Paris without a phone. We have to take *so many pictures*."

"We'll get you a phone. And champagne, and croissants, and baguettes, and all of the cheese."

"I thought you were lactose intolerant?"

"Not in Paris, I'm not."

The production team was scrambling to reset engagement rock, replacing broken candles and adjusting tripods and lighting rigs, preparing for Bailey to arrive on Adam Fox's arm to start the finale all over again. Edie's heart felt warm, thinking about her friends Bennett and Bailey finding the love they both deserved. Edie rested her head on Peter's chest, content. Somehow, against all odds, they'd arrived at their happy ending. Sure, it wouldn't be perfect, but Edie felt like she got it now—love was an intention, an action, an acceptance. And perhaps her optimism didn't need to be psychotic. Perhaps it could be rooted in something imperfect but genuine. In her. And in Peter. However the edit played out, Edie's journey on *The Key* was probably going to make great TV. But all of a sudden, she knew she'd never watch. All the best stuff happened off camera.

And who needs TV when reality is even better?

EPILOGUE

The wedding, of course, was televised.

"I always knew this day would come," Jessa pronounced, handing Edie a beautiful bouquet of cascading orchids. "But, oh my god, if you guys didn't try to kill me along the way. Look up." Jessa inspected Edie's makeup, licked the tip of her pinky, and rubbed away a fleck of mascara. "I named my first gray hair Edie Pepper. Right before I plucked that bitch out. You're welcome."

Edie laughed. "Pretty sure you loved the ratings. Remind me, did we break all the Tuesday night records? Or just most of them?"

"You think you're cute, but eight million people are watching." Jessa pointed at a monitor with a live feed. Social media was already on fire. "Are you ready?"

Was she ready? Every single day since Switzerland, Edie had thought about arriving right here, right now. She smiled her biggest smile ever. "Ready. Definitely."

And then the double doors were swinging open, and Edie Pepper was walking down the aisle while a string quartet played a dramatic cover of Taylor Swift's "Wildest Dreams." An artful display of driftwood and candles separated Edie from the two hundred guests watching with breathless anticipation. For a moment, it seemed absolutely insane that tweeting at Jessa six months ago had somehow turned into all of this. She'd gone from an anonymous, semitragic Midwestern singleton to an instant fan favorite internet sensation, so used to cameras and exposure that now the cameraman trotting backward down the aisle and blocking her view of the altar didn't even seem strange. She just smiled into the lens like a professional. The cameraman broke left, revealing a handsome groom waiting for his beautiful bride. They locked eyes, and a sweet rush of love filled Edie's heart.

"Congrats, Charlie," she whispered. He smiled with that one crooked tooth and, honestly, he looked happier than she could ever remember seeing him. When Edie met Charlie in that kindergarten cafeteria, she could never have imagined all the ways their lives would diverge or the people they'd become. But somehow, at thirty-five years old, Edie felt like they'd really seen each other again, with all their old and new imperfections, and that they hadn't looked away. They were family.

Edie took her place next to Max in the row of bridesmaids.

"Adam Fox has been messing with the crotch of his pants for like ten minutes," Max whispered while looking absolutely gorgeous in her matching strapless, frosé-pink gown. "Like, I'm starting to get concerned about what he's got in there. Check it out."

Edie looked to the altar, where Adam Fox held a padfolio with the ceremony script in one hand and pulled at the crotch of his tux with the other. He rose to his tiptoes and did a little hop. Good lord, Edie could not worry about Adam Fox's junk right now, all she wanted to know was—

"Have you seen Peter?" she asked, searching the crowd.

"Not yet," Max said with a smile.

As soon as Edie and Peter had walked back into the Alpina Gstaad in Switzerland, their plans for a romantic trip to Paris were derailed. They were immediately summoned back to New York and shuttled straight into Carole Steele's conference room in Midtown to begin negotiations. Edie had never seen anything like it, and honestly, it scared the shit out of her. Lawsuits, contracts, NDAs, hundreds of millions of dollars on the line—what the hell did Edie Pepper know about any of that?

But Peter—Peter Kennedy was all over it.

Hour after hour that day, Peter and Carole went head-to-head, breaking only for calls with their respective lawyers, Peter's agent, and the production and public relations teams as they hammered out not only a mutually acceptable plan for the final *Key* edit, but also for Edie and Peter's future.

"We're gonna have to make some concessions," Peter told Edie in the hall later. She couldn't help noticing that the cuffed sleeves of his button-down and single-minded businessman vibe was giving Don Draper, and it was seriously hot.

"Like what?" she asked, feeling Paris slipping further from her fingers just as she wanted more than anything to be—*ooh la la*—slipping into bed with Peter.

"It's manageable. We'll agree to a narrative for the season and then support that narrative when we're asked to. So, if they need you to do reshoots to build the story or do press down the line to reinforce the narrative—stuff like that. Once the season's over the finish line, I'll leave the show and forfeit my bonus and any back-end incentives. They'll agree to no future litigation, and we'll all agree to a clause that precludes the network from talking about us and us talking about the network. The cast, the production team, everyone will be reminded of their NDAs. And"—he ran a hand through his hair and looked away before meeting her eyes again—"we'll agree not to be seen in public together, or have any sort of public relationship, for an agreed-upon period of time."

Edie's eyes went wide. "How long?"

"You know," Peter hedged. "Not that long. A couple of months, maybe."

"How long, Peter," she demanded.

He sighed. "Until Bennett and Bailey get married. Or one year from today. Whichever comes first."

Edie's jaw dropped. "What do Bennett and Bailey have to do with this? Are they even engaged?"

"They are, in fact, engaged. And by all accounts, deliriously happy." Peter stepped closer to her, took her hands in his. "The thing is, the network thinks when it comes out that we're together, it will ruin the show for good. The fairy tale's already tenuous enough, and a producer falling in love with a contestant—it exposes how unreal this reality is. But they think if Bennett and Bailey get married, everyone will be so focused on that that when we say we got together months after filming ended, no one will care. They think because of our ages, it will sort of…make sense."

"Wait, what does that mean? Because of our ages?"

Peter searched for the right words. "You know, just because we're older than most of the cast, it could make sense that we might gravitate toward one another—"

"They're age-shaming me? I'm thirty-fucking-five!" Exhausted and running on little sleep and food, Edie was getting heated now, waving her finger around. "And even if I was ninety-eight, if I wanted to get married, I wouldn't let some fucking TV network tell me—"

Peter took her by the shoulders. "Edie! Come on, this isn't even the important part!"

"What's the important part?" she asked slowly.

Peter smiled. "For one, I love you. For two, I have a plan. A live TV wedding. A total ratings bonanza. Right after the finale airs—the wedding."

"Peter, the finale doesn't air for three more months!"

"Three months..." Peter started nodding like it was perfect. "I can get them to agree to three months. We'll hide out. We'll get Brad Pitt's security team on it if we have to." He looked at her, pleading with those intense green eyes. "It's three months in exchange for the rest of our lives. Trust me. It will work."

Now the three months were finally up. The Beach Club's double doors swung open again and a radiant Bailey started down the aisle. Edie's heart soared—with love for Charlie and Bailey and their happy ending, of course. But also, because over the past ninety days, Peter had proven to Edie, in a myriad of ways, that he meant every single thing he'd said on that mountaintop. She searched for him in the crowd until finally he appeared in the doorway, incredibly handsome in a tailored black tuxedo. Jessa, in a simple black gown and production headset, was whispering to him. He had his head inclined to listen, but his eyes? His eyes were on Edie.

Instantly, her body was on fire. They hadn't been in the same room together since three weeks ago in Connecticut, surviving only on texts, phone calls, and the occasional email Peter would send in the middle of the night containing some of the sexiest content Edie had ever read in her life. Her heart started beating fast, and it took everything she had to stay rooted to her spot. Edie forced herself to focus on the ceremony, on Charlie's eyes filling with tears as he recited his vows, until, finally, it was time to kiss the bride, and the crowd was cheering, and Bennett and Bailey were laughing and smiling and heading back down the aisle. Peter, per usual, was nowhere to be seen—he'd gone *back to work*.

But this time Edie knew he'd be back.

The reception was predictably beautiful, extravagant but tasteful, and Edie let herself be swept up in it all. Reunited with Zo, Aspen, McKayla, and the rest of the season's girls at the cocktail hour, Edie was astonished that everyone was so friendly. Edie supposed they were trauma bonded now. She posed for pictures with the massive bridal party, and then posed for more with former *Key* contestants and friends of the happy couple who were also somehow now Edie's fans. Jessa corralled her into the Beach Club's lobby for an on-the-fly interview where she gushed about how happy she was for Bennett and Bailey and even snagged a hug from her camera guy Ted, who'd been instrumental in Edie's own happy ending. Over the lobster dinner, she gossiped and laughed with Max until her cheeks hurt. Occasionally she'd see glimpses of Peter conferring with the top network brass or striding toward the lighting team to request some adjustment, but she did her best to abide by the contract she'd signed and pretend like she barely knew him, until finally she found herself on the packed dance floor with an entire coterie of drunken *Key* contestants surrounding Bennett and Bailey as they sung along to Miley Cyrus's "Party in the USA." Bennett had his shirt unbuttoned and his black tie strung festively around his head, and Bailey was laughing as he twirled her, the trumpet skirt of her gorgeous lace gown rising and falling as she spun. Wyatt Cash himself was screaming at Edie over the din, something about a "collab," when suddenly a hand cupped the bare skin where her neck met her shoulder, and the heat of his body formed to the back of hers. Instinctively she closed her eyes and leaned into him. He whispered in her ear.

"Let's get out of here." His hand slid forward and down her chest, sending shockwaves through her body. She bit her lip. "Meet me out back in five." And then, before anyone even noticed, he was gone.

"You can do my podcast from wherever!" Wyatt yelled to her as he shimmied. "You can come to the studio, or I can send you a Zoom link—it's super easy! The gays are obsessed with you!"

"Awesome!" Edie nodded. "Can't wait!" and then she was threading her way off the dance floor and directly into Carole Steele.

"Edie Pepper, just the little disruptor I was looking for. This is Christian Brooks," Carole said, gesturing to an immaculately groomed man next to her. "Head of development at RX."

"Nice to meet you," Edie said, shaking Christian's hand. After everything, Carole remained absolutely the scariest woman Edie had ever met in her life, and she felt desperate to escape. "It's so great to see you, but I—"

"Don't be ridiculous, we want to talk to you." Carole took Edie by the wrist and led her to a less-crowded space next to the bar. "So, Edie, have you thought about what's next?"

"In what way?" Edie asked, wary.

"For your career, obviously." Carole rolled her eyes. "Don't tell me you plan to sit around waiting for Peter Kennedy to marry you."

Edie cocked her head but said nothing.

They stared at each other until Carole pursed her lips. "Fine," she continued, slightly chastened. "Edie and Peter forever. But don't be stupid. You're having a moment and you shouldn't waste it. We don't want to see you languishing in podcastville with the rest of the reality stars trying to outrun their fifteen minutes. You're better than that. What we want to talk to you about is a TV show. Late night. On our streaming platform. Pop culture. Comedy. Celebrities."

Edie looked at Carole, confused. "Sure." She shrugged. "I'll come on your show. Just let me know when you need me, and I'll be there."

"No, no, no, no, no," Carole said as Edie tried to escape again. "We're talking about *you*. You *hosting* a show. We're thinking about calling it"—Carole painted the word in the air with a sweep of her hand—*"Famewhores."*

Edie was completely stunned. On the dance floor, the crowd was cheering as Bennett removed Bailey's garter with his teeth.

"Like *Watch What Happens Live*, but with you as the host," Christian added helpfully.

"Wait," Edie said, brow furrowed, "am *I* the famewhore in this scenario?"

Christian crinkled his nose adorably. "Of course not. The *guests* are the famewhores. You're more like a celebrity gossip whore."

"Oh," Edie said, not sure if that was better.

"We want to start ASAP," Carole continued. "I'm in town for two more days. You'll meet us tomorrow for brunch at the Polo Lounge, and we'll discuss details."

Edie was so stunned—*her own TV show???*—that when Bailey's bouquet sailed through the air and smacked her right in the head, even that wasn't enough to snap her out of it.

"See?" Carole gestured at the slack-jawed Edie and the bouquet in pieces on the floor. "This is it. This is the whole show."

"I completely see it," Christian agreed. "A total star."

As Carole and Christian continued to plan—"I want this in production by the time they announce their relationship. That news will go viral, and I want this show mentioned in every single fucking lede"—Edie was swept up in *Key* girls loading her arms with broken pieces of the bouquet. After so many hugs and a big "I love you so much!" kiss from Bailey, Edie finally extracted herself and went to find Peter.

Edie made her way onto the deck and down the stairs to the beach. And there was Peter in his tuxedo, hands in his pockets, staring at the ocean. The water sparkled in the moonlight, and out here, everything felt like magic. Vast and unknowable, but also rooted in everything that was real, right here, right now.

"I thought you didn't stare at the ocean," she teased.

Peter turned around. He raised one brow. "When did I say that?"

"The first day we met. *The Monk of Malibu*, remember?"

Peter laughed. "You never let anything go, do you?" He nodded toward her armful of flowers. "Don't tell me you caught the bouquet."

"Something like that."

"Bad luck, you know." He stepped toward her. "A married woman catching the bouquet." He took his right hand from his pocket and offered her a simple platinum band that matched the one he was wearing.

"You're gonna get us in trouble..."

"What? They're married now, aren't they?" he said, tossing the broken flowers to the sand and sliding the band onto her finger.

Their wedding three weeks ago was nothing like the weddings Edie had spent her life dreaming about.

And it was absolutely perfect.

To lower their chances of being spotted, Edie, her mother, Alice, and Lauren took a red eye from Chicago to JFK. In the middle of the night, Peter's father, Bob, picked them up at the airport and they drove straight to the Kennedy's massive colonial home in Greenwich, which Alice of course instantly approved of, with its immaculate landscaping and traditional interior design. No one left the house for the next three days. Jessa had worked her magic and sent a selection of dresses ahead of time, and Edie, Alice, Lauren, Peter's mother Libby, and his sister Elizabeth had the time of their lives drinking champagne and picking out the perfect dress for Edie to wear. Alice and Libby were fast friends, aligned as they were on most matters, including the menu for the wedding brunch, which would be quiche accompanied by an elegant winter salad. Bob called in a favor from the Honorable George F. Callahan from down the street, who executed the marriage license. On the big day, Elizabeth blew out Edie's hair in the Jack-and-Jill bathroom she and Peter had grown up sharing, and Lauren did her makeup. All the women helped her into her dress, a simple, white A-line with an open back, except for Alice, who didn't want anyone to see her cry, so she busied herself in the kitchen. Peter's little niece and nephew ran through the backyard, looking for flowers in February, until they settled on sticks and a pine cone that Elizabeth tied together with a ribbon that Edie happily carried down the improvised aisle. Bob played "Moonlight Sonata" on the grand piano as she walked, the only song he remembered from his childhood lessons. Peter stood next to the fireplace in a navy suit and surprised even himself when he started to cry. Lauren, of course, officiated, and they wrote their own vows, filled with all the traditional promises, but with the additional grace, gratitude, and wisdom befitting their advanced marrying age. When they kissed, everyone cheered. And then the quiche was served.

Edie was certain there'd never been a happier day in her life.

Edie threaded her hands into his now. They were married.

"By the way," she said, "Carole just offered me a TV show. A late-night talk show. I think I'd get to meet the Real Housewives. Like, all of them."

"Then you have to do it," he said with a smile.

"But what about living in Los Angeles? Would you stay here?"

"Wherever you are is where I'll be. I can write my book anywhere. Besides, a show will give you something to talk about in the press other than how much you love me."

"Peter, I've been waiting for months to talk about how much I love you."

"Happiness is annoying," he said mischievously. "Nobody likes it. We'll stay happy in private. And you, you will be the best late-night TV host they've ever seen."

And then his hands were in her hair, and he was kissing her until her knees were weak.

Finally, they broke apart and Peter pressed his forehead to hers. "What do you think, Mrs. Kennedy? Are you ready for everything that comes next? It's probably gonna get a little crazy."

"Honestly," she said, looking up at him. "I can't fucking wait."

ACKNOWLEDGMENTS

This book exists because of all the amazing people in my life.

Taylor Flory coached me through every single page, and I'm endlessly grateful. She listened to me talk incessantly about the characters, helped me solve story problems, let me text her my favorite lines over and over again, and read every single word approximately three hundred times. Taylor, your friendship has changed my life in a million ways. I love you.

For some inexplicable reason, Elizabeth Gomez has *always* believed I could do hard things. I've learned an insane amount about myself and what I'm capable of from Elizabeth and had a lot of fun along the way. Elizabeth, pretty sure friendship is the greatest love of all.

Rachel Bertsche was the first person who really made me believe I could write a book. "Of course you can," she'd say with a shrug. Rachel, thank you for reading drafts, shepherding me through the world of publishing, and for always believing, especially when I didn't. I'm so glad you came into my life and became my bestie.

I've been trying to be a writer for approximately eighty-five years, and I would've never made it this far without Jeremy Owens and our Chili's lunches. One day we'll have a podcast, *Live from Chili's*, where we eat queso and share all our neurotic ramblings with the world. Jeremy, I love you and believe in you so much! Thank you for accepting my friend request all those years ago and letting me court you until you agreed to be my BFF.

For over twenty-five years, the Delta Zetas have been my biggest cheerleaders. They laugh at my jokes, arrive in packs to my shows, and I'm so grateful for our sisterhood: Heather Seidelman, Jena Cherry, Brie Pio, Christine Formenti, Elizabeth Ruffner, Jinny Forrester, Dana Parr, and Laura Arroyo. Sarah Downing, thank you for being my sis through good times and bad. My Pilates ladies bring so much joy and wisdom to my life: Margaret Guira, Anna Atkinson, Jena Cherry, and Josie Shapely. Team Tuff Muff, your friendship allowed me to be the very worst at something and keep going and I'm forever grateful. Thank you to my creative community; you inspire me every day: Andrea Uptmor, Jessa Heath, Zane Biebelle, Amy Danzer, Andy Fine, Owen Cooney, Mike Copperman, Kim Nelson, Archy Jamjun, Claire Zulkey, Amy Sumpter, and Alexandra Tsarpalas. My Northwestern and Loyola peeps have offered me so much support—thank you so much and please do not choose this book for book club. To the staff at Uncle Julio's Old Orchard, thank you for all the chips and salsa; it fueled more of these pages than you know.

Fan Favorite would still be a Word document languishing on my desktop without Rachael Kelly and the Grand Central team's stewardship and belief. Rachael, thank you, thank you—you made my dreams come true! Your close reading and thoughtful insight made this book so much better, and I'm so grateful. (Also, if you liked the epilogue, thank Rachael, because I tried really hard not to write it, and now it's my favorite part of this book!) Kirsiah Depp and Jacqueline Young, thank you so much for stepping in and bringing this book over the finish line. Lori Paximadis, your careful copyediting truly meant so much to me—thank you! Liz Connor, thank you so much for allowing me to collaborate on the cover, I absolutely adore what you made. Bob Castillo, Leena Oropez, and Lauren Sum, thank you for all your care in bringing *Fan Favorite* into the world.

Marcy Posner, and the Folio Lit team, thank you for believing in me and this project. I can't believe I get to work with you and am so appreciative of your stewardship and care.

When I was a kid, Melody Gunn would take me to Waldenbooks at the mall and let me buy as many *Sweet Valley Highs* as I wanted. Mom, thank you for teaching me to love reading. Jim Gunn has dedicated his life to making and curating beautiful things. Dad, thank you for teaching me to love creating. I hope I'm passing both of these lessons down to my own kiddo.

Max Goldberg, you're my greatest love and greatest teacher. I'm honored to be your mom.

ABOUT THE AUTHOR

Adrienne Gunn is a writer and podcaster obsessed with pop culture. When she's not busy watching reality TV, Adrienne works as a content strategist, performs as a storyteller and comedian, and hangs out with her adorable son, Max, and adorabler puppy, Georgia. Visit her at www.adriennegunn.com.

Visit **GCPClubCar.com** to sign up for the GCP Club Car newsletter, featuring exclusive promotions, info on other Club Car titles, and more.

QUESTIONS FOR DISCUSSION

(This Section Contains Spoilers)

1. The beginning of the novel pokes fun at the state of modern dating. Did the author's commentary on first dates, apps, and break-up texts resonate with you and your own experiences? Why or why not?

2. Edie is shocked to see her high school boyfriend cast as the lead in the upcoming season of *The Key*. Has anyone from your past ever resurfaced in a sudden, almost unbelievable way? How would you have reacted to seeing your ex on TV, and who would have been the first person you called?

3. Edie, especially at the beginning of the novel, is frank—even critical—when it comes to her appearance. When Edie was staring at herself in the full-length mirror, what came to mind for you, as a reader? Did the scene resonate with you? Did it upset you? What would you have said to Edie, had you been standing beside her? Discuss this

in relation to the makeover scene before Edie's "Cinderella" date, and the conversation Edie and Peter have about beauty in the back of the limo.

4. Edie has been an avid watcher of *The Key* for nearly a decade. She describes it as "America's most beloved dating show, the only one that really, truly, believe[s] in love." Compare and contrast *The Key* (inspired by ABC's *The Bachelor*) to your favorite dating show. What about the setup of your favorite show appeals to you, and keeps you coming back season after season?

5. Peter describes the show as a "microcosm that parallels dating in the real world... You have to figure out what [people's] intentions are, what they want, [and] what you want." Did you agree with Peter's assessment here, that millions of people tune in to these kinds of shows to untangle what's real and what's not? Explain.

6. Edie's best friend Lauren is not convinced that joining the cast of *The Key* is a good idea. Instead, she encourages her to "invest" in herself. What did you think of this advice? Had you been in Lauren's shoes in this moment, would you have said the same thing? Or encouraged Edie to take a romantic leap?

7. If you were the lead on *The Key*, and you were being asked to help cast your dream contestants, which qualities—physical and personality-wise—would you share? Who is definitely *not* your type?

8. Lauren tells Edie that she once read an article about young girls being told they can "have it all—careers, husbands, children. And [that boys should] go out and find a nice girl to take care of them." What is the underlying message here

regarding physical and emotional labor, and how do you think it affects heterosexual relationships today?

9. Edie isn't a "typical" cast member on *The Key* because she's not in her twenties and not a size 0. In this day and age, are you surprised that more women like Edie aren't cast on reality TV shows? What does the continued casting of characters who look like Zo say about our expectations as viewers, and of our society at large? Do you think these kinds of shows would benefit from greater inclusion—in all forms?

10. The novel gives readers a behind-the-scenes look at the machinations behind the creation of reality TV. Knowing what you do know now about showrunners and PAs and editing, would you ever consider being a cast member on *The Key*? How does knowing what goes on during the filming of these programs affect your experience as a viewer?

11. Edie and Peter both think about significant exes in their lives over the course of the book. How did this reflection help prepare them to meet each other? What lessons did you/have you learned from dating, about yourself and what you want in your romantic relationships?

12. In the hospital, Bailey and Max have a heart-to-heart with Edie. Despite their different backgrounds and experiences, Max says they're all motivated by the same thing: wanting "to be loved." In life, what do you feel is people's biggest motivator? Is it love? Something else? What motivates you the most?

13. Contestants are placed in "dream date" scenarios throughout the show: formal cocktail parties, team volleyball games, romantic prom reenactments. If you were the

showrunner for *The Key,* what kind of activities (sincere or hilarious) would you orchestrate for the participants? Where would you send them internationally?

14. When Edie leaves the show, she's shocked to learn she's become something of a sensation on social media. According to "most of" the internet, she's an icon for single women everywhere. What are your thoughts regarding the public consumption of other people's lives? Why do you think women, in particular, are often criticized harshly online? Do you think fame and notoriety are fair trade-offs for unkindness online?

15. At the end of the novel, Edie realizes that Bennett was not, in fact, her One True Love. Like Edie, have you ever found it difficult to move on from past relationships? Do you believe in the concept of "One True Love" or "The One That Got Away"? Were you satisfied by Edie's choice, in the end?

EVERYTHING I KNOW ABOUT LOVE I LEARNED FROM POP CULTURE

I grew up in a suburb far enough away from Chicago that going to "the city" was something that happened twice a year when you boarded a school bus and endured a ten-hour trip to the Field Museum. Life in Rockford, Illinois, was strip malls and chain restaurants, and for an unpopular kid whose parents weren't all that interested in dragging her around to activities, I spent *a lot* of time consuming media.

I preferred the hallways of *Sweet Valley High* and *90210* to my actual high school. The hilarious Huxtable family hijinks to my own family drama. I watched *Sixteen Candles*, *Grease*, *Dirty Dancing*, and *The Cutting Edge* on repeat. From the pages of *People*, I became encyclopedic about Hollywood's hottest men. (*Cosmopolitan* provided an education for how to turn them on.) I studied pop culture like a road map that would lead me out of the suburbs and into the fabulous big-city life I was sure was waiting for me. The directions seemed clear: Be pretty, be thin, be fashionable, be charming, be sexy (but not too sexy!), and then, be a girlfriend, a fiancée, and—most importantly—*a bride*.

So, when I got engaged on a glamorous Las Vegas rooftop and subsequently married in an elegant New Year's Eve ceremony in downtown Chicago, I was happy. How could I not be? I wore a gorgeous Monique Lhuillier gown, just like Reese Witherspoon or something! I was twenty-three years old, married to a handsome man, and living in the city—what other fabulous storybook things were about to happen?! Seven years later, when I was in the middle of a very messy divorce and everything was very sad and very terrible, it was like, wait a minute, what just happened? This isn't like *When Harry Met Sally*—like, *at all*.

But the part of me that believed in Bridget Jones and Mr. Darcy and all the other romantic stories I loved was—somehow—still alive and well. I decided my first marriage was a fluke and I might as well start looking for my second! True love was out there! I just had to find it.

But then I started dating.

I quickly realized most of my ideas about dating in your thirties were formed by *Sex and the City*. Even though *Sex and the City* ended before Michael Patrick King could tell us what to do about dick pics and ghosting, I still felt a mix of Charlotte York's romanticism and Samantha Jones's no-strings-attached spirit as I swiped. Imagine my disappointment when I discovered not only that "true love" was probably a myth, but also that Sam's sexy one-night stands were about as realistic as Carrie's fabulous New York City life on a freelance salary. Dating felt so insane and so delusional that, for the first time, I was forced to grapple with just how hoodwinked I'd been by all the representations of love and marriage that I'd gobbled up from books, TV, magazines, and movies. I sought sisterhood with women looking for The One who found only The Asshole. But most of my friends were either married (or getting married), so I had to find my compatriots elsewhere.

Like on *The Bachelor*.

By the time I started watching, *The Bachelor* had already been on for fourteen seasons and had a devoted audience of millions. Generally, I thought the premise—twenty-five women competing for the heart of one man—was misogynistic and ridiculous. Still, I found comfort in watching these gorgeous women rip each other's hair out over the chance to kiss the same mediocre man. I felt certain we were driven by the same bogus ideas about life and love that we'd been spoon-fed since we were kids, and it was cathartic to see that they also believed that if they were pretty and perfect and pleasant enough, Prince Charming would appear and all their dreams would finally come true.

Everything about *The Bachelor*—the roses, the over-the-top dates, the hot tubs and fantasy suites—blatantly traded on outdated heterosexual fairy tales, and it felt like everyone on the show was performing some agreed-upon contract of modern love rather than actually *feeling* it. Every Monday night I'd think the funniest thing in the world would be if a normal person—just a regular gal who eats carbs and shops at the Gap—went on this show and said all the things we're at home thinking. If some regular, thirty-five-year-old woman had to slide into a hot tub of twenty-two-year-old models in her tankini, wouldn't the whole show fall apart? And wouldn't it be amazing?

And thus, Edie Pepper was born.

Like me, Edie's spent her life consuming pop culture and media and has no clue just how much it's shaped her wants, needs, and desires. By the time she sees her high school sweetheart Charlie Bennett on *E! News*, she's fresh off a break-up and agonizing over her quickly advancing age in relation to a possible happily-ever-after. But just like every other woman looking for love on *The Bachelor*, Edie's got enough hope (delusion?) to believe that finding love on a TV show is realistic. But as Edie twists herself in knots trying to become the woman that the new and improved Charlie Bennett is looking for, she quickly learns that real life rarely has anything to do with fairy tales.

(Even when you're on a TV show all about fairy tales!!!)

Edie, of course, is not the only one trying to figure out life and love in a society saturated by Instagram. Peter, *The Key*'s showrunner and top manufacturer of love stories, has his own deep-seated ideas about what real love is, and he's consistently disappointed by the gap between his ideals and reality. Bennett,

The Key's six-packed suitor, is obsessed with crafting himself into The Perfect Man™ and thinks that the perfect woman will also conform to a generic (but widely accepted) idea of what a woman should be. The contestants, of course, are searching for another form of love: fame. And as this motley crew embarks upon *The Key*'s "journey," the show itself reflects and refracts the state of modern love today.

Of course it makes sense to me now that my obsession with pop culture and romantic idealism combined with my own disappointment in the world of love and romance would eventually result in my own attempt at crafting a perfect happily-ever-after. I set out to write a romcom that considered what it's like to search for lasting love in a culture consumed by dumb ideas about romance. My favorite romcoms feel rooted in real characters with real motivations, and I wanted this book to feel like that, too, not just another [insert running through airport scene here]. I wanted flawed people with flawed ideas to have to confront their nonsense but still find their way to true connection in the end. For me, the most romantic moment in *Fan Favorite* is not Edie's fantasy makeover or her epic prom, it's two people sharing Nachos Bell Grande and the truth of themselves as messy and imperfect and confused. And when the man of Edie's dreams—who we know is not actually a Perfect Man™ at all, but really sort of a mess—declares not only his love, but also that he's gonna go to therapy and work his shit out? Now, *that's* a total swoon. And, somehow, through writing this book, the impossible happened—it got me believing in true love all over again.